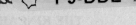

KATHERINE CARLYLE
She runs from the shadows of her past
to seek a new life—
only to find tragedy and hope
in a savage wilderness . . .
and the rugged, dangerous stranger
who is her destiny.

BYRD KINCAID
He lives a solitary existence
in a treacherous land,
sharing his secrets with no one—
until a remarkable woman wins his trust
and his love . . .
and bears him sons and daughters
fated to tame a vast
and breathtaking frontier.

**Bold pioneers of a wild, young America,
they follow their hearts and their dreams west—
and found a glorious dynasty
that will shape the soul and spirit
of a remarkable land
for generations to come.**

THE
KINCAIDS

THE KINCAIDS

RAGING RIVERS

TAYLOR BRADY

AVON BOOKS ♦ NEW YORK

THE KINCAIDS: RAGING RIVERS is an original publication of Avon Books. This work has never before appeared in book form. This work is a novel. Any similarity to actual persons or events is purely coincidental.

AVON BOOKS
A division of
The Hearst Corporation
1350 Avenue of the Americas
New York, New York 10019

First Avon Books Printing: October 1992

AVON TRADEMARK REG. U.S. PAT. OFF. AND IN OTHER COUNTRIES, MARCA REGISTRADA, HECHO EN CANADA

Printed in Canada

UNV   10   9   8   7   6   5   4   3

Chapter One

Northwestern Kentucky, 1820

Even in the best of times, Mud Flats was appropriately named. The small landing on the banks of the Ohio River was wet, dirty, and undistinguished, besieged by black flies in summer, locked in by ice in winter. At spring high water, which it was now, the streets became a foul-smelling mire of churned up mud and offal which attracted free-roaming pigs, carrion birds, and rats. Mud Flats was a stagnant gateway to the passage west, located on one of the busiest waterways in the nation.

Mud Flats was also dying.

The enterprising trapper who first established the trading post on a well-wooded curve of the river in 1783 had thrived for a while, trading whiskey and flour with the Indians for pelts of beaver, fox, rabbit, and muskrat. After the Revolutionary War soldiers who had been mustered out of the army and paid for their services in western land grants had drifted down the Ohio looking for a place to settle. Some got as far as Mud Flats and stayed. They cleared the heavily

1

timbered land, built cabins, and tilled small fields of corn and barley, tobacco and potatoes. They sent back East for their families and, slowly and undramatically, the settlement grew from a population of twenty scattered farmers to a town of almost two hundred people.

Two events in the early nineteenth century changed the trickle of settlers heading west into a mighty flow. The first was the Louisiana Purchase in 1803, which doubled the size of a young nation already bursting at the seams. The second was the end of the War of 1812, which pushed the Indians across the Mississippi and the British back over the Canadian border. The time was ripe for expansion, and thousands of immigrants moved west. Overland travel was difficult and hazardous, and the great rivers, like the Ohio, became obvious highways for the travelers.

For a few years Mud Flats competed with Louisville and Maysville upstream, and Henderson downstream, for river traffic and trade. But the same capricious river that brought wealth and trade to Mud Flats' sister cities decreed that the little settlement's time in the sun would end. The river channel that allowed the heavily laden barges to tie up along the bank began to fill with silt. No efforts of the townspeople could stop the inexorable drift of sand. By 1815, Mud Flats was accessible to larger boats only when the river was in flood and the deeper water allowed the vessels to drift over the dangerous sand bars. The residents of Mud Flats watched prosperity slide past them as more and more boats, even some driven by steam, plied the river. Most pilots passed Mud Flats without stopping, not wanting to risk their hulls on the ever-shifting shoals.

Sometimes as many as five flatboats passed each day. Some carried families headed for the Mississippi River and beyond; others were laden with corn and tobacco, barley and hemp, destined for New Orleans and the ports of Europe. Now and then a whiskey barge drifted past with its cargo of smooth, mellow liquor made upriver in Bourbon County. Kentuckians had learned early on that it was more economical to transport corn in its liquid form, and a barrel bought for twenty-five cents in Louisville sold for two dollars in New Orleans.

Only the occasional keelboat with something to trade, or a trapper's canoe headed upstream to Pittsburgh, ever stopped at Mud Flats. It was a dangerous business trying to maneuver a broadhorn onto a landing, and a waste of time to risk losing the current for such a place. But today was an exception. A man had died at Louisville Falls, and last night at sundown a flatboat had tied up at Mud Flats to let off his widow, who was too overcome with grief and fever to continue the journey west.

The passengers had camped on the riverbank all night and today swelled the population of the town by more than twenty. The women, afforded an opportunity to shop in a real store, didn't care if that store was a ten-by-twelve lean-to that they could reach only at great peril by crossing shaky, half-sunken boards thrown over the mud. The men, glad to feel ground under their feet for the first time in days, didn't care if they were ankle deep in mire. They were glad to mingle with others of their kind, to hear news of the river and the latest word from back East.

They had come from as far away as New York

and Rhode Island, or as near as Virginia and Pennsylvania. They had crossed the Erie Canal or traveled overland in mule carts and on foot. By the time they had boarded the flatboat at Wheeling, many of them had already put a thousand miles behind them, and when they disembarked at Mud Flats they were seasoned veterans of more than five hundred miles of rapids, falls, shallow currents, and treacherous channels. Theirs were weathered, toughened faces, embittered by the hardships they had endured yet touched with cautious jubilation. They had made it this far, and less than two hundred miles lay between them and Cairo, their jumping off point.

The men were attracted by the river-front sign that announced Calhoun Bros. Saloon and were disappointed to learn that for some unknown reason this fine establishment was closed. The women were conversely grateful.

The travelers brought a touch of the exotic to the community. From first light the townsfolk began to gather, treading across swampy lanes and oblivious to the constant drizzle, to mingle with the newcomers. They met in the general store, under the eaves of the livery, or outside the canvas tents that had been set up on shore.

The young boys listened with rapt attention to the tales of adventure being told. The old men turned down the corners of their mouths and thanked God they had more sense than to go off on such a fool trek, while at the same time smothering glints of yearning in their eyes. Those hale of body but weak in spirit, tied to their farms and their wives, talked of failing crops at home and fertile valleys elsewhere, of river pirates and hazardous crossings, and the travelers listened intently for any news that might be helpful to them on the last leg of the journey.

The townswomen, eager for news from upriver, gathered around their wayfaring counterparts, bringing baked goods, admiring the children, and making solicitous noises about the poor widow Mabry who'd lost her husband in the falls and what was to become of her. They saw the weariness in the eyes of the travelers and listened to stories of the hardships they had endured. They smiled at the brittle confidence in the pioneer voices as they talked about the homes they would make across the Mississippi, but the smiles were more of pity than envy, and the townswomen each secretly wondered what kind of woman would leave hearth and home for lands unknown. Privately they counted their own blessings.

It was a day long to be remembered, to store away like a secret treasure and take out later at hard moments. A scrap of conversation, the look in the eye of a stranger—a man would stand over his broken plow and recall those things, and slowly turn his eyes westward. A woman might rub the rime of frost off the window and let her eyes wander over the frozen streets of a dying town toward the sluggish Ohio, and remember. A child would dream, and grow, and plan, and keep his face turned toward the setting sun.

Afterwards, that soggy April day in Mud Flats would be recalled as The Day the Flatboat Stopped, but in fact it had another, even more dramatic distinction. Early that morning Joseph Bacon's boy, who sometimes did odd jobs out at the Carlyle place in exchange for eggs and fruit preserves to help feed his eight brothers and sisters, burst into Sawyer's General Mercantile, white faced and gasping, with news of a murder.

Not that murders were unusual in Mud Flats. Knife fights were more or less regular in the slow season when men got to drinking too much down at the Calhoun Brothers Saloon. There was also the expected violence from the riff-raff that floated downriver and were attracted by the painted wooden sign that promised Good Whisky. Not to mention violence done by the Calhoun brothers themselves, who'd just as soon shoot a man as look at him. Over the years they'd taught townspeople and travelers alike more than one bitter lesson in steering clear of their bad side. But this murder was different. It had been done by a woman, and the dead man was Early Calhoun himself.

By midmorning, folks had gathered in knots from the riverbank to the general store, discussing what was to be done. The travelers, awed to be part of such a drama, gathered close, listening to the tale again and again and absorbing the horror with the same determined distaste with which they might digest a bad meal. Little Joe Bacon, by now a hero, had made his circuit from one end of town to the other and was back in the General Mercantile, perched on a pickle barrel and helping himself to free samples, telling the story again to a rapt audience.

"An' so I sez to her, Miss Kate, what're you doing? Knowing in my heart they weren't but one kind of hole to be dug that deep and that was a grave, and the hairs stood up on my neck coz I ain't never been easy around dead folks. And she sez to me, 'Burying my grandmother,' and I looked in the winda and sure enough, there's the old lady all wrapped up in a quilt and dead as a doorknob, and there's Miss Kate lookin' right white around the gills, and I'm thinkin' it's just on account of the old woman, you know. But then she hands me the shovel and she sez, 'I ain't got the strength to dig more'n one grave today, Little Joe. You're gonna have to help me out.' And I stares at her, thinkin' her mind's gone unhinged, talking about two graves, and then she sez, 'Look around the side of the house.'"

He paused for dramatic effect, crunching on a pickle and letting the juice carve pale green rivulets down his dirty arm. Though this was the fourth or fifth hearing of the tale for some, no one moved.

"An' Lord Gosh Almighty, there he was ... Early Calhoun, all crumpled up against the side of the cabin, sliced to ribbons, and the bloody ax that done it on the ground. His head was jes hanging on by a strop, and his eyes was wide open and starin' straight at me. And Miss Kate she sez, 'I done it, Little Joe. May God have mercy on my soul, I kilt Early Calhoun.' But me, I taken off running and I didn't stop til I got to town, and I swear that dead man's eyes was doggin' me ever' step o' the way."

An almost reverent silence followed the last word, until one brave soul asked, "Dead? You're right sure he was dead?" There was more dread in his voice than outright disbelief.

Little Joe gave the interloper a contemptuous look. "Hell, Lenny, there weren't enough left of him to stuff in my mama's sewing basket! How much deader can you git?"

Among the listeners were four women from the flatboat huddled together in a little group, horrified as was only right, but also as fascinated as any of the town's residents to whom the drama rightly belonged. There was Esther Wiltshire, a narrow, gray-haired woman whose parsimonious nature was reflected in her thin lips and quick, spare movements. Generally disapproving and rigid in her demeanor, she deferred only to her companion, Maude Sherrod.

Hilda Werner also stayed close to Maude, as though for protection. Hilda was gentle and plump-faced, round with pregnancy and quick with a sweet smile, which naturally garnered the affections of the townswomen, who forced sweets and cookies and fresh pies on her "for the baby."

Caroline Adamson was the comeliest of the group, but not so much in her physical appearance as in her manner. She spoke with a soft southern drawl and moved with the grace of a born aristocrat, doing nothing to call attention to herself. Even in her faded calico and frayed bonnet she managed to remind others that they were in the presence of a lady. When she walked into a room, men took off their hats and women straightened their cuffs and brushed off their aprons. Her smile was cool and gracious, and her eyes had the steady confidence of a woman who was so certain of her own strength that she feared nothing . . . except perhaps Maude Sherrod.

Upon the completion of the tale it was predictably Maude who spoke first, with a properly muffled, "Unspeakable! Simply unspeakable!" Maude was a dark-haired, dark-eyed woman with a ponderous bosom and a thickening waist, prone to wearing grays and blacks, which made her more imposing. She was only in her mid-thirties, but her air of self-importance and unmistakable authority made her appear older. She had traveled from Hancock, New Hampshire, with her husband and three children, with an eye toward fortunes to be made across the Mississippi. Eastern papers were filled with stories about golden opportunities for shopkeepers in towns like St. Louis and Cape Giradeau, which outfitted settlers going west. Packed aboard the flatboat was the nucleus of their merchandise, brought from their mercantile store back home: needles and cloth, horse bits and plow tips, nails and hunting knives. Maude had no doubt that these goods could be sold on the frontier for suitably inflated prices, which would set her well on her way to assuming a position of wealth and power in her new home.

Unswerving in her Calvinist beliefs, secure in the social standing she had held in her small, tight-knit New Hampshire community a thousand miles upriver, she had become the unquestioned leader of the flatboat women, who clustered around her like pilgrims around a Messiah. She never smiled, but when she spoke people listened. Even the townspeople regarded her with respect.

Caroline drew her three young children close to her and murmured hesitantly, "Perhaps we should go back to the boat. This is not fit talk for the children."

Hilda, looking rather ill, concurred in a small, thickly accented voice. "I have finished my purchases. I should find my husband."

Esther vehemently agreed. "None of us can be safe on these streets."

But no one moved. They were all waiting for Maude to make the final decision. And Maude was not ready to go yet.

Among the townsfolk gathered in the store and spilling onto its sagging front porch were half a dozen women and perhaps twice as many men. They regarded the flatboat women's uneasiness as a compliment, for in a town as undistinguished as Mud Flats even the ability to provoke fear among strangers was a claim to fame. They took it as their duty to prolong the entertainment rather than apologize for it.

Jake Sawyer, the storekeeper, was particularly pleased by developments, which had brought customers into the store to hear little Joe's story. In a village of less than two hundred, customers were hard to come by, especially when most of the families were practically self-sufficient, not so much from choice as from necessity. For the most part, the forty or so families who lived in Mud Flats and the surrounding area were farmers trying to wrest a living from the rocky soil. The land was tired, and for the past few years the crops had been poor. The settlers had to depend on what they could make themselves. They put up their own preserves and dried apples. The women made dye from berries and roots, candles from tallow or bear grease, soap from ashes. They grew their own potatoes, turnips, pole beans, and corn, and raised a few cows, goats, and pigs.

But there were some things the farmers could not manufacture themselves, and that's why they came to Sawyer's. They came for needles and cloth, hunting knives, new pots and pans, broad-axes, gunpowder, and bullets—and for salt, the most precious commodity of all. Sometimes Sawyer might have special food items, taken in barter from his customers—venison or hare, a cured country ham hanging from the rafters, or special goat cheese made by an old lady living on the outskirts of town. It was a marginal living, though he did better than most folks in Mud Flats, and he could not afford to let an opportunity for doing business pass him by.

Hoping to keep the shoppers' attention a little longer, Sawyer mused, "Reckon somebody ought to go out there and round her up?"

Maude Sherrod gave an approving jerk of her head. "I should certainly think so!"

There was a stirring among the townsfolk, a low discussion about how one best went about dealing with a female murderess, but they were prolonging the moment to achieve the fullest enjoyment both for themselves and the onlookers.

Then somebody else put in warily, "Anybody rode out to the Calhoun place yet? Think Zeke and Abel know?"

A pall fell over the gathering. Little Joe Bacon suddenly became very interested in his grooming, tugging at the pickle bits stuck in his teeth and wiping his sticky fingers on his shirt, studiously avoiding eye contact. It was apparent no one wanted to make the effort—nor did they want to face the distinct possibility of danger that came with telling the dead man's family.

Suddenly, there was a commotion from the porch, excited murmuring and pointing. Somebody said, "It's her! She come her own self!"

The people inside the store forced their way out, spilling onto the porch. The flatboat women were chief among them as everybody strained for a view of the murdering woman.

Her name was Katherine Carlyle, and when she passed, people drew back and stared and followed her progress with awed distaste. They whispered about her with morbid pride, anxious to reiterate the community's one distinction with the newcomers, prolonging the moment for its fullest effect.

"There she is. The killer-woman."

"Early Calhoun hisself, sliced him like a side of bacon."

"Witch-woman, I say. Got the evil eye."

"Them Carlyles was always strange. That old woman, mumblin' and acursin' in tongues. Workin' spells, if you ask me."

"Look at her. There's as bad a one as ever walked the earth."

Katherine Carlyle kept on walking straight down the unpaved mainstreet of Mud Flats. There were no more than half a dozen buildings on either side of the street—the mercantile, the blacksmith, and the wheelwright's shops, the deserted shell of the bank that had failed and fallen into disrepair.

Halfway down the street was the lone church. It served weekdays as a schoolhouse, at least in the rainy season when the children weren't needed in the fields. They were there now, faces pressed to oilcloth windows, crowded in the open doorway. "Witch woman, witch woman!" cried one fair-haired girl.

The other children took up the cry, ignoring the preacher, who also served as teacher and town undertaker, who insisted that no one these days believed in talk about witches as he tried to bring the schoolroom back under control. Paying no attention to his orders to take their seats, the children deserted their schoolroom to join the townspeople and visitors in the street and stare at the red-headed woman.

Finally it was Maude Sherrod who said, "Well, there she is! Why don't you do something?"

Esther Wiltshire added, "Is there no law in this town?"

One of the men dragged his eyes away long enough to explain, "We're our own law this far out, ma'am. No sheriff or nothing."

"She's a killer and you let her roam free?"

"We ain't letting her go free," asserted the man patiently. "We're studyin' on what to do."

"It weren't the killin' that was so bad," put in another with the sagacity of one who is an authority on such matters. "It was the *way* she done it. Downright un-Christian."

The travelers had no answer for that, and spent a few moments in uneasy contemplation of the shifting standards of morality that marked their progress west. It was left to Maude to render the final judgement. Even before she spoke, eyes were turning to her, the people waiting to pattern themselves after her.

Her dark eyes snapped with righteousness. Her bosom jutted. And although it was a mild condemnation, given the circumstances, her words carried the wrath of God.

"Such filth as that," she pronounced clearly, "shouldn't be allowed to walk the same streets as decent folk."

Her voice was loud, and Katherine Carlyle, who was passing not ten feet in front of the general store where the travelers had gathered to stare, would have had to be deaf not to hear. She was not deaf, but she did not pause, nor did she turn. She trudged on, the mud sucking at her field boots, her skirts dragging in the filth. Her head was high, her shoulders square, and she looked neither right nor left as she pursued her determined course down the center of the street.

She was a tall woman, strongly built, with a flash of red hair escaping beneath her bonnet and frizzing in the rain. Her gown was faded and worn, but her apron was clean. A threadbare shawl was wrapped around her shoulders as meager protection against the rain, and a calico-wrapped bundle was flung across her back like a pack. She carried a walking stick made of sturdy hickory, which was of little use to her in the muddy streets but was known to be helpful in the rock- and snake-infested fields at her home. Her proud carriage and the bright, almost unnatural color of her hair inspired both envy and scorn in the women; her hardy build and firm figure elicited an entirely different reaction from the men. It was this—or perhaps the shame of having a private disgrace commented upon by an outsider such as Maude Sherrod—that emboldened one of the townsmen. From the crowd there arose a shout, "Whore!" and a ball of mud splattered on Katherine Carlyle's apron.

She stopped and turned and swept them all with a cool green gaze. From the men outside the livery to the women at the general store to the children squatting in the mud, she touched them all with the quiet force of her eyes. Of them all, only Maude met her gaze. Murmurings ceased, there was an uneasy shifting of feet and some sporadic throat clearing, and then Katherine Carlyle turned and walked on.

Maude Sherrod poked a sharp elbow into the ribs of her fifteen-year-old son, who had been among those on the porch from the beginning and therefore had the best view of the spectacle.

"Stop your gaping, boy! You want the Lord to strike you blind?"

Oliver Sherrod blushed to the roots of his hair and squirmed uncomfortably. He was almost a man now and intensely disliked his mother's insistence on treating him like a boy. But he couldn't tell her that; nobody ever told his mother anything, and Oliver was constantly torn between pretending to be the adult he felt it was only his right to be, and fearing his mother. "Aw, Ma, she don't look so awful bad ..."

"What do you know about bad? I swear to Goshen, I don't know what this land is coming to."

Then someone else said, "Look, she's heading toward the river."

"Maybe she'll drown herself," volunteered another.

There were some uncomfortable chuckles, and a few attempts to resume the conversation, but curiosity was a strong pull. Eventually, one by one, they wound up their business, gathered their children and their possessions, and drifted down toward the riverbank, where Katherine Carlyle had gone.

The rain increased as Katherine approached the river, and the breeze drove needles against the back of her neck. Mud oozed over the tops of her boots, which once had belonged to her younger brother and consequently were too big for her, and her sodden skirts clung to her ankles. The cloying stench Katherine had always associated with this town—a mixture of dampness, waste, animals, and cooking—gradually gave way to the fresh scent of the fast-flowing river. Katherine did not mind the breeze that blurred her vision with rain because it brought with it clean air and escape.

The flatboat was tied up to a spreading oak by two ropes that tugged and strained against the current. It was somewhat larger than most—about sixty feet long, with a narrow, penned off area at the stern for livestock, which included a milk cow, two mules, and a crate of chickens. Such a conveyance was sometimes called a broadhorn, because of the long, flat oar used to steer it, but more often it was known simply as a family boat. It was outfitted with a rude hut in the center of approximately twelve by twenty feet, where the passengers might take shelter from the rain or, in fair weather, sit on the roof and watch the Ohio speed by.

Each available space was packed with canvas-wrapped supplies and household furnishings, and in this manner almost two dozen people had set out from Wheeling, Virginia, to navigate the Ohio to its mouth.

Several men stood on the shore, and all of them looked up as Katherine approached. Some of them she recognized as townsfolk come to chat with the crew. Others were strangers. Her heart was pounding in her chest, for any one of those faces, strange or familiar, could mean destruction to her. Everyone must know about Early Calhoun by now. They could detain her. They could hang her. They could ride for Zeke and Abel Calhoun, or they might have done so already. Her every heartbeat could be ticking off the last moments of her life.

But she kept her head high and her fear to herself. There came a point when fear simply ceased to be measurable, and grief was an effective anesthetic. Her eyes went from one to the other of the strangers until she found the one she sought—a lean, knotty man with graying hair and grizzled cheeks, his skin toughened by weather and his eyes narrowed from hours spent gauging the sun. She walked up to him.

"You are the captain?" The calmness of her voice surprised her.

He straightened up, shifting a wad of tobacco from one cheek to the other, and surveyed her with flat, assessing eyes which had seen too much to be surprised. His drawl was thin and measured. "I'm the pilot, yes'm. Dewhurst's my name."

Ned Dewhurst had lived on the Ohio River all his life. He'd grown up in Cincinnati and worked with his father ferrying settlers across the river from Kentucky. He'd left only once, to fight with Oliver Hazard Perry in the Battle of Lake Erie during the War of 1812; then he'd come back to the Ohio. He knew the river and how dangerous it could be, yet he loved it and enjoyed the challenge of each new trip. The Ohio and Mississippi were constantly changing, and they kept a man sharp and alive. He'd endured fires, collisions, the changing channel of the river, pirates, and an occasional Indian raid. It was the only life he knew, and he planned to travel the river until the day he died.

He especially liked piloting the great barges down the river, ending up in New Orleans, selling his boat for lumber, and then heading home again by way of steamboat, or sailing to New York on one of the great clipper ships. He had a wife in Cincinnati and one in New Orleans; neither knew about the other and Dewhurst planned to keep it that way.

Years of experience had given him a nose for trouble and he had perfected the art of avoiding it. But the minute he looked up and saw the red-haired woman standing there, he knew two things: this woman was trouble, and she would not be easy to avoid.

Katherine said, "I wish to purchase passage on your boat."

The other men stopped their conversation to listen and to watch. People began to wander down from the town in groups of two and three, gathering a cautious distance away. The captain spat on the ground and turned to secure a canvas bundle he was preparing to toss onboard. "You do that in Wheeling. I got a full load."

Desperation pulsed through Katherine's veins, fluttered, and quieted again. She lifted her chin. "You lost a man upstream. A woman just got off. You have room."

The captain efficiently tied the knot and doubled it, lifted the bundle to his chest, and with a grunt—"Ho!"—heaved it across to a crewman onboard. Her gaze did not waver. "You're travelin' alone?"

"Yes."

He spat a stream of juice that left his lips and his lower chin stained brown. "Ain't takin' no lone woman. Nothin' but trouble."

"I can pay." Katherine reached inside a slit in her skirt, to the pocket tied around her waist. The pocket was an old-fashioned but reliable way of securing valuables. She drew out a coin and placed it in the captain's hand.

He stared at it for a long time. "What the hell is this?"

"It's gold."

"I know that." Just to be sure he bit down on it, and looked at it again, rubbing it between his thumb and forefinger and turning it to catch the meager light. He frowned. "What kinda markin's is them? Ain't never seen nothing like this."

Katherine said nothing. She concentrated all her energy on trying to still her heartbeat so that its poundings would not be noticeable to all who observed. It was a losing battle.

The captain looked at the coin again, then at her. His eyes narrowed. "What you so all-fired determined to get on my boat for?"

Katherine took a breath, barely discernible as a slight rise in her chest. Her fists tightened by her sides until they ached, but she barely felt the pain. *Nothing,* she thought sternly to herself. *I can feel nothing, not any more.*

Steadily, she said, "This morning I buried my grandmother, the last of my family in these parts. I've nothing left here. I'm going west to find my brother, who went to make a home for us there. If you had not been here, I would have gone by canoe. Your boat is a convenience, that's all. However, if you won't take me, I'll be on my way."

She knew the captain saw through the brave speech to the desperation that churned inside her, and when she held out her hand for the coin, her fingers were trembling. Katherine was beyond caring. *I will either live or die,* she thought. *But if I die it won't be from lack of trying, and please God, don't let me die here.*

A flicker of astonishment crossed the face of the man who thought he had seen everything. The captain would not have been able to say whether the reaction was caused by the notion of a woman paddling a canoe down the fast-flowing Ohio, or the absurdity of her thinking she could find a single man in the wild expanse of the western lands. But when he looked into her cool, steady gaze and saw the square set of her shoulders and the determined jut of her chin, he thought better of mocking her ambition. A woman like this was not to be trifled with.

"Way I hear it," he muttered, "you buried more than your grandmother."

Katherine did not reply, and when he made no move to return the coin, she lowered her hand.

The captain asked carefully, "How long since you heard from this brother o' yourn?"

"We had word only last year."

The captain shook his head sadly. "Lady, you got any idea how big the West is? He could be dead by now, or holed up with some wild Indian tribe, or God knows where-all. You ain't got a chance in hell of finding him, if you'll pardon my blunt speaking."

Katherine replied with quiet confidence, "I'll find him."

The captain weighed the coin in his hand, indecision clear on his face. Perhaps he knew, or at the very least suspected, that the heavy gold with its foreign writings was worth more than the sum total of the other passengers' fees for the entire voyage. Perhaps he was remembering the gossip he'd heard about her, or was considering his responsibility to his passengers. He had a solid reputation along the Ohio, and when it got out he'd taken a lone woman into the wilderness and dumped her there . . .

Where had she come by such a coin, anyway? It was old, older maybe than even he could imagine, and there were folks in Philadelphia and New York who would pay a high price for it.

His gaze shifted to the dull yellow waters that sped toward the Mississippi. "We got some rough travelin' ahead of us. The river swolled up like it is, and all this rain, it don't make me easy, takin' the folks I already contracted to. We lost a day already, and the water's only gettin' rougher. I don't navigate at night, and that means five-six days you got ahead o' you before Cairo, some of the hardest travelin' you ever done. We got river pirates and snags and planters and sandbars between here and landfall. And when you get there, then what? Cairo ain't much more than a wide space in the bank, and it mostly ain't respectable folk that stop there neither. With no man to look after you, what do you think you're going to do?"

The small lines around Katherine's mouth tightened, but still she said nothing.

The captain swept his eyes toward the bank, a respectful courtesy to the townsfolk who had gathered there. He demanded clearly, "You folks got any use for this here woman?"

There were murmurings and uncomfortable glances, but the consensus was clear: Katherine Carlyle was trouble, and it was the kind of trouble they'd rather not have to deal with in Mud Flats. Privately they may have thought she had done them all a favor by getting rid of Early Calhoun. But when Zeke and Abel found out, there'd be more than a little hell to pay, and every man, woman, and child was within firing range. They didn't much care what happened to her, just let it happen someplace else. Let her go, and solve the problem all around.

Among the townsmen, not one voice was raised in protest.

Maude Sherrod strode down the bank, her dark skirts switching above mud-splattered petticoats, her feet slipping and her chin held high with righteous indignation. "Captain Dewhurst!" She pronounced the name like a condemnation.

She drew herself up before him, her chest rising and falling from her exertion, her eyes snapping with contempt. "I see I have arrived just in time! Surely you aren't thinking of bringing this, this Jezebel among us!"

Dewhurst looked at Maude with annoyance pushed beyond tolerance. He had, after all, traveled more than five hundred miles with the woman. His drawl was deceptively mild. "I was considerin' it, yes'm."

Maude expelled her breath in a whoosh and at the same time managed to puff out her chest so that she looked even bigger. Outrage emphasized the broken red lines around her nose and tightened her already thin lips.

"This woman is a murderess!" she announced in ringing tones. In the distance, thunder rolled, adding a heavenly fanfare to her words. "Have you no concern for the safety of your passengers?"

The crowd on the bank shuffled in uneasy agreement, and Dewhurst looked at Katherine, studying her. Her face was square and strong, her forehead broad and her eyes wide-set and steady. She had a fair, smooth complexion which even now was untouched by the faintest color of shame. Dewhurst prided himself on his ability to read faces, and in the face of this woman he saw nothing bad.

"We are good Christian folks," asserted Maude Sherrod venomously. "We have children among us. We will not tolerate the presence of this viper in our midst!"

From the banks came a louder murmuring of consent and vigorous nodding of heads. Dewhurst weighed the coin in his hand once more. His mouth tightened. "There's a storm a'comin'," he announced loudly, to all assembled. "We'd best be on our way if we're to be making any time today."

He turned to Katherine. "Miss . . ."

"Carlyle," she answered, loud enough so that all might hear. "Katherine Carlyle."

The captain jerked his head toward the pack on her back. "Is that all you're bringing?"

Katherine nodded.

"On board with you then."

She made her way toward the flatboat, ignoring the cries of shock and outrage that rose up around her. The captain, oblivious to it all, began to hoist the remaining supplies on board.

Maude Sherrod grabbed her husband's arm. He was a good four inches shorter than she was and much lighter, a quiet man whose face bore the signs of twenty years of marriage to a domineering woman.

"Are you just going to stand there?" Maude demanded. "Do something!"

An expression of panic fluttered across his features. His pale eyes squinted under heavy, dark brows, and nervously he brushed a few strands of graying brown hair over his balding head. Then, sensing the eyes of all upon him, he cleared his throat and stepped forward. "Woman!" he called, in a voice that was surprisingly strong for a man of his size. And again, "Woman!"

Katherine turned.

Now that the moment was upon him, William Sherrod's courage failed. Waves slapped against the side of the boat, and rain drummed lightly on the leaves overhead. The anchor lines creaked, and everyone waited.

With a determined effort he stepped forward, hesitated, and spoke. "I've one question for you," he said loudly, "and before God and all assembled here I'll have the truth." Maude looked pleased, and even the captain paused in his work to listen.

Emboldened by his own bravado, Sherrod took another step forward. "Did you kill the man?"

The silence was sharp and suspended. Katherine looked at him gravely, and for a moment it seemed she might actually reply. Then she turned away without a word.

She walked toward the boat, and a crewman extended his hand to help her on board.

Chapter Two

T hey left Mud Flats less than half an hour later. The current was swift even close to the bank. Dewhurst at the stern and his crewman Daniels at the bow pushed off with long poles. As the flatboat picked up the current, Dewhurst manned the long broadhorn, using it as a tiller to maneuver the barge out into the river. He called orders to Alex Werner, a passenger, and to Daniels, who manipulated the smaller sweep oars to steady the barge; but it was Dewhurst who controlled the boat and guided it into the swiftly flowing main channel.

Most of the passengers huddled inside the shelter, out of the damp and cold, but Katherine stood on deck, her feet braced against the turbulent rocking of the river, watching home speed away. A tangle of trees on sloping, scrubby banks, the smoke from an occasional cabin, a woman looking up from her wash pot or coming out from her milking to watch the boat slide by ... these were the signs of civilization. Soon they would all be left behind.

Katherine had often wondered how she would be able to walk away from all that was familiar to

her, to leave the little weather-tight house in the
valley, the furniture Pa had made with his own
hands, the temperamental fireplace which sputtered in the winter and set the roof on fire at least
twice a year—the swampy bottomland and even
the stumpy fields that were full of rocks and sapling pines. It may not have been perfect, but it
was home. And now she was leaving it, running
in terror from the memory of spattering blood
and grinding flesh, and the very real danger of
Zeke and Abel Calhoun.

Somehow she had always known this day would
come. Her family had always been exiles. In the
seventeenth century her grandmother's, Fiona
McLeod's, ancestors had been among those rest-
less Scots exiled to Ulster, Ireland, where with the
passage of time they had become known as the
Scotch-Irish, as though they were a breed. More
than a hundred years later Fiona and her family
had been driven out of Ulster and come to the
shores of America.

The McLeods drifted from Maryland to Virginia, and it was there that Fiona met and fell in
love with Hugh Carlyle, a burly Scotsman who
was serving against his will in the British army.
By the time of the Revolution, Hugh had deserted
and been forced to move on, heading toward the
Blue Ridge Mountains that reminded him of his
home in the Highlands.

After Hugh's death, Fiona had moved again
with her son Edward and his wife Margaret along
the Wilderness Road trail into Kentucky. Their
first home was near Harrodsville. Edward made a
living by trading and trapping, but he had a need
to keep moving on. Katherine herself had been
born on the trail in a hastily made lean-to of limbs

and leaves. In that year, 1802, the dawn of a new century, the Carlyles staked a claim to a plot of acreage near the tiny town of Mud Flats. Margaret wanted to stay put for a while and raise her growing family. Edward decided to give farming a try, ignoring the call of the river, which still urged them westward.

For more than ten years the family endured while Edward battled the land, which all too soon was overplanted and underproductive. In 1813, Margaret died of a long, wasting illness. Edward was never the same after that. Gone were his dreams of traveling down the Ohio to the Mississippi. They had died with Margaret.

Death came to Edward Carlyle soon afterward in the form of an itinerant tinker, who passed through Mud Flats selling pots and pans. He left the fever, and Edward and Katherine and two of her brothers came down with it. Fiona, who'd had the fever as a girl, nursed them, making her own remedies from the herbs and roots of the forest. Katherine was the first to recover, driven by a determination to survive. Nine-year-old Sam, big for his age and quieter than the others, was strong and survived. Jamie, at five, was more vulnerable; blond haired and blue eyed, he lay trembling with fever, pale and thin, and Katherine thought surely he would die. But one night the fever broke and very slowly he got better. Edward, though, simply turned his face to the wall and gave up living.

In 1815 Katherine's brother, Boothe, had traveled west to find a new home for them. Gran had sent him. "Boothe Carlyle," she had said, "you are the oldest and the strongest. As Moses sent his scouts to Canaan, I send you to the western lands.

It's a big land out there, and being what we are, we'll have need of a portion of it. Hard times are coming for us, and soon we must be moving again. You go, Boothe Carlyle, and stake us a homestead, and when it's done, you come back for us. But have care. Remember that in the land of milk and honey there were also giants."

Katherine shivered from the cold drizzle and pulled the damp shawl tighter around her. The shores of the familiar landscape were speeding by, and now she was going alone into the land of the giants.

Yes, Katherine had known this day was coming; the time when she, too, would be forced to move on. But she had never imagined it would be like this. How could she leave everything she had ever known for strange and wild lands?

But she already knew the answer. There was little of importance left behind. The crops had been failing for almost two years, and she had turned the livestock out. There was nothing laid by except a two-room house and some farm implements, the stuff of homemaking. And she was leaving the row of graves on the hill—Ma and Pa; the twins, Rose and Ellen, who had taken milk fever before their second year and followed each other out of the world in the same order in which they'd entered; big, husky Sam, who'd been trapped under a log while trying to retreive a fishing net and had drowned; little Jamie, who'd gone last spring from snakebite. And now Gran.

Yet it was hard to leave, even if all you were leaving behind were graves.

When Gran first took ill and Katherine realized she was dying, she wept in bitterness and fear. Gran was all she had left, and Katherine was terrified of being left alone. But Gran had gripped her hand hard and told her, "You are a foolish child. You will never be alone. We will be with you always, your family, watching out for you, taking care of you. Do you think I'd have it any other way?"

Katherine tried to believe in that promise. After all, she wasn't really alone. There was Boothe, waiting for her, somewhere. And there was Gran, looking out for her.

She tried to think how much worse it could be—if Gran hadn't seen the need to send Boothe out West, or if Boothe lay now in one of those graves and she, Katherine, were all that remained of the Carlyles in America. But Gran had been blessed with a vision, and she had seen the need. Because of her, Katherine had a chance. Because of her, she knew what to do.

From the old land and better times Gran had brought into the Carlyle family three treasures. The first was a talisman of iron pounded into a Celtic cross and surrounded by a circlet of bronze, the origins of which were lost in antiquity. This Gran had threaded onto a heavy chain and suspended around Boothe's neck the day he set out for western lands. The second was a leather pouch which once had contained thirty gold coins stolen many years before by Katherine's great-great grandfather from a Spanish captain shipwrecked upon Scottish shores. The last nine of those coins Katherine now carried in the pocket tied around her waist. But the most valuable of Gran's treasures was a power as old as the woodland goddesses, and Gran called it second sight.

The gift of second sight was a legacy passed down through the women of her family since the

old times, when the word *witch* meant wise and
those who followed that calling were revered.
Gran had told stories of those times, the legends
of the forest and of the gifts of the earth, until
they were as much a part of the Carlyle children's
heritage as nursery songs and cradle rhymes. It
was important, Gran had said, that each man and
woman know from whence he came, and she
could trace her family history back to the old
Scottish lords, and beyond. She taught the children to do the same, to remember their mother's
father and their father's great-grandfather and
take note of the accomplishments of them all, to
remember how much had been sacrificed to bring
them to where they were today.

She taught them other things as well. Poetry
from Homer and philosophy from Plutarch, great
tales of courage and adventure from the Greek
and Latin classics and from the Bible. All of this
she kept in her head, for books were a scarcity
on the frontier. Often she spoke words in her
ancestral tongue, which caused suspicion among
the townspeople, but the words were beautiful to
hear. She had no formal schooling, but learning
was highly valued in her family, and she was with
little doubt one of the most educated women in
the area. All the Carlyle children were taught to
read and write as soon as they could walk, for the
pen, she said, was the most important tool of
communication, and communication was the key
to civilization.

When she was but a girl in Ireland, Fiona
Mcleod had foreseen that the husband she was
yet to meet would die at the hands of a naked,
copper-skinned man wielding an ax. She had no
knowledge of Indians or tomahawks, and little

thought of marrying a man who might encounter such things. When she emigrated with her family to America, she met and married Hugh Carlyle, who was killed twenty-five years later in an Indian uprising.

Years afterward, Fiona had known that the swelling in Katherine's mother's stomach was not another baby but a tumor that would eat away her life. And Fiona had known that she herself, like Moses of old, would never see the Promised Land she had sent her grandson Boothe to find.

Gran's second sight had not been passed on to Katherine. Gran had told Katherine that she had other gifts, but to this day Katherine had not been able to discern what they were. At this moment she would have traded them all for just one glimpse of what the future held in store for her.

When Katherine was thirteen, Gran had taken her hand, looked deep into her eyes, and said, "Yours is not an easy way, Katie-girl. You will pass through blood, and water, and fire. But your seed . . ." Her eyes, old and faded even then, were lit with a far-reaching wonder. "Ah, your seed will spread throughout this land, to the shining mountains and the thundering waters and beyond. Your daughters will give birth to a new breed of men, and your name will not be forgotten."

Blood, water, and fire. Already there had been blood. Now there was water. But Katherine did not want to be mother to a new breed of men. She wanted to be warm, and dry, and safe. She wanted to go home.

She shivered again and tightened her shawl. Oh, Gran, she thought longingly, and turned her eyes back toward shore. Pain stabbed at her heart, tightened her throat, and blurred her eyes, for she had not, until this moment, allowed herself to grieve, or to feel how alone she was. I don't want to leave you. . . .

She heard the clatter of the cabin door behind her and fumbling footsteps picking their way along the cluttered, slippery deck. Katherine blinked away the tears and straightened her shoulders, swallowing hard.

Oliver Sherrod came up beside her, shyly offering her a metal cup. He was a long-limbed, gangly youth with brown hair and gray eyes. His mother's stern features were softened on his face, and his countenance was kind, with the uncertain innocence that is often found in boys his age. But despite his youth Katherine could see a strength in him that spoke well of the man he would one day become.

"I brung you some tea, Miz Carlyle. Thought you'd be cold." Awkwardly, he pressed the cup toward her, explaining self-consciously, "Some of it spilt."

Katherine took the cup hesitantly, warming her hands with it. She studied the boy closely. "That's very kind of you. Thank you."

Those few words of encouragement seemed to both embarrass and please him. His neck flushed, and he shrugged his shoulders. "Miz Wiltshire, she keeps a fire going in a skillet all the time, just for making tea. She's mighty proud of that teapot. Says it come all the way from Holland."

Katherine raised the cup to her lips. "Your mother wouldn't like your being here with me."

He didn't look at her. "No, ma'am. I reckon she wouldn't."

"What about you? Aren't you afraid to be alone with me?"

He was silent for a long time, watching the passing landscape, contemplating with the thoroughness of a boy wavering on the edge of manhood. "I been thinkin' on it, ma'am," he said at last, unable to quite meet her eyes, "and I figure if you did kill that man, like they say, he musta deserved killin', bad."

Katherine did not know why, but those simple words from the mouth of a child were like an expiation to her. She smiled at him, hesitantly. He colored bright red, and she turned her attention to the tea. They stood together in the light rain and silently watched the western shores of Kentucky speed away, going fast, out of reach.

And then Katherine knew how you did it. You simply said goodbye, and walked away.

Ezekial and Abel Calhoun stood bareheaded in the drizzle outside the Carlyle cabin, looking down at the remains of the brother they had uncovered beneath a burlap sack. A three-legged hound sniffed nearby, and when it came too close to the body Zeke chucked a rock at it and sent it howling.

The dog didn't have a name. Abel had found it in a fox trap, fiercely chewing its own leg off in an effort to escape. Zeke and Abe had cast bets on whether it would free itself from the trap before it died and had spent one long afternoon watching the dog gnawing and growling, snapping and crying, devouring its own flesh with a single-minded, purposeful viciousness. When the dog finally got free they debated whether or not to shoot it, but in the end they decided to drag it into town and show folks. When the animal was still alive at the end of some weeks, it seemed only natural that it take up with Zeke and Abe. In a way, they were all of a kind.

Zeke muttered, "Bitch. Didn't even bury him proper."

Abe echoed flatly, "Bitch." None of the Calhouns were very bright, but Abe was the dullest of the bunch. He hadn't spoken until he was five, and even then it was in a slow, deliberate, imitative manner that he kept to this day. That, and a badly squashed-in nose that caused him to breathe slack-jawed through his mouth, and an eye that cocked consistently to the left, gave him a perpetually stupid look. But nobody ever called Abe stupid when Zeke was around—or when Early was around either.

Early had been the youngest, and the best looking, and hellfire wild, with a ruthless cunning his older brothers couldn't help but admire. Early liked the ladies, and he took what he wanted, and when he got lickkered up, nothing could stop him. But that Carlyle bitch had stopped him.

"Goddamn it to hell!" Zeke exploded suddenly. He kicked viciously at a clod of rain-soaked earth, and mud spattered over his dead brother's curled-up hand. That hand was big and fierce and sprinkled with coarse black hair, already stiff and lifeless from rigor mortis.

Zeke shouted at the dead man. "I told you, didn't I? Didn't I tell you, you son of a bitch? I said you better steer clear of them Carlyles, they're witchin' folks, but you just laughed, you jackass! Didn't I tell him, Abe?"

"You told him, Zeke." But even Abe remembered that the warning had been in jest, and they had all laughed and talked about how they'd like to have a piece of what was under Kate Carlyle's skirts. Early should just drag her on back when he was through and they'd each have a go. They'd sent Early out laughing and weaving with a fresh jug of corn whiskey under his arm.

Abe figured Zeke must have remembered the way it was too because he screamed again, "Goddamn it to hell!" and the echo of his voice tore through the gray day and made it shake for a moment before it was swallowed up by the fog and by the dull plop-plop of rain dripping off the eaves of the cabin. Zeke whirled away from the body with a sharp, angry motion and strode a few paces away.

Abe followed him. "We gonna kill her, Zeke?" His voice was low and eager, and his thin, slack face was momentarily animated.

Zeke's jaw hardened. His face was long and narrow like his brothers', framed by greasy dark hair and marred by a jutting row of large yellow teeth. His thin dark eyebrows overshot a pair of weasel-sharp eyes, and his mouth was a narrow slash above a crushed button of a chin. It was a lazy face, reflecting generations of inbreeding, not easily given to expression of any kind; even meanness was reflected on his face as more of a habit than a deliberation. But now his eyes narrowed, his lips set, and his features arranged themselves into something that could almost be taken for contemplation. He said lowly, "Damn right we're going to kill her. Kill her deader'n a smokehouse hog."

Abel's simple face fell. "But she's gone, Zeke. Ole man Sawyer sez she went off with them flatboaters." For that piece of information the shopkeeper Sawyer now lay at midwife Perry's, screaming in agony while a gash in his middle was stitched up with sewing thread.

Zeke turned on his brother and grabbed him by the collar, spraying spittle on his face as he shouted, "You think that makes no never mind to me? You think that's gonna stop us from killin' her?" His eyes were wild and his grip was furious, threatening to rip the skin right off his brother's throat.

Abe was not so stupid that he didn't know when to be afraid. He shook his head in quick and adamant agreement. "No, Zeke, that ain't a'gonna stop us. Ain't gonna stop us one bit."

Zeke released his brother's collar. "She killed our baby brother, Abe," he said in a much milder tone. "She done in one o' *us*. We gonna just let that pass, gonna let the folks hereabouts think it's just fine an' dandy to go round cuttin' up a Calhoun?"

"No, sir, we ain't," said Abe vehemently. "Can't have that."

"Damn right we can't."

The dog wandered close again, sniffing at the back of Zeke's hand, and Zeke let off a kick that sent the cur flying and yelping six feet across the yard. Zeke frowned, turning back toward the body, and after a moment Abe did the same.

It wasn't that either of them had any particular affection for their brother. For all that Early could be as spritely as a carnival when he was sober, and they'd sure miss his tall tales about the women he'd had, he had a mean streak two feet wide, and there was no figuring him at all when he was drunk. He'd tried to drown Abe in the river once over a game of cards, and Zeke still

bore a scar on his throat from Early's blade—
which was all right, because Early had a bigger
one from Zeke's knife, right between his ribs. But
he was their brother. As far back as anybody could
remember, the Calhouns had been fighting men.
They were uneducated, unscrupulous, and their
concept of right and wrong was judged solely by
their own gratifications, but one thing they did
know, and that was loyalty to family.

"He woulda done the same for us," Zeke said
finally. "We're Calhouns, and ain't nobody gonna
get away with something like this."

"We'll git her," Abe agreed. "We'll git her
good."

"Yeah." Zeke moved toward the body. "Come
on. Let's get 'im buried."

The rain graduated from an annoying, soaking
mist to a drumming downpour over the next two
days, endangering visibility, swelling the current,
and requiring all the skill of the captain and oars-
men to keep the little boat on course. Years of
experience had taught Dewhurst to read the river.
He knew that long slanting lines across the water
revealed a reef; lines that branched out like a spider's web from the center revealed a small reef
just below the surface, and he was always careful
rounding a point of land. The eddies that flowed
around the land warned of hidden shoals. But
today Dewhurst couldn't rely on his eyes. The
river was too fierce, the water too high. An in-
creasing number of floating logs told him that the
river was rising far too fast.

Even the riverman's bible, Zadok Cramer's *Nav-
igator*, which showed every turn and twist of the
Ohio from the Monagahela to the Mississippi,

couldn't help him today. The charts were marked with Dewhurst's own notations on every spit of land that had eroded away or new reef that had formed, and usually old Cramer saw him through. But today, with the wind and the rain limiting visibility and the fast-flooding waters causing treacherous currents, Dewhurst had to navigate on instinct and a prayer. He ordered his crewman to keep ringing the great bell on the bow of the boat; he could only hope like hell that anything in his path would have the sense to get out of the way, fast.

Twenty-two people huddled inside the shelter, which might have housed a family of four comfortably. Pinched, silent faces marked with the memory of the recent terror at Louisville Falls grew more strained with each violent toss of the boat.

Katherine found for herself a small, dry corner out of the way of the others where she could observe without being noticed. She had lived too long with the angry caprices of the river not to have a healthy fear of it now, but fear was something she had grown accustomed to. She could feel the tug of the channel fighting against the efforts of the crew with the sweep of the oars. Her heart caught when she heard the tearing scrape of a log against the underside of the boat; the vessel gave a violent, three-quarter turn before slowly, painfully righting itself again. When the other passengers cried out and lurched for the door, she remained still. She had learned long ago that panic did not enhance one's chances of survival.

The air was thick with the odors of fear, spoiling food, and unwashed clothes. Mrs. Wiltshire's skillet fire, deemed too dangerous under the present conditions, was put out. The only light came in pale cracks between the boards of the walls and roof—cracks that admitted as much water as light and made the interior thoroughly miserable. The whine of the children and their mothers' irritated shushing was faintly audible over the thunder of rain and river, but attempts at conversation had long since ceased.

Among the passengers there were seven children under ten years of age, six men, eight women, and one boy aspiring to manhood. Katherine, having been cloistered with them for over forty-eight hours, knew all their names and each of their stories, despite the fact that no one except Oliver had exchanged a direct word of conversation with her.

The Wiltshires, Priscilla and Matthew, had traveled from Albany on the strength of an advertisement Matthew had seen in the paper for a position in a St. Louis bank. It was Matthew's mother, Esther, who kept the teapot full, and in fact the family of three looked more like mother, father, and daughter than mother, son, and daughter-in-law.

Priscilla was a diminutive sixteen year old who spent most of her time either pouting or snapping at her mother-in-law, and in such close quarters she alone accounted for a high percentage of the tension. She was almost pretty, which for her was a much greater burden than being truly ravishing or helplessly homely; she had neither the confidence of a beautiful woman nor the modesty of a plain one and was constantly striving to draw attention to herself. Her small, round face was absurdly surrounded by ringlets of golden curls,

which on another woman might have been strik-
ing. Her mouth was tiny and pursed, her hazel
eyes nondescript, and her nose so small that it
was perfectly undistinguished. When she pouted,
her features drew into themselves in such a way
that one was reminded of a small, sullen chip-
munk. Even at her best she looked like a child
masquerading as an adult in her mother's clothes.

Priscilla's husband, Matthew, was a good twenty
years her senior, and even if Katherine had never
met them she could have predicted the consequences of such a marriage. Matthew was a man
of stern angles and harsh movements; his clothes
seemed to hang on his boney frame, and his lank
black hair contrasted shockingly with the un-
healthy pallor of his skin. He had been a bank
clerk in Albany, and not even the weeks of open-
air travel had put color in his face or erased the
aura of dust and fatigue he carried with him. He
was a quiet man, sometimes almost as sullen as
his child bride, and it was clear he was not happy
with the decision to go west.

Matthew's mother, Esther, seemed to delight in
perpetuating quarrels between her son and his
wife. Every time Matthew began to glower or Priscilla to pout, Esther assumed an air of satisfaction
that seemed to radiate, "I told you so." She talked
a great deal about Francis, the son she had left
behind—and obviously her favorite—and every
time she mentioned his name, Matthew's jaw
would knot and Priscilla's temper would boil.

Under normal circumstances, Katherine would
have found this disharmony unbearable, but the
Wiltshires provided a distraction from her own
troubles. As the boat pitched and rolled, and the
fear on the other passengers' faces became more

pronounced, Katherine wondered if everyone else
didn't feel more or less the same way about the
Wiltshires.

Hannah and Job Prescott were sturdy farm
people whose seven-year-old son had an inflam-
mation of the lungs. It was thought that he would
fare better in the clear air of the West. Job's
brother in the Missouri territory had staked a
claim for farmland next to his, Hannah told her
fellow passengers with pride—twice as much
acreage as their little farm in Pennsylvania, and
twice as rich. The chickens and the cow belonged
to them, along with a sensible array of farm
equipment and supplies. They had saved enough
money to buy a mule in Missouri, but they had
heard that chickens and cows were almost impossible to come by west of the Mississippi and had
refused to go into an unknown land unprepared.
If Katherine had been called upon to rate the
chances for success of each family aboard, the
Prescotts would have been high on her list.

Lucretia and Henry Macon had traveled from
Baltimore with their only child, a ten-year-old boy,
to open a school for young gentlemen in Memphis. They had friends in Memphis who wrote of
the need for a school there, and had even found
a house large enough for a classroom downstairs
with family quarters upstairs. Henry Macon was
a quiet man of letters who, even at the height of
the storm, made three trips a day to the deck to
check on the condition of his tarpaulin-wrapped
books. Lucretia, a nervous, chattering woman, divided her time between fretting about the spinning wheel that had been in her family for four
generations, and was now left to the hazards of
the weather under the canvas on deck, and work-

ing the rosary beads she wore around her neck. As Catholics, the Macons naturally aroused a good deal of interest and suspicion, but Lucretia's almost desperate efforts to ingratiate herself to everyone—except, of course, Katherine—had long ago turned the passengers' irritation and caution to pity.

Hilda and Alex Werner, recent immigrants from Germany, were following the trails of other Germans west to St. Louis. He was a brawny, blond-haired man who barely spoke English; she was in her eighth month of pregnancy, and everyone aboard thought her too far along to make the journey. Their dream was to open a bakery in St. Louis, but Alex knew that would take time and money. Meanwhile he would work at any job—as a stevedore along the river, or as a carpenter building houses for rich people, or even cleaning livery stables. He had a strong back, a willing spirit, and a determination to provide for his wife and unborn child. He was working off his passage as an oarsman, and spent every spare hour on the roof, carving an exquisite floral pattern into the cradle he had built for his firstborn.

The Werners were young and cheerfully confident in each other and their future. Hilda spoke with proud determination of how their baby would be born on the first land to be owned by the Werners in over three generations. Sometimes she would smile hesitantly and curiously at Katherine, as though it were her habit to reach out in friendship, until a look from her husband or one of the other women would cause her to drop her smile and look away. Katherine did not know whether it was because of these small, uncertain gestures or for some other, less easily defined reason, but of everyone aboard, she found herself thinking most kindly toward Hilda, and wishing the best for her.

Caroline and Paul Adamson were a puzzle. They came from Virginia with their three children, the youngest of whom was barely two, and Caroline sometimes spoke in her quiet, dulcet tones of plantation life in the rich James valley. Everything about her exuded quiet strength and aristocratic breeding. She kept herself and her children emmaculate, although her clothes were much turned and mended. For the trip west they had brought nothing except one mule and a meager parcel of household provisions. In her gentle, reserved manner she implied wealth and privilege, yet why she had chosen to give up a flourishing plantation for the uncertain lands of the West she never explained, and even Maude Sherrod had enough good taste not to pry.

Caroline's husband Paul compounded the mystery, for he hardly bore the stamp of a successful planter. He had the indolent good looks of a onetime rake upon whom years of dissipation had taken their toll. His personal habits were sloppy, his eyes were tired, and his middle sagged. But he was patient with his children and respectful to his wife, and that, given the trying circumstances under which they traveled, was all anyone could ask.

All of them regarded Katherine with suspicion and a measure of superstitious fear, but only Maude was bold enough to confront her with overt hostility. On the first night she had insisted that, for the safety of the party, the men should take turns standing armed guard. Not one man among them had dared disagree with her. Faithfully they took their turns over Katherine's sleeping form—some with enough grace to be embarrassed, but most with a grim determination to prove their value aboard the boat. Whenever any of the children began to approach Katherine—particularly her own two daughters—Maude would jerk them back with an angry scolding. Once she had boxed Oliver's ear for simply smiling at Katherine.

Katherine endured this treatment with curious detachment. After all she had been through, could anyone make her burden worse? She was only eighteen years old, and already she had lived the lifetimes of three grown women. Sometimes she would notice the way they all looked at her and she would think in amazement, Why they're afraid of me!—forgetting for a moment the circumstances under which she had joined them and the stigma that had been stamped upon her; forgetting that she was no longer simply Katherine Carlyle, Edward Carlyle's daughter and Fiona Carlyle's granddaughter, but a murderess, a criminal, an outcast.

When she did remember, hurt and indignation would fill her and she would think, *It's not fair. I didn't ask for this, I never wanted this, I didn't plan it, and it's not fair that I should be hated for it.* And it became more difficult to ignore Maude Sherrod. Gran would have chided her about compassion and seeing through the eyes of others, but in fact the only people Katherine could feel sorry for were Maude's husband, who had to endure her browbeating night and day, and her children, who couldn't make themselves small enough or quiet enough to escape their mother's notice.

Katherine had lived with rejection and had

grown accustomed to relying on no one but herself, and her family, for companionship, but she could not stand being the object of unrest in such close quarters. She met Maude's dark, resentful gaze across the dim cabin and she thought, Four more days of this. How shall any of us bear it?

She wondered if she would fare better in Cairo, where the rumors would surely accompany her, or on the uncertain journey that lay beyond that. Would her past follow her even into the wilderness?

When she closed her eyes at night, her dreams were invariably blood-soaked and horrific. She would awake with a thundering heart, gasping for breath, imagining the faces of Zeke and Abel Calhoun bending over her, axes in their hands, their eyes glinting with demon fire. Despair would overcome her, and the nausea of fear, and she would shake with it silently in the night with no one there to comfort her, no one to stroke her hair or to murmur soothing words and tell her she was safe. She would think, Oh, Gran, why aren't you here with me? Boothe, why did you leave me? But the slap of water against the hull and the snores of strangers were the only answers to her silent prayers.

The powerful drumming on the roof let up somewhat, and the passengers looked up with hope. But the lessening of the rain only made the creaking and grinding of the boat boards more audible, reminding them anew of how fragile was the vessel to which they had entrusted their lives and all their possessions. Esther Wiltshire clutched her teapot protectively with both arms, and Hilda Werner leaned into her husband's strength. Two-year-old Rebecca Adamson began to hiccough with sobs, and her mother embraced her absently. And then Maude Sherrod opened up her Bible and began to read aloud the story of Jonah and the whale, as she did every day at this time. She had no need of light, for she knew the passage by heart, and her eyes never left Katherine Carlyle.

Katherine leaned against the wall of the cabin and wearily closed her eyes. How much longer?

Chapter Three

Captain Dewhurst wiped his eyes and thought, God sure made a bunch of fools that'd go up against Him in a place like this. Around him the river churned and pulled, spitting up debris and chewed up land as though a hungry monster thrashed beneath the surface. All he could see on either side and behind him was water, rushing and spinning and falling from the sky. The Ohio was a huge, living creature, and the small boat remained afloat only at its capricious mercy.

Throughout the day, as he had grimly fought the current and the storm, he had spared no time to worry. Rain and fog were as much a part of a river captain's life as were the channels themselves. Though at times the rain reduced visibility to only a few yards, Dewhurst guided the boat by feel, by instinct, and by the confidence that came from having made the passage many times before.

It was only now, when the rain had lessened and the channel felt smoother—when he should, in fact, be able to relax and breathe easier—that he was gripped with unshakeable unease. Perhaps it was the strange texture of the sky which, though

47

the rain was drying to a mere sprinkle, seemed even lower and darker, forecasting worse things to come. Perhaps it was the stillness and warmth which seemed out of place on these teeming waters.

He narrowed his eyes to make out an object ahead, and it was as he had feared. A snag had formed in the middle of the channel, collecting everything that swept toward it so that now it was an island of dead branches, tree stumps, broken logs and other debris. It was navigable, but just barely, and in this weather . . .

"Captain, look!"

Dewhurst swept his eyes in the direction his crewman pointed. He could not prevent an instinctive start of alarm when he saw a man's body float by. He had just a glimpse of a blue-white face with wide staring eyes and a scrap of a red flannel shirt before the current sucked the body under. Following close behind were two logs loosely bound by a shredding strip of rawhide. Dewhurst cursed. Another pilgrim trying to negotiate the treacherous waters and without sense enough to tie up in a storm.

He looked again at the deadfall looming ahead, then searched the banks for a likely landing spot. Chances were they could circumnavigate the snag just fine now that the rain had let up and while there were still several hours before dark, but his every instinct told him to make toward land, now.

A roll of thunder crackled in the distance, and he wasted no more time. He spotted a sheltered cove to starboard and lifted his arm toward it. "Land ho!" he shouted.

"But the Lord sent out a great wind into the sea, and there was a mighty tempest in the sea, so that the ship was like to be broken. Then the mariners were afraid . . ."

Thunder clapped close by, causing the passengers inside the cramped cabin to give an involuntary start and frightening one of the children into wailing. Maude continued, unperturbed, "But Jonah was gone down into the sides of the ship, and he lay, and was fast asleep."

Katherine opened her eyes to find, as she had expected, that all eyes were uneasily upon her. Maude's gaze was the most piercing.

"And they said every one to his fellow, Come, and let us cast lots, that we may know for whose cause this evil is upon us. So they cast lots and the lot fell upon Jonah."

There was a sudden stillness; even the child stopped crying. Everyone was staring at Katherine, even Oliver who quickly shifted his eyes away in embarrassment.

Thunder rolled again and the boat lurched. Priscilla Wiltshire gave an elaborate shiver and declared, "My goodness, must we have such a morbid passage on such a day?"

Priscilla was a fastidious girl who, even here, managed to keep her apron spotless and her headdress starched. Her hand fluttered nervously to her hair now, primping one fat curl and securing the tie of her kerchief under her chin. Her mother-in-law glared at her.

"Mrs. Sherrod has chosen a most appropriate sermon for our troubled times," pronounced Esther Wiltshire, her eyes fixed meaningfully on Katherine. "Pray, go on, Maude."

Maude inclined her head graciously and continued, "Then they said unto him, Tell us, we pray thee, for whose cause is this evil upon us?"

She paused deliberately, giving everyone's eyes an opportunity to return to Katherine. Katherine held her gaze and picked up the text in a soft, clear voice, "And he said unto them, I fear the Lord, the God of heaven, which hath made the sea and the dry land."

Maude's lips compressed tightly, and steel came into her voice. "So they took up Jonah, and cast him forth into the sea; and the sea ceased from her raging."

Katherine was silent for a moment, letting the implication sink in. Then she said, "If you are waiting for me to voluntarily leap overboard, I'm afraid I must disappoint you. I've never heard any reports of whales in the Ohio River."

There was a smothered male chuckle which no sharp female eye could pinpoint, and Maude's fists closed upon her open Bible. "Do you mock our meditations, woman?"

"Indeed I do not," Katherine replied. She tried to keep the anger from showing on her face, but she could not keep it from tightening her voice. "But I cannot admire anyone who would twist the Lord's word for her own purpose."

"I have twisted nothing!" Maude closed the Bible and pressed it to her breast. "You've heard it from the Good Book itself what happens when evil comes among God-fearing men!"

Henry Macon, who until this moment had appeared to be absorbed in his own thoughts as he so often was, stirred and cleared his throat. "Actually," he pointed out, stroking his narrow chin, "in the instance you've quoted, Mrs. Sherrod, Jonah was the only man aboard who was God-fearing. He was God's chosen one, if you recall, and he sailed with heathens to escape the call of the ministry."

Katherine barely suppressed a smile, but Maude's temper had been kindled. "Think as you will, sir," she replied with a huff, "but there is no doubt in *my* mind that we have brought wickedness among us and God is at this moment speaking his wrath!"

There were some murmurings of agreement, and Lucretia Macon spoke up nervously. "It *is* in the Scriptures, Henry."

Another roll of thunder sounded, seeming this time to shake the boat in the water. Hannah Prescott was thrown against Katherine and quickly jerked away, gathering her son to her. Hilda Werner huddled against her husband, murmuring to him in rapid German, her arms protecting her bulging abdomen. When she glanced at Katherine, her eyes were frightened.

Katherine got to her feet, steadying herself against the low roof as the boat listed violently. She could better endure the rain on deck than the hostility here. She cast one long glance around the room and said, "Perhaps if you search the Scriptures further, you will find another useful passage. From St. John, chapter eight, verse seven: Let he who is without sin among you cast the first stone."

She started to move toward the door, but suddenly it was flung open and a young crewman stood there, dripping with rain and taut with authority. "We're tying up for the night," he announced. "Captain says all passengers must disembark."

It was immediately apparent from his tone that

this was no ordinary request, and a ripple of panic went through the passengers, which they tried to disguise with protests and questions.

"What's this?" Matthew Wiltshire got to his feet, exercising his prerogative to take out the frustration caused by his wife and mother on anyone who happened to get in his way. "It's only a little past noon! Has the captain gone daft?"

"I won't take my baby out in this storm!" chimed in Hannah Prescott. "He'll get the fever for sure!"

"Clearly," objected Henry Macon, "these are hardly the best circumstances in which to be making camp!"

"Well, I'm not setting one foot out of this cabin!" Maude Sherrod declared. "The captain must be mad to think I would. Is this what we paid passage for? All manner of indignities and inconveniences! I declare . . ."

"At least we're somewhat dry in here!" said Caroline Adamson, to a chorus of agreement. "I simply can't imagine . . ."

The crewman interrupted impatiently. "Get the womenfolk and children off first, then we start off-loading the livestock." He strode across the deck, leaving the door open to the river mist and wind.

Thunder rolled again, and Katherine slipped the straps of her pack over her arms.

"Well, I never!" exclaimed Priscilla Wiltshire with widened eyes. She turned to her husband. "Matthew, I'm not going out in that nasty weather, and that's final!"

"I'll just go speak to the captain," Matthew said.

Katherine started moving toward the door, and Job Prescott spoke up gruffly, voicing her thoughts. "Lightnin', you fools!" He was a man of few words and precise common sense. "There's a storm a'brewin' and we're sitting on this river like a lone duck at a target shoot. Hannah, get the boy and start moving!"

That galvanized them. The only thing that puzzled Katherine was why it had taken so long. They had all seen lightning fires, watched livestock be struck down in open fields and ships fried to skeletons in harbor. Still, Gran had always said there was nothing like fear to slow a person's thinking, and these people must be more frightened than they let on.

It took some time for the women to gather up the children and the few personal possessions they carried with them—reticules, sewing baskets, small valises that held a change of clothes and items of value. The men headed for the deck to help with the tying off, and the women shrilly snapped instructions and herded the children. Katherine, who was closest to the door, found herself being stepped on, shoved back, and ignored. It was like being trapped in a henhouse during a high wind, and if it hadn't been for the children she would have done some shoving herself, if only to escape to fresh air and sanity.

By the time she reached the deck the weather had worsened. The sky was a bruised yellow and fat drops of rain were falling slow and hard. A gust of wind caught her skirt and as she watched, lightning bisected a low-hanging cloud. Katherine felt a measure of panic herself as a clap of thunder followed quickly. She did not want to be caught on the water when the full force of the storm broke.

The boat was tied to a half-submerged cypress.

The water level was so high that the bank was barely a leaping step up. But the current was fast and the boat was lurching; a misstep could be dangerous. Daniels the crewman was on shore, receiving the children who were passed to him. Dewhurst stood ready to help the women over but so far only two, Hannah Prescott and Maude Sherrod, had been brave enough—or frightened enough—to make the crossing.

"I can't!" cried Priscilla Wiltshire as the captain urged her forward. "I'll fall!"

Her mother-in-law pushed impatiently in front of her, holding the crewman's outstretched arm with one hand and her precious teapot with the other, and heaved herself on shore. Caroline Adamson followed.

On shore Hannah Prescott called, "You get my cow, Job Prescott! Little Joel's gonna need that milk tonight!"

"My spinning wheel!" cried Lucretia Macon, and made to turn back.

"Blast the cow, woman!" Precott shouted angrily. "You get back from them trees!"

"Everybody move back!" Dewhurst commanded. Lightning crackled audibly and thunder almost swallowed his words. "Get away from the banks!"

"Oliver Sherrod, you get over here and take care of your sisters!" Maude ordered. "Hilda, don't you be afraid, honey, we're not going to let anything happen to you or that baby. Captain, help that poor woman!"

With a backward, despairing look at her husband and a great deal of assistance, Hilda pulled her cumbersome form safely to shore. Henry Macon pushed his wife forward next, assuring her,

"Leave the spinning wheel be. It's drier under the tarp. I'll just check my books . . ."

"Blast it, Maude Sherrod," Captain Dewhurst shouted. "Can't you get those women to move back?"

"I can't do it, Matthew," shrilled Priscilla. "I'll break my neck for sure!"

Katherine moved toward the edge of the boat then, reaching for the crewman's hand, but he had turned to usher away some children who had wandered too close to the bank. "Confound it, woman," exclaimed Matthew Wiltshire, dragging his wife forward. "You heard the captain—everybody off!"

There was a great commotion behind them, a squealing and a braying, and Captain Dewhurst exclaimed, "Who let that goddamn mule loose?"

Katherine pressed against the wall of the cabin to avoid being swept overboard as the mule came charging by, hawking and flinging froth. Someone shouted, "The stock's going crazy! He kicked down the pen!"

The mule ran around the deck once, trampling cargo and kicking his heels, and then, in a move that would have been comical had the situation not been so desperate, the animal leaped off the boat toward the bank. His front hooves slipped and he sank half into the water, but with the surefootedness that had made him an invaluable servant of man, he righted himself, dug in again, and scampered up the bank and off into the woods.

Paul Adamson shouted to his children, "Benjamin! Martha! Don't let that mule get away! Caroline! I'm not spending half the night rounding up that animal!"

For whatever else the mule's unexpected escape might have done, his appearance on shore did move the crowd back, and several of the women and children pushed through the woods, calling the mule.

Matthew Wiltshire turned angrily to his wife. "All right, I'll go first and pull you onshore. Grab my hand."

He sprang onto the bank, and Priscilla, thus ordered, meekly caught his hand. She cried out as he hauled her roughly off the boat, and when she landed on her hands and knees in the mud her cry turned to outrage. "Matthew, look what you've done! My gown!"

The rain was coming harder now, and Katherine moved again to the edge of the boat. Oliver Sherrod sprang in front of her. "I'll help you, Miz Carlyle," he offered, extending his hand from shore.

Someone shouted, "All right, I'm bringing the cow! What about these chickens?"

Katherine reached for Oliver's hand, but something shoved her; she faltered and stumbled. She saw the alarm on his face as he grabbed for her arm and caught it. She felt him slipping in the slick tracks the mule had made and she tried to pull away but was too late; his weight dragged her forward and into the current.

Matthew was the closest. He saw Oliver fall and drag Katherine with him; he heard Maude's piercing scream. Instinctively he grabbed the low branch of the tree and leaned toward the water. No one was quite certain what happened then.

Children standing as far as ten yards away felt their hair stand on end. Priscilla shrieked as her silk petticoat—her pride and joy—billowed upward of its own accord. The air burned and tingled, and in that instant—before Priscilla's shriek was half-formed and before a startled child could lift his hand and point at his playmate's dancing hair—the air split apart with a tremendous crack.

Matthew Wiltshire shot back through the air as though propelled by a cannon, his feet flying, his hands outstretched, his eyes wide open and locked in an expression of surprise. The great cypress was sliced in two like butter under a hot knife and tumbled forward into the river.

The crewman died instantly, his neck snapped by a heavy branch. Dewhurst turned to see a rushing screen of twisted limbs and green foilage before the weight of the tree crushed his skull and flung him into the water. The boat snapped under the impact of the fall like a child's toy. Henry Macon, standing on the roof of the cabin checking that his books were secure against the rain, was swept into the current by the descent of the first branches. The others never knew what hit them. Impaled by sharp limbs, crushed by the falling trunk, smothered by debris, or flung into the rushing water, they each met a swift and merciless death.

Katherine knew none of this. She knew only dark brown water rushing into her mouth and spinning past her eyes, an explosive pressure against her lungs, and the violent speed of the current dragging her along like a helpless doll. She surfaced through no act of her own and flailed wildly. Her hand caught a root protruding from the bank and tangled in it, but the rest of her body was pulled sideways with such force that she thought her arm would snap from its socket. She got one gasp of air before river water slapped her face again and submerged her, but she came up choking, looking wildly for Oliver.

At first she saw nothing but water and more water, dark, angry, churning. Then a splintered plank spun by, and what looked like a broken china plate, and then water slammed into her face again.

When she opened her eyes a face was floating before her. It was a ghastly thing, cruelly mis-shapen, stained pink with rivulets of blood. But the features were recognizable. It was Captain Dewhurst.

The current sucked the corpse away. Katherine was not aware of the wild, animal-like noises she made as she struggled to secure her hold on the branch, clawing her way further up the bank. A fingernail peeled backwards and shot fresh agony through the arm she had thought was numb. The river pulled at her feet and tore at her clothing, and every time she managed to lift her head a few inches she would sink back down again, swallowing water.

Panic flooded her as swift and as powerful as the river around her. *I'm going to die*, she thought. *Gran Boothe ... I'm not strong enough ... I'm going to die!*

From far away, like an echo, came the words, *We are with you always.*

Gritting her teeth, she slowly unwound one set of fingers from the branch. The current tugged at her, but she held fast with the other hand, and slowly she began to work the strap of her pack over her shoulder until one arm was free of it. She paused to breathe a sigh of relief before the current slammed into her again, catching the heavy pack and flinging her backwards. She screamed

out loud as she felt her grip slipping, and she
choked as scalding lungs inhaled water. She
grasped the branch again with both hands and
held on. It was a long time before she could make
herself release the other arm and work the strap
of the pack off her shoulder.

The calico bundle surfaced for an instant and
then was gone—and with it, all she possessed. A
change of clothes, the family Bible, some cookware, a sampler Gran had embroidered with a
coat of arms and her family ancestry. Gone.

But around her waist the coins dragged heavily,
and she was still alive. Slowly, painstakingly, she
inched her hands upward, one over the other, on
the branch. Her shoulders strained and throbbed,
and the muscles in her arms began to quiver, but
she was strong from years of farm work, and
eventually she was able to swing her feet forward
and touch the rocky bank of the submerged shore.

She dragged herself onto the muddy ground,
shaking and gasping. For a long time afterwards
she knew nothing but the drum of rain on her
shoulders and the roar of thunder, echoed by the
explosive beat of her own heart. Faintly, she
thought she heard a voice, far away, calling. She
pulled herself to her knees, and as she did, Oliver
stumbled through the undergrowth toward her.

He was as soaked as she was, smeared with mud
and river slime, and his face was white and frightened. His expression sagged with relief as he saw
her, and he gasped, "I saw you . . . couldn't get to
you. I was only pulled down a little way, hit the
bank . . . Miz Carlyle, we've got to get back to the
boat. I think something bad has happened. I . . .
I saw the cow in the water. It was dead."

Katherine let him pull her to her feet, but dread

weighted her down now as the hungry waters had only moments ago. She thought something bad had happened, too. And as they turned and stumbled upriver, she was afraid of what they were going to find.

Chapter Four

A pallid sun filtered through the foliage overhead, its light seeming to waver and drip like the remnants of moisture that slithered from the leaves—slow, faint, and deliberate. The morning found sixteen women and children huddled in a loose circle around a cluster of graves on the riverbank. The one male survivor, Matthew Wiltshire, sat with his back propped up against a nearby tree, his eyes wide and staring, his once black hair now snow white.

Only three bodies could be recovered for burial: the crewman Daniels, who had died on shore, Alex Werner, who had been flung onto the bank by the impact of the falling tree, and William Sherrod, whose body had floated downriver a hundred yards before becoming entangled with some remnants of the raft in the undergrowth that protruded from the edge of the bank.

The deadfall in the center of the river was gruesome testament to the fates of at least three of the other men. Broken and crushed bodies waved like horrific banners against the tide, their hair floating on the current, their clothing billowing around them. Distance and the ever-surging current made positive identification impossible, which was perhaps a mercy, but one thing was certain: those who now stood on the bank were alone.

They had scraped out the graves from the muddy soil with broken planks rescued from the boat, and it had taken most of the night. Now they stood, too exhausted by shock to feel grief, their faces still and blank, and stared at the results of their handiwork. No one seemed to know what to do.

Katherine thought, Someone should say something. These men shouldn't go to their Maker without having some words read over them. But the eyes of those who wouldn't have the benefit of a Christian burial seemed to stare at her from the deadfall, and she suppressed an involuntary shiver. Who would pray for those men? And would praying do any good anyway?

She looked at the faces of those who survived, her eyes going from one to the other. Caroline Adamson, straight backed and still, stared deliberately over the graves and into the forest beyond. One hand rested on the shoulder of her oldest, Martha, and another on five-year-old Benjamin, who was the man of the family now. Two-year-old Rebecca clung to her skirts and whimpered with exhaustion and confusion.

Priscilla Wiltshire's blonde curls straggled about her face, her hands were black with mud, her eyes were swollen and red-rimmed. Her mother-in-law, Esther, staunch and straight, still clutched her teapot. Their only male protector, son and husband, had not spoken a word or moved an inch of his own accord since the bolt of lightning had flung him through the air. He had quite obviously lost his mind.

Hannah Prescott held her seven-year-old son in her arms, oblivious to his weight, stroking his hair as one might pet a kitten or a puppy, taking more comfort than she gave. Lucretia Macon likewise held her sleeping son over her shoulder, staring at the river with a dazed detachment and something akin to calm disbelief.

Maude Sherrod gripped her Bible in one hand and the hand of four-year-old Amy in the other. Oliver stood beside her, holding his sister Judith in his arms. Behind the lines of experience and fatigue now etched on his face, his eyes were those of a frightened little boy. Next to them was Hilda Werner, her damp gown clinging to her protruding abdomen, her plump face aged with exhaustion and grief. Who would care for her baby now? What would become of her?

What would become of all of them?

The silence wore on, broken only by the drip of the leaves and the occasional whine or hiccough of a child. Katherine could feel another outbreak of hysteria building. Lucretia Macon swayed on her feet and looked close to fainting. Priscilla's lips tightened and twisted as she staved off fresh tears. The longer they stood there, helpless and silent, the more the thin composure that had bound them together through the night threatened to break. Katherine knew they would not welcome her interference. Yet no one else seemed to have the spirit to to do anything.

It was Oliver who finally broke the silence. He cleared his throat as he set his sister on her feet, then went to his mother and took the Bible from her unprotesting fingers. Awkwardly he began to thumb through the pages. He found the passage he wanted and stepped forward, a gangly boy suddenly thrust into adulthood, the oldest, the man.

"Let not your heart be troubled," he read. His voice was small and he looked around anxiously, as though uncertain he had chosen the right passage. But the eyes of the women turned to him, they patted their children into quiesence, and he continued more strongly, "Ye believe in God, believe also in me. In my father's house . . ."

His eyes fell upon the fresh mound of earth that contained the body of his father and he faltered. Katherine's fists tightened as though to physically impart courage.

His Adam's apple bobbed, and he blinked hard. Then he took a breath and continued in a clear voice, "In my father's house are many mansions; if it were not so, I would have told you. I go to prepare a place for you . . ."

An hour later they were still hovering around the gravesites, forming separate islands among themselves as grief worked its way through each of them. Caroline Adamson had had some sweets in her reticule for her own children; she had distributed them among the others, but it wasn't enough. The children were hungry and cranky and whined intermittantly, but even their limited understanding told them that much greater problems faced them now, and on the whole they were remarkably subdued.

Maude Sherrod could not make herself leave her husband's grave. She looked down at the narrow hump of freshly turned earth and thought bitterly, For this. Everything . . . for this.

She knew in her heart she should spend these moments contemplating a life cut too short, the time they had had together, the mistakes they had made, the joys they had known. She felt regret, sorrow, and unrelenting pain, but what she felt most of all was anger.

William had left her. He had left her and the children alone and helpless with everything they had ever worked for destroyed, with nothing left to build on and no hope for the future. All her life Maude had had to guide William, to wheedle and complain, to push and command. He was a weak man through no fault of his own, and it had been up to her to take charge. She had run his mercantile shop, nursed him, dictated his future, kept them all safe. Now he was gone.

Perhaps the only place in the world where a man was indispensible was in the wilderness, she thought, where only he could trap and hunt and defend. The only time a woman really had need of a man was when she was defenseless and impoverished and homeless, when she was without the things only a man could provide. Now, for perhaps the first time in her life, Maude Sherrod needed her husband, and he was gone.

Without warning, guilt pierced her. William hadn't wanted to come west; it had been Maude's idea. Everything was Maude's idea. If she had not insisted, if she had not badgered and cajoled and finally taken it upon herself to scrape up their savings and book passage, none of them would be here today. William would be alive, and she and the children would be safe . . .

But no. Guilt was one thing Maude could not afford, not now, not here. She had always done the best for her family. All she knew was taking care of her own, taking charge, making decisions. Someone had had to do it, and the task had always fallen to her. She had done what she thought best.

Now she was alone. Oliver, her little man. She had been so proud of him when he took up the Bible. He was growing fast, but he was still just a boy, with the best years of his life ahead of him. Her two precious girls, Judith and Amy ... she had such hopes for them. What would become of them now? How would they get by? What future did they have?

We have nothing, she thought. Maude had to keep repeating that to herself, trying to make herself believe it. Nothing is left.

Her eyes moved over the bedraggled group and tried to summon up the strength to offer encouragement or advice. They would expect it from her. Who else could they turn to? But just now Maude was so tired, so stricken, so numb in spirit that she had no words for anyone.

A flash of frizzy red hair caught her attention and with it came a surge of resentment so powerful it made her ill. It wasn't fair that this hussy should survive while her William was gone. A wolf among innocents, and who should endure but the wolf? Because of that murderess, Maude had almost lost Oliver too, and now she simply squatted there on the riverbank, picking through debris like nothing had happened. Untouched, unfeeling, and alive. The hatred she felt for Katherine Carlyle was a pure thing, and it brought scalding tears of fury to her eyes. The tears made her feel weak and she couldn't afford to give in to them. She turned her back on Katherine Carlyle and walked away.

Katherine had gathered up some of the debris that had floated to shore—a child's nightgown, a good-sized piece of canvas, a cooking pot and two cups; nothing of much value. If they stayed here much longer they could doubtless make themselves almost comfortable on the refuse that washed ashore from their own and other wrecks. But staying was out of the question. Already the rising river had obliterated the original site of the accident, and the flooding showed no signs of abating.

The mule had wandered back into camp sometime after sundown and someone, probably Oliver, had had the presence of mind to tie him up. If worse came to worse, they could always eat the poor creature.

It would be days, perhaps weeks, before the river lowered enough to permit the passage of other boats. Besides that, the captain, in making his decision to tie off, had moved out of the well-traveled channel and into a smaller, narrower inlet. Even if other boats did pass, it was unlikely they would see any signal from the band on shore or hear their cries.

Food and shelter were the first necessities, and neither would be easy to come by here. Katherine tried to think how far they had traveled in relation to the distance between Mud Flats and Cairo. Fifty miles? Sixty? She had never heard of any settlements between here and Cairo, and Mud Flats lay on the other side of the river.

Katherine had been raised on hard luck and hard times, and she knew how to survive. But these people . . . she let her eyes wander over them again. Hilda Werner aroused the most sympathy in Katherine. Since the tragedy she had barely made a sound, nor had she drawn any attention to herself. On her hands and knees, she had helped to scrape out her husband's grave, and now she sat on the ground, tears streaming down her face, trying to fashion a cross out of two broken boards and strips of muslin torn from her petticoat.

Hannah Prescott had wrapped her son in her shawl and continued to hold him in her arms even though he complained of being too hot and squirmed to get down. She did not take her eyes off the deadfall. Oliver tried to keep his two sisters busy gathering firewood. His eyes kept darting anxiously to his mother, who sat on a broken log, unnaturally quiet, stroking a piece of red calico that was inside a waterproof bundle on her lap.

Esther Wiltshire was kneeling over her son, patiently wiping saliva from his chin and speaking to him soothingly while Priscilla stood by, wringing her hands and making incoherent sounds that expressed both horror and helplessness. As Katherine watched, a spreading wet stain appeared on the front of Matthew's pants, and she turned her head away, embarrassed.

Lucretia Macon was kneeling before her ten-year-old, Ulysses, combing his hair with her fingers and wiping the grime from his face, as though she were cleaning him up for Sunday meeting. "My poor spinning wheel," she murmured sadly. "Thank God mama never lived to see this day. She got it from her mama, who saved it when the British came and burned their house. She hid it in the woods and buried it with leaves. Did I ever tell you this story, dear? I think we'd best not mention this to your father. He knew what store I put by it, and he's going to be beside himself when he finds all his books wet. He's like to pitch a fit when he gets back, but we simply must be patient. We'll all just have to be patient . . ."

Caroline Adamson stood looking out over the river, her expression composed, holding the hands of her children on either side of her. "Everything is going to be all right," she told them calmly. "We'll just wait here for another boat."

"I'm hungry," ventured her daughter Rebecca, in a small voice.

"It won't be long," Caroline assured her. "Today . . . or tomorrow. We'll just wait for another boat."

"Yes," Maude Sherrod said quietly.

Nothing had changed for Katherine. Boothe, a home, a chance for new life lay across the Mississippi, and she still had a long way to travel. She got up and went to untether the mule.

"What are you doing?" Caroline said sharply, following Katherine's movement. "That's my Paul's animal! You leave it be!"

Katherine calmly unwound the rope from a low branch. "If you're staying here, you'll have no need for the mule. I plan to borrow it and go downriver for help."

All eyes turned on her in a mixture of horror and disbelief. Clearly, such a plan had never occurred to them.

"You're mad!" exclaimed Caroline.

"We'll be rescued before you're out of sight!"

"You leave my husband's mule be!"

"Let her go," advised Maude in disgust. "We're better off without her. She'll see her own foolishness soon enough and pay for it."

Katherine pressed her lips together and retethered the mule. "Very well then, I'll walk."

"You can't go out there by yourself!" Oliver exclaimed.

His mother snapped, "Hush up, boy, let her be!"

Katherine looked deliberately at Maude. "No boat is going to come for you," she said. "Look." She gestured toward the river. "Already the water has covered the landing. By tonight the ground on which we stand will be covered. I've seen this river flood too many times to take its temper lightly. Those men foolish enough to try to navigate these waters will pass through the channel on the other side. How do you imagine the boats could cross over and stop for you, even if they could see you? Perhaps in a week, or two ... but in the meantime all the game has been driven away by the floodwaters, and you have no food." She paused and shook her head. "I'm going."

Her words seemed to cause some doubt among the women, for the silence that followed was tense with worry. Some of them reached for their children, others bit their lips as the immediacy of their problems momentarily overcame grief.

Then Oliver spoke up. "She's right, Ma. It's dangerous to stay here. Cairo can't be more'n a week away by land—and by the time another boat comes by we could already be in town."

Maude frowned.

Katherine turned to go. "I'll send help back for you."

It was that phrase that sent consternation through the group. Katherine was escaping while they remained helplessly behind; she would go while they waited at the mercy of fate. For the first time the reality of the situation hit them.

With the typical urgency of adolescence, Oliver was the first to respond. He squared off his shoulders and puffed up his chest. "I'm the man of the family now, Ma," he said, "and I say we go. Pa wouldn't want you to stay here and die."

"You're just a baby!" Maude snapped back, glaring at Katherine. "Hush up!"

"We can't stay here!"

"That woman's bewitched you! Can't you see she's the cause of all our problems? Now you'd follow her into the wilderness?"

"Ma, how can you say that?" Oliver's voice cracked with incredulity. "She didn't have nothing to do with the wreck! She weren't even on the boat when it happened."

"We travelled all the way from New Hampshire with nary a mishap!" Maude cried, a note of hysteria in her voice. "We were doing fine . . ."

"What about the falls?" Oliver objected, but she didn't hear him.

". . . until we took this . . . this Jonah aboard! The wrath of God struck us down, it couldn't be plainer, and now all our men are . . . are gone."

Her voice broke harshly and she covered her face with her hands. Caroline went to her, making soothing noises, and Oliver stood by helplessly. Katherine started to walk away.

It was Hilda's voice, small and uncertain, that stopped her. "Where . . . will you go?"

Katherine hesitated. Until this moment she had been convinced of the rightness of her decision, simply because it was in her nature to act rather than meekly be victimized by fate. But now, confronting the truth of what she was about to do, she was not so certain. Perhaps they were right. Perhaps they would fare better together here on the riverbank than she would alone in the wilderness.

She answered with far more conviction than she felt. "I'll follow the river as far as I can, then keep moving west. I'm bound to find a settlement somewhere, or if not, Cairo can't be very far away."

Esther stood up. The contempt in her voice didn't mask the uncertainty in her eyes. "You've got no food, no weapons. There are savages in these hills and all manner of beasts. You'll die."

If there was one thing that would push Katherine to try the impossible, it was being told she could not do it. She lifted her chin and squared her shoulders. All doubt left her eyes. "Then at least I shall die trying," she said purposefully.

Hilda rose awkwardly to her feet. "Wait."

She came over to Katherine, her plump face white and streaked with tears, but with a new calmness in her eyes. "My babe shall not be born on the muddy riverbank without a roof o're its head. I promised it a home, and a home it shall have." For a moment her eyes flooded and her voice wavered. "My Alex would have wanted it so."

She took a breath and steadied herself. Katherine could only guess at the courage it took for her to say the next words. "I will come with you."

Katherine felt her chest tighten with alarm, and although she drew in a breath for protest she found she could say nothing. How could she take a pregnant woman on a grueling journey through the wilderness, a journey that even Katherine feared might fail. But if she refused her, if she left Hilda and her unborn child on the banks of the river to await whatever fate might have in store ...

Oliver picked up his sister Amy and stepped forward, an almost manly set to his jaw. "So will we."

Maude pushed away Caroline's consoling arms and got to her feet. "Now you wait just a minute ..."

Oliver turned on her. "We've got no choice. We don't have any food, either, and at least out there there's a chance of finding some. Will you stay here and let these children starve?" His voice was rising. "I'm not going to stay behind to bury the rest of my family!" His voice broke and his eyes glistened with unshed tears.

Oliver ducked his head, embarrassed. Maude lifted her hand in a faltering gesture to reach for him, but he turned away. The stubborn set to Maude's jaw wavered, and Katherine saw uncertainty in her eyes for the first time.

Esther was looking at her son. His tangled snow-white hair gave him a ghoulish appearance, and the blank and staring eyes were unsettling to say the least. "We've got to get him to doctor," she said quietly.

Priscilla recoiled as though struck, her voice high with alarm. "You mean walk? All the way to Cairo? I can't do that! There're snakes, and bugs, and—wild things in those woods! We'll get lost! We ..."

"You shut up!" Esther hissed. Her eyes flashed with such venom that Priscilla took an involuntary step backwards. "Haven't you caused my son enough pain? Isn't there a caring bone in your body? We're taking him to Cairo for help, and as much as I'd like to leave you behind, I won't! You'll do as I say, do you understand me?"

She turned her back on Priscilla's wordless gape and went over to Caroline. Her voice gentled only a fraction. "Caroline, we'd be obliged to you for the use of the mule. We'll send it back as soon as we can."

Caroline stood slowly, reaching for her children. For a moment her expression revealed her doubt, but gradually it composed itself into lines of calm acceptance. She had known hardship. She had had her life torn apart before. She knew what it felt like to teeter on the brink of disaster with hysteria nipping at her heels, threatening to push her over ... and she knew the danger of giving in to it.

Under different circumstances she never would have dared go against a woman like Maude Sherrod. She knew the folly of insane risks, the sting of derision, and she had sworn long ago never to expose herself or her children to that kind of punishment again. Until yesterday, the most important thing in the world to her had been to avoid Maude's disapproval, or that of anyone else she met. But that was yesterday.

She had never been alone before. Not completely, utterly alone. She saw suddenly, and very clearly, that what they were facing now was more than just a tragic loss, more than just a storm cloud of misfortune that would soon be righted. This was a matter of life and death. She was afraid. She still wasn't certain it was the right thing to do, but she knew if she hesitated she could spend the rest of her life waiting on the riverbank for rescue that might never come. She had spent too many years already hoping and waiting.

She could no longer afford that luxury. None of them could.

She said quietly, "That won't be necessary, Esther. We'll come with you."

She walked over to Hannah Prescott, who had never once turned her gaze from the river. "Hannah?" she said softly.

A tear rolled down Hannah's wrinkled face and caught on her lip. "I can't," she said. "My Job ... he might come back. He'll be looking for me, and I'd right better be where he left me. I can't leave." Caroline's face became taut with pain, but before she could say anything Hannah said sharply, "No. Until we find his body ... there's hope. I can't leave."

"We'll wait," Lucretia Macon added calmly. "You go on if you must. And if you see Henry, tell him where we are."

Caroline looked at them both helplessly. No one could say for certain that they had a better chance waiting here than the others did moving on. Esther stepped forward and embraced both women, one after the other. "If a boat stops, tell them what became of us. We'll send somebody back as soon as we can."

Then Maude said briskly, "Oliver, help get Mr. Wiltshire on that mule. Judith, you go hold your sister's hand. Mama's too tired to carry you today."

Just like that, the decision was made. Within minutes six women, six children, and one desperately ill man had gathered themselves together. They had no food, no weapons, not even a clear idea of where they were going. There were no trails to guide them, yet they were preparing to follow a woman they did not like or trust into the wilderness, to what could quite possibly be their deaths. But their options were limited, and they had made the best choice they could.

Weary and helpless, they huddled together, waiting for someone to make the first move. Oliver looked up at Katherine.

"Which way?" he asked simply.

At the far end of Mud Flats, just where the river began to bend, stood a three-sided lean-to. The charcoaled lettering on a board nailed to a tree identified it as Calhoun Bros. Saloon. It was little more than a shack with a plank laid across two barrels for a bar, a mud floor, and strips of canvas battened over the open front wall to keep out the cold in winter and the flies in summer.

About a dozen men sought refuge from the drumming rain beneath the tarpaper roof, cursing the foul weather and each other in low, ugly tones, gulping down homemade whiskey, and playing with a deck of battered cards. Occasionally they wandered off to relieve themselves on a corner of the floor before staggering back to one of the rickety barrel tables, looking for trouble. A couple of tallow candles flickered in cracked saucers, and misery hung over the room as thick as smoke.

Among the customers that day were three particularly unpleasant characters, frequent visitors to Mud Flats. Since the first keelboats had started coming down the river, men like these—river pirates by trade and proud of it—had become common. The past few years had seen more and more of their ilk on the Ohio, floating down in keelboats and canoes and following the mass of westward immigrants like wolves salivating after a herd of sheep. They lay in wait on the banks or beached themselves on sandbars or floated in apparently empty canoes toward hapless travelers. There was no law on the river, and nothing short of vigilante power could stop them. They murdered, raped, and pillaged indiscriminately, and their victims were the weak, the innocent, and the unwary.

This band was only one of many who roamed from the Allegheny to the Mississippi, but in recent years they had established territorial dominance over this part of the Ohio. Their leader was a broad-faced, narrow-eyed man named Snake McQuaid, who was missing one ear and had a mouth full of black stumps for teeth. He wore a woven chain around his neck which he claimed was made from the hair of the women he'd raped. Today Snake was drunk and mad-dog mean.

"Oughta carve ever' one a ya up," he muttered to the dregs of whiskey in his cup. "Take you on one by one and feed you to the river snakes. Zeke!" he bellowed, flinging his head back. "M' goddamn cup is empty!"

Under ordinary circumstances Zeke would have broken a bottle over Snake's head and driven him out into the rain; he had tangled with the pirate before and wasn't averse to doing it again. Rarely in Zeke's life did good sense prevail over impulse, but this was one of those times. He had other plans for Snake McQuaid.

"What's the matter with him?" Zeke asked Snake's cohorts, who were leaning against the bar. They had been staying as far from Snake as possible.

"Don't like to be crossed, is all," muttered one.

"Lost Hickock and Jones upriver," put in the other.

"Overboard?"

"Hell, no! Murdered in their sleep!"

"Emptied out the goddamn hold, too. Best haul we ever took."

As low-down as he was with his own misery, Zeke was hard put to repress a grin at the thought of Snake being outdone by one of his own kind. If he had been smart enough, or ambitious enough, Zeke might have given it a try himself. As it happened, the circumstances couldn't have been better for his own plans.

Zeke went behind a curtain and came back a moment later with a jug of whiskey—the real stuff, not the doctored-up version he served behind the bar. He set it squarely on the table before Snake, and when the man looked up bleary-eyed, he wasted no time. "We're j'inin' up with you. Me 'n' my brother Abe."

Snake glared at him with hands coiled and muscles poised to spring, and Zeke felt the comfort of his own knife in its holster at the back of his neck. Then Snake threw back his head and roared with laughter. Spittle flew from his lips on a cloud of foul, whiskey-scented breath.

"Is that a goddamn fact?" Abruptly the laughter ceased and Snake pried open the jug, sending the cork flying across the room. "I got me some killin' to do, Mister," he growled. He fixed Zeke with a pair of deadly cold eyes. "And the way it is right now I ain't too particular about who I kill."

"I got killin' on my mind too," Zeke said, meeting him stare for stare. "And I got to git down-river to do it. Same as you."

Snake's eyes narrowed. He flung the jug over his shoulder and drank, wiping his mouth on his sleeve as some of the contents sloshed onto the floor. "Heard about that petticoat that done in your brother."

"An' I heard you got took in the dark by a cut-throat better'n you."

Snake threw down the jug and leaped to his feet, his mouth drawn back in a gaping, animal-like roar. Zeke held his ground and once again the roar turned abruptly into laughter. Snake slapped him hard across the back. "You'll do, you filthy son of a bitch! You'll goddamn do!" He dropped back to his chair and scooped up the jug, which was now half empty. His eyes were shrewd. "Hear tell that goddamn petticoat's got more than tits stuffed up under her dress."

"Gold," Zeke said. "Gold coins. She paid passage with one. They're yours."

Snake nodded, accepting that as his due. "And before you kill her?"

"She's yours too," Zeke conceded reluctantly.

Snake grinned and sat back, offering Zeke the jug. "I reckon I just took myself on a couple of partners."

Chapter Five

Katherine found a heavy oak branch, stripped off the twigs with her hands, and used it to clear a path through the woods. The undergrowth was thick in places and eventually drove them back from the river, but Katherine used its rushing sound to guide her steadily westward. The sun never quite broke through the gray sky, and the forest was dark with close-growing hardwoods, fallen trees, and mossy boulders. A brief rain-shower soaked them all and caused the mule to balk, and Katherine spent almost an hour, Oliver pushing and herself pulling, trying to get the stubborn creature to move on.

The children cried with hunger and stumbled constantly. Hilda, who had bravely walked with Katherine at the head of the group for the first hour or so, now lagged far behind. She didn't complain, but Katherine could tell the exertion was proving too much for her.

Abruptly Maude insisted, "We've got to find something to eat. We can't go on like this."

"Yes, please, the children haven't eaten since yesterday," Caroline added, "and they're so tired. We've got to stop."

Katherine did not look back. As far as she was concerned, they could all stop. But she was going on.

Over and over she asked herself, Why? How did this happen? A crazed and helpless man, half a dozen children, and women who had never known any hardship their husbands could not remedy. What were they doing here, following her, looking to her for guidance?

Nothing in her previous life had prepared her for such a predicament. As the middle child in a large family, she had lacked distinction. Boothe was the strongest, the twins the prettiest, Jamie the brightest. Katherine . . . was just Katherine. She did what she was told and dealt with what came her way the best she could, but she was not equipped to deal with this.

Why had these people followed her? Didn't they know that everything she touched turned to dust? Maude was right; the townsfolk of Mud Flats had been right. She was a Jonah, cursed. Left in her care, her family had been struck down one by one and her fields had turned to stone. When she had nothing to lose, she had turned away, but disaster had followed her even here. And these fools hadn't any more sense than to trail her footsteps, looking to her for salvation when all she could offer them was an uncertain death.

By noon Katherine estimated they could not have made more than three miles, and she knew this was not going to work. Alone, she might have had a chance, but with all these children, with poor Hilda, and Matthew, and Maude's constant complaining—it was simply impossible. If any of them were going to survive, Katherine would have to go on alone and pray that she could find help.

Tonight, while they slept the sleep of exhaustion and dark grief, she would steal away. She would find a secure camp for them and hope that Oliver would be able to find food and that Maude could keep them together, and she would leave. And if it was a sin to abandon them helpless in the woods, then a sinner she would be. She had done worse. This was a matter of survival.

Just when Katherine thought the going could not possibly get any slower, she came upon what she had most dreaded. Skirting deadfalls, boulders, and undergrowth, they had followed a circuitous course that had taken them farther and farther from the riverbank. Now Katherine pushed aside a low-hanging branch and heard the near and immediate sound of rushing water. Before her lay a sharp gully, and at the bottom of it a fast-flowing stream.

She stopped and stared in dismay as the little group drew up around her, following her line of vision. Maude pushed herself forward, puffing with exertion. Her face was flushed, but her mouth was set with grim satisfaction as she demanded, "Well. What are you going to do now?"

In the best of times, it would have been difficult to get the mule, not to mention the children, down the steep bank and up the other side. But now the creek was swollen to half again its normal size, reaching almost midway up the banks, and crossing it was out of the question. Katherine narrowed her eyes and looked to the north.

"We'll have to go upstream," she said, "until the creek narrows enough to cross."

"But that's the wrong way!" cried Priscilla.

"I thought you said we were going to find food," added Esther angrily. "We can't go any further until we've eaten. My Matthew has got to have some nourishment. Can't you see he's ill?"

"We'll turn back," Maude announced. "At least as long as we were near the river there was a chance someone would find us. We can't just keep going further and further into the woods. These children have got to have something to eat. They can't keep going like this ..."

Caroline interrupted quietly, "My children are just as hungry as yours, Maude Sherrod. But I haven't come this far to turn back now. She's right. We go upstream."

Katherine felt a brief stir of gratitude for Caroline's support, though she didn't know why. It would have been easier for everyone if they had turned back and left her to go on alone.

Katherine's empty stomach cramped as badly as any of theirs, her muscles ached, and her head throbbed with weariness. Perhaps it was cruel of her not to let them stop to rest, but she had asked none of them to follow her. They had to find a campsite; it had to be near water and possible game, and the only way to find it was to keep moving upstream.

In the hours that followed food consumed her every thought—the need for it, the worry about it, the fear of what would happen if they could not find it. It was April, too early for berries and too late for the hickory and pine nuts that must litter the forest floor in autumn. How was she to provide for these people?

Katherine was raised on a farm. She knew how to bake bread and make cheese and preserve fruits; she knew how to plant and harvest and cure a hog and dress rabbits and squirrels. She knew nothing of hunting and killing her own game. The men in her family had done that, and when they were gone, she and Gran had traded in town for meat and fish. No one had ever taught her how to shoot or build a snare or even how to fish without fishhooks and nets.

If I had a long rifle right now, I'll bet I could shoot something, she thought, grimly. And she resolved then and there that if God granted her mercy and she lived through this and bore daughters, they would grow up knowing how to do the things a man did to feed his family.

Gran had once said to her, "God didn't give us this earth for a playground. He gave us the soil to till and the trees for shelter and the creatures and water for sustenance. He set us down with everything we need to live. It's all here, in the earth, in the river, in the sky. All we have to do is use it."

But what was she to do without weapons, without knowing how to trap? When even the seasons had turned against her and the trees refused to bear fruit?

Eventually the dense forest began to thin and the ground underfoot grew less rough. The banks of the gully melted and evened out and the creek, though still too deep to cross, did not flow as fast. Katherine realized they could not put off the search for food much longer. They would have to camp on this side of the stream tonight.

She reached a spot where the creek pooled up near an abandoned beaver dam and the trees were far enough apart to clear the area for sleeping. She stopped. "We'll make camp here," she said.

Amid groans and murmurings of relief Katherine studied her surroundings, dreading the in-

evitable question, "What will we do for food?"
What *would* they do? If they waited long enough,
would God rain manna from the sky?

The flash of movement in the pooled water
caught her eye and an idea began to form. It was
a feeble notion at best, and what she had seen
might have been nothing but a reflected shadow,
but she had to do something. *It's all here, in the
earth, the sky, the river. All we have to do is use it.*

She was not prepared to stand here waiting to
be pommeled with questions that rose out of
helplessness and despair. She said briskly, "Oliver, go upstream and gather the biggest rocks you
can carry, and some big tree limbs. One of you
women take the older children and hunt along
the shore for nests—duck eggs, or quail, anything
you can find. The smaller children can start gathering firewood. The rest of you take off your
shoes and stockings and help me dig a ditch."

She expected incredulity, protests of fatigue,
arguments of all sorts. Indeed, from the looks that
went around the group, she might have had a
rebellion on her hands if Caroline hadn't stepped
forward at that moment. "I thought I heard quail
calls over behind that copse," she said, and even
though her face was pale and lined with fatigue
she managed to make her voice sound energetic.
"Martha, Judith Sherrod, you come along and
we'll have a hunting party, shall we?"

The girls, excited at the prospect of a "party,"
scrambled to obey, and Katherine glanced at Caroline gratefully. For all the fuss she had made this
morning over the mule, she had turned out to be
the most dependable. Underneath that demure
ladylike exterior was a woman of iron.

Following Caroline's lead, everyone else took

up various tasks. Oliver began prying up loose stones from the creek bank and Hilda organized the youngest children into a foraging party for firewood. Even Maude listened without objection when Katherine explained her plan. Everyone seemed relieved to have someone take charge.

Within an hour they had scraped a narrow trench out of the creek bank which filled with water almost three feet deep. Using the natural barrier of the beaver dam on one side and Oliver's stones and branches on the other, they had formed a pool of their own, impenetrable except for a gap left in the stone barrier they had built. Katherine had been heartened to notice while they were digging that the flash of shadow she had seen earlier had not been her imagination— the creek was thick with fish. But the water was too deep and fast for them to hope to catch any unless her plan worked.

"I remember Pa telling me about the Cherokee fish traps," she said, pressing a muddy hand against the small of her back and regarding their handiwork with far more confidence than she felt. "The fish swim through the opening in the dam, and when enough have gathered, we close it off. Then we should be able to just scoop them up."

Priscilla stared at her. "With our hands?"

Maude looked equally skeptical. "You expect fish to just swim in there because we want them to? Lord, child, you're crazier than I thought."

Katherine turned slowly to Maude. She was tired, she was hungry, and she didn't want to fight anymore. It took every ounce of energy she possessed simply to push aside despair. She couldn't fight Maude Sherrod for her right to survive. "Do you have a better idea?" she asked.

Maude's dark brows shot together. "You should have asked me that when we were back at the river. If it was up to me we'd still be there, that much I'll tell you!"

"Mrs. Sherrod, please," Hilda said anxiously.

But Katherine could not remain silent, nor could she endure any longer the constant brooding hostility that Maude Sherrod generated. "I didn't ask you to come with me," she said plainly. "No one is asking you to follow my every command."

"A very good thing!"

Katherine faced Maude squarely, ready to put an end to it. "Why do you hate me so?" she demanded. "What have I done to you?"

Another woman might have flinched from such directness, but not Maude Sherrod. She seemed, in fact, to welcome the chance to answer. "You are a killer," she replied flatly. Her face was sharp and tight with repulsion. "If there had been one man fit to wear pants in that town you came from, you'd be swinging from a rope right now. The devil alone knows what kind of woman it takes to hack a man to bits like you did, what kind of evil must be breeding in your soul. I'm sure *I* don't understand it, nor do I want to. God save us all from the likes of you."

"Do you want to be in charge?" Katherine burst out, the frayed ends of her cautious composure finally snapping. "Is that what you want—everyone looking at you and listening to you and turning to you for help? Because you're more than welcome to it! It's none of my affair *what* you do!"

Almost as though by invitation, Maude too let go of whatever control she had been exerting through the day. With her words she fairly spat venom. "No, indeed, why should you? You're nothing but a common criminal, out to save your own worthless hide!"

Oliver carefully straightened up after placing a rock in the pool and looked at his mother, anxious and concerned. He seemed to want to say something, but Maude didn't give him a chance.

"You've lost nothing," Maude hissed at Katherine. "You care for nothing. And you have nothing to lose! What becomes of us is none of your concern. Why don't you just leave us be?"

Katherine merely looked at her. *Lost nothing.* The words kept echoing in her head. Lost *nothing?* But she could never expect Maude Sherrod to understand what she had lost.

Shock and horror overcame Hilda's timidity. "Mrs. Sherrod, you cannot mean that!" she exclaimed softly. "We mustn't say such cruel things to each other!"

Hilda's quiet outburst produced a slight flush in Maude's cheeks. Hilda's gentleness made Maude's behavior seem crude, and Maude did not like to be made to appear crude.

Hilda persisted, "Katherine has brought us this far . . ."

"Into the very heart of the wilderness?" asserted Maude scornfully. "I could have done as well!" But there wasn't as much heat to her tone now, and after a moment she had difficulty meeting Hilda's eyes.

Hilda said simply, "And do you know how to catch the fish?"

Maude's silence grew uncomfortable. She plucked at the bodice of her dress, pushed the hair from her face, and gazed into the distance.

At last she said shortly, "Do what you like." And she walked away.

Katherine wished it could have been she, not Maude, who walked away and kept on walking. But the other women were looking at her, waiting, and Katherine had no choice but to turn back to the problem at hand.

"We need something for bait," she said.

"Will this do?" Hilda dug into her reticule and pulled out a crumpled piece of butcher paper. "One of the women in town gave me some teacakes. There's nothing left but crumbs. I ... I didn't get a chance to throw it out."

Katherine took the paper carefully, not wanting to spill any of its precious contents. "Well, let's hope the fish like teacakes as much as you do," she said, and Hilda laughed shyly. The sound of laughter was a wonderful thing, and everyone smiled. For a moment Katherine thought that those smiles, that fleeting instant of comaraderie, were almost more satisfying than any fish they could catch. They almost made up for Maude Sherrod. Almost.

Katherine scattered the crumbs on the water and left Oliver to guard the opening to the dam, knowing it might be hours before any fish were drawn to the trap. She moved the group away from the bank and then set about building a fire, praying all the while that someone would produce something to cook over it.

It had been a long time since Katherine had started a fire with flint and stone, and at first she despaired of even finding a flint with which to begin. The hazy sun was barely a glimmer through the trees by the time a spark finally caught on the small bed of dried leaves and pine straw she had prepared. The group whispered a soft cry of wonder as hesitant tendrils of smoke curled upward.

Hilda quickly and carefully began to feed small sticks into the tinder until a flame appeared. Katherine sat back on her haunches, weary to the bone but satisfied that next time the procedure would be much easier.

"Miss Katherine! Miss Katherine, it worked!" Oliver came running up, his pale face shining with triumph. "That trap is plumb full of fish. They took to them teacakes like hogs to fresh slop!"

Leaving the children to tend the fire, the women ran to the pool. The trap was not exactly teeming with fish, but there were five or six good-sized trout swimming around, anxiously seeking escape. At first the women lay on the bank and tried to scoop up the fish with their hands until Katherine showed them how to wade into the pool and hold their aprons like a net. When a fish swam near, only one quick movement was required to fling it onto the bank.

The experiment was not without its failures, however. Hilda was too ungainly for the maneuver, and on her first attempt fell backwards in the pool and dislodged part of the trap, allowing two of the biggest fish to escape. When a fish swam into Priscilla's apron, she screamed and flung it backwards into the stream, whereupon her mother-in-law twisted her ear so viciously that she sank to her knees, sobbing. In the end, four fresh fish lay flopping on the shore, hardly a meal for thirteen hungry people, but better than Katherine had ever dared hope. Oliver speared the fish on the end of a sharpened stick and went to roast them over the fire.

Caroline and her foraging party returned with only a double handful of wild mint, which Esther was delighted to make into tea, and—to Katherine's astonishment—a huge mud turtle, which gentle, refined Caroline dragged behind her in her apron.

The turtle proved to be valuable in more ways than one. Once Oliver figured out how to crush its head with a stone and pry the meat from the shell, it provided its own cooking pot. As the sun sank below the trees, mint tea was steeping in Esther's Dutch teapot, turtle stew was bubbling in its own shell, and four trout were roasting over the fire.

Caroline approached Katherine privately, her hand open to reveal half a dozen hairpins. "I was thinking," she suggested, "if we bent the pins into hooks and used the drawstrings from our petticoats—mightn't it be easier to catch fish next time?"

When Katherine thought of the hours wasted digging the trap, poor Hilda chest-deep in icy water, Priscilla screaming and flinging the fish over her head, she didn't know whether to laugh or cry. But she smiled and said, "You're right. We'll do that to catch our breakfast tomorrow."

But Katherine wouldn't be here tomorrow. The others would be all right, or as all right as they could ever hope to be. They had water and fish, and the trees would provide some shelter from the weather. It was more apparent now than ever that Katherine couldn't hope to make it to civilization with this rag-tag bunch trailing after her. They would do as well without her as with her. She must go on alone.

The children had watched how much fun the

adults had had playing in the stream and were
clamoring to do the same. "It's a swimmin' hole,
ain't it, Oliver?" four-year-old Amy Sherrod insisted. "An' you built it just for me! Can't we go
swimming? Please, Oliver?"

"Don't be ridiculous, Amy," her mother returned shortly. "You'll catch your death."

Hilda, who was sitting close to the fire to dry
her clothes, gave a laugh. "Then we shall all catch
it together," she said cheerfully. "Look ... I was
as wet as a fish, but I'm drying quickly."

Oliver's eight-year-old sister, Judith, tugged at
his sleeve. "Please, Oliver, take us swimming,
please?"

Oliver looked hesitantly at his mother, then at
Katherine. "Miss Katherine, you think you'll be
needing any more fish from that hole?"

She suppressed a smile at his expression, which
was almost as anxious as the children's. "No, not
tonight."

Benjamin Adamson climbed into his mother's
lap. "Can I go, mama? Let me go!"

Caroline stroked her towheaded child affectionately and glanced at Maude. "They've had
such a hard day, Maude," she said gently. "I really
don't think it would do any harm to let them play
a bit."

Maude frowned, once again finding herself in
the uncomfortable position of being outvoted. "I
can hardly keep my children out, Caroline Adamson, if you are going to let yours go in."

"Hooray!" Benjamin squealed, and wiggled out
of his mother's lap, tugging off his shoes as he
ran for the pool.

Amy and Judith looked up at Oliver. "Take us,
Ollie, please!"

Oliver glanced at his mother, heard no objection, and then gleefully scooped up his sisters, one under each arm. "Sure I will, darlin's! You know I made that swimmin' hole just for you! What you been waiting for?"

Katherine felt something warm touch her heart at the sight of Oliver's affection for his young sisters, and theirs for him. He reminded her of her brother Sam, who, for all his formidable strength and gruff manner, was never too busy for his younger siblings, always making them surprise gifts or taking them on unexpected jaunts into the woods to see a bird's nest or a litter of fox pups.

Or Boothe, who never failed to reserve time at the end of the day to tell the young ones stories. She could almost see him now, sitting in the big oak chair before the fire, a child on each knee and three others gathered at his feet, his face painted with firelight and animated with the quiet drama of the tales he spun. A lump came into her throat and she had to blink the mist from her eyes. So much love, she thought. How could it all have ended?

It wasn't fair. All she had ever treasured in the world was gone. Her family, her home, her simple way of life ... it would never come back again. No matter how hard she wished or prayed, it was gone. She was eighteen years old and she had never been married, nor had she children of her own, and now she probably never would. It wasn't fair that life should be so hard, or hurt so much.

The faces of the other women softened as they watched the children's careless play, each touched by her own memories of easier times.

"How innocent they are," Caroline murmured. "They just don't understand."

Hilda smiled. "Would that we all could be more that way, don't you think?"

Stripped down to the skin, the children crowded into the pool like jumping trout. Oliver rolled up his pants legs and jumped in with them, laughing and splashing as loudly as the youngest. Katherine's heart ached with memories of her own brothers and sisters and her own lost youth.

Abruptly she stood up, removed her shoes and damp stockings, hitched her skirts up around her knees, and headed toward the pool.

She heard a gasp or two, and disapproving murmurs from the women behind her. The children's chatter died down as everyone stared at her. She waded knee-deep into the water with the uneasy, wide-eyed scrutiny of the children upon her.

Then Benjamin Adamson said shrilly, "Look! The witch-lady's going swimming!"

Katherine sat down flat on the sandy bottom, immersing herself, fully clothed, to her neck. "She certainly is," she said.

After a moment, Benjamin howled with approving laughter.

Amy Sherrod gave a mischievous squeal and splashed water in her face, and Katherine splashed her back. Martha Adamson scooped up a handful of sand from the bottom and dribbled it over Katherine's hair. Katherine laughed and grabbed for her. Soon she was deluged by naked, slippery bodies, all laughing, splashing, winding their tiny arms around her neck as they hopped up and down in the water.

Oliver laughed and sank to his knees, trying to

rescue Katherine from some of the more boister-
ous players. His eyes were sparkling and his face
was gentle with wonder as he said, "You're really
something special, Miss Katherine."

She flattened her palm against the water and
playfully sprayed his face. Oliver laughed and returned the gesture, and the little ones screamed
with delight as they indulged in a free-for-all.

Sometimes tragedy can enhance the wonder of
the plainest experience, Katherine thought. The
uninhibited embrace of children who had not yet
learned how to hate, the careless play, the moments of laughter—from such things came sustenance for living. They were without price.

Katherine would remember the sound of Oliver's laughter, the innocent warmth in his eyes, the
children's exuberance. She would look back on
that afternoon in the days to come and take
strength from it. She would remember the moment as one in which she felt briefly at peace.

Gran had had a custom of murmuring words
of thanks and respect to the animal that had given
its life to fill her plate—a tradition from the Old
Country and one that Katherine had later learned
also was common among some American Indians. Katherine's father, a modern man, had dis-
dained the custom and always said a proper grace
over the table, but tonight Katherine found herself reverting to the old ways. As the first morsel
of trout touched her tongue and seemed to melt
there, spreading its strength through her body
and promising life for another day, a reverence
filled her for the ways of nature and the provisions it made. She thought, Thank you, fish, for
coming to us. The little prayer startled her, and

she wondered just how much of Gran was in her after all, and how thin were the layers of civilization that separated her from the old ways.

The children were fed first and bedded down under the canvas Katherine had saved from the wreck. There was only enough food left to whet the adults' appetites, but it was more than they had expected to have, and for the moment they were content. As darkness wrapped around them and the pulsing night sounds sealed them in, they huddled close to the fire, passing around the turtle shell half-filled with mint tea and contemplating the accomplishments of the day.

Katherine's clothes were dry, and she sat a little away from the fire, leaning drowsily against a tree. The pleasure of the pool lingered, helping for a time to keep bad memories at bay. The familiar creakings and groanings of the night did not frighten her, but it was not so with the other women. Their voices drifted to her.

"We must have been mad," Esther said, her voice high and tight with nervousness, "Crazed with grief to ever come out here. Who knows what could be lurking in those woods."

"Praise the Lord," Maude said with low relief. "Somebody's finally seeing the light!"

"Hannah and Lucretia were right," Esther went on anxiously. "We should have stayed by the river where someone could find us. If we live through the night, we must turn back in the morning."

Caroline's voice was cool. "Do you know the way back?"

Priscilla broke in, her voice quavering. "Nobody asked me whether we should stay or go. Nobody cared what I thought. Well, I hope you're all happy. We're out here in the middle of the wilderness with a woman who'd as soon murder us in our sleep as not."

Against her will the vision swam before Katherine's closed eyes. The wet, heavy dawn. The sound of her ax ringing on wood, two satisfying thumps as the split log fell to the ground. Early Calhoun's hands on her waist, spinning her around. Early Calhoun's leering grin, whiskey tainted breath, muttered obscenities ...

Katherine jerked her eyes open, shivering.

Oliver was saying, "Ma, you don't know that. None of you know what really happened. I wish you wouldn't ..."

"Then ask her," Esther challenged. She turned her eyes toward Katherine and held them there. "We've got a right to know the truth."

All of the women at the fire turned toward Katherine. Some of them, like Oliver's, were reluctant; others, like Hilda, embarrassed; some were afraid and others defiant. But all of them were curious, almost greedy with it.

There was no stopping it now. The nightmare played itself out in a few quick flashes of heart-stopping color and mind-wrenching immediacy: Early Calhoun's yellow teeth, sweaty face, blazing eyes. His hands groping at her breast. Her own voice crying out. Her instinctive swing of the ax in self-defense. Her surprise when a gush of blood spurted from his leg; the shock on his face and his roaring growl as he lunged at her again. Then a rush of madness, of blind terror and yes, a swift, enveloping flood of hate as she lifted the ax and swung again and again.

Blood flowing, screams very much like her own coming from far away and oh, the madness. . . . A blow she struck for the insults Early Calhoun had hurled at her on the streets; another for the terror that tightened in her chest every time she walked to town, knowing he would be lying in wait for her; another blow for Simple Jim, who used to smile at her, whose throat had been slit by Zeke Calhoun's knife; and then she was raging at God and swinging blindly, for Jamie, for the twins, for Sam, for all the injustices in her life and the fear that she simply couldn't bear any more.

Then Early lay lifeless at her feet. She was covered with blood and small, frail Gran, who had dragged herself from her sickbed with a butcher knife in her hand, was pulling on her arm, guiding her away. It was the last act of love Fiona Carlyle would ever make, for she had died less than an hour later.

And now a voice was coming to Katherine, defensive, belligerent, and she could not even reason to whom it belonged. "Well? Will you tell us the truth?"

Katherine dragged herself back to the present through a fog. She looked at the firelit circle of faces, a primitive tribunal ready to judge her beneath the stars just as their skin-clothed ancestors might have done a thousand years ago. She wanted to ask them, Why? So that you can decide whether I'm fit to die with you? Shall I be excommunicated if I give the wrong answer? What would you have me tell you? And she almost smiled, sadly, wearily.

It didn't matter whether they understood or not. Whether she redeemed herself in their eyes or not was of no importance in this far away place. She did not need their sympathy; she did not ask for their exoneration. Guilty or not, justified or not, the burden of those few violent moments was one she alone would have to bear for the rest of her life.

Katherine answered quietly, "No."

Maude sucked in her breath. "Well," she declared with satisfaction. "That's as close to a confession as we're likely to get, if you ask me. We're good Christian folks, all of us. We don't have to associate with this . . ."

"Oh, for heaven's sake, Maude," Caroline interrupted. "This is not a drawing room in Boston and we're not discussing who is fit to be invited to tea! We're here, don't you see that, and we're all in this together. Nothing else matters now, and all this foolish talk about what did or didn't happen in the past is worthless!"

"No," Katherine said. "Maude is right." All eyes fixed on her in stunned silence, and she got up and brought a few more sticks to the fire, feeding it carefully. "We'd all be better off if I went on alone, and that's just what I'm going to do. You can go back to the river or wait here. I'll make sure someone comes for you."

There was a confusion of mixed reactions. "Miss Katherine, you can't . . ."

"Good, I say!"

"We already decided . . ."

"Now do you see . . ."

And then suddenly Caroline said sharply, "Hush!"

Everyone turned to her, startled. Even as Katherine registered her alert, wary manner she heard it too. Something was stirring in the bushes. Terror seized everyone gathered there.

"Something's out there," Hilda whispered, pressing a fist against her abdomen.

Priscilla clutched her mother-in-law's arm and Esther's eyes widened. "Someone's come," she said. Her voice rose as she peered over the fire into the darkness. "They've found us! Someone . . ."

Katherine shot to her feet, her hands spread to urge silence, but even as she moved, a huge shape materialized in the darkness at the edge of the woods, bigger than a man. It threw back its head and roared.

There were screams, movement, and a dozen thoughts raced through Katherine's head. The children sleeping outside the circle of the fire; Matthew Wiltshire, unable to protect himself; their camp situated between the woods and the stream where all sorts of animals might be accustomed to drinking; the fish scraps thrown carelessly on the ground. Even as she cried, "Don't move! It only wants the fish! It won't bother us if we don't . . ." Esther drew back her arm and, with a mighty cry, threw the teapot.

The fragile china and its scalding contents shattered against the bear's shoulder. The fury of its scream shook the very tree-tops, and it reared up on its hind legs again, casting a shadow over the fire that was twice its height. The children, awakened by the noise, were sobbing and stumbling, their mothers running toward them, the shrillness of screams and the terror of the beast filling the night.

Though Katherine knew it was not common for a wild animal to approach a fire, the bear had been attacked, and bears were among the most fearless of creatures when provoked. Shaking its head furiously, the bear took two running steps toward the camp, stopped, and reared up again to attack.

Katherine looked frantically around for a weapon—a club, a stone, anything. She swept the ground for her walking stick but tripping, stumbling feet had pushed it away. Fear tasted hot and metallic in her mouth as the bear roared again, and she reached into the fire and grabbed a flaming log.

She didn't feel the pain of her scorched hand, and she didn't stop to think or fear or choose. She held the flaming log high overhead and charged the animal.

She was so close she could smell the bear's fetid breath and see the gleam of its yellow teeth. Saliva sprayed her arm and face as the bear shook its head with one more deafening roar, then dropped to its four paws and loped away.

Katherine dropped to her knees, shaking. The log fell to the ground and rolled away, and she cradled her burned hand, rocking back and forth, her eyes squeezed tightly shut.

Voices and sobs blurred around her. Shadows of horror danced on the screen of her closed eyes. And then she felt someone drop down beside her. A trembling arm went around her shoulders. Hilda embraced her, whispering, *"Mein Gott.* You are so brave. What should we do without you?"

Katherine opened her eyes; she wanted to fling the woman away, to scream, *No, I'm not brave! I'm just as scared as you are! I don't want to be brave!*

But she said nothing. She rested her face against Hilda's plump shoulder, and thought, Let it end, dear God, just let it end. Let me be safe again. Let me go home . . .

Hilda made a soft exclamation of sorrow as she

lifted Katherine's burned hand. "Oh, your poor hand! I will get a wet cloth." She moved away quickly, and Katherine remained where she was, listening to the slow, heavy beating of her heart and trying hard to think nothing at all.

Across the campfire, Caroline was busy soothing her children. She looked up and met Katherine's eyes. After a few more murmured words, she left the children and came over to Katherine. Her hair was untidy, her gown stained, and her face was so pinched that the two pockets of flesh under her eyes looked like swollen bruises. There was nothing of the aristocrat in her appearance now.

Caroline sat beside Katherine on the ground, and for a long time she was silent. Then, very quietly, she said, "You can't leave us."

Katherine thought dully, Can't I?

But much against her will her eyes were traveling over the ruins of the camp. Esther, dazed, was gathering up shards of broken china, murmuring, "My teapot. My poor teapot. All the way from Holland . . ." Babies were crying, Maude was clutching Oliver, her face buried in his chest as though it were her last refuge. Priscilla was sobbing into her husband's shoulder, while he made no movement or sound. Tonight they had known only a taste of the dangers that lay ahead of them. They thought it was over, but it had just begun.

What would they do? Katherine thought bleakly. What would they do without her?

Caroline noticed her gaze and followed it. "You mustn't mind what they said," she said gently. "They're frightened, alone, and they say things they don't mean. Besides, . . ." her face seemed tense, and she dropped her eyes to her hands. "We all have secrets."

Katherine wanted to argue, she wanted to protest. All her life she had been taking care of people, being brave and quiet and good while the people she loved were torn from her grasp. She was tired, hungry, scared, and she didn't want to do it any more. Who was going to take care of *her*?

But as she looked at the women and heard the children's frightened hiccoughs, the burden fell heavily onto her shoulders. She pushed slowly to her feet.

"We'd better get some sleep," she said. "We must start out early in the morning."

Chapter Six

Byrd Kincaid lay flat on his stomach in the undergrowth outside the cave, watching the movement below. His buckskins were stained and soiled to the color of the earth so that he seemed to melt into his surroundings, and he was so still that a rabbit wandered within an inch of his moccasined foot before suddenly catching the man's scent and hopping off. A long bow lay ready at one hand, and a rifle, its barrel dusted with dirt to deflect any revealing gleam, was loaded and cocked under the other. Byrd had been lying there, listening and waiting, for over an hour, and if need be he could lie motionless for hours more, for the ways of the wilderness had become second nature to him.

The narrowing of his eyes was the only indication of his astonishment as the first of the band came into view. A tall red-haired woman was leading a mule with a slumped man upon it. A young boy carrying a child walked beside her. They followed singly or in groups—women leading or carrying children, old, young, middle-aged, and one swollen to the point of birth. Byrd released the faintest of whispering breaths and relaxed his finger against the trigger of the rifle. He stared, still finding it hard to believe his eyes.

He counted thirteen of them, including the old man on the mule. Women and children, alone in the middle of the woods. Where were their men? What the hell were they doing here?

Their shoulders were bowed with fatigue, and their footsteps were stumbling and shuffling. They didn't talk much, but the children whined and the mule snuffled and they made enough noise crashing over the forest floor to roust a goddamn army. Byrd swore silently and slid back from the overhang, flexing his cramped muscles and sitting up. He could still see them, but even if they had sense enough to look up, they wouldn't see him.

The last thing Byrd needed now was to draw attention to himself. In the cave behind him were enough goods to set himself up in style in New Orleans, and he had gone to too much trouble stealing them to risk losing them now. He was safe here, at least for awhile. But those women were leaving a trail a blind man could follow, and even as he sat there watching, a sense of danger breathed hot fumes down his neck.

Women. Children. What were they doing here?

He entertained a brief notion that they would move on, far enough and fast enough to pass him by. But their men had to be somewhere. Scouting for game, waiting for them up ahead, following behind. They couldn't be out here alone. And who knew what manner of men theirs might be?

Thirteen of them, he thought. Now there's an unlucky number if ever there was one.

Byrd had lived on the edge of danger long enough to know one thing: ignorance was his worst enemy. He had no choice but to find out who those women were and what they were doing here.

It took him only a few moments to clean his camp so thoroughly that only the sharpest of trackers would have been able to detect a sign of his passing. He buried his ashes, sifted dust and leaves over his footsteps, and checked to make certain that the entrance of the cave was so well concealed by brush that even an Indian couldn't find it unless he was looking for it. Then he shouldered his long rifle and his pack and, as silently as a panther, he started down the incline after the women.

It was their third day on the trail. Fording the creek had taken longer than Katherine had expected; they had had to travel almost a full day before they were able to find a spot shallow enough to cross. Now they were deeper into the woods than Katherine had ever expected to go and were roughly following the stream back toward the river.

Some of the children had diarrhea from eating green acorns, and their diet of fish and bird eggs was proving far from adequate for any of them. Often Katherine's thoughts flitted ahead to how much further along she would be if she only had herself to feed, if she could ride the mule instead of leading it, if she didn't have to stop so often or move so slowly. She could have sent help back to them in a matter of days.

There were other ifs too. If only she had refused to let them follow her; if she had stayed at the river and waited for the water to go down or taken the chance that some passing boat might spot them; if Early Calhoun hadn't come bursting out of the dawn back in Mud Flats.... But none of those exercises were good for anything other than passing the time. The fact was they were here, they were together, and nothing could be done except to go on.

The Katherine Carlyle who had so desperately boarded the flatboat for regions west in search of her brother and unknown lands seemed very far away now. The Mississippi River, the Missouri Territory were nothing but amorphous phrases with little meaning, and the memory of Boothe's face faded and became a blur. Even her terror of the Calhoun brothers wavered and grew indistinct. When it took all of her energy to put one foot in front of the other, Cairo seemed as far away as the shining mountains, and just as unobtainable. Everything else faded into the background.

She dreaded the nights most of all. In this respect Katherine was no different from any of the other women: nighttime spent under the open sky aroused a primitive uneasiness in her that she could not dispel. Even those women who had traveled hundreds of miles before boarding the flatboat had always had the comfort of their husbands at night, a wagon bed beneath their backs, and a canvas roof to cover them. There was something uniquely terrifying about sleeping on the naked ground, vulnerable to the elements and the night prowlers, knowing there was no one and nothing to ward off disaster but oneself.

After the incident with the bear, Katherine always made camp well away from the stream and buried all food scraps, but she lived in constant terror that the animal would return. Often in the mornings she would find animal tracks by the stream and was reminded that they were the intruders in this place and at the mercy of the creatures who inhabited it.

Sleep came slowly, her fitful rest disturbed by terrifying dreams. She saw the blood and felt the man's body breaking apart beneath the force of her hands. Blood in her mouth, in her hair, soaking her dress and skin ... blood on her hands. Then she would wake up, her heart pounding and her breath raspy; she would feel the wetness of her clothes and think it was blood, but it was only sweat, and then she would stare into the darkness and think, Is this my punishment, then, God? The terrors of the night, the despair in the eyes of these women, the hungry crying of the children day after day without end?

There had been so much blood all over everything when Early Calhoun lay at her feet. Gran had made her wash the blood from her dress, and Katherine had scrubbed her body and her head until they burned from the lye and the skin was raw in places from the boar-bristle brush. Gran had dragged herself back to bed with the last of her failing strength and commanded Katherine to sit beside her. Katherine had hugged herself to stop the trembling and said, "I'm going to go to hell. I've sinned. I've done murder and I'm going to burn in hell."

Gran had taken her by the shoulders and looked her in the eye and said sternly, "Now you listen to me, girl. The only hell you've got to look forward to is the one you make for yourself. You did what you had to do and that's no sin. God doesn't punish people for doing what they've got to do."

Those were among the last words Gran had ever spoken to Katherine, as though, having done the best she could for her grandchild, she was finally able to close her eyes and slip peacefully to rest. Katherine would always remember the words, but she wasn't sure, even now, that she believed them.

The battered keelboat moved clumsily down the Ohio, sometimes floundering, sometimes shooting through newly formed rapids, sometimes listing violently to avoid sandbars and bobbing sawyers. Snake McQuaid and his crew—now increased by the two Calhoun brothers—did all they could to keep the craft in the channel. Their efforts were accompanied by much swearing and threats of violence; tempers were running high and the mood was foul.

The storm had delayed them, keeping them on land for three days before the river was minimally navigable again. Even now it was a death trap of whirling eddies, rushing currents, and charging debris. The day before, they had taken a lone keelboat, but its cargo had been lost to the storm, and Snake had ordered the keelboat's crew murdered for their trouble. For the most part the waters were barren of traffic; remnants of shattered canoes and broken flatboats swept by, but no living prey. No one but the pirates would chance the river in its present condition, for they valued their own lives as little as they did those of their victims, and this was what made them so ruthless.

The going was slow and hard, but anger and greed drove them on. Snake McQuaid did not doubt his mission would be successful. He pri-

vately thought the girl on the flatboat was probably dead, but he made a point not to mention
that to Zeke Calhoun. He needed the extra man-
power, and besides, there was a more than even
chance of finding her body and the treasure she
carried. As for his own quarry, Snake could practically smell him. He was a clever bastard and too
mean to die in anything as paltry as a storm. No,
it would take somebody like Snake to finish him
off proper, and that was exactly what he meant
to do.

Suddenly Zeke, who was standing on the roof
working an oar, shouted, "Starboard! Look!"

Snake squinted into the wind and spray and
could hardly believe his luck. Two scrawny
women and a couple of brats were standing on
the bank, waving their shawls and leaping up and
down, shouting into the wind. Snake threw back
his head and laughed. Things were beginning to
look up, and a lot quicker than he'd hoped.

He gave the order and turned the boat out of
the channel, toward shore and the welcoming
cries of the frantic, grateful women.

They made camp three hours before sundown,
for it took at least that long to scavenge a meal.
The older children were dispatched to the creek
bank with fishing lines made of hairpins and
muslin. Earlier in the day Oliver had improvised
some snares, and now he ran back down the trail
to check them. Katherine and the other women
scouted for birds' nests and firewood while Hilda
stayed behind to tend the children.

Supper that night consisted of two small fish,
four robin's eggs, and a cooking pot full of boiled
dandelion greens. Oliver's snares had turned up

empty and he was frustrated. If only we could have killed that bear, Katherine thought longingly. The meat would have been enough to last us til Cairo.

She was not going to miss another such opportunity. While the others sat around the campfire talking, she sought out a sturdy green branch and, after some struggle, managed to tear it off at an angle. Then she knelt beside the fire and repeatedly charred and then scraped at the end with a sharp rock, trying to form a point. It might not be a very professional weapon, but she was certain if she got hungry enough she could make it an effective one. And she was just that hungry now.

Esther returned to the fire after feeding Matthew the last of the broth. "He's getting weaker every day," she mourned, wringing her hands in her apron. "I don't know how he can make it the rest of the way."

Katherine thought Matthew Wiltshire's chances of lasting even a few more days were very slim, but she said nothing. He slowed them down and his condition was demoralizing for all of them. It would have been best all around if he had died on the river, but Katherine felt guilty for even thinking that.

Esther turned on Priscilla, who had unbound her hair and was trying to comb out the tangles with her fingers. Her once lustrous curls were now dull and stringy. "And you," Esther accused her, "you're no help at all. Don't you even care what becomes of your own husband?"

"What can I do?" Priscilla cried. "He doesn't even know me! When I try to feed him he just spits it up again ... just like a baby!" Her face twisted with disgust.

"He can't chew," Katherine pointed out. "You have to chew his food for him, and then put it in his mouth."

All the women stared at her. "That's disgusting!" Priscilla exclaimed.

"You selfish, worthless little viper!" Esther hissed, whirling on her. "Don't you ever think of anyone but yourself?" And then her shoulders slumped with misery and she sank onto a log near the fire. "Oh, if only I'd listened to Francis. He told me not to come, he had a vision of what would happen. My precious Francis, I'll never see him again. Oh, if only he were here now. He'd know what to do."

"Oh, yes, Francis," Priscilla said venomously. "Your first-born son, perfect Francis, noble Francis. Well, *I* wish you had listened to him, too!"

"We wouldn't even be here if it weren't for you! The only reason Matthew ever agreed to come west was to make a better life for you. You with your constant demands!"

"Me!" Priscilla jerked her fingers through her hair, her eyes glittering. "I never wanted to leave my home for this Godforsaken place! I had everything there. I was the most popular girl in town, I ..."

Oliver couldn't stop himself from breaking in. "She's just a little girl, Miz Wiltshire. I don't think you should ..."

Instantly Esther turned on him. "This is none of your concern, Oliver Sherrod ..."

And Maude, appalled at her son's bad manners, snapped, "You stay out of this, Oliver. This is a family matter."

Oliver's cheeks reddened, but he didn't back down as easily as he once would have. "We're all family now, ain't we?" he insisted. "I mean, we're all we've got. Seems to me that what happens to one of us should concern everybody."

For a moment the women were taken aback by his simple wisdom. Hilda and Caroline regarded him with gentle smiles, and Maude didn't seem to know whether to reprimand him for his impudence or praise him for his charity. Not even Esther had a ready answer to his interference now, and after a moment she said stuffily, "The least you can do is make yourself useful, Priscilla. Go get some more deadwood before the fire dies down."

"With pleasure," Priscilla said, and flounced off into the shadowed woodland.

Oliver saw a lecture building up in his mother and figured he'd better not push his luck. Besides, having gone to so much trouble to defend the girl, he felt some obligation to see it through. "I'll help her," he muttered, and hurried off after Priscilla.

She hadn't gone far, as Oliver knew she wouldn't. Priscilla was afraid of the dark and didn't like the woods. Still, she looked rather forlorn and neglected, poking around in the dark for twigs and fallen branches, and Oliver, now that he was here, didn't know what to say to her.

She must have heard him come up, for he made no secret about it, but she didn't look around. She kicked delicately at a stick with her toe, then bent to pick it up. Oliver looked around for something to pick up himself, just to look busy as the silence grew uncomfortable. His Adam's apple felt like a big knot in his throat.

Then, still without looking at him, Priscilla said, "I'm not a little girl."

It was such a relief to hear her say something that Oliver didn't mind her miffed tone. He answered, half-grinning, "Well, you're not full-grown either."

"I'm older than you," she asserted. Turning, she dumped a meager collection of twigs and branches in his arms.

Oliver felt his cheeks sting again. "Not by much," he muttered. "A couple of months."

She tossed her head. "I'm a full married woman."

Before he had met Miss Katherine, Oliver had spent a lot of time looking at Priscilla because, though she wasn't what he would exactly call beautiful, she was sure the best thing to look at on the boat. That pretty gold hair, the turned up nose, the flash of a tiny slipper, all had a certain appeal. Of course, she was a married woman, and when she scowled and pouted she wasn't the least bit attractive. But now, in the starlight, standing with her shoulders back and her head tilted to one side and one hip thrust forward flirtatiously, she looked right pretty. Oliver didn't trust his voice and so didn't speak for a minute.

He juggled the wood in his arms and almost dropped it. He cleared his throat, making a big fuss over straightening the wood without looking at her. "That don't make you a growed woman," he said uncomfortably. "Anybody can get married."

But Priscilla wouldn't give up. "Don't I look like a woman to you, Oliver Sherrod?" she demanded.

Oliver was taken by the spark of challenge in

her eye, the little bow mouth. He couldn't help himself; his eyes drifted lower, to the way her bodice strained over tight, apple-shaped breasts, and the heat that flamed in his face went all the way down inside his pants and stiffened him there. He looked away quickly and miserably. "Yes'm," he managed after a moment, "you do."

An interminable time, filled with the roaring of crickets and the pulsing of treefrogs, passed before he was able to venture a glance at her. When he did, he was relieved to find she was smiling. "Thank you," she said demurely.

She dropped the flirtatious pose and turned away, searching for more wood. Relaxing a little, Oliver went with her.

She found a broken pine branch and bent to pick it up. Oliver rushed to help her and almost dropped the wood in his arms again. She smiled at him. Hesitantly, he smiled back.

"I like what you said about family," she said. Her voice was sweet and smooth when she wasn't screeching at somebody.

"I reckon it's true," he agreed. "I mean, we've all lost . . ." He swallowed hard and couldn't finish. "I reckon we've all got to stick together now."

"Yes," Priscilla agreed softly and rather sadly. She glanced at Oliver, and again he had a glimpse of a quick, hesitant smile, which was quite nice. "I guess I don't act so grown up sometimes."

Oliver didn't figure it would be polite to reply to that.

She sighed, a breath that caught on the end with a small, muffled sound. Her voice was very low. "It's just that I'm so scared sometimes."

Oliver sensed that her distress was genuine. Without thinking, he reached to pat her hand, then withdrew. He said what only seemed proper at times like this, what everybody was saying to each other. "It's going to be all right, Miss Priscilla."

Her eyes were big in the starlight, wide with worry and sadness. "But it's not," she said. "Everyone says it's going to be all right, but nothing's ever really going to be all right again, don't you see that? What are we going to do when we get to Cairo? We have no money, nowhere to go . . . and my husband . . ."

Her face tightened and Oliver was terrified she was going to cry. But she caught her breath, tightened her fists, and went on. "Mama Wiltshire is all I've got left and she hates me. I just don't know what I'm going to do. I don't know what *any* of us are going to do."

Oliver looked at her with uncertainty and confusion. No one had ever talked about what would happen when they got to Cairo. He supposed they'd all known they would have to face it sooner or later, but they had been so busy just trying to keep moving that that very real problem had been pushed far back in their minds. It gave him a sick, empty feeling to think about the future, about his mother and sisters with nobody but him to provide for them in this strange new land. What *was* going to happen to them—all of them?

And poor Priscilla. What could he say to her? He felt he should offer comfort, or reassurance, but he had none to give her and she knew it. At last all he could say was, "I reckon we got enough wood."

They were silent and thoughtful as they walked back to camp.

* * *

"Paul was going to establish the first tobacco plantation along the Mississippi," Caroline was saying, her dulcet tones drifting over the campfire. "Of course we had a lovely place back in Virginia, but we were doing so well Paul said to me, Why not expand? Of course I was reluctant to make the trip with the little ones, but Paul said it would be educational for them. We didn't intend to be gone very long, only to mark off the land and find a place to build, then we would bring over the slaves and our household furnishings . . ."

Something in that story did not ring quite true to Katherine, and she suspected the others felt the same. But this was the first time Caroline had ever volunteered anything about her background, and everyone was too intrigued, or polite, to question her. No one could imagine why the gentle lady would want to tell a lie.

"Men and their foolish notions," put in Maude bitterly. "Always looking for something better, never satisfied with what they have. Why, we had the finest mercantile shop in town, the best neighbors anyone could ever hope for. My house was filled every night with folks stopping by to chat or visit or ask me for some little advice. My daughters would have made matches any mother could be proud of, and my Oliver, . . ." her smile was benevolent. "Well, his future was secure."

Oliver looked as though he wanted to say something, but Maude did not give him a chance. "We had everything!" she repeated, her voice growing tight with resentment. "But no, that wasn't enough! Why did he want to throw it all away?"

Katherine had to bite her tongue to keep from saying something. The poor man was rotting in his grave and his wife still criticized him. Privately Katherine thought he was better off, and wished Gran had been able to impart some of her compassion to her granddaughter. She swung a vicious blow at the half-formed spear with the rock, and missed. She didn't know why she allowed Maude Sherrod, above all others, to provoke her.

Katherine was in the process of turning her back on Maude in disgust when suddenly she froze. There, standing just outside the shadows of the campfire, was the biggest, fiercest man she had ever seen.

His feet and legs were wrapped in buckskins. His coat was caped and fringed and fell below his knees, belted at the waist with a strip of rawhide from which hung a small ax and several strips of deerskin. A powder horn and pouch were slung over his shoulder, and around his neck was another slender pouch which held a knife. His face was covered with a thick black beard, and long dark hair trailed beneath a cap of reinforced homespun. His eyes were a startling shade of pale blue, surrounded by fine white scars which, rather than detracting from the beauty of his eyes, actually enhanced it. He wore a pack on his back and carried a Kentucky rifle under his arm.

He had materialized out of the woods like a ghost and stood surveying them now with cautious detachment. The other women's shock was as absolute as Katherine's, and for a long moment no one moved. Then Rebecca Adamson, barely two, wriggled out of her mother's lap and toddled across the camp straight toward the man, her arms outstretched. "Papa!" she cried.

The man gave a laugh that seemed to rustle the

trees with its merriment, and dropped down on one knee to receive the child. "No, lovely, I'm not your papa, but I'll hug a sweet thing like you any day of the week." Caroline gave an involuntary cry of alarm as he swung Rebecca up and perched her on his hip, but he swept off his hat and bowed around the circle. "Ladies. Byrd Kincaid, at your service."

Chapter Seven

As though something physical had snapped, everyone began talking and moving at once.
The children ran toward him and stopped a few
feet short, gaping up at him. Even Oliver's face
shone with admiration as he noted the rifle and
the shiny hilt of the knife and the rugged woodsman garb. There were tears on Hilda's face as she
pressed a hand to her breast and whispered,
"Praise be to Gott, praise be! We're saved!"

The other women rushed him with breathless,
half-sobbing questions:

"How did you find us?"

"Where did you come from?"

"What are you doing here?"

". . . news from the river?"

"You must help us . . ."

"Please, come to the fire . . ."

"Thank God you're here, we were so afraid."

Only Katherine held back, and for no certain
reason. Perhaps it was her natural suspicion of
strangers. Perhaps the days of fighting the wilderness had honed her senses to a more acute level.
Perhaps life had taught her too well that God
rarely granted favors in such a concrete form. She

was uneasy about this man. His eyes kept returning to hers, and what she saw there might have been a hint of admiration, or respect, or perhaps simple curiosity. She held his gaze each time, studying him.

He smiled around the group. "I reckon you got about as many questions about me as I do about you. But first ..." He set Rebecca down and shrugged his pack off his shoulders. "I don't like to come callin' without bringing a little something." He loosened the pack and drew out a haunch of venison. "I hope you folks can make use of this"

An almost reverent silence greeted his gift. Even Katherine felt her vision mist over briefly with the power of hunger. Then, in a rush, there were cries of delight and gratitude, a few muffled sobs, and everyone was talking again. Oliver quickly built a spit and used the spear Katherine had been working on to place the venison over the fire. The children drew the stranger over to the log they had been using for a bench, and Maude said warmly to the man she once would not have allowed into her pristine drawing room, "Sir, you must forgive our manners. I am Maude Sherrod, of Hancock, New Hampshire. This is Caroline Adamson of Virginia, Esther and Priscilla Wiltshire from Albany, and Hilda Werner of Germany."

Byrd Kincaid's eyes lit again on Katherine, but he made no mention of her omission. "Well, I'm mighty pleased to meet you all. But if you don't mind my askin' ... where's your menfolk?"

There was a stricken silence, and in a clamor they told him about the accident, their losses, the foolish journey into the wilderness. Byrd listened intently and asked astute questions about the height of the river and the details of the accident and whether or not any other boats had been similarly stricken. It might have been Katherine's imagination, but it seemed he was perhaps a bit *too* interested in the tragedy they had left behind.

"So you're all alone out here?" he said, and Katherine looked at him sharply.

The women murmured that they were.

"What happened to him?" he said, nodding toward Matthew.

"Lightning," whispered Esther, dabbing at her eyes with her apron.

Byrd nodded soberly. "I seen a man struck once. Knocked him clear across a crick as big as this one. Didn't do nothing but jabber day in, day out, for near a month, and not a thing he said made sense. Then one day he woke up in his right head again and didn't remember anything that'd happened. Went back east, raised him a family, started writing for the dailies about his adventures out west. He's a right prosperous fellow now, I hear."

This seemed to give Esther hope, but Katherine didn't believe a word of it.

"I don't reckon you run into anybody out here," Byrd said.

"Lord, no!" exclaimed Maude. "You're the first living soul we've seen since we left the river."

"And you say you left a couple of other women and children back there?"

Katherine moved forward to turn the meat on the spit. "You ask an awful lot of questions, Mr. Kincaid."

He looked at her steadily. "Yes'm, I reckon I do. It's the best way I know to find out anything."

Benjamin Adamson, who had been snuggling up to Byrd and examining the fringe on his coat, wrinkled his nose and backed away. "You smell funny," he announced.

"Benjamin!" reprimanded his mother, appalled, but Byrd let loose another one of his full, tree-rattling laughs.

"Well, little soldier," he said, "I can see how I just might smell a mite peculiar to you. But to an Indian or a bear I smell just like home, and that's how come they leave me be."

Benjamin regarded him with new respect. "We saw a bear," he told him proudly.

"Did you now?"

Benjamin nodded enthusiastically, and Oliver added, "Miss Katherine chased him away with a stick."

Byrd cast his eyes toward Katherine. "I can believe she did," he said softly.

"You never did tell us, Mr. Kincaid," Katherine said, "what you're doing out here."

"Just passing through, ma'am, just passing through. I'm a trapper by trade and on my way upriver to sell me a load of furs."

Katherine tightened her lips, but said nothing.

"That meat smells nigh done, and we'll need something to wash it down with." Byrd dug into his pack again and pulled out a small leather pouch. "Chickory," he explained. "Not as good as the real thing, but it'll give a fair impression of coffee if you're not too particular."

The women made appropriate sounds of pleasure and Caroline sent her Martha to fill the cooking pot with water while Byrd instructed Oliver in the art of peeling tree bark for cups. Katherine, more than a little disturbed by all she had heard, took the pot from Martha and went down to the creek herself.

She tried to be sensible about the uneasiness that plagued her. Byrd Kincaid was the first living being they had seen. He came at a time when hope was almost gone. He brought food, weapons, and the reassurance of male strength and competence. He was their salvation. He was also a liar.

No self-respecting trapper would try to make a living this far south; that much she knew from Boothe. The river valley had been depleted long ago, and the only furs left of any value were far to the north and west, in Canada and the Territories. What was this supposed trapper doing this far south, and headed upriver instead of down? Five years ago Byrd Kincaid's story would have been perfectly plausible, but Boothe, who once had made his living as a trapper, gave them news of the changing industry in his last correspondence.

So why had Byrd lied? And why was he so unnaturally interested in their numbers, in whom they had left behind, in the condition of the river when they had left it? If he were really on his way upriver, he would have known the conditions of travel, and what was he doing this far from shore? Katherine had heard tales of white slavers she had hardly credited, and even now she rejected the notion as soon as it was formed. But *something* was wrong about Byrd Kincaid.

She was just lifting the heavy pot out of the stream when his shadow fell over her. "I haven't the pleasure of knowing your name," he said.

"Katherine Carlyle," she replied without turning, bracing her arms to lift the pot over the bank.

He swept down and took the pot from her hands effortlessly. "Did you lose your husband, too?" Her hair was falling beneath the confines of her bonnet, and she pushed a length of it over her shoulder as she turned to look at him. "No," she replied. "I travel alone."

If he felt any surprise at the announcement, he masked it well. He simply looked at her thoughtfully and intently. Katherine didn't mind, for she was studying him in the same way, each of them searching for the truth.

"You're different from them others," he said at last. "You don't belong with them."

That drew a small, tight smile from Katherine. "There's some who say I don't belong anywhere." She met his gaze without fear, warning him, or simply informing him. "I killed a man, Mr. Kincaid. They call me a witch woman, a Jonah, a murderess. No decent society will have me."

She was faintly startled to see him smile. His eyes left her and traveled over the darkened landscape at leisure. "You know, when God kicked ole Adam and Eve out of Paradise, I think he must've sent them west. Can't think of any better punishment for a couple of sinners, myself. Is that what happened to you—got yourself kicked out of Eden?"

"The Bible says they went east."

He looked at her again. "I'm an unlettered man, Miss Kate. Don't know about the Scriptures. But this much I do know—there ain't a man or woman alive who belongs out here, and nobody comes by choice. Maybe it's the law, maybe it's the church, maybe it's just an all-fired restlessness in their souls, but the folks that come out West are the ones that couldn't make it back East. They were pushed out, they were drove out, but they're all outcasts in one way or t'other, and I reckon if a woman like you is ever going to belong anywhere, it'd be here."

She thought of Caroline Adamson with her cultured accent and her gracious home in Virginia, and Maude Sherrod with her prosperous store and position in the community, and Katherine could not agree. But she said nothing.

"Was it your idea to walk these folks along to Cairo?" Byrd asked.

"It was."

He nodded. "A good one, too. The river's a dangerous place." His eyes wandered off again. "Maybe more than you know."

Alarm tightened Katherine's muscles. "What do you mean? We left two women back there. What do you know?"

"Maybe nothing." The expression in his voice and eyes was mild. "Probably nothing."

He changed the subject smoothly. "You got any particular reason for heading to Cairo, or do you just enjoy the traveling?"

"My brother has gone west. I intend to find him." She lifted her chin defiantly, expecting the same incredulity she had gotten from Captain Dewhurst.

But Byrd only said, "Your brother wouldn't happen to be Boothe Carlyle, would he?"

Her heart lurched. "You know him? You know my brother?"

"Heard of him, ma'am. It's a big land out West, with few people, and we kinda cling to each other. If a man's honest—or not—you hear of him. If a man's good to ride the river with, or if he'll kill you for your boots, you hear it." He looked Katherine over slowly, appraisingly. "If you're Boothe Carlyle's sister, I reckon you'll do."

Katherine stiffened, her patience worn thin with the man's maddening habit of talking without revealing anything. "Who are you, Mr. Byrd Kincaid?" she demanded coldly. "What are you doing out here?"

He looked at her for a time without answering, his face placid and, it seemed to Katherine, faintly amused. "I got a few pieces of advice for you, Miss Kate, and you're going to want to heed them if you plan to get much further down the trail. Don't stare into your campfire at night; it blinds your night vision. Don't be so quick to tell a stranger everything you know; you're giving away your defenses. And don't ever ask a man questions you don't really want to hear answered."

He lifted his arm to gesture the way back to camp. Katherine snatched the cooking pot from him and walked back alone.

The children, replete for the first time in days, slept around the fire, as content as puppies. The women sipped the bitter chickory brew from bark cups as though it were the finest of China teas. Byrd was putting the final touches on the spear Katherine had started, and the women watched him with the drowsy satisfaction that can only come from knowing that a man is near and doing the things a man does to make the world safe for women.

Byrd handed the spear to Oliver. "Now you remember, son, it's in the aim more than the power behind it. I've seen an Indian half your size fell a deer with one of these, and there ain't no reason you can't do as well. Take your time, site your target. That's all there is to it."

Oliver took the spear and examined it with admiration. He certainly couldn't fault the man's workmanship, but he felt somewhat overawed by the events of the evening.

Byrd Kincaid's arrival had been strange and fortuitous, and it aroused mixed emotions in Oliver. He didn't know whether he was supposed to be welcoming the rugged stranger or defending the womenfolk against him. Everything about Byrd, from his dress to his weapons to his language, inspired a boyish hero-worship in Oliver which he tried hard to overcome, because he was supposed to be a man now. He had never met anybody like Byrd. He could have sat for hours at his feet listening to his tales, and there was no doubt that he could be the answer to all their prayers. But something about him made Oliver uneasy.

He didn't like the way Byrd looked at Miss Katherine, for one thing, seeking out her eyes over the fire, studying her from afar, his gaze lingering when it ought not to have lingered. Nor did he like the way Katherine looked back. And what was he really doing way out here in the first place? Why hadn't he made his presence known sooner? How long had he been stalking them?

All evening Oliver was caught between suspicion and admiration, ashamed of his mistrust and knowing he should be grateful for Byrd's help. But he couldn't help thinking that when it got right down to it, things might have been simpler all the way around if Byrd Kincaid had never shown up.

And then Oliver's suspicions were borne out.

Byrd reached for his rifle and got to his feet. "Well, ladies," he said, "it's been a pure pleasure passin' the evening with you."

"What are you talking about? You're not leaving?" Maude said, startled.

"Yes'm, it's about time I started back for my own camp."

For a moment absolute incredulity paralyzed the group. Even Katherine could hardly believe her eyes as she watched him swing his pack on his back and prepare to go. Then they all burst out at once.

"But you can't leave us!"

"You'll be back . . ."

"You must help us get to Cairo! You won't leave us here to starve . . ."

"We were counting on you . . ."

Byrd said, "Well, I'd like to help, ladies, really I would. But like I said, I'm headed upriver, and you're headed down. You just keep on trailing west, and you'll hit Cairo in no time."

They stared at him as though he were the proponent of a particularly tasteless joke, their stunned faces white in the firelight, their eyes slowly filling with horror. Then Priscilla took a stumbling step toward him and made as though to clutch his arm. "You can't leave us out here!" Her voice contained a note of hysteria. "You can't!"

"I thought you were a gentleman, sir!" Caroline said stiffly.

As Esther cried, "What about my Matthew—the children! Surely if there is a shred of decency in your soul . . ."

"Miz Wiltshire," Byrd Kincaid said, "I don't know what your son was thinkin' about, bringing you out here, but if there's one thing a woman your age ought to know, it's this: life is rough, and where you're going it's going to get rougher. Out here you either learn to take care of yourself or there's nothing left to take care of, and there's not a thing in this world I can do about that. I'm sorry for your loss, all of you." His eyes swept the group and settled on Katherine. "But you're in good hands, and if you just keep on moving the way you have been, you're gonna be fine. There's nothing more I can do."

He walked over to Katherine, who rose slowly to her feet to meet him. Her face was hard with cold contempt, but she said nothing.

"I can't spare my rifle," he said, "but I'll leave you this." He pulled out his knife, and Katherine's hand closed around the hilt. A glint of amusement shone in his eyes as he added, "I reckon you know what to do with it."

Maude heaved herself to her feet, her nostrils flaring with rage. "You vile abomination! God will have his vengeance on you! You'll burn in hell for this night's work! Deserting helpless women and children to the dangers of beasts and savages! You should die of shame!"

"Ma'am," Byrd Kincaid said politely, "there's a lot I've got to be ashamed of, and I reckon the good Lord will have a word or two for me on Judgement Day. I won't argue with you there. But I've got to say I've rarely run across a woman less helpless than you. My sympathies are with the beasts and the savages."

He turned, and in an instant was swallowed up by the darkness.

Byrd walked for awhile, then lengthened his strides to an easy, loping run. His vision was acute in the darkness, his steps sure and all but silent.

It was a loathsome thing he was doing, leaving those women back there, and though he rarely felt guilt, he felt it now. He knew with his head that he had no choice; he would bring them far more danger by staying than by leaving. The men who were trailing him would think nothing about raping those women and killing them when they'd had their fill and carving up the children just for sport. Byrd would be in a far better position to prevent that if he stayed away from the women's camp. At least alone in the wilderness they would have a fighting chance.

But knowing that didn't keep him from feeling as low as a mud snake, and his thoughts kept returning to the tall, red-haired woman. Katherine. There was a lot in her he admired and a lot in her he feared, and he reckoned that just about summed up the state of things between a man and a woman at the best of times. If matters had been different, if *he* had been different, he might have been running in the other direction. As it was . . . Kate Carlyle. She would be all right. She would have her hands full with that pack she had taken on, but if anyone could get them through to Cairo she could. Byrd didn't doubt that.

And then he saw something that gave him pause.

He stopped and retraced his footsteps, bending low to the ground and carefully examining what he saw. His frown grew deeper, for the moon was bright and there was no mistaking what his eyes told him. Eventually he straightened up and swore softly.

He stood there for another moment, as still as

the shadows that enveloped him, eyes narrowed, head cocked, ears listening. His thoughts raced ahead to a hidden cave and the river beyond. But when he turned, his footsteps took him as swiftly as he had come back toward those he had just left.

Chapter Eight

The moon was setting when Byrd arrived back at the women's camp. Their fire, reduced to glowing embers, provided enough light to allow him to make out their sleeping shapes at its perimeter: children murmuring and shifting in the depths of dreams, their mothers still and heavy with exhaustion, the senseless man snoring loudly. Oliver, looking more like a vulnerable child than a half-grown man, had drawn his knees up; his hair was falling over his eyes, and the spear Byrd had given him was propped up against a tree, well out of reach.

If Byrd had been a hungry wolf, he would have eaten well tonight. If he had been a murderous pirate, he could have dispatched the lot of them before the first cry was uttered. If he had been a Shawnee . . .

He drew in a silent breath of disgust and anger through his teeth and went forward on silent feet. *Byrd Kincaid,* he told himself clearly, *you are a fool. You're that far from a boat to New Orleans that'll make you a rich man. You've got killers on your trail and enough trouble just trying to save your own hide.*

What the hell do you want to get mixed up with a bunch like this for?

He had no trouble discerning the glint of Katherine Carlyle's red hair. He dropped down swiftly beside her and covered her mouth with his hand. All he needed was for her to start screaming and create a panic in the middle of the night.

But even he could not hold back a sharp gasp of astonishment when he felt the pressure of a knife blade against his belly.

Katherine had come awake the instant his shadow fell over her, her heart pounding strength and awareness to every inch of her body. Only the familiarity of the bearded face kept her from driving the weapon home; still, she did not release her grip. Her eyes were wide and glittering, her nostrils flared above the heavy pressure of his hand, her chest was heaving. She held the knife hard against his abdomen but delayed the thrust. She did not know why.

Perhaps hesitating was a mistake, and one that, if she had been in the wilderness only a week longer, she would never have made. She thought of Byrd Kincaid's lies, his mysterious appearance, his unconscionable abandonment. But she also remembered the meat he had brought and the weapons he had left, and there was enough of the civilized woman left in her for things like that to matter.

Byrd must have sensed as much. In an instant the hard expression that had followed his first look of shock faded, and he murmured, "I knew I was leaving that knife in the right hands."

He relaxed the fingers that gripped her face, but only fractionally. "Miss Kate," he told her, "you're quite a woman. But I ain't about to let myself be carved up by any kind of woman, especially with my own knife, and I reckon you're smart enough to know it. I come back to talk to you, and I don't want to wake the others. So come away from the camp."

Slowly he took his hand away from her face, watching her as he got to his feet. Very cautiously, still maintaining her grip on the knife, Katherine followed.

He led the way, exposing his back to her, and Katherine allowed herself a wary confidence. Her heart was still pounding from the abrupt awakening, and she didn't foget for a minute the vulnerability of those she was leaving back at the camp, or what could happen to her out here in the woods at the hands of Byrd Kincaid. She flexed her fingers on the hilt of the knife and appreciated its weight.

Well out of earshot of those in camp, yet not completely out of their sight, he turned. Katherine stopped a good four paces before him.

"You've got to pack up your people and get out of here," he said without preamble. "You've got to do it now, and you've got to do it without a sound."

Katherine said nothing.

"That trail you've been following is a Shawnee hunting trail. They don't use it much anymore, and normally I'd say you'd be just fine, but the river flooding must've turned their course, because there's ten or twenty of them not half a day behind you."

Katherine's breath stopped, then resumed again in a slow, fluttering course. The knife went slack in her hand, and for a moment she forgot

Byrd Kincaid and whatever nebulous danger he might pose.

She had been raised in the Ohio River Valley, and the word "Shawnee" could not help but strike fear into the heart of anyone over ten years of age. She was old enough to remember Tippecanoe and the years of slaughter that had preceded it. She knew about Tecumseh and his relentless war against the encroachment of the white man, and his brother The Prophet, who was considered even more dangerous because of his fanaticism. They had drawn together the fiercest of the tribes and for years had been conducting an organized and nearly successful war against white settlers.

Katherine's father had once traded with the Shawnee and had found them to be honest and trustworthy. But she also knew about the families who had been massacred at their firesides, the bodies hacked to pieces and the remnants looted and scattered. She knew the Shawnee habit of stealing quietly by dawn and leaving nothing but death and smoking rubble in their wake. She knew the tales of torture and abduction.

"But we're not at war with the Shawnee," she said weakly. Then, with more conviction, "They were defeated at Tippecanoe. There are no Shawnee in this part of the country."

Byrd didn't bother to disguise his impatience. "Are you daft, girl? This *is* their country. Where do you think they went after the final battle, up in smoke?"

He dismissed her naivete with a brief shake of his head. "If it was a bunch of men out here, I'd say they'd be apt to leave you alone; this is nothing but a hunting party, and they're not looking for trouble. But like it is ..." his gaze narrowed. "The Shawnee need women," he said bluntly. "And they take what they need. As for the young'uns ... well, to their way of thinking, they'd be doing them a favor by takin' them into their village and raising them like their own. I don't know whether the young'uns would consider it a favor though, or their mothers either."

Katherine swallowed hard. A dozen women and children and a pathetic hull of a man, with only one knife and a hand-carved spear between them.

"Are you saying we're in danger of an attack?"

"No, ma'am, I'm not saying that at all. I'm saying you're going to be *took* if you stay here, and that's all there is to it."

No! Not this too! her mind screamed. There were too few of them. They were defenseless, with no weapons or battle skills. They weren't prepared for Indians. *She* wasn't prepared. Byrd could be lying. This couldn't be happening.

Byrd was watching her carefully, impatient with her hesitation. "Maybe you figure you'd be better off as Shawnee prisoners."

Katherine looked at him sharply. "Maybe we would be." She flexed her fingers on the knife at her side, and the feel of the metal against her skin gave her a measure of courage. "Maybe we'd be better off almost anywhere than with you. Why should I believe a word you say? You're no more a trapper than I am, and you've done nothing but lie since you came into our camp."

There was a slight tightening of the skin around his eyes, but his tone was mild. "Is that a fact?"

Katherine kept her voice low, but the words came rapidly, every syllable clear with purpose. "This is some kind of trick. I don't know what, but I know you're a liar and I know better than to trust a man who'd leave a bunch of women and children stranded in the wilderness. We've gotten along just fine so far without your help; why should we listen to you now?"

He held her challenging gaze, soberly assessing her. "Because," he answered simply, "I'm all you've got." And he made as though to turn away.

"Wait!"

The moment she said it, she despised herself for the weakness that made her call him back. But suddenly she was unsure, terrified that he might be telling the truth, alarmed at the thought of him disappearing into the night and leaving her alone again with all these people looking to her for guidance.

He turned to face her and her jaw tightened. Her fist closed again around the knife, revealing her tension. "Why did you come back?" she demanded.

He took a step toward her, and Katherine had to force herself to stand her ground. He was so close that even in the moonlight she could see the fine black hairs on his cheek where his beard began. He lifted his hand and touched the corner of his eye. "You see these scars?" he said. "I got them from a Shawnee brave who held a burning torch to my face just to see how long it would take me to scream."

Unwillingly, Katherine's eyes followed his hand to the fine network of scars that outlined his eyes like a mask. She swallowed hard.

He dropped his hand.

"I was captured by the Shawnee 'bout four, five years ago," he went on. His voice had a flat, matter-of-fact drawl. "Stayed in their camp a whole winter before I finally managed to break loose. While I was there, I saw half a dozen white women—Shawnee slaves—used like squaws and worse. They were a miserable bunch, some of them so far gone they'd forgot what it was to live in the white world, others of them pleading with me to help them. But there was nothing I could do. Not a blessed thing."

Katherine was surprised by the bitterness in his voice. The muscles clenching in his face conveyed his effort to keep pain at bay. She had not guessed that a man like him would feel deeply about anything, and somehow this brief display of emotion, however tightly controlled, reassured her.

"When I got out," he went on, "I rounded up some men and went back, but it was too late. They'd already moved. We never did catch a trace of them."

His voice was bleak. When he looked at her again, his expression was bland, his tone calm.

"I ain't good for much, ma'am, and that's the truth. But there's some things I'll allow and some I won't, and if I can keep that from happening to just one more woman, then I'm obliged to try."

Katherine tried with all her might to reject his words. But the idea kept coming back to her— what if he was telling the truth? What if she sent him away and at dawn they awoke surrounded by Shawnee braves? What of Hilda, and the innocent children, and Oliver? What if he was right?

She didn't want this responsibility. If she went with Byrd, she could be leading them all into a trap. But if she refused to believe him, the blood of a dozen innocents might be on her hands. How could she take that chance?

She knew the danger of hoping too much, of

trusting too much. But she had no choice. When she spoke she was aware that she was putting her life, and those of all who followed her, in his charge. "What should we do?"

"I can get you to a safer place. After that, we just hole up and wait. But it's got to be done before sunrise and with as little racket as possible."

Katherine swallowed hard, and nodded. She turned to go back to camp, and stopped. She looked back at him thoughtfully. "Mr. Kincaid?" she said. "How long did it take you?"

"For what?"

"With the Shawnee—how long did it take you to scream?"

He regarded her with the indulgence a parent might give an inquisitive child. "I didn't," he explained. "That's how come I'm here to tell about it."

Katherine felt a shiver grip her spine, and the night suddenly seemed twice as dark. She turned abruptly and led the way back to camp.

There was a great deal Byrd hadn't told the women about the Shawnee. He ran his fingers across his scars and remembered. He was lucky to be alive.

Five years ago he'd been traveling upstream by foot along the north bank of the Ohio, heading toward Cincinnati. He wanted to run one more keelboat that autumn before the winter ice set in. He'd stopped at a stream to get a drink, his rifle on the ground by his side. He was tired and careless, and before he could raise his head from the stream, the Shawnee were on him, six braves who seemed to materialize out of the shadows of the oak and hickory trees. He didn't have a chance to reach for his gun.

They'd marched him back to their camp, stripped him to the waist, tied his hands with strips of rawhide and made him run the gauntlet, the Shawnee custom with captives. The whole village had participated, men, women and children, flailing out at him with sticks, clubs and switches, trying to strike his head and shoulders as he sprinted between the two rows of taunting, shouting Indians.

He'd tried to keep on running out of the camp and into the dark comfort of the forest, but two braves grabbed him, turned him and forced him to run the gauntlet once more. The Shawnees crowded closer together, almost closing his path, lashing out with their weapons. Byrd decided to go down fighting. He lowered his head, closed his eyes, and plunged forward, kicking out, pushing against unseen bodies with the thrusts of his shoulders, bulling his way through the gauntlet. He felt the blows as the villagers flailed away at him, but he kept on fighting. Byrd knew he'd held his own as the villagers shouted their approval of his courage, much admired by the Shawnee.

Two braves used the rawhide cords to bind him between saplings, and while the chanting Indians watched, a powerfully built brave taunted him with a firebrand, circling, moving away, then closer, and closer. Byrd kept his eyes straight ahead, his face impassive. He knew they weren't going to kill him, not then. When the Shawnee burned captives alive, they did it with great ceremony and ritual. No, they didn't plan to kill him. They were testing him again.

Byrd didn't flinch, not when he smelled the acrid scent of his burning hair or felt the heat of the firebrand and the searing pain as the flames licked at his flesh. The sun sank behind a dark band of trees; the torches glowed menacingly in the twilight as the brave circled Byrd, feinting at him with the flaming torch, waiting for him to break. The flames reflected eerily on the brave's nose ring and earrings and cast deep shadows on his strong nose and high cheekbones. It was a war of wills, a battle of nerves. Byrd was a statue, unmoving, unblinking, fighting to keep his breath shallow and even. Indians prided themselves that they never groaned or showed pain, not like the white man who was no better, they said, than a screaming woman.

Byrd set his teeth and made no sound.

And then it ended. The chief called out a few words; the brave untied Byrd and took him to a wigwam where a woman attended his burns with a soothing salve. Another woman brought him a meal of corn, beans, and roast squirrel meat. Feet and hands bound once more with rawhide, Byrd slept under a rug of raccoon fur that night, as he would for the next one hundred nights.

The village was small, composed of no more than fifty related family members, wintering together. The eight or so wigwams that made up the camp were rectangular in shape, a dozen feet wide and perhaps twenty long, built of strong poles overlaid with deer hide, the winter covering.

The Shawnees were nomads, who traveled deliberately and slowly through the eastern forests. The women built warm weather wigwams of bark and poles, and in the summer the smaller winter bands would join together to form a larger group. Game was more plentiful then, and often the Indians might stay in one spot during a corn plant-

ing and harvesting season before moving on.
During the winter, they followed the animals,
moving their village when the game in their
camping area was depleted.

Byrd wasn't the only white person in the camp.
There were the women, kept as slaves, who were
used sexually by the unmarried braves as the men
wished. A white child, a little boy, had been captured and adopted into the tribe. He watched
Byrd with curious eyes but kept his distance, as
did the other children. They were Shawnee. Byrd
was the outsider.

He ate their winter food of deer, rabbit, and
squirrel stew flavored with wild onion; dried nuts
and fruits, cherries, plums, and grapes. He wore
their winter clothing of deer skin moccasins and
leggings to the top of his thighs, a breech cloth
between his legs, and a long loose shirt of deer
hide. He was not given the brightly colored cloth
turban of the Shawnee male nor necklaces of
dyed porcupine quills or brightly colored feathers. He didn't want those. Neither did he want
their nose rings or feathered ear decorations, but
he was grateful for the warmth of the clothes
when the snows came. He slept in the wigwam
with the unmarried braves and hunted with the
men for bear, raccoon, otter, deer, and rabbit.
There were no better woodsmen or trappers than
the Shawnee, and Byrd watched and learned.

He also watched covertly the white women and
tried to talk with them, but soon learned his attempts only resulted in beatings for them. The
white captives worked along side the Shawnee
women. They cooked and cleaned the game the
men brought in; they mended the deerhide clothing with sinew and needles made of porcupine

quills; on warmer days they sat in the sun and
wove baskets of reeds, wild grape vines, and the
bark of the hackleberry tree. The Shawnee had
no horses or wagons. The women moved most of
the band's belongings from camp to camp, either
on their backs or in the sturdy baskets they had
woven.

The Shawnee men, when not hunting or trapping, worked with wood and carved spoons and
bowls from the knots of hardwood trees. They
made shelves and stools of wood for their wigwams and sleeping platforms for their fur rugs
and traded blankets. Byrd was allowed to sit
among the men and whittle small wooden animals for the children, just to relieve the tedium
of his days. The children always took the toys sus-
piciously, their huge dark eyes questioning and
grave, but they played with the trinkets, and that
gave Byrd a feeling of satisfaction.

Even though the Shawnee fed him and clothed
him, took him on hunts, shared their fire, and
taught him their language, he was still a prisoner
and a slave. All he wanted was a chance to escape.

It came during a trapping foray. Byrd and three
braves were setting traps of wooden sticks and
deer sinew along the edge of a frozen lake. A
young Indian, a nephew of the chief, had been
playful and filled with the exuberance of youth.
He ventured out onto the ice, trying to slide
across the slick surface on his moccasined feet.
He fell heavily, and his laughter, which had rung
out across the cold air, turned suddenly to shouts
of fear as the ice broke and he tumbled into the
cold lake.

Byrd knew the Shawnee would rescue the boy
and take him back to camp before they came

looking for him. He melted into the thick forest and began to run east toward the sun. Three hours later, his luck still held. A snowfall obliterated his tracks. A day later he reached the Ohio River. Five days later he stumbled upon a settlement.

He had survived.

By dawn Byrd realized that whatever chance he had of getting the group out of Shawnee territory without detection was almost nil, and his respect for Katherine Carlyle and the task she had undertaken increased tenfold.

They had broken camp with surprisingly little fuss. The word "Indian" was enough to strike white-faced fear into the eyes of the women, and that fear, communicated in raw proportions to their children, resulted in a frantic, nearly silent flight. They doused the campfire, bundled up their little ones, snatched together their meager belongings, and were gone almost before anyone had a chance to question why.

There was one bad moment when Byrd insisted that Hilda ride the mule and Matthew walk. They had barely gone a mile when it became clear that Hilda was incapable of keeping the pace they had set, slow though it was. If she should fall and injure herself, they would be slowed down even further.

Esther was appalled. "Matthew can't walk! He's ill!"

"I will not be trouble," Hilda insisted. "I will walk."

A determined sigh escaped Byrd. "No offense, Miz Werner, but we just don't have time for you to prove you're not going to be any trouble. The quicker we move, the better chance we all have for getting out of here, and you'll be safer on the mule."

Hilda hesitated, seeing the reason in that, but Esther cried, "What about Matthew?"

"He either walks, or we leave him behind."

Esther drew in a strangulated breath. "You wouldn't . . ."

"Yes, ma'am, I would. There's no room out here for a man—or a woman—who can't take care of himself."

Esther burst into tears and called him wicked and heartless, but the response she received from the other women was mixed. They might not have approved of Byrd's methods, but they all agreed with him one way or another. In the end Hilda rode the mule and Matthew trailed behind, guided by his mother with a rope tied to his waist.

Still, by dawn, they had gone only two miles.

The children had awakened cranky and frightened. The mothers were nervous and exhausted; they snapped at their children and stumbled over their own feet. Matthew had fallen twice, and each time Byrd had to go back and put him on his feet again. Katherine kept looking nervously over her shoulder.

"No point in that," Byrd told her. He had a flat, low drawl that reminded her of the Cumberland Gap region of Kentucky, the kind of voice that was never raised and never harsh. "You won't see them unless they want to be seen."

"We can't go any faster," Katherine whispered. "They're going to find us."

Byrd did not tell her that, no matter how fast they moved, the Shawnee would find them if they were determined to. "The only thing we got to be thankful for is that they move even slower than we do. We'll still be half a day, maybe a day ahead of them. The Indians see time different from the way we do, and they're not in any hurry."

"Why should they be?" Katherine said grimly, and with surprising perception. "We're leaving a trail clear enough to drive a wagon through."

Byrd gave her a brief glance, but said nothing.

Katherine dropped behind, setting her pace with Oliver's. Benjamin Adamson was whining to be picked up so Katherine lifted him into her arms. She felt a stab of protective anxiety as the tiny legs wound around her waist and the weight of a human life settled in her arms. What if she had made the wrong decision?

Oliver was carrying his sister Amy, who was asleep against his shoulder. He glanced at Katherine, and she could tell he was trying hard to keep his expression noncommittal. "Where do you think he's taking us?" He spoke in low tones, both to avoid waking Amy and to prevent his words from carrying back to Byrd.

"I don't know," Katherine answered worriedly. "But we don't seem to be going in the right direction."

The expression of Katherine's face gave Oliver the confidence he needed to express his thoughts. "Just because he brought meat to the fire, everybody's supposed to follow him like he was the head ram and they was a bunch of sheep. I don't like it."

Katherine didn't know whether to be reassured or alarmed because someone else shared her doubts. "Perhaps he's all right," she murmured uneasily.

Oliver glanced at her. "Do you think so?"

Katherine's struggle was briefly visible on her face, but in the end she was unable to convince herself of the lie. "No," she admitted with a sigh.

Satisfaction showed on Oliver's face. Katherine found his glance of protective adoration both amusing and endearing. "Don't you worry, Miss Katherine," he assured her. "I'll keep an eye on him. He makes one wrong move and he's gonna have me to deal with."

Katherine smiled gratefully at him, but she wasn't in the least bit reassured.

It was clear to Byrd that he could do nothing to protect the women out here in the woods; he was only one man with a rifle and a longbow. Nor could he get them out of danger before danger found them. The best he could do was hide them and prepare for the worst.

The safest, most easily defensible place he knew was back on the ridge where he had made his camp. That was back toward the river, and another kind of danger. But for the time being, he had no choice.

The ridge could only be reached by a steep climb over broken branches and slick, leaf-covered banks, and Byrd knew even as he guided them that he would never be able to erase all the tracks they were making. He tethered the mule in a grassy area by the stream at the bottom of the incline, knowing full well that when the Shawnee came, the animal would be the first thing they would take. It was left to Byrd to carry Hilda up the bank, much to her mortification. He returned several times for the children and finally for Matthew. Maude slipped and fell halfway down the bank, dashing her head against a low branch, but the other women made the climb with little more than scraped hands and knees and a few scratches.

"This is a horrible place!" Priscilla exclaimed in dismay, looking around at the thicket-covered, heavily wooded ridge. "There's no place to lie down, and if we want water we have to go all the way down the bank again, and *anything* could be hiding in those bushes . . ."

Byrd took the hatchet from his belt and handed it to Katherine. "Miss Kate, you womenfolk start cutting branches from the other side of the ridge and dragging them up here. We'll use them to build a screen." He jerked his head at Oliver. "Come on, son, let's see if we can't scare us up some breakfast."

An uneasy silence, broken only by the murmur of children's voices, settled over the group as they watched him walk away. Caroline took the hatchet from Katherine. "Come along, ladies," she said briskly. "She can't do it by herself. Hilda, you stay here with the children. The rest of us will bring back the branches and start building a fort."

Byrd met Oliver at the bottom of the ridge. He was carrying two rifles, and a long bow was slung over his shoulder. Oliver looked curious. "Where'd you get the other gun?"

Byrd handed the rifle to Oliver. "No man should go into the wilderness without a good fire-arm in his hand."

Whatever suspicion Oliver might have felt at the neat way in which Byrd sidestepped the question was mitigated by the solid feel of the Kentucky rifle in his hands. Byrd had called him a man. And with a weapon like this, he felt like one.

Oliver checked the barrel to make sure it was loaded, and noticed Byrd's approving glance as he did so. His pride swelled another degree as he swung the rifle over his shoulder.

"A woodsman never uses his rifle unless he has to," Byrd said as they started walking. "Makes too much noise. Scares away the game and attracts attention. You see that big oak over there?" He said, lifting his arm. "We don't hunt any further than that to the east, or past the stream on the west, and never any closer in than half a mile from our camp."

"How come?"

"You got to stake out your hunting grounds. You hunt too close to your camp and you're going to drive out the game, and you might need it in an emergency. You go wandering too far away, and like as not you'll run into a pack of redskins. And don't go near the river no matter what." His tone was harsh.

Oliver stared at him. "Why not? It's bound to've gone down by now. Seems to me like we ought to . . ."

"Just do as I say," Byrd said shortly. He forestalled further protests by slipping his longbow off his shoulder and smoothly notching an arrow. "You ever shoot one of these?"

Oliver shook his head, unable to suppress his excitement. "Never even saw one, not a real one, before. We lived in town."

He watched as Byrd drew back on the string and released an arrow that was one moment invisible and the next quivering in the knothole of a tree fifty feet away. Admiration filled Oliver to the core. Whatever else Byrd Kincaid was, he was a *man*.

Byrd retrieved the arrow and strode back to Oliver. He handed him the bow. "Let's see what you can do," he said.

Oliver took the bow and arrow, looking at them with wonder. He was so excited, he didn't think he'd be able to keep from dropping it. But he had watched Byrd carefully, and he was a good imitator. The first arrow flew straight.

To his great disappointment, Oliver missed the target. But Byrd merely retrieved the arrow, offered a few simple words of instruction, and advised Oliver to try again. By the third time Oliver hit the tree, by the fifth he actually hit the target.

Byrd walked forward to examine the hit, pulled out the arrow, and returned it to Oliver. "You got good eyes for a city boy," he said, and the pride that swelled within Oliver was the best thing he had ever felt in his life.

Over the course of the next half hour's walk, Oliver began to reevaluate his opinion of Byrd. His own father had been a busy man, not much given to any but the most rudimentary outdoor pursuits, and he had never had much time to spend with his son. Byrd Kincaid was the kind of man you read about in the newspapers, or heard about in legends—like Daniel Boone or General Anthony Wayne. He was the kind of man a boy like Oliver only dreamed about meeting, and here he was teaching Oliver how to hunt and shoot a long bow, and talking to him like he was one of his own kind.

Six months ago Oliver would have taken it all at face value and been completely enthralled. But a lot had changed since he'd started the trip west, and more particularly since his whole world had been turned upsidedown on the Ohio River. He had learned to be cautious. It might not be right or fair, but there was still something about Byrd Kincaid that made him uneasy.

About an hour later Byrd spotted a wild turkey in the brush and let fly an arrow that felled it so neatly that its mate, pecking at the ground not five feet away, didn't even notice what had happened. Silently, Byrd paused the bow to Oliver, and though he was so eager and afraid that sweat broke out on his brow and threatened to blur his vision, Oliver's arrow hit true. He wanted to whoop out loud with triumph, but restrained himself just in time.

The two of them went to collect the prey. Byrd had to hide a grin when he saw the pride and thrill of accomplishment in Oliver's expression and how hard the boy tried to mask it with a nonchalant, "I reckon that ought to do it."

"Make a fine meal," Byrd agreed soberly, concentrating on strapping the two birds together by the necks with a rawhide thong. "Not bad for a couple hours of hunting."

"Reckon we ought to be headin' back," Oliver said. "Shouldn't ought to leave the womenfolk by theirselves too long."

Byrd flung the turkeys over his shoulder. "Oh, I wouldn't fret about them much if I was you. Miss Kate'll take care of the camp."

Oliver glanced at Byrd sidelong, and in the newfound camaraderie of hunters in the wild, he figured now was as good a time as any to bring his concern out in the open, man to man. They walked for several minutes before he found just the right way to say it.

"You think right smart of Miss Katherine, don't you?"

"That I do. See that?" Byrd pointed to the trunk of a pine tree, where some of the bark had been rubbed off about five feet up. "Black bear, scratchin' hisself. Them scars are about five days old though. He's moved on by now. You see anything fresher, you want to steer clear.

"Yep," he continued as they walked on. A ruminating tone had come into his voice. "A man could do a lot worse than a woman like Miss Kate." Through the corner of his eye, Byrd saw dismay cross Oliver's face, and again he had to keep himself from smiling. That boy would never make a poker player.

He glanced at Oliver. "But I reckon you already know that."

Oliver swallowed hard and straightened his shoulders. A determined look came over his face, and he faced Byrd squarely. "You're right. Miss Katherine is one of the finest women I ever knew, and I wouldn't want to see anything happen to her."

The signs of adolescent puppy love were so painfully clear that Byrd wanted to laugh out loud. Instead he squinted into the sun, nodded seriously, and allowed, "That's a right fine attitude, son."

"I'm not going to let anybody hurt her," Oliver reiterated.

"That sounds like a warning."

"Maybe it is." Oliver screwed up his courage and stood his ground. "Maybe there's a few things about you I don't rightly trust."

Byrd chuckled. "Suspicious, are you?" The amusement died down, replaced by a shrewd look. "Well," he decided, "that's not a bad quality in a man. All in all, you'll probably live a lot longer if you stay a little on the suspicious side."

He clapped Oliver on the back and gestured the way up the hill, leaving Oliver more confused than ever, but somehow feeling all the better for the morning's work.

Chapter Nine

For the remainder of the morning Katherine sawed at green branches with her knife while Caroline hacked away with the hatchet. The other women gathered the fallen branches and dragged them back to camp, a slow and often irritating process. Once, Priscilla saw a snake and screamed, startling the creature, which slithered off into the underbrush without so much as a hiss of warning.

Katherine was careful to vary their positions as they cut the branches, knowing that a stripped forest would be as revealing of their presence as if they had never bothered to build the screen at all. And all the time she knew that whatever measures they took to hide themselves wouldn't be enough.

By the time Byrd and Oliver returned, the women had made a good start on weaving the branches together into a rude shelter against the side of the ridge. The screen would provide not only protection from the elements and a filter for cookfire smoke, but also an adequate hiding place in case of attack. When seen from a distance, the man-made cave would look like an extension of the woods.

Byrd glanced at their handiwork without comment and set to work building a fire under the shade of a giant oak, using dry wood and trusting that the leaves of the tree would disperse the smoke enough to leave no trace of their activities. While the turkeys cooked, Byrd efficiently lent his hand to finishing the shelter.

"It'll do," he pronounced at last, eyeing the structure critically. "I want the young'uns inside here day and night, and the same goes for Wiltshire. The rest of you should stay with them unless you've got some reason to be outside. In case of trouble, each of you will have a post to defend. Otherwise stay out of sight."

Maude glared at him. She had a nasty cut on the side of her head, her clothes were torn, and she felt badly used by the morning's work. "We can't keep these children penned up inside there like animals!"

"You will if you want to keep them at all," Byrd said indifferently.

"But it's damp in there," Esther protested. "My Matthew needs sunshine, he . . ."

"Any of you know how to shoot a gun?" Byrd asked.

In the moment of startled silence that followed it seemed as though the absolute reality of what they were facing descended like a physical thing. This was no longer an uncomfortable, inconvenient trek into the wilderness. They were being called upon to defend themselves with weapons, and they were only women.

"I think you're lying," Maude stated abruptly.

All eyes turned to her in shock and confusion. She continued heatedly, "Last night you were ready to abandon us to the wolves, but now suddenly, just because you say so, we're supposed to follow you God-knows-where, just like we followed the other heathen who got us into this mess in the first place!" Her glittering eyes shot to Katherine before sweeping around the group. "I don't think there are any Indians out there at all!"

"And even if there are, what makes you think they'd bother us?" Esther added. "Everybody knows that the Indians never started any trouble until they were pushed. And it was people like *him*"—she pointed an accusing finger at Byrd—"who did the pushing! All they want is to be left alone, and if we don't start any trouble we'll be just fine. We should have kept moving, kept minding our own business. If we sit up on top of this ridge pointing long rifles at everything that moves, we're just asking for trouble."

Katherine listened with dismay. Why hadn't they spoken up sooner? If she had known how they felt, she never would have allowed Byrd to lead them on this pointless jaunt to nowhere. Why hadn't she discussed it with them? Why had she taken the full burden of decision making on herself? Now, if anything went wrong it would be she, and she alone, who was to blame.

Esther was right. The war had been forced upon the Shawnee by the settlers' relentless encroachment into their territory and by numerous broken promises. But the war was over now. Perhaps if they had just kept moving they would have been allowed to pass unmolested. Or perhaps that was only what she, Katherine, like the rest of the women, wanted to believe.

Byrd regarded them with lazy amusement laced with contempt. "Well now, ma'am." He spoke to Esther, but his words were for all of them. "I know that back east there's a lot of talk about the poor, put-upon red man and how bad he's been done wrong, and I'm not saying I don't agree with it, to a point. But if you're going to show respect for the Indian, you'd best respect him for what he is, not for what your fine preachers and newspaper writers want you to believe he is. You think it's been hard on you, this little time you've been wandering around in the woods, trying to stay alive on what there is to eat out here, trying to stay dry in the rain and warm at night and fighting off bears with a stick? Well, ma'am, the Indian's been doing that for hundreds of years before white men ever set foot on this soil, and if you think that don't make for a bunch of dirt-tough, snake-sly men, you'd better think again.

"What the Indian is, is the fiercest fightin' animal God ever put on this earth. If he wasn't, he wouldn't be around today. A brave gets moved up in his tribe according to how many coups he's counted on his enemy, and mercy is considered a weakness. He goes out of his way to find a fight, because that's what he's been trained to do. That's how he's survived all these hundreds or thousands of years ... by conquering. The Indian don't want your pity, Miz Wiltshire, and he's sure not going to give you none."

He paused and looked around the ground once more. This was the longest speech he had uttered. His eyes maintained the same flat, disinterested expression. "When the Shawnee come up on this camp—and yes, Miz Sherrod, they're out there, maybe watching us this very minute and making out their plans—when they come up here, they ain't gonna see a bunch of harmless women and children that just want to be left alone. They're going to see squaws for their camp and white braves they can raise up as their own. They're going to look on you like you was a herd of buffalo waiting to be shot down, only worth twice as much. They're going to see the glory it's going to bring them, dragging you back to their camp, and the hero's welcome the village is going to turn out for them."

He shrugged, a subtle gesture of dismissal that was all the more effective for its simplicity. "I've said what I've got to say. If you ladies still want to take the chance on them Indians leaving you alone, all I've wasted is a day. You go right ahead and do what you think's best, but I've been inside a Shawnee camp, and I've got the scars to prove it. I ain't particularly anxious to try my luck again."

The women were glancing at each other uncertainly, but no one seemed to have anything to say. Eventually all eyes went, as they always did, to Katherine.

She took a breath. "We're here now," she said. "We're all tired, the children need to rest. We have no choice but to make camp and wait and see what happens. If there's no sign of trouble in a couple of days, we can move on."

That was the best she could do, and if anyone else had a better idea they seemed to be keeping it to themselves.

Byrd started to walk away, and Caroline spoke up quietly. "I can shoot."

"Me, too," Oliver added. Then, blushing a little, he amended, "Well, not very good. But I can generally hit a target three times out of five."

Byrd swept his glance across each of them, slowly. No one else said a word, and neither

Maude nor Esther met his eyes. "All right then," he said at last. "Before the day is done, the rest of you are going to know how to shoot, too."

Katherine had to speak up. Everything Byrd had said made sense, but she still couldn't completely trust him. She knew that if fighting was the only chance they had, then they didn't have any chance at all.

"There are only two rifles," she pointed out.

Byrd met her gaze evenly. "Yes, ma'am, that's right. But when it gets down to dirt, I don't know which one of us is going to be left standing up to fire them. So everybody's going to know how to shoot."

They could not afford to waste ammunition any more than they could afford to give away their hideout by shooting loaded rifles for target practice, so the day's instruction consisted of the mechanics of loading powder, patch, and shot, then sighting imaginary targets down the barrel. Caroline proved to be every bit as competent with a rifle as she claimed. When this aroused suspicion among the others, she merely tossed her head and replied that riding to the hounds was considered a genteel occupation for young ladies in Virginia. Katherine privately wondered if Kentucky rifles were used for sport in Virginia, but the others seemed to accept her story. Besides, it didn't really matter how or why Caroline had learned to handle a rifle, only that she could. If the worst happened, at least they would have one among their numbers who knew what she was doing.

Priscilla rebelled against learning to shoot, as she did against everything else. "I don't know why we should have to do everything," she complained. "You're a man, you'll take care of us."

"There's only one of me," Byrd replied, "and thirteen of you."

"But it's a man's duty to take care of women!"

Byrd stared at her with surprise, then gave a brief shake of his head. "Maybe back east . . . but out here on the frontier things is different."

"I don't know why I should have to do a man's job when there's a perfectly capable man around to do it himself!"

Byrd's eyes narrowed, as though he was finding it difficult to resolve what he saw with what he heard. Then he drawled, "I'll tell you what, ma'am. You just keep on whinin' about it and you're gonna have a camp full of Shawnee braves to take care of you. The way I look at it, they'd be getting about what they deserve."

Priscilla gasped with fury. With a strangled "Oh!" she flung the rifle on the ground.

Byrd's hand went around her arm so quickly and with such force that she cried out in alarm. Instantly all eyes were upon them. Even Esther took a half step, as though to defend her daughter-in-law, before thinking better of it.

A menacing look came into Byrd's eyes. "I know you're just a scared, half-witted little girl and you got your problems same as I got mine. But that there rifle might be the only thing that stands between me and my Maker, and *nobody* throws a fine piece of weaponry around like that without a damn good reason, do you understand me, girl?" He gave her arm a fierce shake which wrenched a terrified sob from Priscilla.

"If . . . if my husband were able . . ." she stammered.

"If your husband was able, he'd turn you over his knee," Byrd said, and released her arm with a jerk. "And if you don't stay out of my way, I'm apt to favor him by doing it myself."

Priscilla's lip quivered. "Oh, you hideous man! I wish you'd never found us!" She burst into sobs and ran away, nursing her bruised arm. No one seemed inclined to offer her any comfort, and when she saw that she had no one to turn to except her husband, who was sitting on the ground staring sightlessly into the distance, she flung herself away and covered her face with her hands, sobbing even harder.

Hilda stepped before Byrd. "I will learn now, if you please," she said.

Byrd dusted the debris off the rifle barrel and turned to look at her. The tension on his face slowly gentled at her quiet courage. "I don't think that'll be necessary, Miz Werner," he said. "This old Betsy packs a powerful kick, and it'd be better if you just stayed low and minded the young'uns."

"I will learn," Hilda insisted. Her hand moved unconsciously over her abdomen. "My babe will be born a slave to no man, and I have much to protect."

Byrd looked at her thoughtfully for a moment and then nodded and handed her the rifle. "Yes, ma'am, I reckon you do."

With the other women involved in practicing their shooting skills, Oliver felt at loose ends. There was nobody to brag to about his hunting conquests, and in fact, nobody to talk to at all except Priscilla, who was sitting under a bayberry bush crying her eyes out. He felt kind of sorry for her, even though she had acted like a dang fool with the rifle, and Oliver privately thought she was lucky Byrd hadn't hauled off and belted her one. But she was just a girl, and nobody even took time to pat her shoulder or tell her to stop crying. Since their conversation the night before Byrd had arrived at camp, Oliver felt he understood her better than anyone else. For the moment, they were two of a kind, since nobody seemed to have time for either one of them.

After a while Oliver went over and sat down beside her. Awkwardly, he patted her shoulder. "There now, Miss Priscilla, it ain't all that bad."

Her voice was muffled in the skirts that covered her drawn up knees and strained with angry weeping. "Oh, he's such an awful man!"

"Well now, I wouldn't say that. He just wants you to be safe, that's all."

A minute later Oliver was sorry he'd been so quick to defend Byrd. Byrd had turned over the job of teaching Hilda to Caroline and had walked over to Katherine. He took the rifle from her, and Oliver strained to make out his low words as he demonstrated siting a target. All the while, Katherine never took her eyes off Byrd's face.

Priscilla dried her face on her skirts, sniffing a little. "I suppose you think I'm horrible," she said.

Oliver dragged his attention away from Katherine and Byrd. "It don't matter what I think. You've got a lot on your mind."

Priscilla's reddened face slowly relaxed into a shy smile. "You're nice, Oliver."

Oliver shrugged, trying to resist the temptation to look back at Katherine. "I just don't like to see a body carrying on so, is all."

Priscilla let the tension go out of her shoulders and occupied herself with picking at a loose thread on her apron. "Nobody else likes me."

"They all like you, Pris. They just don't have a lot of time to show it right now."

Priscilla glanced at him quickly. His intimate shortening of her name thrilled her more than she wanted him to know. She was glad he was looking at something else just then and couldn't see the warmth in her eyes. "You're the only one who understands though," she said softly. "The only one I can talk to."

She turned her attention back to the loose thread, suddenly too shy to meet his eyes. "It's just that I've never been on my own before, you know. First there was Papa, and then there was Matthew, and now ... well everybody else is so ... well, they all know just what to do, and what needs to be done, just like a real matron should. They're all so brave and I'm so scared and oh, Oliver, sometimes I ..." She reached hesitantly for his hand, but the gesture faltered in midair. Oliver didn't even notice.

His attention was fixed on something across the clearing, and he was frowning so fiercely that Priscilla realized he hadn't heard a word she had said. Hurt and puzzled, she followed his gaze until she found what had captured his attention. Byrd Kincaid was standing with his arms around Katherine Carlyle, helping her to balance the rifle against her shoulder, bringing his head close to hers as he lined up the sights. Her face was half turned to him. Priscilla watched Katherine's lips curve in a small, reluctant smile at something Byrd had said.

At first, not understanding, Priscilla looked back at Oliver. The expression on his face told her all she needed to know. Fresh tears misted her eyes, but she swallowed them back. When she stood and walked away after a moment Oliver wasn't even aware of her departure.

As dusk fell, Katherine walked away from the camp, a little way into the woods. She stopped where a cluster of pines fought with a red oak for soil and sun, and leaned back against the oak, tilting her head up toward the leaves. She was too tired to be wary of the creatures that might slither around the trunk or drop from the branches or burrow inside her clothes. She felt the rough bark beneath her hands and the firm support against her spine and simply rested.

After supper was over, the children prepared to bed down on leafy pallets inside the shelter while the women gossiped and worried, and Byrd and Oliver worked on making a new bow. Katherine could smell the cooksmoke which clung to her clothes and hear the chattering voices that echoed in her head even as she enjoyed the coolness and solitude of being outside by herself. The burdens of the day always seemed to grow heavier as sunset approached.

Her back ached, her eyes were gritty with fatigue, her burned and blistered hand throbbed, and her feet were caked with the dried blood of broken blisters caused by her too-large shoes. She wanted a bath, a warm fire, a mattress, and a pillow. She wanted some of Gran's fresh johnnycake and milk warm from the cow. She wanted to sleep . . . and never dream again.

What was to become of them? For the moment they at least appeared to be safe and well fed. But uncounted miles lay between here and Cairo, and what if Byrd was right about the Shawnee? They couldn't stay here forever. Tomorrow or the next day she would have to make a decision about moving on.

Perhaps by then the river would be safe again. But what did that matter since they had neither a boat nor a pilot? Some of the children were already developing coughs from sleeping on the exposed ground. What if one of them became seriously ill? And what about Hilda, whose time could now be measured in days, not months? Could any of them expect to make it to Cairo alive?

An awful weariness came over her, as thick, as subtle, as overpowering as the dropping curtain of night. *How much longer can I stand it?* she thought. *Will it never end?*

"You should be inside the shelter."

Katherine tensed at the sound of Byrd's voice. "I needed to be alone."

He came toward her, his steps barely a whisper on the leaf-padded forest floor. He stood beside her for a long time in silence, sharing the stillness of the evening. At last he said, "It's not easy, is it?"

She looked at him "What?"

His face was painted in shadows, but there was an openness in his expression that Katherine found comforting. "Staying, when you want to go," he said.

She drew in a breath, of surprise, of protest, then let it filter past her lips in impotent silence. With Byrd Kincaid, of all people, there was no point in pretending, and no grace in lying. She didn't have the energy for it anyway.

She rested her head against the tree again, letting her eyes wander over the woodland thicket with its tricks of light and shadow and hidden menace. "I never wanted this," she said. "The worry, the responsibility, all these people. All I wanted was to go west and be safe. I didn't ask for any of it."

"Then let's do it," Byrd said suddenly.

He stepped before her, startling her. His eyes were hard with purpose, and his voice was low and smooth. "We can slip away tonight and be well out of here by dawn. We'll leave a rifle behind, and the boy's gettin' right good with the long bow. They'll do all right." He paused before continuing. "I'll take you to the Mississippi and from there down to New Orleans if you want, or up the Missouri. It's a fine land, Miss Kate, and a cryin' pity for a woman like you to live out your life without seeing it. The Mogollon Rim, the Yellowstone, the Shining Mountains . . . I can show you wonders you wouldn't believe." The corners of his lips turned down—with amusement or the beginning of a challenge. "Who knows? We might even run up on that brother of yours, holed up in a hollow somewheres. Wouldn't that be fine?"

Katherine felt a little breathless. She studied him intensely. "You'd do it, wouldn't you?" she said at last.

"You give the word, Miss Kate. You just give the word."

For a moment her head spun with possibilities. To leave this very night, just to walk away and keep on walking. . . . They would be safe, the two of them, much safer than they would be trailing a herd of whining women and children. Byrd would take care of her; he would feed her, shelter her, protect her from danger. For once in her life she would be able to depend on someone else instead of everyone else depending on her.

His strangely beautiful pale eyes were intense, searching her face, probing inside her head. "You and me'd be quite a team, Miss Kate," he said huskily, "and you know it, don't you. Folks like us was meant for this land—to fight it, to know it, to make it our own."

His hand came up and touched her face, his rough palm cupping and brushing her cheek, her jaw. She turned to the caress like a starving kitten seeking its mother's milk. So odd to feel gentleness from such a big man. So wonderful.

Yes, she thought. Let it be. Let him take me away ... The strange, lyrical-sounding places he had spoken of, the ragged mountain peaks, the fast-flowing rivers, the endless vistas all meant freedom, escape. She wanted it all with a ferocity that brought the taste of tears to her mouth.

She held his gaze. "But I don't trust you."

"Does it matter?" he asked, a faint smile playing upon his mouth.

No, Katherine thought, and the realization did not surprise her. No, it didn't matter, because she wanted to believe in him more than anything in the world. If at that moment he had offered to show her a silver road that swept upward to the moon, she would have gone with him gladly, never doubting that he would deliver on his promise, that he would help her escape.

"I am so tired," she half-whispered. And then, without conscious decision, she let her body relax. Byrd's strong arms came around her, and she rested her cheek against the soft buckskin that covered his chest. For the first time in what seemed like forever, she felt safe.

He was right. They were two of a kind. Both lawbreakers, both runaways, both willing to turn their backs on a dozen helpless women and children and never look back. She could do it. She *would* do it. This might be her last chance, and she must take it.

The crickets chirped, the nightbirds began to sing, the branches rustled with the soft whispers of the dying day. The shadows deepened from gray to violet then to hues of midnight blue. Byrd held her, and Katherine leaned against him.

Then another sound filtered through the stillness, distant and muffled, at odds with the perfect harmony of the twilight. It was the sound of a child's cry. Katherine tried to ignore it, to concentrate on the thump of Byrd's heartbeat, the warmth of his arms, the vistas of freedom that swept before her. But it tugged at her, dragging her back, tearing her dreams to shreds. She pulled herself slowly away.

"I can't," she said.

A slow, sad smile touched Byrd's lips, and she understood.

"You knew it, didn't you?" She looked at him with new eyes, though still not completely understanding what she saw. That was why he had made the offer, painting such beautiful, tantalizing pictures in her head: he knew that only when she saw clearly what she wanted would she realize, finally and completely, what she must sacrifice for it. Now, once and for all, there would be no more wishing, no more what-ifs, no more looking back. She couldn't leave these people.

"I reckon I always knew you had the makin's of a hero in you," Byrd said. "It just took a little something to bring it out, is all."

Katherine tightened her lips, shaking her head.

"I don't want to be a hero. I just want to be home, and safe, and free of all this worry."

"Katherine Carlyle." Byrd caught her face and held it firmly, turning her eyes up to his. His voice was low and gentle, his expression sadly amused. "You know what a hero is? Nine times out of ten it ain't nothing in this world but a man—or a woman—just doing what he has to do to get by."

Katherine held his gaze for a long time, trying to recapture that sense of rightness she had felt in his arms, the hope that had so briefly been hers. But the child's cry continued, the darkness lengthened, and weariness crept into her every bone.

She pulled her face away from his hand, shaking her head. "Funny," she said dully. "That's the same thing that made me a criminal in the first place."

She turned and walked back to the camp, slowly and alone.

Oliver waited until she had entered the shelter and Byrd had moved on into the brush before he stepped out of the shadows. His lips were grim and his eyes were burning with the vision of Byrd Kincaid's arms around the woman he, Oliver, loved.

It was arranged that they would each take turns standing watch at night, though the dictum excluded Priscilla, whom Byrd declared wasn't fit to be trusted, and Hilda, who could no longer take the strain. Katherine relieved Caroline at her post outside the shelter shortly after midnight and settled down with the rifle across her knees, its heavy, unfamiliar weight more frightening than reassuring. She flexed her fingers on the stock, not wanting them to grow numb with disuse, and wondered doubtfully if she would have the quickness of reflex to aim and fire if she had to.

Byrd had taken his bedroll outside the shelter, higher up on the ridge. Katherine could not see him, but she knew he had chosen the best position for defense in case of trouble. That should have made her feel better, but it didn't. The scene between them earlier was so far away it might never have happened at all, and, once again, Katherine felt alone and afraid.

The woods were immense and powerful, teeming with alien life, in the midst of which the band of women and children were like insects waiting to be scooped up by a giant bird of prey. They did not belong here, any of them. They were intruders into God's ancient land and He could sweep them off the face of the earth with the same careless gesture with which a man might swat a fly. It was a strange feeling to sit beneath a vast, inky sky and breathe the time-aged air of a river older than man, where a hundred forests had risen and fallen, and to know one's own smallness.

Katherine heard a stirring in the shelter behind her and gave a startled jerk. Before she could lift the rifle, a whisper came to her, "It is only I, Hilda."

"Are you all right?"

"Yes."

Katherine relaxed as Hilda moved a little way into the woods to relieve herself. She did not like to think how quickly it would have been over had it been a Shawnee brave behind her.

After the scene this morning, most of the women had agreed that Byrd's plan for defense was the best one. But Katherine was accustomed to relying on herself, and she knew there had to be a better way. She turned the problem of their vulnerability over in her mind, finding no solution, until Hilda returned.

She sat beside Katherine with a shy smile. "The babe grows heavy," she said, as though apologizing. "I must go to the woods more than the others."

The baby had dropped noticeably in the past few days. Hilda was very near her time. It could be a week, maybe two.

"Why did you start off on such a journey in your condition?" Katherine asked.

Hilda laughed softly. "Ah, but it wasn't such a condition when we started! We mis-guessed the size of your America, I think, and the time it would take to get from there to here."

She pressed her hand into the small of her back, flexing, and smiled wistfully. "My Alex, he was a stubborn man. Quiet, but strong." She glanced at Katherine. "Like our Mr. Kincaid, I think, but perhaps not quite as . . . strange."

Katherine made a muffled sound of amused agreement as Hilda went on. "It was the land, you see. In Germany, the cities are close and full— living here, you cannot imagine such fullness. My Alex, he worked in a shop selling breads and sausages and giving most of his money to the owner, though it was Alex who made the breads and stuffed the sausages and fed the households of all who came in. Still, he managed to put some by, for our marriage.

"My Alex was slow to anger, but he was very big and strong. Bruhauser, the owner of the shop, went to him one day and accused Alex of stealing.

There was a fight, and they were going to put poor Alex into prison. That night he came to me, wet with running and out of breath but with a fire in his eyes like none I'd ever seen. He said to me, 'Hilda, we will go to America.' And we did." A proud, achingly sad smile curved her face. "We were married on the boat and left without even saying goodbye to our families. Sometimes I am sorry for that.

"When we got to America, we must work to live, as we only had money for our passage. My Alex, he did not speak English very well, and in the cities there was little to do. Everywhere we went, it was the same. No place for us, no one who wanted us. So Alex said to me, 'Hilda, we will go west, where there is land. We will have our own shop, and we will raise cabbages!'" She laughed, a soft, melodious sound that wrapped together memories in a brief, shining parcel and then, on the same breath, released them gently to the floating winds.

"And so we come. Alex for his cabbages, and me for a roof over my babe's head, a roof that is my own and that no one can drive me from. Alex . . . ," there was a catch in her voice, "he will not have his little shop after all. But me . . . ," she folded both arms over her abdomen, holding it with protective pride. "I will have this. For always."

The darkness and the silence, which only moments ago had seemed so threatening, were now beneficent. Katherine listened to the gentle carol of the wooded life around her and realized why she had always felt a kinship with Hilda: it was because she, like Katherine, was an outcast looking for a place to call home.

After a time, Hilda spoke again in a surprisingly different vein. "This Mr. Kincaid, he is very odd, is he not?"

Katherine sensed there was more to the subject than idle conversation and listened alertly.

"Fierce like a bear," Hilda went on, "but kind too. He has many secrets, I think."

"Yes," Katherine agreed. "He has his secrets."

Hilda seemed to be encouraged. "Today, when you were all away, one of the children ran away and I went to follow. I saw Mr. Kincaid coming out of a—" she struggled for the word. "A hole, but one that is in the dirt?"

"A cave?" suggested Katherine, interested.

Hilda nodded. "A cave, hidden behind a bush with red leaves. He seemed very . . . careful. When he went in he had one rifle. When he came out, he had two. I don't know why he would be such a mystery with it, do you?"

"No," admitted Katherine thoughtfully. "I don't." But she thought it might not be a bad idea to find out.

Hilda smiled. "The others—they say you are mad. They are angry at you sometimes for bringing us here, and they think we would have no problems if you weren't here. Silly women. I would never have been brave enough to go into the woods without you. But because you went, my babe will have a home." She leaned forward and kissed Katherine lightly on the cheek. "You will be my friend forever for that."

Hilda got up and went into the shelter. Katherine sat there alone, listening to the dark, thinking about Hilda Werner's dogged, foolish optimism and still feeling her kiss upon her cheek.

Chapter Ten

The morning dawned quiet and clear, and with it came a resurgence of Katherine's doubts. She watched the women go about the morning chores—stoking up the fire, hauling water, grooming their children, divvying up the leftover turkey for breakfast, and she found it difficult to believe this was not just a routine morning in an ordinary camp. There was nothing about the scene to suggest they were all fleeing in terror from a Shawnee attack.

That morning, Katherine's thoughts flowed clearly as she carefully reasoned through the events of the past two days. She didn't like the picture that eventually formed. To all appearances they were safe here with Byrd. They were fed and sheltered and armed. They had a man who knew more than they did, who planned better than they did, who seemed to make it his duty to take care of them. It was difficult to give up that security for the doubts that crowded her, but logic and her own sense of responsibility demanded she do so.

Were there Indians out there? They had no proof of it except Byrd's word. Then why was he keeping them here, feeding them, sheltering them, and paralyzing them with promises of an attack that never came?

Unless ... He had admitted he had dealt with the Shawnee before, claiming to have been a prisoner against his will. Suppose his relationship with the Shawnee was of a different nature altogether?

The Shawnee were an honorable, fair-dealing tribe, and it was said that their word, once given, was never broken. As they moved from place to place, it was traditional for them to ask permission of occupying tribes to pass through their land or to use their hunting grounds, and they paid for the privilege with goods or services. Might they not expect the same sort of payment from a white man who wished to pass in peace through *their* lands?

Twelve women and children could buy a great many favors from the Shawnee.

Unbidden, memories of the night before came back to her. The warmth she had felt in Byrd's arms, the rightness, the safety. No man had ever held her like that, said such things to her, or made her feel what he made her feel. She had been willing to go with him in the dead of night, to leave everything behind for the sake of his promises. Yet he had not seemed worried about the Shawnee when he made the proposal, had he?

Though she hated the possibility that she might be right, she had to know. Her duty to the others must outweigh the preferences of her heart. She wished she had inherited Gran's second sight.

When Oliver and Byrd were out hunting that morning, she seized the opportunity to explore the cave. It was not easy to find, especially since

Katherine did not want to alert Hilda to her suspicions by asking for directions. She had searched for what seemed like hours, the sun was growing high, and Byrd would be back soon. She decided to search the ridge wall once more before giving up. And then, finally, in a place she had passed half a dozen times, she found it.

She might have passed it once more had she not noticed that the shrub was withering at the roots. When she brushed up against it, it moved and fell aside. There was more brush behind it, which she carefully pushed away until she felt the touch of cool, dank air.

The cave was not large, more like a crevice in an overhanging rock. Katherine had to get down on her hands and knees to crawl inside, and when she tried to stand she could feel the top of the wall brushing her shoulders. She heard the rustle of small, dark-dwelling creatures but gritted her teeth and tried to ignore them.

She crouched there for a moment, letting her eyes adjust to the dark. Enough light filtered through from the entrance to allow her eventually to see that the cave was not as small as she had first imagined; it was simply crowded. Surrounding her on three sides and reaching down to the ceiling were large, irregularly shaped bundles wrapped in what felt like buckskin and tied with strong rawhide thongs. Those bundles could contain furs, of course, which would make Byrd Kincaid an honest—though highly unusual— trapper. More likely there were rifles inside those buckskins, and ammunition. Byrd Kincaid would not be the first white man to trade arms with the Indians for his own profit or safety.

Working until sweat rolled into her eyes and

her blistered fingers began to throb, Katherine finally managed to loosen one of the thongs on the closest bundle. She sat back on her heels to ease the cramping in her calves and reached inside, pulling out one item after another. When perhaps a dozen items were piled up before her in the dim light of the cave entrance, she had to sit there for a moment, letting the impact of what she had discovered sink in.

There was a silver plate worked in elaborate filigree, a handful of jewelry set with winking stones, a ship's compass, a woman's fur muff, a gold locket with a miniature of a young girl inside and elaborately scrolled initials on the back. Further back inside the pack she touched a bolt of material that felt like silk and a pair of soft leather boots. Among the jewelry were several gold wedding bands, with inscriptions inside them she could not read in the dimness. In this bundle alone were enough treasures to fill Alladin's cave, and all of them belonged to other people.

Byrd Kincaid was a thief!

She retied the bundle and left the cave hastily, careful to rearrange the bushes and to erase her footprints by sifting leaves and pinestraw over the area as she had seen Byrd do. She was too stunned by what she had found to consider what it meant in terms of her own safety and that of the others. But one thing was clear. The people to whom those treasures belonged had not parted with them willingly, and it was more than possible that there was a body moldering in the river for every item that Byrd Kincaid had stuffed into his packs. A man capable of stealing the boots off a dead man's feet and wedding bands off women's fingers was capable of anything.

What was he planning for them now? And what could she do to prevent it?

She was almost back at camp, heavy with worry over this new development, when a piercing shriek stabbed her ears. Her heart slammed against her chest and she thought, *No! Too late* . . .

She burst through the bushes with her knife drawn, her blood pounding a violent rhythm through her limbs, her eyes searching wildly for signs of attack. What she saw caused her to stop and stare.

Priscilla was standing outside the shelter, sobbing and shaking her head, wildly raking her fingers through her hair with little moans of horror and disgust. Esther exclaimed irritably, "For the love of the blessed savior, girl, will you stop that caterwauling?"

"Priscilla Wiltshire, you hush your mouth!" Caroline scolded. "Do you want to bring every Indian in these woods down on us?"

"But they're everywhere! I can't get them out!"

Byrd was casually propping his rifle against a tree, but the scattered brace of rabbits at his feet bore testament to his initial startled reaction. He looked at Katherine as she burst through the woods, at her white-knuckled grip on the knife, her heaving chest, her fierce, terrified eyes, and he said flatly, "Bugs. She's got bugs in her hair."

Katherine went weak.

"Oh, for pity's sake, let her wash her hair!" Maude said sharply. "I'll go down to the creek myself if it'll keep her quiet."

Katherine let her arm drop shakily to her side.

Bathed in a clammy sweat, she felt her muscles quivering with residual energy, and her side ached from running as she struggled to get her breath. "I'm going to strangle that girl," she said, her voice was low and determined.

Byrd picked up the string of rabbits and handed them to her, amusement in his eyes. "Here, put that knife to good use. I dropped a mess of squirrel on the way in, too." He glanced back at her as he started toward the woods again, and something in that look did peculiar things to Katherine's insides. "It's good to know I wasn't the only one ready to come in fighting."

Katherine took a deep breath and dropped down to her haunches. She pulled the first rabbit off the rawhide string and began to gut it, her hand still shaking so badly she almost cut herself.

Hilda went over to Priscilla. "Here now, I will help you."

"No!" Priscilla slapped Hilda's hands away, her voice shrill and angry. "Just leave me alone! Everyone ... leave—me ... *alone!*" She burst into sobs again.

"Spoiled child," Maude muttered.

"Ungrateful little wretch," Esther agreed.

Priscilla caught her breath on a sob and lifted her swollen face in defiance. Her eyes flamed anger and hatred. Without another sound she strode over to Katherine and snatched the knife out of her hand.

Katherine lurched after her in alarm as the other women shrank back. The shock in their faces turned to gasps of dismay. Priscilla grabbed her hair at the nape of the neck and furiously began to saw it off.

"Oh, my dear!" Caroline said softly.

In a horrified whisper Hilda echoed, "Poor thing!"

Even Esther's face was momentarily creased with consternation as the limp yellow curls lay scattered on the ground. Cutting off the infested hair was the only wise thing to do, of course, but Katherine would never have imagined that Priscilla, of all people, would have the courage to realize that. She knew what this sacrifice cost her.

As the last curl fell, Priscilla let the knife slip to the ground amidst the scattered yellow tresses. Tears were streaming down her cheeks. What hair remained on her head clung in spikes and tangles to her scalp. Her eyes were swollen almost to slits, her face blotched and twisted as she swept them all with a glittering glance. "I hope you're happy now!"

She turned and ran, half-stumbling, to the shelter, Hilda following.

Byrd returned with six fat squirrels which he dropped to the ground beside Katherine. He noticed the shorn hair without comment, picked up Katherine's knife, and returned it to her. He sat down beside her and quickly and efficiently began to dispose of the squirrels' heads and tails with his hatchet.

Hilda was making soothing noises to Priscilla and her sobs gradually ceased. Esther and Maude went in and out of the shelter, tending the children. Byrd and Katherine worked in silence side by side.

How was it possible to be so torn about a man? Katherine wondered. Two days ago she had not even known of Byrd Kincaid's existence, yet now her life, as well as the lives of those in her charge, revolved around him. A word, a silent embrace, a pair of oddly perceptive pale blue eyes, and she had been willing to abandon her future and her honor to his whim. The moment of madness that had come over her in the twilight was forever laid to rest now, yet the hold he had on her reason had not diminished. Despite all she had learned, she still needed to believe in him.

Maude came over to collect the rabbits Katherine had skinned. Suddenly she stopped and looked around. "Where's Oliver?" she demanded sharply.

Byrd looked up. "He's not back yet?"

A thread of panic tugged at Maude's stern mouth, and the yellowing bruise on her forehead stood out starkly. "He was supposed to be with you!"

"No, ma'am," replied Byrd mildly, "he's supposed to be out huntin'. Ain't no use in both of us covering the same ground."

The skin around Maude's eyes seemed to pinch and tighten. "Do you mean ... you let that boy go off on his own?"

"He's no boy, ma'am. He's a man with a family to provide for."

"Out in those woods where anything could happen!"

Katherine's heart was beating heavily. Oliver, alone in Shawnee territory, armed with nothing but snares and a bow he hardly knew how to use. Oliver with his quick, sweet smile and his sudden bursts of adolescent courage, big with bravado and prey to all sorts of dangers. . . .

The other women had been drawn by the conversation, their expressions anxious. Even Priscilla looked up with red, puffy eyes. A tense stillness descended on the group. Everyone liked

Oliver. Everyone knew this could be the beginning of what they had dreaded and feared and fought against.

Katherine slowly wiped her knife on her apron and started to rise. Byrd's hands closed tightly around her wrist.

"Now, you just get that notion right out of your head, Miss Kate," he said calmly. "You too, Miz Sherrod." Byrd looked around the group, his expression calm and reassuring. "The boy's all right. He knows the safe boundaries for hunting. If he's not back in a couple of hours, I'll go look for him. Meantime, the last thing we need is a bunch of women tramping around out there, making noise and getting lost. You all just calm down now and go about your business."

Caroline touched Maude's sleeve hesitantly. "He's right, Maude. There's no need to think the worst."

"He'll be fine," Esther said with more confidence. "There's a smart boy if ever I saw one."

"He will be hungry when he comes." Hilda took the rabbits from Maude with a bracing smile. "We'd best start cooking."

Maude was not reassured, but she pretended to be. There are some mother's nightmares that are just too horrible to come true, compelling a woman through a sort of superstitious terror to deny the possibility and therefore refuse to give it life. But her heart was like an anvil in her chest, and her veins felt filled with ice water, and for a moment, she could hardly see for the terror that gripped her.

Had she failed her only son? Oliver, so anxious to grow up, so determined to become a man ... She should have been more careful, she should not have allowed him such freedom, she should have drawn a tighter rein. But since that Carlyle woman had come into their lives, Maude's control had been slipping; no one listened to her, no one obeyed her, and if Oliver was lost now, whose fault would it be?

The dull thundering of her heart answered, Yours. It will be your fault and yours alone. But there was fury and accusation in her eyes as she turned to Katherine.

"Hurry up with those squirrels, girl," she said sharply. "I've got water boiling for stew."

Katherine stripped the hide from the last squirrel and handed it to Maude. The accusation on the woman's face as she snatched up the carcass bore the familiar, hateful look that said, If it weren't for you ... Katherine set her jaw and forced herself not to respond to the challenge. She was worried too.

An hour passed, and Oliver did not return. The group grew quiet and tense. Katherine could feel despair straining and stretching inside her like a strip of rawhide pulled to its finest extension. Every time she heard a rustle outside, every time Maude rushed to the entrance of the shelter and then returned with the hope gone out of her eyes, the strand twisted and tightened and threatened to break.

The children sensed the anxiety that permeated the adults and grew quarrelsome. Benjamin Adamson spilled his stew and Caroline slapped his bottom so hard that he wailed, then she gathered him close, hugging him until he sobbed from breathlessness. In the corner of the shelter a squabble broke out between Amy Sherrod and Rebecca Adamson, which resulted in Amy's pinching the younger girl so viciously that she howled. Katherine, with an instinct born of years of mediating fights between her younger siblings, immediately separated the two girls, scolding Amy sharply. Maude caught her arm and spun her away. "You keep your hands off my child, you vile creature! Haven't you done enough?"

Caroline abandoned Benjamin and flew to Rebecca, crying, "What a hateful little girl! Maude Sherrod, you'd best learn to control this little monster, or I'll do it for you! Look at that, my poor baby. She's got a black and blue mark!"

Katherine jerked her arm away. The children's shrieking was exacerbating everyone's nerves, and Katherine was no exception. She felt heat rising to her cheeks and flashing in her eyes as the culmination of the past weeks' tensions left her light-headed, teetering on the brink of control. She turned those flashing eyes on Maude.

"I didn't ask for you and your passel of brats," she said with barely suppressed rage. "You've been nothing but trouble from the day I laid eyes on you, and if I could have left you behind I would've done it long ago! You are a bitter, dried up old woman who brings nothing but misery to everyone around you, and I'm tired of it. The only thing you ever did right in your life was give birth to Oliver and now he's gone—and probably better off with the Indians than living with you!"

"You wretched, Godless creature," Maude whispered. Her eyes were churning with hateful emotions and her voice was choked. "You dare . . ."

"I dare," Katherine shot back tightly. "And it's blessed time somebody did." She could feel the stares of the other women on her as she pushed past Maude, past caring whether their sympathies were for or against her. She turned back briefly at the entrance to the shelter. "And another thing," she said, cold with fury. "Don't you ever touch me again."

Katherine pushed out into the warm humid air and found Byrd standing there, listening. His mouth was upturned in a wry smile and his eyes sparkled. "Give 'em hell, Katie-girl," he murmured, and ducked to enter the shelter in her wake.

Katherine strode a few angry steps away, hugging her arms, furious with herself for her loss of control. Gran always said that every evil thought came back to wreak vengeance on its owner, and Katherine could fear a mighty vengeance from this day's work. Still, perhaps this time it had been worth it.

She could hear Byrd's voice inside the shelter. Through the corner of her eye she saw him lift Rebecca onto his knee. "I won't say for sure," he drawled, "but it just might be that if some little girl put her hand in my pocket she might find something special."

There were giggles, and a child's voice asked, "What is it?"

"It's a buckeye. Very rare, very valuable. You hold onto it, now, and it'll bring you luck. Of course, there's an old Indian legend that says only good youngsters can find one. I wonder if we got any more good youngsters in here?"

There was the sound of scrambling feet and more giggles; Katherine walked away. What a strange, unfathomable man he was. Obviously a thief, possibly worse, ready to abandon them all one moment yet returning to shepherd them to safety the next; taking on the burden of feeding, sheltering, and protecting them all and for reasons that could be either good or bad. . . . He had scared the hellfire out of Priscilla, but was as gentle with the children as though he were born to it. He allowed Oliver to become lost in the woods with Shawnee roaming about and made no move to find him. Undeniably, though, his presence brought comfort to them all. What manner of man was he? And how much longer could Katherine allow all of their lives to remain in his hands?

She moved around the campsite, gathering deadwood for kindling, noticing how the voices inside the shelter were calmer. Apparently Byrd had succeeded in mitigating some of the fear. Once again the women were talking in quiet, almost natural tones about the things they always talked about—what they had left behind. Caroline and her plantation suppers, her horses and her slaves; Priscilla and her parties; Hilda with cheerful reminiscences of her discovery of America; eventually, Maude spoke of her Sunday socials and her prosperous business. But under the soothing cadences of normal conversation was a thread of fear Katherine could feel even at this distance. They avoided talking of the present, of the future . . . of Oliver.

In a while she felt, rather than heard, Byrd exit the shelter and come up behind her. He bent to take the armload of deadwood she held. "You're looking mighty thoughtful, ma'am."

She had a lot to be thoughtful about. She could have answered anything, or nothing. She placed the wood in his arms, brushed off her sleeves, and straightened to look at him. "Sometimes I think you are a good man."

His face was strong and sober, and as unread-

able as ever. "Well now, ma'am, that's where you'd
be wrong." He took the firewood over to the shelter and added it to the stack Katherine had already made. "I'm a mean man, rough clear
through, and if I wasn't I wouldn't be alive today.
I'm out here for the same reason you are—because
nobody else'd have me."

He turned his head toward the westerly sun,
squinting a little. "If he's not back by the time the
setting sun hits those trees, I'm going after him.
If I'm not back by dawn, you get these women
out of here. Go west, like you was going, and *stay
away from the river!*"

Katherine swallowed hard. *Oliver,* she thought
desperately, *Come back. Don't do this to us.* Despair
swelled in her chest and threatened to choke her as
she searched the thicket, almost as though by force
of will she could make the boy's familiar, gangly
figure appear. The woods, of course, remained still.

She released a shaky breath. "What can have
become of him?"

Byrd did not remove his gaze from its thor-
ough contemplation of the woods beyond. "Well,
ma'am." He seemed to be chosing his words carefully. "There comes a time in every man's life when
he has to put boyhood behind him. Like as not,
when that time comes, there's a woman involved."

Katherine looked at him, puzzled.

Byrd met her eyes. "The boy was out in the
woods last night—watching us. Now, you might
not have noticed it, but seems to me he's had his
mind made up to stake you for his own, and I
reckon he didn't rightly approve of the competi-
tion. I'd estimate he thought it over and decided
that the only way to win your heart was to prove
hisself a better man than me."

The information struck Katherine like a blow
to the chest, leaving her feeling stunned and hollow. She tried to deny it, but hadn't she seen with
her own eyes the way Oliver looked at her, how
his face flushed when he spoke to her; hadn't she
noticed the constant little favors he'd been doing
for her?

No, it couldn't be true. Because if it was ... if
it was true and Oliver never came back, it would
be her fault. Don't let this be her fault too. Not
Oliver.

She searched Byrd's face anxiously, for hope,
or reassurance. "But," she stammered, "but I
never did anything, I ..."

"You didn't have to," Byrd said gently. "A fine-
looking, good-hearted woman like you ... it's
enough to tear the heart out of a grown man,
much less a pup like Oliver." His eyes moved back
toward the woodlands. "The boy's not a complete
fool. I didn't see any Shawnee sign this morning,
and as long as he does what I told him, he'll be
all right. I wouldn't fret so much if I was you. Not
yet, anyhow."

Katherine let the words sink in, holding onto
the certainty in Byrd's voice. If Byrd wasn't worried, she mustn't be either, even though she knew
it was unreasonable to trust his opinions when
she was filled with such doubts about his charac-
ter. She couldn't help it. She had to believe in
him for a little while longer.

He turned back to her, studying the way the
sun reflected off her hair. He lightly brushed a
strand of it with his big, rough knuckles, a gesture
that made Katherine's breath come faster.

She met his thoughtful gaze. "I been alone a

long time, Miss Kate, and it's a fine thing to feel
something this soft and pretty on my hand."

Katherine's heart began to pound.

His eyes were opaque with light, the small scars
around them clearly etched upon his dark skin.
How strange it was to see such lovely eyes on such
a rugged, bearded face, how hard to look into
them and see such quiet sincerity there. How
could those eyes hide a lie of any kind?

"I meant what I said last night, Katie-girl," he
said. "We would make some kind of team."

The touch of his fingers was warm against her
neck; the strength in his eyes seemed to hold her
like a caress. She wanted to answer him, to say a
dozen things to him that she was not free to say,
that she could not trust him enough to say. And
after a moment of looking at her, he guessed her
feelings.

He reached behind her to the bonnet that had
fallen onto her shoulders and pulled it up over
her head. "You'll want to keep that fine head
of hair covered from now on, ma'am," he said.
"The Shawnee ain't likely to've seen many red-
headed women, and if they catch a gander at
yours, you'll be the biggest prize they ever took."

He began to tie the strings of her bonnet with
broad, clumsy movements, until Katherine lifted
her hands and placed them atop Byrd's wrists.
His hands grew still beneath her touch and she
searched his face, his eyes, probing for some small
hint of the truth that was hidden deep within him.
Gran, she thought, *help me.*

"Who are you, Byrd Kincaid?" she asked softly.

His eyes dropped to her hands. He took both
her hands in one of his and turned them over.
Slowly, almost absently, he ran his thumb over

her palm, tracing the blisters, the callouses, the work-worn flesh. "I'm just a poor mountain boy from up Cumberland way, getting along the best I know how."

"You're not a trapper."

A small smile flickered beneath his beard. "No, ma'am," he admitted, and dropped her hands. "Not exactly."

From inside the shelter Esther's voice came. "And in the evenings, Francis would read poetry to me. Such a fine boy, he was. Everyone said so."

Byrd walked away from the shelter, and Katherine, by tacit agreement, followed him. He paused beside a fallen pine overlooking the bank that swept down to the stream and though his manner appeared absent and purposeless, Katherine knew he was studying the terrain intently. After a moment he began to speak.

"When I was a boy, 'bout young Oliver's age, right after my pa and ma died, I went out along the Wilderness Trail with my Uncle Nate. In St. Louis we hooked up with a man by the name of John Colter—"

"I've heard of Colter," Katherine interrupted. "Boothe used to talk about him."

"That don't surprise me none. John Colter was quite a man. Traveled and scouted with Lewis and Clark back in '06. He stayed out west, did some trapping and exploring. You know, Miss Kate, it's men like Colter and your brother who're opening up this land of ours, not the government with their map makers, not the army. Just plain folks like us with feet that won't stand still."

"Feet that won't stand still . . ." Katherine smiled. "That sounds like Boothe."

"Colter was one of the best, so my uncle and

me hired on with him to work for a man named Manuel Lisa. Now there was a rascal if ever there was one. Old Lisa decided to change the way things was done. No more trading for furs with the Indians. He hired his own trappers, mountain men and wanderers like me and Nate. He bought the furs from us, then shipped 'em down the Missouri to St. Louis and sold 'em for a nice profit. Lisa took all kinds of fur—otter, marten, fox— but the one he wanted most was beaver. Rich men couldn't get enough of them top hats, and prime beaver fur gives the best beaver wool.

"So Lisa counted up the money from furs while we waded through snow and fought off the Blackfeet and dragged them beavers out of traps in water so cold it froze a man's blood. That winter we holed up in a little tent made out of deer hides stretched over poles, wondering if we'd ever be warm again and trying to kill enough deer and rabbit to keep us alive. It was harder on Nate than it was on me; he got mighty sick and we knew then we wouldn't spend another winter trapping beaver for Manuel Lisa."

Katherine listened, fascinated, her mind filled with questions but not wanting to speak and interrupt Byrd's unexpected flow of words.

"Yep, Lisa was a smart 'un, but it was Colter we all looked up to; he was a man to ride the river with. And I did see some country. I'm telling you, Miss Kate, there's mountains so tall a man could climb straight to heaven if he was a mind to, and still, quiet meadows that never been trod on by human foot."

A passion came into his voice as he spoke, low and powerful, charged with visions Katherine could not even imagine. She sat on the fallen tree at his feet and listened intently.

"There's streams locked into them mountain passes up so high a man has to work hard just to breathe, and the rivers that run through them hills, flinging white water and crushing bolders as big as this ridge, make the Ohio seem like a fledgling creek. There's places where steam shoots right up out of the ground, boiling up like it's cracking open the mouth of hell and spraying scalding-hot water a hundred feet in the air." As her eyes widened with disbelief, he shook his head slowly and agreed, "It's a wonder, ma'am; it surely is."

He squatted down on his haunches beside her, and she noticed that as he spoke his hands were working three of the strips of rawhide he wore around his neck into a sturdy braid.

"We sold our furs to Lisa at his fort at the mouth of the Bighorn, and then we did a mite of trapping up the Yellowstone that spring. But me, I've always been the loose footed type, and it wasn't long before I took off on my own again after Nate died. The coughing and the aching chest from the cold just never went away."

Boothe paused for a moment, his eyes far away and remembering. "So I buried Nate up there on the Yellowstone and headed back to this part of the country and met up with old Mike Fink, and him and me spent a time running keelboats down the Ohio and Mississippi to New Orleans. Ain't done much trapping since then, but I reckon you already guessed that."

Katherine sensed that he could tell a hundred stories she yearned to hear and might never have a chance to listen to. She asked, "You piloted a New Orleans boat?"

"Yes'm, that's right."

Katherine had heard that the keelboat pilots were among the most daring and skillful men ever to set course down the Ohio. The tales of Mike Fink's exploits were legendary; the men associated with him were reknowned for their courage, their recklessness, and their determination. Had God himself opened up the skies he could not have sent a more suitable man to a group of stranded women desperate to negotiate the Ohio. Yet until this moment, Byrd had made no mention of his skills, much less volunteered his services. Katherine thought she knew why.

"And was that when you took to piracy?"

He looked at her without surprise or alarm. Katherine poised for what he would say next. If he denied it, she would know him for a liar. If he confessed ...

But just then there was a commotion inside the shelter and they both looked up abruptly as Priscilla stormed out. "I mean it!" she cried. "If I hear another word about your sainted Francis, I'll scream until my voice gives out and I don't care *who* hears!"

Esther was quick behind her, heaving with the righteous indignation of a woman who had been pushed too far. "You dare blaspheme the finest man who ever lived!"

Priscilla gave a high, ugly laugh, and Caroline came after them, making soothing gestures. "Ladies, please, your voices!"

In a moment Hilda and Maude had joined the fray. Katherine cautiously let her tense muscles relax, not knowing whether she was relieved or irritated by the distraction. Byrd made a muffled sound beside her which she thought might have been amusement. She started to rise, but he laid a hand lightly on her arm. "Leave 'em be," he advised. "Folks got to work things out in their own way."

"I won't stand by and listen to this . . . this *hussy* . . . speak ill of the only son I've got left!" cried Esther. "After all I've been through, to spend my last days saddled with this unspeakable little she-cat—it's more than any mother should have to bear!"

Priscilla's face was strawberry red and her eyes glinted with malice. She clenched her fists at her sides. "The only son you ever had is sitting inside messing on himself and choking on his own spit and it's *your* fault he's there—yours and your precious Francis'!"

Esther went white. Her voice was a ragged hiss. "You shut up!"

Priscilla shot a wild, triumphant glance around the group, her expression filled with bitterness, hatred, and the sharp edge of hysteria. "Shall I tell them about your Francis, Mama Wiltshire?" she demanded. "Shall I tell them about fine, noble Francis with his poetry reading and his wisdom of the ages? He was a drunk," she spat, "a falling-down street drunk who never held a job in his life and ended up in jail for raping a white girl and *that's* why we had to leave Albany. Because you couldn't hold your head up in the street and you begged Matthew to take you!"

"Slut!" Esther's hand shot out and slapped Priscilla across the mouth so hard that it knocked her to the ground. Esther stood there, as still as a statue and just as gray, her trembling hand falling limply by her side.

The silence was absolute. Hilda clutched her throat, her face twisted with helplessness as she forced herself to keep from reaching out to either woman. Maude moved away, deliberately avoiding meeting either woman's eyes. Even Katherine felt the agony of embarrassment for the pubic humiliation she had just witnessed. For all the shame and pity they felt, there was also fear. They had all just seen how thoroughly and quickly the pretenses and refinements that had bound them to an old society could be stripped away. The vision of what they could so quickly become was frightening.

Caroline moved to help Priscilla to her feet, but with some dignity the girl brushed her away. She stood, wiped the blood from her mouth in a deliberate motion, and turned back inside the shelter.

"With every step you take into this wilderness," Byrd said, "you leave a little something of yourself behind. Sometimes it's good ..." He looked at Katherine, saying more with his eyes than with his words. "Sometimes it's not. That's just the way it is."

"Oliver!" Maude's voice shot out, breathless and quavering. "Oliver, thank God!"

Chapter Eleven

Maude was running toward the woods, where a heavy rustle of movement could be heard, her face slack with joy and her arms outstretched. Byrd snatched up his rifle and Katherine leapt to her feet, but before she had taken two running step, Oliver pushed through the undergrowth.

His face was drawn with fatigue and marred with scratches and white streaks where sweat had carved rivulets into the dirt, but otherwise he appeared unharmed. Dragging a calico bundle of some sort behind him, he strode into the camp with a proud confidence that immediately turned to dismay as his mother hurled herself on him.

"Oliver, you wicked boy! I've been half mad with worry! How could you do such a thing?"

Katherine stopped a few steps before Oliver, weak and nauseous with relief. She found herself scolding him, too. "Where have you been? Don't you know we were ready to start searching for you?"

Maude was running her hands over him, trying to scrub his face with her apron, alternately praising and deriding him. The other women descended upon him as well, with exclamations of joy and relief. Oliver looked from one to the other in confusion and embarrassment, trying to fend off his mother as he demanded, "What's all the fuss about? Can't a fellow bring home the bacon without all tarnation coming down on his head?"

"You watch your mouth, boy," Maude warned, and Katherine interrupted again.

"Where have you been?"

"Hunting," he said defensively. "Only, the pickin's weren't too good hereby, so I went downstream a little." He looked uneasy for a moment before he bolstered his courage by bringing forth the bundle. "Well, look! Look what I brung for supper."

He untied the loops in the calico and let its contents spill to the ground. The bundle was filled with mussels, dozens of them.

A reverent silence spread through the group as the women stared. Someone murmured, "Shellfish!" And another, "But where . . ."

"Have you been to the river, boy?" Byrd demanded.

Oliver looked frightened, and when Katherine glanced at Byrd she knew why. A tight white line bracketed his lips, and his eyes were as hot as coals. His dark brows formed two descending arrows over his eyes and his entire body seemed to swell with menace, making him seem twice as large as before. He was a man whom Katherine thought incapable of anger, and now he was furious. It was enough to frighten any right-thinking man—or boy.

"Well, yeah, but—"

"Didn't I tell you to stay away from the river?"

Oliver shrank back a little. "It weren't no great piece, and I didn't see hide nor hair of trouble . . ."

Byrd took two heavy steps forward, forcing himself to restrain his anger. "By God," he said with a voice like thunder, "if you were mine I'd strop the living daylights out of you!"

Maude whirled on him. "Don't you talk to my son like that! Can't you see you're scaring him?"

Oliver jerked away from his mother's embrace. "For gosh sake's, Ma, stop treating me like a baby! I'm here, ain't I? I brung supper, didn't I?"

"Oliver, you could've got yourself killed," Katherine said tightly.

The confusion in Oliver's eyes was laced with hurt at her sharp tone. "But I did it for you, Miss Katherine. I thought you'd be happy to serve up something different for supper, the way everybody's always complaining about being hungry . . ."

So, Byrd was right. Katherine felt ill at the thought of the chances Oliver had taken; if he hadn't come back, it would have been because of her.

Maude's eyes blazed. "That woman again! I might have known."

"Well, somebody's got to help her out," Oliver asserted angrily. "You sure don't! It seems to me somebody in this family ought to show their appreciation for all she's done, and Miss Katherine depends on me!" He stood glaring at his mother, then, with a gesture that signified he was tired of arguing, he strode away.

Katherine knew she had to do something when she saw the justifiable outrage in Maude's eyes, and the somber knowledge in Byrd's. She still felt queasy with the aftermath of worry and near-disaster, and somewhat stunned to realize that once again it was all falling on her shoulders. She turned to follow Oliver, with no idea what she was going to say to him.

He was standing half in profile to her, absently picking the bark of a pine tree, scowling fiercely. For a few moments, Katherine simply stood there, letting him grow accustomed to her presence. Finally she said, "You're right, Oliver. I do depend on you—perhaps too much."

He turned to her. His scowl was gone, and faint color touched his cheeks. "Aw, Miss Katherine, I'm pleased to do it. You know that."

She smiled at him. "You're a thoughtful, good-hearted boy, and I'm very fond of you."

Disappointment crossed his face at her use of "boy."

"You remind me a lot of my little brother," Katherine went on wistfully. "He's dead now. Maybe that's why I . . ."

"I don't want to be your brother."

The words were out before he knew it. Afterwards, he would never know where he got the courage to say them. It seemed that everything that had been locked up inside him came surging up and spilling out, and it was all he could do to keep from gripping her hands.

"Miss Katherine, don't you know how I feel about you? I love you with all my heart, and there's nothing in this world I wouldn't do for you!"

His adoration-flushed face filled her with dismay. He must have taken her silence for encouragement for he went on eagerly. "You're not that much older than me, you know. I know we haven't known each other that long, but things are different out here, and I was thinking when we get to Cairo . . ."

Katherine was sorry she had let it go this far, for the hurt she would cause him. "When we get to Cairo," she said, "I must go on, and you must stay behind to take care of your family."

There was a faint frown on his brow. "Ma can take care of the family."

"Oliver, listen to me," Katherine insisted. "Your mother is a strong woman, but not as strong as she pretends to be. She needs you, and she loves you very much. *She* depends on you. Your sisters depend on you. You're all they have left."

"But . . . what about you?"

"A real man," Katherine said firmly, but as gently as she could, "takes care of his family first."

"And you . . ."

She shook her head. "No, Oliver. Not me."

He looked quickly away, and swallowed convulsively. When he turned back to her, there was such hope and despair in his eyes that Katherine wanted to enfold him in her arms.

"I'm not good enough for you, is that it? Because I can change, Miss Katherine. There's nothing . . ."

"Oh, Oliver," she said, shaking her head. "You have so many years ahead of you. Someday you will find a woman who deserves you, and you will make her a wonderful husband. But—"

"But it won't be you," he said dully.

"No," she whispered. She leaned forward and kissed him on the cheek, then turned to leave.

Maude was standing only a few feet away. There could be no doubt but that she had heard and seen everything. Katherine readied herself for a stiff reprimand or a scathing criticism, but Maude only looked at her with a strange, unreadable expression in her eyes—half puzzlement, half uncertainty. Then she, too, turned and walked away.

Priscilla hated collecting firewood, but today she didn't mind. It got her away from the close, dank-smelling shelter, from the horror of Matt's blank eyes, from the animosity between herself and her mother-in-law. She didn't care that the other women thought she was horrible. She had told the truth; she had exposed Esther's hypocrisy and vanity in the same way Priscilla herself felt exposed by her shorn, ugly hair. But she didn't feel any satisfaction from her achievement. She was miserable. She felt hated and hate filled, and cast aside by everyone.

The last thing she expected when she entered the woods was to hear someone sobbing. Her brow creased as she stopped and listened, for it did not sound like a woman crying. Hesitantly, she pushed her way through the brambles and undergrowth. She ducked beneath a low spruce branch and tore her skirts on a clinging thistle bush. She stopped.

"Oliver!" she said in surprise.

He was sitting on a flat rock, his arms crossed over his drawn-up knees, his head buried against them, his shoulders shaking. When she said his name he looked up. His face was streaked with tears, his eyes red and watery. He twisted his body away. "Go away, Pris!" he said harshly. "Get out of here!"

But Priscilla did no such thing. Oliver had always been so calm and in control. Even after the boat wreck he hadn't cried, and seeing him now, hearing those awful sounds coming from his throat, sent alarm through her that almost stopped her heart.

She went to him and dropped to her knees beside him. "What happened?" She grabbed his shoulder. "Oliver, what's wrong?"

He jerked away, hunching his shoulders against her to hide his face. "Nothing. None of your business. Leave me alone!"

She allowed herself a small measure of relief. If it didn't concern her, then it couldn't be too bad. No one had died. But there was Oliver, looking so small and miserable, *crying,* and when she saw him like that she wanted to cry too. "Oliver, please . . ." Her voice gentled, and she stroked his shoulder. "What is it?"

He remained stonily silent.

"Don't send me away Oliver. Please talk to me."

He spoke without looking at her. "I feel like a darn fool, is all. Now git on."

Priscilla was silent for a moment. When she spoke her voice was sweet and persuasive and earnest. "After all the times I made a fool of myself and you made me feel better, what kind of friend would I be if I went away now? I don't think less of you because I've seen you crying, Oliver. We're friends, aren't we?"

He wanted to shout at her, *No!* He wanted to push her away and run like a six year old from an angry mother; he wanted to rant and rave at her and at Katherine and at the whole world; he wanted to curl up into a ball and die. But he scrubbed his face with his sleeve and kept his back to her, staring blearily at the thicket.

"Oliver, please talk to me."

He could not imagine putting his feelings into words. The love he felt, once as pure and brilliant as sunlight sweeping through the sky, had been defiled and made small by her rejection. He could not tell Priscilla that. He couldn't make her understand. Instead he found himself saying tonelessly, "Miss Katherine . . ." He took a breath, and it caught in his throat. The next words were hardly a whisper, and rich with aching.

Priscilla did not know whether the stab of hurt she felt was for Oliver or for herself.

"She doesn't love me back," Oliver said. "She thinks—I'm just a kid."

Priscilla didn't know what to do except to reach out and take his hand. He did not object. Together, they sat in heavy silence for a long time.

"Maybe you're lucky." Priscilla said at last. "I don't even know what love is."

Surprise and confusion filtered through his black sorrow. "But . . . you're a married woman."

Priscilla smiled sadly and shook her head. "That doesn't have anything to do with love, Oliver Sherrod," she said, sounding suddenly much older and wiser than her years. "Matthew—well, he swept me off my feet. He was so much older, and more worldly, and, you remember, he was nice looking. He worked in a *bank*. I just thought I was the luckiest girl in the world when he came courting. He had his own buggy, and he always brought flowers. Mama said he would buy me pretty dresses to keep me in style. It all sounded so fine. But after we got married, all those things didn't seem to matter so much."

She frowned a little, as though she still didn't understand how things had come to be. "He never loved me," she said. "He never wanted to talk to me, he never laughed, and I just couldn't seem to please him no matter what I did. After a while I realized I didn't love him either. It's a horrible thing, Oliver Sherrod, to live with somebody you don't love."

Oliver nodded. "It's worse," he said, "to love somebody who doesn't love you back."

Priscilla's eyes were soft and hurting as she whispered, "Yes."

She put her arms around him, and it was the most natural thing in the world for him to open his to her. They held each other in simple comfort and understanding, and Oliver was glad she was here. She hadn't made him feel better—nothing could make him get over Katherine—but she understood and shared his unhappiness. Somehow that made the burden lighter. It was good to feel small, warm arms around him, a soft woman shape against him, soothing him, giving him strength. It was so good.

Without his knowing it, his hand strayed to her hair, stroking it absently, and suddenly he pushed a little away from her. "What happened to your hair?"

She colored and dropped her eyes. "I cut it," she said miserably. "I know it's ugly."

He smiled faintly, and let his fingers play with what remained of her shorn curls. "I don't know. I think it's kind of sporty, like those French girls you see in the magazines."

"Do you really think so?"

She looked so young and defenseless with her short, tangled curls and her big, expectant eyes with a V of worry between her eyebrows and her lips parted with question. He was going to ruffle her hair, or pinch her cheek, or say something to make her smile. Instead, he lowered his face to hers and kissed her mouth.

Oliver had never kissed a girl before, not like that. He hadn't planned it or expected it, but he tasted her soft flesh melting against his and ecstasy shot through him, followed by shock. He was kissing her. She was a married woman and he was kissing her ... and it was wrong! Quickly, he pulled away.

He stared at her, his breath short, his hands gripping her shoulders as though he might either fling her away or draw her close to kiss her again. He couldn't believe what he'd done. He could still taste her. And there she was, face flushed, eyes wide, looking as surprised as he was.

He let go of her. He started to stammer something. She took in a breath as though she might say something too. Then both of them went rigid as a woman's cry reached them from the camp. Their eyes went dark with dread. By silent agreement they scrambled to their feet and ran back toward the camp.

Katherine was scooping up a handful of mussels, intending to shuck them outside before taking them to the fire inside the shelter when Esther said, "Hannah!"

It was a low exclamation, hardly more than a whisper. "Oh, my dear Lord." Esther was staring fixedly at a piece of calico on the ground, the material in which Oliver had wrapped the mussels. For a moment, it occurred to Katherine that Esther's mind had snapped. Then, her face twisted, she lifted a shaking arm toward the calico and screamed, "Hannah!"

Katherine moved toward her at the same time that Caroline pushed forward. Her eyes, too, were fixed on the calico. Slowly, with a reluctance to her movements that seemed to radiate loathing, she bent down and picked up the material, holding it before her. It was a woman's dress.

"Hannah's gown!" whispered Maude.

A sickness went through Katherine, and she had to close her eyes as the trees and the sky and the sun blurred into a swimming, bilious color. The truth could not have been more clear, or more repugnant, had it been a bloated and battered corpse Oliver had dragged into camp. For a long, horrible moment no one spoke.

Byrd glanced at Katherine. "One of the women you left at the river?"

Katherine could only nod.

Just then, Oliver and Priscilla burst through the undergrowth. "What happened?" Oliver demanded.

Byrd stepped forward taking the dress from Caroline's unprotesting fingers. "Are you sure?"

"I always admired her stitchwork." Maude's voice was small and tight, very unlike her own. "So tiny, so neat. Look." With shaking fingers she turned over the collar. Visible to all were the initials HP embroidered in muddy white against the dark blue print.

Hilda's gaze went to Katherine, then Caroline's followed, and finally Esther's. There were varying degrees of fear and grief and disbelief in each set of eyes, but one silent message united them: What if . . . ? What if Caroline, whose idea it had been to wait for a boat, had stayed behind with her children? What if Hilda had not had the courage to step forward and volunteer to go with Katherine? What if Esther had allowed Maude to talk her into staying behind? And Katherine, for all those times she had wanted to steal off into the night and leave them behind, felt bruised inside and hollow with guilt.

Only Maude refused to meet Katherine's eyes. She cleared her throat, her voice came somewhat steadier. "Is there any chance that—that she's still . . ."

"Alive?" Byrd shook his head. "This dress was torn off her." He examined the ragged pieces of the bodice. "The men who did that ain't likely to have set her free when they were done."

Hilda went very pale. She turned abruptly and stumbled off into the bushes; after a moment they heard the sounds of her soft retching.

Caroline's voice was very calm. "Indians?"

"No, ma'am, The Shawnee don't rape their prisoners. Leastwise, not right away. And they don't generally murder women."

Oliver's eyes were dark with shock in his white face. "Then who?" he asked.

Byrd was studying the material, turning it over and over in his hands, and he seemed not to hear the boy. Finally, he looked up. "Tell me where you found this. Exactly."

Oliver's Adam's apple bobbed as he struggled to remember. "I followed the stream to its mouth . . . went west a little piece to a shallow bank where the diggin'd be good, you know . . . then I saw this flash of blue off in the woods about twenty feet . . ."

"Did you see anything else?" Byrd demanded.

"Just junk, up from the flood, nothin' worth saving. Except . . . ," he swallowed again, and nodded toward the dress. His voice dropped. "This."

The muscle in Byrd's jaw knotted. "Somebody ought to see to Miz Werner. The rest of you better start shuckin' them mussels, if we're gonna have them for supper."

He turned and strode some distance away from the others, still holding the dress bundled in his hands. Katherine followed him.

After a time he spoke. "I was coming up with an empty hold from New Orleans when I ran afoul of a sandbar." Without looking up, he kept turning the material over in his hands. "Pirates was lying in wait and we fought it out. I lost my crew and they lost their pilot. So I joined up with 'em, biding my time. I'm not saying I didn't see some horrors on my way upriver, or do some things I ain't proud of, but I stayed alive. One night they left me and a couple of others with the boat while they went upriver to make camp. They do that, you know, pretending to be stranded travelers to lure a boat ashore. I waited 'til the others were drunk asleep, then I slit their throats and emptied out their hold."

"You knew they'd be tracking you," Katherine said, not knowing whether to be dismayed by his foolhardiness or to admire his audacity.

"I figured I'd do best to face 'em down on my own ground. I didn't figure on having a bunch of women and children with me. But that boy's tracks are going to lead 'em right to our camp."

He looked at the material in his hand for another moment, then abruptly bundled it up and tossed it away.

"We move out at dawn," he said.

Chapter Twelve

Dawn came too late.

Byrd lay flat on his stomach in the brush, positioned to overlook the stream. Between the thready limbs of trees he could see the shadow of the mule, its head lifted to crop leaves from a low branch. The night sky was pale and thin, gunshot gray and as still as the grave. Daylight was slow in coming.

Byrd kept thinking about the torn calico dress and the fate of the woman who had worn it; somehow she kept getting mixed up in his head with the women he had left behind in that Shawnee camp all those years ago. He should have gone back to the river as soon as he'd learned of the women who had remained there. He should have known what would happen; he *had* known. But he was only one man. How much could he be expected to do?

More, he thought grimly. More than this.

The camp was packed and ready to go. There would be no fire this morning, only a cold breakfast.

They would move out when it was light enough to travel. They would head westward, away from the river, deeper into the wilderness. Before they left, Byrd would make certain the booty he had stashed would be easy to find. That would stop the pirates for a time, possibly for good. They were an ignorant, lazy lot; without the promise of immediate reward they weren't likely to exert themselves to go after the kill. If the pirates had their stolen goods, if Byrd could move the women far enough and fast enough away, they might escape pursuit.

If.

His eyes were in constant motion, searching the landscape sector by sector, thoroughly, methodically. His eyes returned again to the stream, his first focal point, and stopped.

The mule was gone.

His gut tightened. He cursed without making a sound. Swiftly and silently, moving like a shadow among shadows, he slid down the incline toward the shelter.

Katherine lay awake in the darkness, shivering in the aftermath of a dream of blood, screams, and water that burst into flames. The regular breathing of the others all around her gave her some comfort. A creature rustled in the drying leaves of the shelter, an insect or a field mouse, and a child murmured in its sleep. Today we move, Katherine thought. Out of the path of the Shawnee, away from the murdering river pirates . . . I'll make Byrd build a raft and pilot us to Cairo even if I have to do it at knife point. We won't stay here and wait for death to overtake us. We'll outrun it, go downriver, find Cairo. We'll finally be safe. Then the nightmares will stop.

But the dread she felt in the pit of her stomach

wouldn't let go. Deep in her heart she knew she would never be safe again. How could she be, having done what she had done and known what she had known?

Hannah Prescott's face kept forming before her eyes. A tallow-faced woman, silent and humorless, not easy to know or to like. She would not have died instantly. She would have lain in the woods for days in slow, helpless agony until finally succumbing to the ravages of the wilderness. Had the fate of her companion been any kinder? And the children, two innocent, little boys ... Katherine's stomach tightened and rolled when she thought what might have become of them.

Would it have been different if she had stayed behind? Should she have tried harder to make them come with her? So much death, so much terror ... must this be on her conscience too?

She became aware that Hilda, who lay near her, was watching her. "Katherine," she whispered, "are you awake?"

"Yes," Katherine whispered back, without moving her head or bothering to meet the other woman's eyes. "I am."

"I've been awake for some time. The baby gives me little sleep." She tried to shift to a more comfortable position. "When it is hard to sleep and my back aches so, I think about when we get to Cairo, and the baby comes."

It was soothing, listening to Hilda's soft voice, her innocent imaginings about the future. The very fact that anyone could foresee the day when they would get to Cairo was heartening to Katherine. How was it Hilda always knew the right thing to say and do?

"I have a little money—not much, but Alex was

always such a scatter-head, it was up to me to keep
our purse. I was thinking . . . when we get to Cairo,
the first thing we must do is hire a strong boy to
cut logs for a house, and make it nice and snug
for the baby, with a good fireplace and a shingled
roof. I shall bake pies and cakes and sell them,
and soon I shall send away to the city for glass
windows. And I will plant flowers outside the windows so I can look at them all day while I do my
baking."

Katherine's face softened with the vision. Yes,
a home, a fireplace, flowers in the yard. The
aroma of baking in the kitchen. She practically
ached with longing. "It sounds wonderful," she
whispered.

"Katherine . . ." Hilda's eyes searched her face
in the darkness. "I was wondering . . . I hoped . . .
you would honor me by sharing my house."

Katherine was so touched that for a moment
she couldn't speak. She stared at Hilda in disbelief. "You want . . . me?"

Hilda's plump cheek dimpled. "You are my
dearest friend. Who else should I want?"

Katherine swallowed the lump in her throat.
Friend. Had she ever had a friend like this, so
open, so willing, so completely ready to accept
without question all that Katherine was, and to
love her without reservation? Could she ever ask
for anything more?

"I . . . I have to go on, to find my brother . . .
He's my only family now."

Hilda reached shyly for her hand and squeezed
it. "But I will be your family, too, if you will have
me. And by the time you return, my flowers will
be blooming. We will be waiting for you and your
brother, my baby and me."

Tears misted Katherine's eyes and she didn't know what to say. So she simply squeezed Hilda's hand in the dark, and for one brief moment she felt content.

The entrance to the shelter rustled as Byrd crept in, waking Caroline and Oliver, who slept closest to the entrance, with a light touch on their shoulders. The truth hit Katherine even before he spoke.

"Get into position," he said. His voice was low and urgent. "Don't make a sound. Miz Werner, you keep those children quiet. There's Shawnee braves on three sides of us and they're moving up the ridge."

Byrd and Oliver were armed with rifles, and each woman was hidden in the thicket, separate from the others. Should Byrd and Oliver be unable to hold back the attack, some, at least, would have a chance to escape. If they remained quiet and hidden, they could not all be taken at once.

From her position deep in the woods Katherine could see Oliver, flat on his stomach behind a fallen log, but no one else. She knew Byrd was in front of her, and Caroline behind. Priscilla was slightly to the left of Byrd, and Maude and Esther were higher up on the ridge. Nothing, no one, moved.

"You doing all right back there, son?" Byrd asked, his voice barely a whisper.

Oliver flexed his hand on the barrel of the rifle, his eyes glued to the sights, his finger on the trigger. His voice was low, too, imbued with determination. "Yes, sir. Ready to kill me some injuns, sir."

"Good man. Hold steady now. Nobody moves till I give the signal."

Oliver's hands grew sweaty on the stock, but he dared not wipe his palms. His legs were beginning to cramp. He didn't know how long they had been lying there. The sky was a bleached gray now. Daybreak arose by inches, and nothing stirred to greet it—no chirping birds, no scurrying squirrels, no chattering chipmunks. That was the worst part, the silence. For it seemed a hundred eyes were hidden in that silence, watching, waiting, stealing forth on soundless feet to take them unawares.

He thought about Katherine, he thought about Priscilla, and he vowed not to think about either of them. Yesterday seemed so far away and tomorrow might never come. He was glad he had kissed Priscilla. He wanted to be ashamed, but he was glad.

The sky lightened as the first pale rays of the sun stroked the trees, turning the undersides of the leaves a bright green, then cool yellow, until finally shards of light pierced the foliage. A drop of sweat gathered on Oliver's brow and rolled slowly down the bridge of his nose, but he could not lift his hand to wipe it away. A wood spider crawled up his sleeve toward his collar; a gnat caught in his eyelash and he blinked it away. His throat ached from dryness, and every thump of his heart was like a stab to his midsection. He waited. They all waited.

Suddenly from the shelter came a loud, querulous voice. "No, I won't! Where's mama?"

Oliver's heart stopped, his breath stopped. For a moment the morning was very bright—every leaf, branch, and blade of grass etched in stark detail, still, suspended. He thought, *This is how the world looks just before you die,* even as another part of him frantically insisted that it hadn't happened. No child's voice had split the silence to give away their position; no child's footsteps were even now stumbling over the earth inside the shelter; nothing had happened, everything was still, he hadn't heard a word ...

Amy Sherrod stumbled out of the shelter, rubbing her eyes and whimpering, "Mama!"

Byrd made a soft, angry sound. In an instant he left his cover, dashing across the small clearing toward Amy. He was two steps in front of her when he fell face down on the leaf-covered ground. No one had heard or seen the arrow fly. Even as Amy let out a horrible wail, Hilda was dragging her back into the shelter. Suddenly the air was thick with a dozen swooshing arrows. Then nothing.

It was so still Oliver thought everyone must be dead. Dead beneath the onslaught of quick, silent arrows. Only he had survived. Sweat was pouring down his face and stinging his eyes. His tongue was dry and swollen against the roof of his mouth. He tried to think what to do. His eyes moved to Byrd, lying motionless in the dirt. It was up to him now. He had to do something. Move? Stay hidden? The one person who could have told him lay face down with an arrow in his back. He was on his own, he had to *think* ...

Suddenly from behind him a high rattling scream, embodying the very essence of terror, shattered the silence, piercing the day like a bolt of lightning. Oliver whirled and dropped the rifle, which hit the ground with a dull thud. Terrified it would discharge, he scrambled to retrieve

it. That's when he saw Priscilla being dragged forward, her face white and her eyes frozen in terror, a thick brown arm around her throat. Oliver
couldn't move.

He saw Priscilla clawing at the arm around her
throat. He heard her choked animal sounds of
terror. He saw the brave who held her, his buckskin leggings, taut brown skin, colorful calico shirt
decorated with feathers and painted beads. He
had an impression of blues and reds and purples,
of a brightly turbaned head and long misshapen
ears pierced with decorated feathers, a fierce face
made even more terrifying by painted stripes and
metal nose rings. Oliver had never seen an Indian
before, though he had formed a dim vision of
strange costumes and alien decorations. This first
sight of one in the wilderness, armed with bows
and long rifles and sharp knives, surpassed all his
worst nightmares.

His heart was pounding so hard he couldn't
move, he couldn't think. Time seemed to slow,
and he saw everything in waves—Priscilla stumbling along and sobbing with dry, choked breaths
as the Indian brave prodded her with his rifle.
Byrd with an arrow in his back. The rustle of a
bush where Katherine was hidden. Far off a voice
in his head commanded frantically, *Up to you . . .
do something . . . they're depending on you . . .* But he
couldn't move.

Suddenly there was another brave standing not
ten feet before him, pointing a rifle and muttering in clipped gutteral tones to his companion. A
female voice cried, "Shoot, Oliver!"—Katherine's? His mother's? But they were everywhere,
the Indians had surrounded them, they were all
going to die . . .

Somehow he managed to get his hands around the rifle. The voice, "Shoot, Oliver!" kept echoing in his head. Priscilla was sobbing. The brave with the rifle had noticed him. Oliver saw his eyes, fierce, dark, piercing. *Shoot,* Oliver! Oliver lifted the rifle to his shoulder. He got his finger around the trigger. The brave was advancing on him. He tried to pull the trigger. Another three steps and the brave would have him. *Shoot . . . shoot . . .* The savage, painted face swam before his vision, and he tried, he tried . . . but his fingers wouldn't work. He couldn't pull the trigger. He was going to die. They all were going to die.

Suddenly the day was split apart by a sound so loud and infinitely sustained that it seemed to come from the very earth itself.

It was a high, screeching wail, shrieking with power and fury, unreal, alien. Matthew Wiltshire burst out of the shelter, screaming with the force of a demon.

His hands were outstretched into curved talons, his face was twisted with rage, his eyes wild and mad. With his brittle white hair, his blank, glowing eyes, his mouth open with that soul-grating, inhuman screech, he resembled an underworld god, a devil incarnate, an ancient creature of unspeakable evil and unrestrained power. He charged forward, his hands clawing the air, his sightless eyes fixed on Priscilla and the brave who held her.

Oliver felt the blood drain from his veins, his muscles go slack with shock, yet some part of his consciousness noticed the same reaction on the face of the Indian before him—alarm, consternation, fear. Matthew rushed forward, screaming, clawing, bent on retrieving Priscilla. The Indians warily moved back and suddenly the closest one lifted his rifle and fired.

Matthew staggered; a red stain blossomed on his shirt, but he kept coming and his scream grew higher, more terrifying. There were swift sharp words in Shawnee, fearful looks flashed from one Indian to the other. The brave who held Priscilla flung her to the ground and reached for his bow, but already other arrows were flying from the woods. One hit its mark, then another and another until five arrows pierced Matthew Wiltshire's body. Still, he staggered on.

The brave with the rifle wore red-tipped feathers in his sagging earlobes. He barked out a few harsh words that sounded like a command or an incantation; he lifted the rifle and fired again.

The thunder of gunfire drowned out the screeching. Matthew Whiltshire's face exploded into a mass of blood and bone and spattering flesh. He fell backwards and lay still.

In that same instant, the Indians were gone. Oliver sank helplessly to his knees and began to retch.

Chapter Thirteen

The scene was emblazoned onto Katherine's mind like a painting: Priscilla crumpled on the ground, clutching at leaves and dirt and making tiny, mewling sounds; Byrd's body stretched out a few yards away; Oliver heaving behind the rock; Matthew Wiltshire's body riddled with arrows and drenched in blood, lying face up toward the sky. From the shelter came the sounds of children crying hysterically for their mothers. And the sun rose, unaffected by the horrors its gentle rays revealed.

Katherine felt dizzy. She felt as though she were awakening from a nightmare, not quite able to make herself believe it was over. It had all happened so fast. But this was no nightmare, it was real and it wasn't over; it had just begun.

Her fingers that clutched the knife were numb, and the other hand, which had held a death grip on her walking stick, was so slippery with sweat that when she tried to use the stick to push herself forward she lost her grip and banged her elbow on the ground. She squirmed out of her hiding place and got to her feet, but her knees barely supported her and she stumbled twice, hardly aware of it, as she ran toward Byrd.

"Priscilla," she shouted, "take cover! They may be back!"

Children began to stumble from the shelter, Rebecca Adamson hiccoughing shrilly, "Mama . . . mama . . . mama!" Benjamin clung to one of her legs, and Amy screamed, "Stop it, stop it, make it stop!" with her hands over her ears. The other women were running from their hiding places with white, blank faces and fevered eyes. Katherine fell to her knees beside Byrd, knowing she should order them all back to the shelter but knowing no one would obey her, thinking frantically, *Not dead, don't let him be dead . . .*

Esther collapsed next to her son's body, clutching her throat, her eyes bulging in a paste-white face and her lips moving with incoherent sounds. Priscilla dragged herself on her hands and knees like a wounded thing, whispering, "Matthew, Matthew . . ." She didn't seem to notice her husband's shattered face or pierced body; she fell at his feet and pressed her face against the hem of his pants and moaned over and over again, "Oh, Matthew, please no, Matthew, Matthew . . ."

"Caroline—help Hilda with those children!" Katherine called. "Get them back inside!"

She saw Caroline's skirts flying toward the shelter, and she thought, *I've got to move Byrd, I've got to get him out of the open . . .* She grabbed his shoulders and tried to turn him over, and the muscles felt stiff to her, and cold. She twisted her head around and screamed, "Oliver, help me!"

Oliver got to his feet, but he didn't seem to hear her. His eyes were dazed. He turned and moved like a sleepwalker in the opposite direction.

Out of the corner of her eye Katherine saw Maude catch her son's arm and say something to him, but Oliver kept right on walking. Maude called, "Judith, Amy, darlings, go back inside with Mrs. Adamson. Mama will be there soon. Do as I say!"

Then Maude dropped down on her knees beside Katherine. "Is he dead?"

"I don't know. I don't know . . ."

Maude grasped Byrd's shoulder and lifted him a little, half-turning him, but she could not roll him flat on his back because of the arrow sticking out of his shoulder. There was a swollen, bloody gash on his forehead where he had struck a rock when he fell. The arrowhead had penetrated his shoulder; Katherine could see an inch or so of stone protruding through the front of his shirt, and the ground beneath him was soaked with blood. A wave of weakness overtook her and for a moment she couldn't move. He was dead, and she was all alone. He was dead and . . .

"No," she whispered, and stared hard at his face. His eyes were flickering, trying to open. The movement was faint, but unmistakable. "No," she repeated frantically. "He's alive. We've got to get him to shelter."

"Can you pull the arrow out?" Maude asked.

Katherine shook her head. "No, it's the arrowhead . . ."

"Then we'll have to break it off on this side," Maude said. "Give me your knife."

Between the two of them, they managed to saw and twist and bend the resilient wooden shaft until it splintered two inches above the entry point. Maude took his shoulders and Katherine his ankles and they managed to get him propped up against a tree a few feet away. Even their combined strength was not enough to move him all the way to the shelter.

The pain of their clumsy handling brought Byrd to the edge of consciousness. He moaned several times, and when they placed him against the tree he forced his eyes open, slowly, as though it took all of his strength to do so.

His face was a horrifying shade of gray; Katherine had never seen skin that color on a living man and it terrified her. His eyes were glazed and unfocused, the color of sky seen through a dull layer of clouds. He frowned as he tried to form words. "Indians . . . what . . ."

"They're gone." Quickly and briefly, Katherine explained about Matthew.

Byrd swallowed and managed to nod. His voice was husky and thick, hardly intelligible. "Gone to make . . . medicine. Magic. Indians . . . afraid of craziness. They'll be back, at dawn." He caught his breath on a spasm of pain and closed his eyes.

Katherine looked at Maude, uncertain whether to trust Byrd's logic in his present state, but Maude nodded shortly. "Makes sense. We've got that long to get out of here."

She had started to gather up her skirts to go warn the others when Caroline came running toward them. Her hair was half down around her shoulders, her lips were bloodless, and her skirts were hiked immodestly up around her knees, showing threadbare stockings and dingy petticoats. "I need help," she gasped. "Hilda . . ."

Katherine started to get up, but Maude gestured her down again. "Do what you can for him," she ordered brusquely. "I'll go."

Katherine watched the two women leave, torn between wanting to help Hilda, who needed her, and Byrd, who didn't look as though he'd live out the hour. What was wrong with Hilda? Was the baby coming? Oh, God, she couldn't have her baby now, not with the Indians coming back. And what was she to do for Byrd? How could she help him? Hysteria was rising in noxious, paralyzing waves. She wanted to scream, she wanted to cry, and then Byrd gripped her arm.

The strength of his fingers startled her, bringing her sharply back to herself. His eyes were narrowed with concentration and his breath came in heaving gasps. "Listen, to me," he said tightly. "No time. You've got to . . . get out of here. Leave me. Get these women . . . out of here."

Katherine's eyes went from him to the shelter, to Oliver and the two women bending over Matthew Wiltshire's body. "No," she said. "You're hurt. I have to get that arrow out of your shoulder."

He grimaced sharply, but she could not tell whether it was from pain or anger. "I'll live." He released her arm and fumbled at the wound, bloodying his hand. "Leave me be. Go."

"We're not leaving anybody behind."

"Goddamn you, Kate Carlyle."

"Shut up!" She began to search the ground for something she could use to push the arrow through his shoulder. Her hands weren't strong enough.

"This is your only chance . . ."

"I told you we're not leaving anybody behind!" she cried and whirled on him, eyes glittering and fists clenched, daring him to challenge her again.

He said nothing, and then it seemed a light of admiration flickered in his eyes. "Goddamn it," he muttered, "if you ain't the stubbornest woman God ever invented . . ."

Katherine found a flat rock and closed her fingers around it. "Get a grip on the tree trunk," she said shakily. "I'll have to push the arrow shaft through so I can get a hold on the head."

He wrapped his arm around the trunk and pressed his face into the bark. "If you're gonna do it," he ordered lowly, "do it quick."

Even as Katherine lifted the rock with both hands, she didn't know if she could do it or if she would kill him in the process. "You can scream if you want," she said, her unsteady voice almost a whisper.

He tightened his grip on the tree and braced himself. "Katie-girl," he murmured, half-delirious, "if we get out of this alive . . ." He took a long, shaky breath that was choked off at the end, and Katherine thought he'd lost his train of thought. But he finished thickly, "I just might marry you."

She brought the rock down against the protruding shaft; his face contorted and then went still as he passed into unconsciousness. As Katherine lifted the rock again it was she who had to try very hard not to scream.

Esther had covered Matthew's face and body with her apron. If either she or Priscilla was affected by the bloodstains that soaked through or the way the quill-like arrows disarranged the material, they gave no sign. There is a point at which horror refuses to register, a point both women had reached. Their movements were slow and heavy. Neither could make herself move away from the body.

With her fingertips, Priscilla stroked the back of Matthew's hand. "I was never a good wife to him," she murmured. Her voice sounded small and far away. "I tried to be ... but I never was."

"I knew you wouldn't be," Esther said. "I tried to tell him, but ... he was so smitten with you."

Priscilla lifted her eyes to her mother-in-law. The older woman was sitting on the ground with one leg awkwardly and immodestly beneath her, just as she had fallen when she reached Matthew's body. Her bonnet was askew and her gray hair fell in clumps around her face. The lines of her face had never looked more severe, but oddly enough there was a softness in her eyes that surprised Priscilla.

"He ... loved me? Truly?" Priscilla asked hesitantly.

"Oh, child." Esther sighed. "He loved you to distraction from the moment he first saw you. That was his first mistake."

Though she thought she was beyond shock, beyond pain, a new knot twisted in Priscilla's chest. Longing and sorrow mingled in her for a time gone that could never be recaptured. "But, he never ... I didn't know. I ..."

The shadow of a smile crossed Esther's lips. "No, I suppose you didn't. Matthew waited so long to marry and he knew so little about pleasing a wife. You were so vivacious and energetic, and he was so reserved, he simply didn't know how to tell you how he felt. Or perhaps he thought you'd think less of him for it. But he did adore you. And I didn't help matters much," she added. "I could have, but I was so afraid ... for both of you."

Through the agony, Esther's words brought a measure of wonder to Priscilla. The anger, the resentment, the misery she had known living with her mother-in-law ... it all seemed insignificant. Now when she looked at Esther she saw only a woman, just like herself.

"You never talked like that before," she said.

Esther lifted her hand and lightly touched Priscilla's cheek. "You were such a pretty little thing when we started out."

Priscilla dropped her gaze. "That was a million years ago."

She touched her husband's hand one last time. The stiff, dry flesh did not repulse or frighten her. It simply filled her with an ache so large and so all-inclusive that her frail body could not contain it. "He died for me. He tried to save me and they killed him. After everything that's happened, he died for me ..."

Esther's hand dropped to Priscilla's shoulder and closed there gently. "It was the way he would have wanted it, child, and we shouldn't grieve for his choice. Better to die now, a hero, than to go on living like he was. You know that, don't you?"

Priscilla lifted her face to her mother-in-law. Esther opened her arms, and Priscilla fell into them.

Byrd was unconscious. Katherine managed to get a grasp on the arrowhead and with fingers slippery from blood, she pulled it through, feeling the resistance of bone and muscle and seeing, in dim flashbacks, another blood-soaked scene and feeling terror like a memory, distant and detached. Afterward she sat there, perhaps for minutes, perhaps for hours. She listened to Byrd's erratic breathing, the mumbles and moans he made as he drifted in and out of consciousness, and distantly she heard other sounds— muffled cries of pain from the shelter, a woman's sobs, a child's hiccoughs. They registered dimly; Katherine knew only one thought and it was repeated over and over again in her head to the beat of her own heart, *He will not die. I won't let him die. I can't ...*

At some point Caroline was beside her, pressing what looked like a clump of moss into Katherine's bloody hands. "Pack this in the wound," she advised. "It will stop the bleeding. If he doesn't lose too much blood, he should be all right."

Perhaps it was the sound of Caroline's calm voice, or merely the presence of another rational being, because from that point on Katherine began to think more coherently, to move with more precision. She cleaned the wound, examined it, and realized that, despite all the blood, the arrow had not pierced a vital organ. He would live.

She packed the wound with moss and bound it tightly with strips of buckskin sliced from Byrd's tunic. Then, somehow, she and Caroline managed to rouse him to the edge of consciousness and get him to his feet, leading him toward the shelter.

As they lowered him to the ground beside the

fire, Katherine had a blurred impression of the dim, smokey interior, smelling of damp forest and human fear; of frightened, white-faced children huddled near the door, and of low moans coming from the corner where Hilda lay, attended by Maude.

"Hilda?" Katherine asked, gasping a little from fear and exertion.

"She's in labor, thank God," Caroline replied, kneeling beside Byrd. "You'd best go to her. I'll stay here. All he needs is warmth and liquids now."

Katherine stared at her. *Thank God?* No, this was the worst time for Hilda to have her baby. She couldn't be in labor now . . .

Katherine took a few stumbling steps toward the corner where Hilda lay, but she moved like a sleepwalker mired in quicksand. The entire world seemed to rock, to shift on its axis and swing slowly back down again. Even in the dim light that filtered through the branches she could see the blood that soaked Hilda's apron. That wasn't right; there shouldn't be blood. Katherine could see the whiteness of Hilda's face, so bright it was like a reflection in the darkness, and she could see the sunken look in Hilda's eyes. It was a look she had seen before, in Gran's eyes, and in her dying baby sisters' . . .

She fell hard to her knees beside Hilda, jolting her and causing her teeth to clack, but she didn't feel the pain. "She was hit," Maude said tightly. "When she . . . when she ran out to get Amy. It tore a gash in her, but I can't tell how bad . . ."

It was bad. *No, don't let it be bad, not Hilda . . .* But there was too much blood, and when Kath-

erine grasped Hilda's hand, it was cold. "No . . . ,"
she whimpered and Hilda's eyes flickered open.

As her eyes focused, Hilda strained to form the
very weakest of smiles. "Ah . . . Katherine, you are
here. I'm glad. You make me . . . strong."

Hilda's face contorted with pain and Maude
moved quickly to stroke her forehead. "Hold on,
child, we're going to get you through this. It's going to be all right."

Katherine clasped Hilda's hand tightly, wanting
to say words of comfort, wanting to calm and
soothe her like Maude was doing. But she couldn't
say a word. She was afraid if she opened her
mouth she would start to scream, and the screaming would never stop.

Oliver did not remember when he had taken
the spear and started to scrape away dirt with it,
but it must have been long ago because the sun
was dropping below the tops of the trees and the
hole he had made was deep. The sun had raised
a burn on his face and sweat had soaked his
clothes through. He heard sounds of sickness
and suffering from the shelter, and he saw
women move in and out, and none of it registered on him. He was moving dirt, opening the
earth with muscle and sweat because that's what
you did when somebody died. You dug a grave.

Inside him was blackness, a dark, empty hole
deeper than the center of the earth to which Matthew Wiltshire was about to be relegated, vaster
than a starless sky; it had opened up inside him
and swallowed him whole, and all that he had
ever known about himself was gone. Inside that
blackness was a tiny pinpoint of truth that pulsed
and throbbed like an old toothache which, when

touched, flared pain through the emptiness and filled Oliver with loathing.

He was a coward. Oliver had kissed another man's wife, and now that man was dead because of him. He had done murder. It was Oliver's job to protect, to defend, and when the moment came and lives depended on him, he couldn't pull the trigger.

Byrd Kincaid was lying in the shelter with his life's blood slowly seeping away. Someone had said Hilda was in bad shape from an Indian arrow. Priscilla's husband was dead. It should be Oliver who was dead, but God was not so kind. It would be his punishment to go on living and remembering, and if he lived forever, he still would not have suffered enough to make up for this day's work.

He carried Wiltshire's body to the grave and began to cover it with dirt. He thought of his father. On that day long ago when he had stood over his father's grave he had thought that his father's death was the worst thing that could happen to him, that life as he knew it was irrevocably over and nothing would ever be the same. But there had been worse in store. The worst was to go on living.

When the grave was filled, he was aware of Esther touching his shoulder. He flinched from her, from the touch of any human being and most especially from the mother of the man he had killed.

She pressed his mother's Bible into his hands. "Would you read a few words?" she asked unsteadily.

It was like that other day, that far away day, and perhaps it was that memory, the sense of destiny, that caused Oliver to open the book and flip through the pages. *I go to prepare a place for you . . .*

He sensed Priscilla's presence, across the grave from him, and some driving need for self-punishment made him raise his eyes to her. Her small face was composed, her eyes calm. There was no hatred there. No accusation. The black agony rose up inside Oliver and blotted everything out—the sunlight, the smell of turned earth, the innocent face of the girl he had made a widow—and he couldn't do it.

With a muffled sound that might have been an oath, or a sob, he flung the Bible onto the grave and ran away.

Sometimes Katherine thought they had been inside the shelter for days, at other times she thought surely only a few moments had passed. A second fire had been built because Hilda was shivering with cold; sweat rolled off Katherine, and the smoke made her eyes water and her nostrils clog. When the sun was high overhead and the gnats and flies buzzed against the leaves of the shelter, seeking the blood they smelled, Katherine thought they would all surely die from heat, from lack of air, from fear.

The wound in Hilda's side was now only oozing blood, thanks to Caroline's ministrations with mud and moss, but Hilda was hemorrhaging from internal injuries; her clothes and the ground beneath her were dark with blood. She drifted in and out of consciousness, rousing fully only when the pain wrenched a moan or sometimes a scream from her as her womb worked stubbornly to ex-

pell the child within her, which even now might
be dead.

Caroline moved between Byrd and Hilda, and
Maude never left Hilda's side. The children had
been sent outside. The smaller ones clung to
their older sisters and brother and all of them
huddled, mute and large–eyed, just outside the
entrance.

Katherine blotted Hilda's brow when exertion
made droplets of sweat break out upon it, and
chafed her hands and arms to warm them when
she went into shivers again. Over and over she
thought, Soon. Dear God, let this baby come soon.
She can't hold on much longer . . .

But she did. Sometimes her breathing was high
and shallow, sometimes so slow as to be almost
inaudible, but Hilda clung to life tenaciously.
Even when it seemed that the last of her strength
had long since been depleted, she always gathered herself one more time, meeting the pain,
working with it, then subsiding again into dry
sobs and moans of exhaustion.

Though her grip on Katherine's hand had
rubbed it raw, only once did she voice her suffering out loud, and that was when she looked at
Katherine helplessly between onslaughts and
asked, "Why does it have to hurt so much?"

"I don't know, love," Katherine whispered,
stroking her brow. She tried to keep her voice
from choking. "I don't know."

If she could have taken Hilda's pain, she would
have. Katherine knew pain; she could bear it. But
Hilda was so weak . . .

Katherine became aware of Maude's eyes upon
her, not for the first time during the long ordeal.
She was beyond wondering what the other woman

was thinking. Maude spoke to Hilda. "You're a very brave young woman, dear. You're doing fine."

Another of Hilda's faint, faltering smiles moved her lips. "This baby will come, whether I am brave or not ... and I do not feel brave." She caught her breath on another spasm of pain and her hand crushed Katherine's. Katherine squeezed it back hard, setting her teeth and tensing her muscles, trying to will strength to Hilda.

"I can see the head!" Maude said sharply, and Caroline came quickly to kneel beside her.

Hilda was breathing hard and her eyes were fever-bright; the color in her cheeks was unnaturally dark against the shiny pallor of her face. Her grip on Katherine's hand tightened. "Promise me," she whispered urgently.

"Hush, now, save your strength. The baby is almost here. You need ..."

"Promise me, Katherine!"

"Yes, of course dear, whatever ..."

"You'll take my baby." She searched Katherine's face. "You'll love it, and take care of it the way you have me. You must promise. You must ..."

Katherine swallowed back the heavy swelling in her throat. "Don't be silly, Hilda, we're all going to live in our house together and bake pies and cakes, remember? You promised me. I'll mind the baby while you're busy cooking, and in the evenings we'll all go out on the porch and watch the dew settle on the flowers ..."

Hilda relaxed a little. "Then it is a promise?"

Katherine's eyes ached with scalding tears, and she did not blink for fear they would brim over. "Of course it is. I won't leave you, you know that."

Hilda's expression lost some of its urgency, then faded into a fretful frown. "My cradle," she murmured. "Poor Alex worked so hard and now it's gone. What shall we do for a cradle, Alex? I must have . . ."

"We'll build another one," Katherine assured her. She slipped her arm beneath Hilda to hold her head. "It won't be as fine but . . ."

Pain contoured Hilda's face again and Katherine's arm tightened about her. "Try, Hilda," she urged. "It's almost over. Try."

"Can you push, Hilda?" Caroline asked. "Please try, just one more time!"

"So tired," Hilda sobbed, and then she began to cry something in German, pulling Katherine's hand, leaving bloody marks with her fingernails, tossing her head back and forth.

Caroline moved quickly over Hilda and pressed down on her abdomen. Katherine held Hilda tightly, pressing her face to Hilda's and squeezing her eyes tightly closed, whispering prayers that were no more coherent than Hilda's German.

Then Hilda's body went limp, and in a moment Maude said, "It's a girl."

Katherine had a glimpse of a still, dark form, and everything inside her went cold. "Is it . . ."

Maude did not reply. She quickly forced the tiny mouth open with her fingers, then held the infant by the ankles and shook it hard. There was nothing, nothing but the labored breathing of three women and one smaller, quieter stream of breath fading rapidly against Katherine's cheek. Maude forced her fingers into the child's throat again and slapped its legs, and there was a faint, sputtering mewl, and Maude whispered, "Alive."

Caroline took Katherine's knife and cut the cord. Katherine continued to hold Hilda, rocking her back and forth, murmuring, "It's over, you have a girl, a lovely baby girl, you're going to be all right now ..." But Hilda's skin was cold and her breath was very faint, and when she opened her eyes, they were almost lost beneath the pockets of sunken skin. They seemed to look at Katherine from very far away.

Maude knelt beside Hilda, the baby wrapped in her apron. "Here she is, dear. A fine girl." Maude's stern face seemed to strain at smiling. "She has a little scratch on her shoulder from the Indian arrow, but otherwise she seems just fine."

Hilda moved her eyes toward the bundle and tried to lift her hand but could not. Katherine took the hand that was still wound around her own and placed it lightly against the infant's cheek. A thin, fluttering breath passed Hilda's lips, and she murmured, "Poor ... dear. You had your first ... battle ... before you were even born. Not a very good ... beginning."

"Nonsense," said Katherine. "That only means she's a strong girl, like her mother."

Hilda's hand fell weakly away from the baby's face. She struggled for the next words, and Maude had to bend close to hear. "I ... will call her ... Kat ..." But she couldn't finish the word. Katherine's chest constricted.

Maude made a gruff sound in her throat. "Cat. Looks more like a kitten to me."

"Kitty," Hilda whispered, and she tried to smile. Her eyes closed.

Katherine felt her slip away, just as Gran had done, quietly, simply, and on a breath. First there was life, then there was not. And just as she had with Gran, Katherine let her go.

Caroline sobbed. Maude's face was very still and hard, and her eyes glittered in the firelight. Slowly Katherine eased Hilda's weight to the ground and rose to her feet.

There was a pressure inside her chest that felt like a dam straining to break. The pressure closed up her throat and pounded behind her eyes so that she saw everything through a hot, blurred film. She made her muscles rigid and stared at the fire until she could see again. She said quietly, "Give the baby to me."

Maude's head was bent over the infant, her expression hidden. "Poor little thing. It doesn't have a chance."

"Give the baby to me," Katherine repeated.

Maude looked up.

"She's mine now, Hilda gave her to me."

"She can't live. She . . ."

In a single, swift move Katherine snatched the child from Maude's arms. She shouted furiously, "Don't you dare say that, you cruel, hateful woman! She's mine and she will live, do you understand that!" She pressed the baby to her breast and felt its warm, wet body, its tiny movements, its kittenlike sounds, and what she felt was fierce, blinding, and soul-invasive. Life. Life was what she held in her arms. "I promised Hilda that nothing is going to happen to this baby, do you hear me?"

Caroline lifted her tear-streaked face. She tried to touch Katherine's shoulder, but Katherine jerked away. "There's no milk. We can't . . ."

"No!" Katherine cried. "I won't listen to you!" Then, more calmly. "No." She lifted the corner of the apron which cradled the baby's face and stroked its tiny cheek with her forefinger. "I'll take care of her," she said softly. "I promised."

And with the baby in her arms, she walked out of the shelter and into the cool light of the dying day.

Chapter Fourteen

As darkness fell, Katherine sat on a stump at the edge of the forest, rocking baby Kitty back and forth. She had bandaged the gouge on the infant's arm with a strip from her petticoat, but the wound was deep and would probably leave a scar. The scar on Katherine's soul was just as deep, and just as permanent.

No one had the strength of body or spirit to dig Hilda's grave, so the women and children had moved outside for the night. They were a silent, shadowy group, huddled outside the shelter without a fire, staying close together and speaking little. Caroline stayed with Byrd at the edge of the shelter and nursed him faithfully, offering him sips of water and sponging his fevered brow with strips of damp muslin. Occasionally his moans or delirious mumblings drifted out to Katherine, but she noticed little else of what went on around her. She concentrated all her energy, and her thoughts, on the baby in her arms.

For all that she had gotten a rough start in life, little Kitty Werner was a determined infant. Despite the gruelling journey, the lack of proper food, her mother's grief and exhaustion, Kitty had

held on. She had been attacked and wounded before she had even left the womb, but still she had
fought for life. Now she waved her small fists and
stretched her toes and emitted tiny peeping wails
of triumph: she was alive, and she was strong.

"Poor darling," Katherine murmured, and
brushed the small bald head with a kiss. Kitty was
sleeping now, her fist curled against her cheek,
her lips pouting, and her small nostrils moving
regularly with each breath. "You wanted so badly
to be born. Well, anybody who would fight that
hard to live deserves a chance. And I'm going to
see that you get it." She traced the curve of the
baby's pale eyebrow with her finger. Kitty's eye-
lids fluttered, but she didn't wake. "That's right,
baby, sleep. I'm going to take care of you now."

Three days, that's how long she had before Kitty
would need to nurse. Within that time they would
reach Cairo, they would find a wetnurse, Kitty
would be safe. Whatever Katherine had to do to
make that happen, she would do. No power in
heaven or hell would stop her. This newborn life
was hers.

So much death. Everyone Katherine had ever
loved was gone. But it ended here. Kitty Werner's
small life was in Katherine's hands, and she would
not lose this one. *Not this one.*

She stood up, all eyes upon her when she
moved. She walked over to Caroline, and placed
the baby in her arms. No one said a word.

Katherine searched the darkness until she
found Oliver, sitting alone in the shadows of the
shelter, his arms crossed on his drawn up knees
and his face resting on his wrists, staring at nothing. "Oliver, I need your help."

It took a long time for him to respond. And

then he spoke very quietly, and without emotion. "No, ma'am. I'm no good to you. It's best you just leave me alone."

"You're all I've got," she said sharply.

Maude half-rose, as though to defend her son, then stopped. Oliver turned his head toward Katherine.

More calmly she said, "Come with me, Oliver. I can't do this by myself."

In his rational moments Byrd knew he had been in worse shape on other occasions. But throughout the night, when the fever raged and licked his body with burning tongues of flame, when time slowed down and spun out incredible images in his head, he could not remember any worse times. Sometimes he was fighting the white water of the Louisville Falls; sometimes he was in the high plains with Hap McKinley, trying to wave back a herd of buffalo, choking on dust and going deaf from the thunder while Hap disappeared beneath the mammoth hooves.

Sometimes he was dozing inside a cathedral formed of towering trees, inhaling the rich, sweet fragrance of cedar and spruce, watching shafts of light filter like a divine halo through the green filigreed ceiling. Sometimes he was touching a woman's face, a face surrounded by hair the color of a northwest sunset. And sometimes he was calling her name or shouting at her, trying to warn her of mortal danger. Sometimes he was pulling at her hand even as she slipped further and further away from him, and he didn't understand why her face was so calm, her voice so soothing and quiet when danger was so close he could smell it.

He knew a woman was dying; he could hear her cries of torture. The Shawnee had Katherine bound hand and foot, and they were holding a burning torch to her eyes. She pleaded with him to help her, she begged him not to desert her, but he could do nothing because he was bound too. He bellowed in rage, but the scream came out a whisper, and when he opened his eyes it was not Katherine bending over him but another woman with sad, quiet eyes and a gentle voice.

He gripped the woman's arm hard. His voice was a croak. "Where is she?"

"Hush, now, Mr. Kincaid, you're feverish."

The cloth on his brow felt like ice and he tried to twist away.

"Katie . . ." he demanded hoarsely. "Is she dead? Did they get her?"

"Katherine is fine. She can't come to you now." Sadly she added, "We lost Mrs. Werner."

It came back to him then, in bits and pieces. A trail of women and children wandering through the woods. A stash of treasure in a cave. Snake McQuaid and his band of cutthroats. Why hadn't he stayed in hiding? Why had he brought those women here? Now they were going to die, all of them.

He plucked at Caroline's sleeve. "Tell her . . ."

Caroline leaned close. Her voice was like a summer breeze. "Tell her what?"

"Tell her . . ." But the fever was outrunning him again, and the words deteriorated into incoherent mumblings. He dreamed of a Shawnee village filled with white women prisoners, their faces haggard and their eyes pleading. He dreamed of Snake McQuaid and his flashing eyes. Throughout his dreams he called and called for Katherine, but she never answered.

The smell of woodsmoke woke Byrd. Panicked, he thought *No! Don't light a fire, you'll give away our position!* Then he remembered it didn't matter anymore. The Shawnee already knew where they were and were just biding their time until they returned for them.

His arm felt like a log strapped to his side, and he was so parched inside that when he moved even his skin seemed to crackle. His eyeballs felt like stones in a dry creekbed and his head throbbed. But his mind was clear. He remembered everything.

A woman's hand touched his face and he knew it was Katherine's. "He's cooler now."

Someone placed a wet cup to his lips and he drank greedily. But he couldn't open his eyes. The lids were too heavy.

The sound of a baby crying, very close, startled him. Then he remembered Mrs. Werner. She had apparently been delivered of her child before she died. The thought did not make him glad.

It was too late to run, to hide. Dawn would be here soon and the Shawnee would return to capture their prize. He couldn't move his arm. He wasn't even sure he could stand.

He heard Katherine say, "Everyone stay outside, and go about your business. We can't afford to show fear. We'll be all right if we don't let them know we're afraid."

Byrd had to open his eyes. It was a slow and painful process, but he managed it.

Katherine's figure swam before him and gradually took shape. She was standing beside him, her back straight and her head high, her magnificent hair tucked securely under her bonnet. She was holding the mewling bundle that was Hilda Werner's child.

"Why did you stay here?" he asked.

She turned, and, shifting the baby to one arm, knelt beside him. "Would you have deserted us?" She touched his forehead lightly again and smiled. "The fever has broken. How do you feel?"

"Not up to fighting Indians." He got one arm beneath him and managed to sit up, though the effort made every joint in his body creak and left him dizzy. When his head cleared he found Katherine's arm around him, supporting him. She removed her arm when he looked at her.

Byrd's eyes went to the bundle in Katherine's arms. "I'm sorry about Miz Werner."

"Yes," she whispered. She touched the baby's small flailing fist. "Her name is Kitty."

Byrd tried to flex the fingers of his injured arm, but even so small a movement caused excruciating pain. The sky was lightening already. Soon it would be gray, and even if they left now, they would not get very far.

"Were there any other losses?"

Katherine shook her head. "Matthew Wiltshire and Hilda."

Byrd's eyes began to focus, and he saw more than just Katherine's face. He saw the children, all safe and accounted for. Four women, and Oliver. And then he saw something else. He stared.

His eyes moved painfully back to Katherine. "What the hell do you think you're doing?"

Katherine had no need to ask what he meant. It had taken her and Oliver four trips to the cave, but they'd retrieved all the bundles Byrd had stashed there. They were arranged in a circle around the fire, their bindings cut, their contents spread out in clear view. Silver, jewels, clothing, bolts of silk, cookware—a veritable treasure trove.

She met his eyes steadily. "The Shawnee are traders. They understand the meaning of a bargain. I propose to bargain for our freedom."

Byrd wanted to shout at her, to catch her by the throat and shake her, to spring to his feet and retrieve the bundles himself and put them back where they belonged. But even if he had had the physical strength for any of those actions, incredulity still would have left him impotent. He stared at her, and she stared back, proudly, defiantly.

"Lady, you are out of your mind."

"We have no choice. The Shawnee took our rifles yesterday, and even so we were in no position to fight them off. This is our only chance."

Anger made Byrd's muscles ache and his head spin. Anger at her, at the Shawnee, at his own helplessness, at the women and children. "They'll take what you offer and you too. They'll laugh at your bargain."

Katherine stiffened. "The Shawnee are known for their honor. They won't break their word."

Byrd gave a short, ugly bark of laughter. His one good hand closed on her arm and his eyes churned. "To another Indian, maybe! But breaking their word to a white man *is* a matter of honor to them, their greatest source of pride! Blast it all woman, don't you see what you've done? You're walking into a trap!"

Uncertainty flickered through Katherine's eyes, but was quickly gone. The baby began to whimper and she bounced it gently. "This is our only chance. It has to work."

Byrd closed his eyes in defeat. The worst of it was, he knew she was right. They had no more choices.

As the first streaks of gray touched the sky Oliver found himself counting the minutes remaining in their collective lives like heartbeats. The strange thing was, now that the time was upon him, he found he did not really want to die.

He hated himself for that. How could anyone want to go on living after what he had done? Yet as night gave way to day, it seemed the woodlands had never smelled sweeter, the air had never tasted sharper, and life had never been more precious to him.

"It never stops, does it?" a soft voice said beside him.

It was Priscilla. Her presence registered like a lead weight inside his chest. He made himself turn to look at her. She wasn't sixteen any more. She was a woman with quiet, thoughtful eyes and tired shoulders.

"Just when you think the worst is over," she went on, "it's there to do all over again. Oh, Oliver, was life meant to be so hard?"

He did not want it to be hard for her. He wanted a snug little house for her, in town with a rose-bordered fence and a big porch from which to watch the sunset. He wanted long, uneventful years in which the memory of these days would dim and fade until they were nothing more than oft-repeated hearthside tales for her children and grandchildren. Priscilla did not deserve this. But then, did any of them?

"No. I don't think so," he said. "Whenever folks

start moving out for something new it gets hard, I reckon. Kinda like growing up."

She looked at him without accusation in her eyes, without hate. Just a solemn understanding.

She looked back toward the fire and the bundles of treasure Katherine had arranged around it. "Do you think Miss Katherine's plan will work?"

A moment ago he would have said no, and that it didn't matter anyway. None of them had a chance. But now suddenly and desperately he wanted it to work.

"Priscilla," he said hoarsely, "I'm sorry. I know you don't want to hear it and I don't have any right to ask you to forgive me, but you're a widow because of me and I just had to say . . ." His voice broke there, but it was just as well, because Priscilla was looking at him with such surprise that he couldn't have gone on anyway.

"But it wasn't your fault," she said in a small voice. "The Indians . . ."

"No." His throat convulsed, his fists tightened. "I was a coward. If I had shot . . ."

Priscilla seemed genuinely puzzled. "But there were dozens of them. You couldn't have shot them all. You might have been killed. You couldn't have saved Matthew." And then, with a catch in her voice, "No one could."

That quiet exoneration should have filled Oliver with relief. Instead it compounded his guilt. He couldn't even look at her, but chose a point in space to stare at, and forced himself to say the next words. "I lusted after you." It was a hoarse whisper. "I wanted another man's wife, and now he's dead and nobody can make that all right."

"I wanted you too, Oliver."

What he saw in her eyes was not forgiveness, not blame, but shared guilt and pain. More than compassion. Understanding.

Suddenly, Oliver saw what he had lost in Priscilla. Katherine had told him he would one day find a girl, but he had been too blind with hero worship to see that that girl was right here, all the time. It could have been so different for them. He wished mightily he could make it different.

Priscilla, reading his thoughts as easily as if he had spoken them out loud, said, "I guess . . . it's something both of us will have inside of us for the rest of our lives."

"And between us," he added hoarsely.

"But it wasn't wrong, Oliver." Her eyes were big, and sad, and touched with pleading. "It wasn't completely wrong."

"No," he said. "And maybe, between the two of us, knowing that inside, it won't be so bad."

He reached for her hand and held it, and she did not pull away.

Katherine placed the sleeping Kitty on the ground inside the shelter, arranging a layer of leaves and light branches to cover her. "Be very quiet, darling," she whispered, "and don't cry. I'll be back soon and then we'll all go away from this horrible place, I promise. Just sleep now."

The baby moved her head a little in her sleep, but made no sound. Katherine got up quietly and left the shelter.

When she stepped outside the sky was turning pale with the day's first rays and Indians were soundlessly surrounding the camp.

There were eight of them, all with bows drawn and arrows in place, forming a loose circle around the outskirts of the camp. In the center, near the fire, stood their captives. Maude and Caroline stood with their children pressed against their skirts. Esther's eyes were cold enough to freeze hell. Byrd had pulled himself up against a tree trunk and stood erect, his knuckles white with the exertion. Oliver held Priscilla's hand, and they tried not to allow their fear to show through. Katherine was so proud of them that strength coursed like molten lead through her veins. She walked slowly to the fire, feeling the swing of a drawn arrow following her every step of the way.

She knelt and flipped back the flap of buckskin that partially covered the largest bundle, exposing its contents to view. She did the same with a second and a third. When she straightened up, she could see no discernible change of expression on any of the dark faces, and for an instant—an instant only—she felt a thread of panic. This might not work. Byrd might be right. They might spit on her bargain and take them all prisoner. Or they might take the trade and return in the night to rape and murder them.

It had to work. Please let it work.

Her eyes moved around the circle, resting on one face and then another, until finally they stopped on one brave with a yellow turban on his head and black and red stripes painted on his cheeks. Judging from the number of feathers he wore in his ears, which she knew were badges of honor, she assumed he was the leader. His bow was not drawn, but arrogantly slung over his shoulder.

It was difficult to sound fearless when looking into hard, alien eyes, aware of the arrows aimed at her heart, not knowing whether they would understand the words of peace she spoke. Everything inside her was trembling, but her voice was loud and clear.

"Among my people," she said, "the honor of the great warrior Tecumseh is well known. I will see now if his tribesmen follow the ways of their fallen chief."

The arrows did not move, and the expressions remained hard. But on the face of the leader Katherine thought she saw a slight change at the mention of Tecumseh. Grasping that frail hope, she went on.

"I have gathered gifts"—she gestured to the bundles behind her—"for brave hunters who will let us pass in peace."

For a long, long time nothing happened. Then the Indian with the many feathers said, "You speak for all?"

Katherine's heart registered a thump of relief to hear the words spoken in English. He had understood. It was going to be all right.

She spread her hands as though to embrace the women and children around her, but she kept her eyes steady on the Indian's face. "Yes," she said clearly. "These are my people. I bargain for them."

A measure of disdain came into the leader's eyes. "You are chief?"

From behind her Byrd said a few words of strong, clipped Shawnee. It was all Katherine could do to keep herself from whirling on him in surprise. He came forward slowly and stood beside her. "She is priestess," he repeated in English, his eyes stern on the leader's face. "She speaks for all."

It seemed to Katherine there was a new respect

in the leader's gaze, and she made herself stand tall beneath it. Her throat was so dry she couldn't swallow, and the morning was so silent she could hear Esther's soft breathing a few feet behind her.

Then the leader, never moving his eyes from her, spoke a few short words of Shawnee, and the braves lowered their arrows. Three of them came forward and began to gather up the bundles.

Relief swept dizzily through Katherine. Her knees wavered and threatened to buckle. She had done it! They were going to take her bargain and leave them in peace. It was truly going to be all right, they were safe.

The leader gave another order so quickly that Katherine hardly saw the movement. A brave had grasped Byrd's arms and placed a knife at his throat. Simultaneously, another grabbed Oliver and pushed Priscilla forward; others surrounded Caroline and Maude, and Esther gave a muffled cry as she was shoved to her knees.

Katherine's eyes went wide in terror and disbelief. This couldn't be happening. It couldn't! She couldn't lose, not now, not after so much. Fury filled her at their betrayal. She wanted to fling herself on the Shawnee leader, to claw at his eyes and beat him with her fists, screaming her rage in his face.

Byrd must have read her intention. Before she could draw breath he shouted, "I spit on you, Little Wolf, and on the honor of Tecumseh! Is this how you keep your creed? A woman is a better brave than you and has proved it this day!"

The Indian who held Byrd's arms pressed the knife deeper into his throat and a trickle of blood stained his beard. The last of Byrd's color drained as the Indian wrenched his shoulder, but he remained standing tall. Katherine made a small, supplicating gesture toward him, but his eyes narrowed, warning her to stay still, not to do or say anything that could further endanger them.

But Katherine did not see what further harm she could do. Esther was being dragged forward, biting her lips to keep from screaming, her eyes wild with terror. The children were crying. The pain that flooded her chest was like a jagged knife sawing through her heart and she kept her eyes fixed on Byrd, silently pleading, praying . . .

And then something else came to her. A distant memory of Byrd's fingers stroking her hair. *"You'll be the biggest prize they ever took."*

Her head snapped around. She met the Shawnee leader's scornful gaze and held it. She walked forward until she was standing no more than a foot in front of him. She untied her bonnet strings and jerked the bonnet off her head, letting her bright hair fall free. She spoke in a loud, strong voice.

"Me," she said with a broad gesture, "for all of them. A last chance to save your honor, and to be known forever as the noble seed of Tecumseh."

There was a gasp behind her, a soft cry of protest, but Katherine hardly heard. She was watching the one Byrd had called Little Wolf, her heart thundering so loudly in her chest she could hardly breathe.

Even after it was done she was not certain what she had expected. She had appealed to their honor, Byrd had shamed them, she had tried to bargain and had been ignored. Would they covet her oddly colored hair enough to trade five women for one? Would they be so impressed by her courage that they would keep their word?

What she did not expect was the reaction that followed. Little Wolf reached forward and took a handful of her hair, examining it closely. He said something in Shawnee and the other braves responded to it with wariness and curiosity. Some of them cautiously left their prisoners and gathered around Katherine, muttering among themselves.

Katherine cut her eyes helplessly to Byrd, and she saw that the brave who held him had taken the knife away from his throat. Byrd seemed just as perplexed by the Shawnee's reaction as she was. "They're talking about something called a firebird," he told her. "Does that mean anything to you?"

She started to shake her head but stopped. A picture formed in her mind. Boothe, coming up from the river with the sun setting behind him, playing like flames on his brilliant head of hair; Gran standing beside Katherine on the porch and smiling fondly. "Now, ain't that a sight? All that red hair in the sunlight, looks just like a firebird lit on his shoulder."

Katherine reached up and deliberately released her hair from Little Wolf's grasp. She knelt on the ground and cleared a space free of leaves; her hand was shaking so badly she had to hold her breath to keep it steady. With her index finger she etched a circle on the ground, and inside it a Celtic cross.

A murmur of excitement went through the gathered Indians, and some of them took cautious steps back, staring at her. Katherine released her breath, but it came so thinly that she had to remain on the ground, breathing shallowly for some seconds before she could speak.

We are with you always . . .

God had intervened. He had not forgotten His children in the wilderness. Thank you, Gran. Thank you Boothe. She rose shakily to her feet. She looked Little Wolf in the eye. "The Firebird is my mother's son," she said. "Tell them, Byrd," she commanded, her voice breathless with excitement. "They're talking about my brother!"

After only one moment's startled hesitation, Byrd repeated the words in rapid Shawnee.

Little Wolf scowled at her, but it seemed his ferocity was mitigated by respect and perhaps a trace of what could have been awe—or fear. He barked out a sharp order, and the braves released their prisoners.

He looked at Katherine sternly. "The Firebird is a great warrior. We accept the bargain of his blood." With a sharp signal he turned away, and the braves began to tie up the bundles of plunder.

Caroline stumbled into Katherine's arms, hugging her hard and trying not to sob. Esther was close, touching her sleeve, and the children clung to her skirts. Katherine let their weight support and buffer her, but she felt it all through a haze, hardly daring to believe what had happened, or why. They were safe. The Indians were going away and they were safe.

And then she heard a sound that froze her blood. The tiny, sputtering wail of a newborn baby.

A Shawnee brave walked past her, carrying baby Kitty in his arm. Katherine followed his progress with wild alarm though her feet seemed rooted to the spot and her arms hung like weights at her sides. The brave went to Little Wolf and they exchanged words; Little Wolf looked at the baby and nodded.

Katherine looked frantically at Byrd. The expression on his face was dark and pained, and it made her heart lurch in her chest. "He told Little Wolf the baby's mother is dead," Byrd said, "and has no milk. Little Wolf said they will give her life, and make her theirs."

"No," Katherine whispered. She turned as in slow motion, fighting a fog that chilled and paralyzed her. Immediately desperation pushed aside numbness, and angry strength flowed into her limbs.

She pushed forward, her arms outstretched for the child. "Give her to me," she commanded.

The brave placed Kitty in Little Wolf's arms. She was still crying and waving her fists. The Indian was holding her too tightly.

Katherine fought to keep her voice steady. "Give her to me." She started to take another step forward.

Byrd grabbed her arm. His face was twisted with agony. "Dammit, girl, they're trying to do you a favor!" he said. "It's a gesture of respect."

Everything about Katherine was shaking, her arms, her legs, her voice. She fought it. She tried to keep her voice low and calm, but she was screaming inside. "They're not taking my baby."

Caroline's hand was pressed to her mouth, her eyes dark smudges of pain and pleading. "Katherine, please!" she whispered. "We have no milk. She'll die!"

"No!" Katherine jerked away from Byrd. Fever burned in her eyes, her head; she couldn't see for the force of it and she flung herself toward Little Wolf. "You're not taking my baby! Give her to me!"

Byrd caught her around the waist, a band of iron crushing her ribs, his face vividly white above hers, his eyes a smear of blue ice and cold fire. She struggled against him, but he said, "Katie! Let her go!"

The words were torn from him like part of his own flesh, and not even Katherine would ever guess how much they cost him. The faces of the women prisoners in the Shawnee camp surged to mock him. His soul cried out for promises made and vengeance exacted, for he had sworn it would never happen again. If it meant his life, it would not happen again.

But it was happening. And though a force older than manhood and stronger than honor demanded that he stop it, that he sacrifice anything to stop it, the voice of reason held him, and tore at him. Would he condemn an innocent babe to death for the sake of his honor? The agony of the choice was almost too much for him to make, the strength of will it required crushed something inside him almost to the point of death. He had no choice.

"Let her go," he repeated. "I swear to you and before God that I will bring her back, if it takes the rest of my life. But you have to let her go! It's her only chance!"

Perhaps some small part of Katherine knew he was right, knew they all were right, but it was too much, and she fought it with all her strength. Not Kitty. Not again, not this too. Not her baby. She screamed, fighting wildly, "No! You can't have her! She's mine! You can't!"

Little Wolf stared at her coldly, then turned and stepped into the woods, the wailing infant in his arms.

"No!" Her cry echoed and re-echoed. "No!"

Katherine broke away from the restraining arms. Someone shouted at her; she took a few running, stumbling steps and a weight hit her hard, forcing her to her knees. She fought with her fists and clawed with her nails, screaming, battling. It was a woman who dragged her down when she tried to get up, a woman who held her arms and pushed her onto the ground and wouldn't let her go even when her screams deteriorated into wild, wordless sobs.

Maude Sherrod held her shoulders and shook her hard. "Stop it! Stop it, she's gone! Stop it, I say!"

As a gray-white blur Katherine saw the woman above her, her hair wild and tangled around her shoulders, her face smeared with dirt and marked with red blotches from Katherine's nails and fists, her eyes burning like coals. Abruptly, the hysteria drained from Katherine; the anger, the pain, the betrayal seeped out of her like the blood of life to leave only emptiness. She was gone. Kitty was gone. Everyone she loved, everyone she touched . . .

She closed her eyes and felt herself sinking until her face touched the ground. She had no strength left to fight. Something essential in her had died today, never to rise again. But it didn't matter.

Maude said, "Come on, child, get up." Her voice was brusque. "We have to move out of this place."

Katherine did not stir.

She felt a hand on her shoulder. "Don't you think I know?" Maude's voice said gruffly. "Didn't I bring that baby into this world with my own hands, didn't I give her her first breath of life? Do you think I wanted this to happen? First Hilda, now the baby ..." Her voice caught before she was able to go on, strongly, "But she's *alive*. We're all alive, and we have a chance to stay that way. But we have to keep moving. The sooner we get to Cairo the sooner we can send a search party after that baby, and that's just what we're going to do. Now get up."

"No," Katherine said dully. Her voice sounded far away, fighting its way through layers of weariness as thick as quicksand. "No, I can't do it anymore. I'm tired, and I can't take any more. Go—without me. Leave me alone."

Maude grasped Katherine's shoulders and pulled her up with such a jerk that Katherine's head fell back. She looked at Maude blankly. Her face was very close, set and hard, her eyes crystalline with an intensity that bored tiny pin pricks of consciousness into Katherine's lethargy.

"Listen to me," Maude said without gentleness or compassion, just the hard edges of truth. "I still don't like you. I don't approve of you. But we couldn't have made it this far without you." Her face tightened, and even Katherine, deep inside her self-protective shield, could see how much that admission cost her. "Before God," she said lowly, "none of us would be alive today if it weren't for you, and I'm not going to let you give up now. We need you. *You will go on.*"

Maude's words battered against all of Katherine's determined defenses and broke them down.

The pain began to swell; her eyes flooded. She shook her head helplessly.

"No," she said. Her voice was high and tight, her face torn with pleading. "No, I can't. Don't make me go on . . ."

Maude's face softened. "Child, you have to."

The tears spilled over and Maude drew Katherine into her arms, rocking her gently while Katherine wept against her breast. The sun rose over the trees, the birds came out of hiding and began to chatter, the earth rotated on its axis. Time moved on, and so must Katherine. She had no choice.

Chapter Fifteen

They buried Hilda beside Matthew and marked each grave with a wooden cross. Katherine stood a long time over Hilda's grave, renewing promises and strengthening vows. Byrd stood beside her, saying nothing, but Katherine knew his pain. For whatever else happened, what they shared in that moment looking down at a grave in the wilderness would bind them together for the rest of their lives.

They camped one more night on the ridge while Byrd regained some of his strength, but when the morning sun rose Katherine knew a decision must be made. Every moment they delayed reduced their chances of ever finding Kitty again. They had to get to Cairo, and quickly.

Caroline handed Katherine a bark bowl warm with Byrd's weak chickory brew, and Katherine said abruptly, "We're going to the river."

Everyone stared at her.

"The water has gone down by now," she stated calmly. "We'll build a raft and float it down. Byrd knows the river; he will pilot us."

"Lady, you've lost your mind," Byrd said. "You wouldn't even get to the banks before the pirates got you. What we've got to do is move further back."

"No." Katherine's voice was quiet, but firm. "We're not going to run anymore. We're not going to cower and hide and starve and wait for the worst to happen. This time we're going to fight."

Silence followed her words, heavy with uncertainty. "It's suicide," Byrd said. But even his voice lacked conviction. He, too, had known too much defeat of late to sit back complacently and wait for it to happen again.

Katherine regarded the others solemnly, one at a time, then asked simply, "What do the rest of you want to do?"

The women looked at each other uneasily. Perhaps they were remembering Katherine's hysteria yesterday and wondering about her state of mind. Perhaps they were recalling her words to the Shawnee leader: "These are my people." Or perhaps they were thinking of the moment she had flung aside her bonnet and volunteered to trade her life for theirs.

Then Esther said, "I'm an old woman, and tired. I just want a bed to sleep in and a hot meal in my belly."

Caroline stroked Benjamin's dirty, tangled hair. "The children can't go on like this much longer. And," she added softly, "I'm not sure I can either."

Maude gave a decisive jerk of her chin. "We go to the river."

Byrd's eyes went around the group, and he knew the futility of arguing. Perhaps he even saw the logic in the course they had chosen: best to face an enemy you know than to be taken defenseless in your sleep, running from a nameless fear.

He tried to flex the fingers on his injured arm and was gratified to see a small movement, though the pain was enormous. He wouldn't be much help to them, not for some days, but he could try. He started to get to his feet. "I'll go scout the path," he said.

"No." Katherine shook her head. "You're too weak, and we're going to need you at your best when we get to the river."

Incredulity roughened his voice. "You can't just push in there blind!"

Oliver looked at Priscilla, and then, hesitantly, at Katherine. "I'll go, Miss Katherine. I've been there before, and I know the way."

Katherine saw Maude bite her lip in protest, and she saw Oliver's look of gratitude when his mother kept silent.

"I'll go with you," Katherine said.

"No. It'd be best if I was alone. Less noise, in case ..."

Byrd glanced at him with an almost imperceptible nod of approval. Oliver's shoulders straightened in acknowledgment. "The boy's right," Byrd said. "The less folks out there tromping around, the less chance for trouble."

Katherine knew what it cost Maude to reply, "Oliver is a sensible boy. He'll be just fine."

Without another word, Oliver got to his feet.

Katherine went to him, and for a moment she didn't know what to say. She tried to remember the starry eyed boy who had reached for her on a storm-tossed boat, who had promised her his devotion, who had poured out his heart to her in a wilderness glade. But that boy was gone, and a young man had taken his place.

In the end, Katherine only handed him her

walking stick and said, "You be careful, Oliver Sherrod. We're counting on you."

He smiled at her. "I know you are, Miss Katherine." He took up the stick in a firm grip. "I'll be back before sunset."

The hours wore on as they waited for Oliver—not without worry, but with a strong sense of excitement too. The end of the journey might really be in sight. It might almost be over.

If Oliver returned with a report of all clear, Katherine thought, they would make camp on the riverbank tonight. Tomorrow they would begin building the raft. It would take a day, maybe two, and then they would be on the river, safe and at Cairo in a matter of days.

She had not forgotten the tattered remnants of Hannah's gown. She knew the pirates were out there, possibly waiting for them, possibly stalking them even now. She knew she may have sent Oliver into danger, or even to his death. But she no longer had the luxury of fear. If there were pirates, she would do what must be done. And she would do it when the time came.

Early in the morning Oliver had helped Byrd set out some snares and fishing lines, which caught half a dozen catfish and three rabbits. As the women sat around the fire cleaning the catch, they talked in hesitant voices about Cairo—what it would be like, how far away it was, how long it would take to reach. For perhaps the first time Cairo was a real and viable possibility, a concrete place rather than a nebulous dream, and they spoke as though they hardly dared to believe it, as though if they said the word too loudly, it all might go away. Then Maude asked what everyone was going to do when they got there.

Esther spoke first. It was evidently a matter to which she had given some thought. "I'll go back east on the first boat, I reckon," she said. She tucked a strand of hair behind her ear with a wan smile. "This country, it isn't for me. And I've got a lot back home that I left unfinished."

Her eyes found Priscilla's, and a moment of quiet understanding passed between the two women. Priscilla's gaze wandered over the ridge, toward the trail Oliver had taken into the woods. Her expression was sad. "I'll go, too," she said softly. "I need my Mama and Papa. I miss them so."

Esther squeezed Priscilla's hand briefly. "I know, child. I know."

She turned to Caroline. "I suppose you'll be glad to take your children back to Virginia. Your folks must be worried sick about you."

Caroline dropped a freshly skinned catfish into a shallow bark dish of water without looking up. "My folks don't even know where I am," she said quietly. "They disowned me before Rebecca was born."

The shock was such that everyone, even Katherine, stopped what they were doing to stare at her. Caroline sat back on her heels and wiped her hands on her apron. Her smile was faint and laced with sorrow.

"It all seems so silly now," she said, with a slight lift of her shoulders that might have been apology or embarrassment. "There was never any great plantation, or slaves, or grand house—at least not where Paul and I were concerned. I was raised in such a place, it's true, but when I was sixteen I fell in love with Paul, the son of our overseer. White trash, they called him, and it was simply unheard of. But Paul had been in the army, and he came back full of fine airs and grand talk and, my, but he was the handsomest man I had ever seen . . ."

Her eyes softened at the memory, gentle with a young girl's dreams. "Oh, my folks were fit to be tied. They did everything but lock me in my room. Maybe they should have, because we ran away one night and got married before a justice of the peace in Suffolk County. Martha was born six months later. When we returned, my folks barred the door to me and even the servants turned their backs. I never saw them again.

"Things were never the same for Paul after the army. He had *been* somebody, fighting the Indians alongside lieutenants and colonels, and having men follow him into battle. But with a wife and baby and no roof over his head, he was just poor white trash again. He tried clerking in a store, but he hadn't much head for figures. For a while we scratched out a living on a little hill farm, but Paul wasn't much of a farmer either. We never had any money, and by then there was Benjamin, too, and Paul started drinking too much and talking about going west as though it would solve all our problems. So we begged and borrowed what we could for passage and started out. It was our last chance."

She mustered a smile, but it faded at the corners. "So you see, I have no place to go back to. And even . . . ," the smile was lost in a thoughtful frown. "Even if my folks would take me back now, I'm not sure I would go to them. I'm not the little girl they locked out of the house anymore."

She took a soft breath and spread her hands. "I've made it this far. Nothing Cairo has to offer can be much worse. I'll stay, I think, and try to find work that will earn me enough to go on to New Orleans or Natchez. Surely there I can find a milliner or a dressmaker who would give me employment. Or perhaps some nice family that needs a teacher for their children. I'd like that."

For a time no one spoke. Caroline's confession was not a complete surprise to anyone, but the courage it required to tell it touched everyone deeply.

Katherine thought Caroline's plans for finding employment were a bit grandiose, but she also suspected Caroline knew it. She, like Katherine, had simply learned to take one thing at a time. And she was a survivor. She would be all right.

Priscilla, who sat closest, put her arm around Caroline's shoulders and hugged her. Caroline squeezed Priscilla's fingers in brief gratitude. Wishing to break the uncomfortable, emotional silence her words had caused, she turned to Maude.

"What about you, Maude? Will you be going back with Esther?"

Maude opened her mouth to give an automatic reply. But then her eyes met Caroline's, and something inside her seemed to change. She dropped her gaze to the rabbit she was cleaning and focused her attention on plucking its skin free of clinging fur.

"Well, maybe I painted too rosey a picture of the way things were back in New Hampshire," she said somewhat gruffly. "Fact is, we never had many friends there. Bad to mix business and social life, you know. People take advantage. The past few years things hadn't been going so well. A man named Henderson opened a store across the street and started handing out credit right and left, and of course we couldn't compete with that. Fact is . . ." She placed the rabbit on the grass and busily wiped her hands on her apron. "We sold everything we had just to pay our debts and get this far, and I can't see any sense in going back. So we'll settle at this end of the river, I guess, and make do with what we have."

How strange, Katherine thought. All of these women had seemed so different when she had started out. So proper and set in their plans, their choices willingly made. But, in fact, they had been driven west just as she had, not out of choice but of necessity.

So much had been left behind. A china teapot, a handworked cradle, a treasured spinning wheel, their husbands . . . and now their pasts. They weren't the same people any more. For the first time Katherine felt a part of them. It was a warm, welcome feeling, but at the same time she didn't quite know how to react to it.

She stood up and wiped her hands on her apron. "I'll go cut some green boughs to roast the rabbits on," she said.

Byrd, who had been listening outside the circle of fire, followed her. He held the thin branch of a sapling for her as she took out her knife. "Time was," he said thoughtfully, "I'd've been the first to say there's no place west of the Mississippi fit for women and children by themselves." He shook his head. "I'm not so sure anymore. I think they might do just fine."

Katherine smiled. "Most women have more

strength inside themselves than you men ever dream of, Mr. Kincaid."

"I know that for a fact," he agreed.

Katherine sawed off the branch and he bent down another one for her. His tone altered slightly, not enough to give alarm, but enough to remind Katherine that the ordeal was not over, that the worst danger might be yet to come. "If we run into trouble," he said, "I'll do what I can to stop them. It's me they're after, anyhow. You just keep the women headed toward the river. I'll try to get the pirates out of your way."

Katherine twisted the branch until it tore. "You think what we're doing is very foolish, don't you?"

"Yes'm. But with no rifles and only the boy left who can even shoot a bow, I don't think you've got much choice. So I'm bound to do what I can to help you out."

With his good hand he pulled off the stubborn branch and handed it to her. Kate let the knife drop to her side and turned to him. "I misjudged you," she said. "I want you to know I'm sorry."

His lips turned up at the corner and he shook his head. "You weren't so far off as that, Katie-girl. I've been a scoundrel, that's for sure, and a thief and a liar as well. Maybe it was only pirates that I stole that stuff from, but I had no con- science about it, and I was going to use it to make myself a fortune. I've been alone too much of my life, used to taking care of nobody but myself. The last thing I wanted was to get hooked up with a bunch of helpless females, and I would've left you that night in the woods if I could."

"But you didn't," she said, searching his eyes.

He lifted his hand, and cupped it around her

neck. The movement brought him closer to her. His eyes were very blue. "How old are you, Kate?"

She dropped her eyes and gave a tired smile. "Old," she answered, and her voice dropped a fraction more. "Very, very old."

His rough, calloused hand stroked the back of her neck beneath her hair. "I've seen thirty summers," he said. "I've been lots of places and known lots of folks. But I've never met a woman like you, who could make me think the way you do, or make me say what I'm about to say." He took a deep breath. "Miss Kate, I reckon we might find a preacher in Cairo, and I'd be honored if you'd stand before him with me."

Katherine's eyes flew to his face and her heart seemed to have lodged, surprisingly and uncomfortably, somewhere between her breastbone and her throat. She scanned his face urgently, and what she saw there only made the lump that was closing off her breath tighten. It was simple honesty, tenderly offered.

"I know I've been light with the words before," he admitted. "Maybe because I've got no use for pretty flatteries and I'm ashamed I don't know how to say them proper to a woman like you. I'm not an elegant man, Miss Kate, and I can't promise you riches. But I can show you a world you've never seen before, from high plain meadows to canyon valleys where man hasn't walked in a thousand years, spaces so wide and so beautiful it makes your eyes ache to look at them. I can make them a present to you, Kate, a safe place, a free place, and you won't have to run anymore. I will raise up your sons and defend your daughters." He paused only briefly. "Your enemies will be my enemies, and I will love you as best a man ever loved a woman."

The ache in her chest spread to her eyes and made them burn. She took his hand, curling her fingers around his where they rested against her neck. "A girl waits all her life to hear words like that," she said. "And if you had come to me a year ago, or a month ago, I would have said it sounded like the finest thing in the world."

Her voice was close to breaking. She had to take a moment to swallow the yearning, the awful need to go into his arms and rest there, forever. And though it seemed the hardest thing she had ever done, she took his hand and lowered it to his side.

"Oh, your world sounds grand, Byrd Kincaid," she said softly. "But I've seen all I want to see these last weeks and I can't go any further. All I want is a hearth fire and a rocking chair and never to move again. The rushing rivers, the shining mountains—you belong there, and you'd never be happy anywhere else. You don't belong under a roof, and you couldn't sleep unless you had the ground beneath your back. But me ... once I get a roof over my head I don't care if I never see the stars again, and my children will be born on a feather mattress, not ..." Her voice caught. "Not in a lean-to under the trees."

She touched his bearded face. Tears spilled over and wet her cheeks. "I'm sorry, Byrd Kincaid. More than you can ever know."

The hard planes of Byrd's face softened and lengthened with sorrow. "Katie Carlyle," he said huskily, "I reckon you're a pretty smart woman."

He leaned forward and kissed her gently on the

mouth. When they parted, his eyes were sad. "I'm sorry, too."

"Somebody's been here, all right," said Ford Bricker, scuffing back into camp. "Tracks all in the mud upriver—a boy, maybe, or . . ." He looked at Zeke Calhoun. "A girl wearing boy's shoes."

Snake glared at him. "Well? You follow them?"

"Hell no, I ain't no tracker. 'Sides, once the mud is gone, so's the tracks. Could be anywheres by now."

Snake swore and threw his knife so close to Bricker's shoulder that it knicked off a piece of his shirt before lodging in the tree behind him.

"Hey, what the hell are you doing? You tore my goddamn shirt, you son of a bitch!"

"Be careful it ain't your ear next time," growled Snake. He strode over to retrieve his knife but didn't sheath it. He was ready to draw blood and it didn't matter whether the blood belonged to one of his men or a stranger.

This run was turning out to be less than satisfactory despite the luck that had led them to the stranded women the second day out. They had learned that Katherine Carlyle was alive and off in the woods with a bunch of other women and kids, but Snake hadn't been able to torture a word out of their terrified victims about his own quarry. Neither one of them had had anything worth stealing—except that beaded cross which Snake, in disgust, had flung at Preacher Jones (so called because he was the only one among them who could read and write)—and the pleasure afforded by the two terrified women and boys had not lasted long.

Downriver, they had found nothing more than

a floundering keelboat filled with whale oil from Boston. They had loaded the cargo onto their own boat, but the barrels were too heavy for their hold and slowed their progress considerably.

Two days later, having seen no sign of either the women or the thieving keelboat pilot, they had turned and begun a ponderous journey up-river again, retracing their route. It was becoming increasingly obvious that if they wanted their quarry they were going to have to take to stalking it on land, a prospect that appealed to no one— except perhaps the Calhoun brothers, who were turning out to be more trouble than they were worth.

Abe Calhoun was stupid and Zeke was sullen and quarrelsome. Neither one of them was good for much but killing, and even in that they lacked a certain enthusiasm as far as Snake was concerned. More than once it had come to knives between them, with Zeke arguing about how the redhead was getting away and Abe flat-out refus-ing to do his share of the work. Snake didn't know why he hadn't shot both of them in their sleep long before now, except that with the oil barrels weighing down the boat he needed all the oars-men he could get. But if Zeke Calhoun came up against him one more time, Snake decided, he was going to shoot him and be done with it. He'd dump the oil if he had to and pick up something better downriver. It wasn't worth the aggravation.

Perhaps Zeke knew he'd been pushing his luck, because when Bricker came stumbling in with news of the tracks he didn't even look up. He was sitting on the bank, whittling down a piece of hickory, his narrow brow creased in a frown of concentration. Snake waited, knife in hand, for

Zeke to launch into his usual spiel about beating the woods for the woman, but he said nothing. After a moment Snake sheathed his knife, satisfied.

Abe squatted next to his brother. He knew what he wanted to say, but it took him awhile to get the words right. Zeke kept on whittling. "Think it's her, Zeke?" he finally said.

Zeke took his own time replying. "Could be," he said at last.

Abe looked at his brother anxiously. This next thought was even more complicated, and he wasn't sure he even wanted to say it out loud. But he'd kept it inside too long, and he thought he would bust if he didn't tell somebody. "I wish we was home, Zeke," he mumbled miserably. "I don't like this business, and I got a feelin' something bad's gonna happen."

Zeke sliced a shaving off the hickory with a particularly sharp twist of his wrist; the corner of his eye twitched convulsively, but he said nothing. Truth was, he wasn't enjoying being one of Snake's band as much as he thought he would. Pirating was hard work, and work was something the Calhouns had made a point of avoiding whenever they could. The whole business was beginning to turn his stomach. He didn't mind killing, not even killing women, but killing kids . . . well, a man had to draw the line somewhere. And Zeke couldn't see the sense in going to so much trouble killing folks without any reason.

His appetite for tracking and murdering Kate Carlyle was beginning to lose its edge, and it was all Snake McQuaid's fault. Now Zeke could almost taste the kill, but there wasn't much satisfaction in it. He and Abe would've been a lot better off if they had never hooked up with this bunch.

Concentrating hard on his whittling he said, "Come tomorrow noon, you ain't gonna have to worry about it no more. We're leaving and going in the woods after that red-headed witch. We don't need no help. It's our fight and we shoulda kep' it that way. I said all along she's around here somewheres, and we're gonna find her and finish it."

He examined the fine point of the hickory stick with satisfaction and threw it, making it stand up straight on the riverbank ten feet away. "Then," he said, casually wiping his blade on his pants, "we're going home."

Oliver slipped stealthily from his hiding place behind a deadfall, turned on stockinged feet, and began to creep away. When he had gone far enough to be sure he wouldn't be heard, he stopped and put on his shoes. Then he began to run, his heart going like a hammer, the words of the pirates pounding in his ears.

"Oliver, for the love of heaven, slow down!"

After the first flurry of excited greeting, Oliver had poured out his story in incoherent gasps and sputters. Between the bombardment of questions and his own frantic efforts to regain his breath, no one caught much of what he was saying. Priscilla was clinging to his arm, Maude kept smoothing his sleeve, and the children were all over him. Katherine stood with her hands pressed tightly before her and Byrd was beside her studying him thoughtfully.

"Now start at the beginning. Slowly," Katherine said.

Patiently, Oliver repeated it all, making an effort to recall every detail and to faithfully reproduce each scrap of conversation he had overheard. Katherine's face changed as he talked, seeming to lose a fraction of its color, her brow drawing into a tight, knotted frown. But her eyes remained calm.

"Can you describe what they looked like again?"

Oliver did. He added reluctantly, "One of them was wearing Miz Mason's rosary necklace."

Caroline closed her eyes and Esther pressed her hand to her mouth, but Katherine seemed to be thinking about something else. She looked worried.

"It's McQuaid's bunch, all right," Byrd said grimly. "And I guess I know what they're looking for."

But Katherine could not help but recognize the description of Zeke and Abe Calhoun, and if she had any doubts, Oliver's quotes about the "redhead" had dismissed them. So, she thought, with a peculiar lack of dismay, We have come full circle. There's no running away, after all.

She said to Byrd, "Maybe you don't know what they want. Those last two men Oliver described— I know them."

Before Byrd could reply, she turned back to Oliver. "You say the boat was tied up nearby?"

"Yes, ma'am. The pirates, they had their camp up on the bank, but the boat was tied up in a shallow cove about fifty yards upriver."

Katherine's eyes narrowed thoughtfully. "You

get that notion right out of your head, woman," Byrd said sharply.

Katherine ignored him. "I think we can take it."

"With all these young'uns?" Byrd hissed. "A bunch of women with no rifles and one knife amongst us!"

"Mr. Kincaid," Caroline said clearly, "with all due respect, and knowing that your only concern is for our safety, we've been running and we've been hiding for a long time now, and we've all learned to do things we never thought we'd do. If there's a chance, however small, of getting out of this place, I think we are obliged to take it."

Katherine was thinking too hard and too carefully to speak her gratitude. "It will be dangerous," she said slowly, her gaze moving over the group, "and it might not work. But if you're willing to try ... I have a plan."

Chapter Sixteen

The night was brilliant with stars, rhythmic with the muted chirping of crickets. Because of the proximity of the pirates, they did not build a fire and bedded the children down after a cold supper. None of the adults intended getting any sleep for themselves. They sat in a loose circle on the ground or on logs, close to each other for comfort and reassurance, absorbed in their own thoughts. The journey was almost over; it had begun on water and it would end on water.

Katherine looked at the faces she had come to know so intimately, the people with whom she had shared the most intense moments of life and death, and she found it hard to believe that they had ever been strangers to her. Caroline, with her gentle manners and lilting drawl, always ready to lend a hand to whatever task needed to be done; Esther, facing down a bear with a china teapot; Priscilla, who had grown into a woman before their very eyes; Oliver, who had left more than boyhood behind. Maude, who had so frightened and angered Katherine at the beginning . . . who had only wanted to protect her own and who had turned out to be the strongest of them all. There was an empty place in the circle which no one could ever fill, but Hilda was as much a part of Katherine's destiny tonight as she had been that first day on the riverbank when she had pulled herself to her feet and said, "I will go with you."

These people had become Katherine's family. They would be a part of Katherine forever, and the love she felt for them had been forged through fire.

She felt no fear for what tomorrow would bring, and no dread. Katherine had no intention of dying. The youngest member of the family was still missing, and she had a vow to keep. If for nothing else, Katherine must live to see Kitty Werner brought home to her.

Byrd was sitting next to her, and Katherine thought how natural it seemed to have him at her side. In the bottom of his pack he had found some tobacco weed and had rolled it to smoke. The pungent aroma drifted through the night, and that seemed natural too, comforting and masculine.

"Sure is peaceful out tonight," Byrd said.

Caroline murmured agreement, and Katherine smiled faintly. It occurred to Byrd that, considering what they had been through and what still faced them, peaceful was the last thing any of them should have been feeling. And he was surprised to realize that rarely had he felt so peaceful as he did in that moment.

Once, he had thought there could not be anything so fine in a man's life as the stark loneliness at the top of a mountain pass, listening to the sigh of the wind and feeling the sun on his face and watching, sometimes for hours on end, the solemn gaze of an antelope or the graceful play of a creek otter. There was no peace so great as that in a misty spruce meadow at sunrise, where man and God were one. Yet tonight those places seemed far away, and the memory of them not so grand.

It had something to do with the companionship of women, the gentleness of their faces, the softness of their voices; the sound of children murmuring in their sleep. The starlight seemed clearer, the night easier, even the taste of tobacco smoke against his tongue richer for the presence of females and children around him. It didn't make sense, and he couldn't think why it should be so, but it was true.

The matter confused and disturbed him, challenging him in ways he did not want to be challenged, and he tried not to think about it at all. But he couldn't get over the notion that when he was parted from them, as inevitably he must be, the emptiness inside him would take a long time to fill.

He looked at Katherine, wishing he could give her something of himself that would last. He would carry the memory of her with him forever, and the thought of leaving her stabbed at him inside with a pain as sharp as any physical wound he had ever known. But he had nothing to offer her. Nothing ... except this small part of himself, and a promise she knew he would keep.

"The Shawnee will make their camp in the fall," he said quietly, "and that's when I'll go after the baby. She's not gone, Miss Kate, she's alive and that was the best thing we could do for her, no matter how hard it was. But I promise you if it takes the rest of my life, I'll bring her home safe to you." He looked at her solemnly. "You know that, don't you?"

"Yes," she said, "I know."

How far away the mountain passes seemed now. How distant, and unimportant.

After a moment Katherine said so that the others could not hear, "Do you think we have a chance tomorrow?"

Byrd smoked the last of the tobacco and cast the stub into the fire.

"More than a chance," he answered. "I think we're gonna pull it off."

He laid his hand over hers, and after a moment, her fingers tightened about his. They stayed that way, in warmth and silence, while the moon rose. When Katherine grew tired, she laid her head against his shoulder and slept.

From the top of a heavily wooded incline that fell toward the banks of the river, the group had a good view of the land below. It was exactly as Oliver had described. Directly below them was a shallow cove with the keelboat drawn close, anchored to the bank with sturdy lines tied to trees on shore. Less than a hundred yards to the west, on a narrow strip of beach, was the pirate camp. The view of the camp was somewhat obstructed by the pre-dawn light and heavy foliage, but Katherine could make out a pair of booted feet protruding behind a bush, and another shadowy shape of a sleeping man. If she listened carefully enough she could almost hear the snores above the soft slapping and gurgling of the river. A wisp of woodsmoke from a smoldering campfire tinged the damp morning air.

Katherine looked from the camp back to the boat. Until this moment she had not fully believed it could be this easy. They were going to make it: creep silently down the bank, wade through the water, climb onto the boat, cut the lines, and push off. They would drift past the camp and into the misty morning before the pirates even stirred.

Her eyes met Byrd's and she saw silent agreement there. They were going to make it. Without a sound, Katherine moved around to the front and began to lead the group down the incline. They had all been instructed over and over again about the importance of these next moments. They all followed her as silently as wraiths.

Byrd and Oliver brought up the rear, keeping a watchful eye on the pirate camp. Byrd knew that if they were discovered there was little he could do; he had no gun, and his arm was still useless to him—he wouldn't even be able to draw the bow that was flung over his shoulder. His hatchet and Katherine's knife would be of little use against the boarding pistols and long rifles the pirates carried. Everything depended on their silence.

And then he saw something that made his blood run cold. At the edge of the cove, previously hidden from view by the bulk of the boat, was another campfire—the kind a man might build himself to ward off the chill through a long night of guard duty. That boat was not deserted.

He grabbed Oliver's arm, but Oliver had already seen. His eyes were dark and his face was drawn. Frantically Oliver looked toward the group that had preceded them, but they were too far ahead to warn. Byrd started to move

ahead. Just then they saw what they most dreaded:
a man, touseled and bleary-eyed, came around the
side of the boat, rubbing his yawning jaw and
scratching his chest. He squatted on the ground
and began to poke at the fire.

Byrd looked up ahead, where Esther's bonnet
could just be seen disappearing behind a clump
of trees. He looked back at the man by the fire.
He slipped his bow off his shoulder and handed
it to Oliver. The message in his eyes was clear.

Oliver thought, *No. No, not again.* It couldn't be
happening again. A cold sweat broke out on his
brow and trickled down his arms. His throat felt
lined with tarpaper. Byrd held out the bow and
his eyes were stern.

Moments ticked passed. The women and children moved closer to the pirate boat. Too late to
shout warning, too late to stop them. The man
beside the campfire would raise the alarm and it
would be a massacre . . . a massacre.

Oliver's hand closed around the bow, but he
couldn't feel the wood against his fingers. He took
an arrow from Byrd's quiver with a hand so slippery with sweat he almost dropped it. He tried to
center the arrow. His hand shook in time to the
pounding of his heart. He saw in his mind's eye
the face of the Shawnee brave closing in on him.
He saw Matthew falling in an explosion of blood
and thunder.

He drew back the bow string, and his arm
quaked with the effort. Sweat rolled into his eyes
and he couldn't see. Time was running out. At
any moment now Katherine and her band would
emerge from the cover of the woods. At any moment the pirate would look up from his fire . . .

Oliver remembered what Byrd had told him

about lining up his target with the quill of the arrow. The quill kept moving, and the blurry target that bounced back and forth before his eyes was a man. He remembered the feel of his finger on the trigger and how his muscles wouldn't move. He thought about Katherine, and Priscilla, his mother and the children moving unawares of their deaths. And he concentrated all his strength on calming his trembling and sighting his target.

He let the arrow fly.

Katherine crouched low beneath the last of the branches that divided woods from the shore, and froze. Before she could lift her arm in warning to those behind her, Abe Calhoun pitched backwards away from the fire, an arrow piercing his throat.

Shock, horror, and relief congealed in Katherine's muscles and paralyzed her for an endless moment. When she snapped her head around, Byrd and Oliver were creeping down through the woods to join them. The bow was in Oliver's hand, but there was no pride on his face for the heroics that had just saved all of their lives. He merely looked frightened and white-faced with relief.

There was no time for words of praise or gratitude. The sky was growing lighter, and the pirates would soon begin to stir. Byrd knelt beside Abe Calhoun's body and quickly wrested the pistol from his belt, thrusting it into the quiver on his shoulder. On a quick signal from Katherine, the women and children began to file into the water, making not a splash as they waded toward the boat.

The children, matured before their time by all

they had experienced, were as stealthy and brave as trained infantrymen as they climbed aboard the boat. Not even Rebecca Adamson, barely out of diapers, uttered a whimper as her mother lifted her out of the water and over the railing into Esther's waiting arms. Her knees banged the hull, and Esther had to drag her through the railing by her armpits, but she made no sound.

Byrd sliced the lines with his hatchet, then he and Oliver pressed their weight against the bow, pushing the boat off. It wouldn't budge. It was resting flat on the river bottom, and their combined strength couldn't move it.

Katherine, watching anxiously from on deck, immediately spotted the problem. Lashed inside the hold and strapped to the rails were perhaps twenty barrels of cargo that even she could tell were too heavy for such a small boat. With the added weight of the passengers, the boat had settled in the mud. They would never be able to push it free.

Byrd sprang lightly on deck and followed Katherine's silent, frantic gesture. He cut the ropes that bound one of the barrels to the deck and used his hatchet to pry off the lid. He swore softly. "Oil."

He handed his hatchet to Caroline, who was the closest. "Start dumping this stuff, quick. I need a couple of you to help push."

Without hesitation Katherine and Maude followed him over the rail and slid into the water. Caroline started cutting the ropes on the barrels.

It quickly became apparent to Caroline that, even with the combined strength of all on board, they would not be able to lift those barrels and throw them overboard. They would have to roll them to the rail, pry off the lids, and pour out the contents. Whispering as much to Esther and Priscilla, and recruiting even the older children to help, she pushed the first barrel forward and onto its side.

It hit the deck with a thump and a clatter which sounded like thunder on the still morning. In the water Katherine's eyes met Byrd's in a moment of raw awareness. The barrel rattled like the beginnings of an earthquake as it rolled toward the rail.

Sound carried with the clarity of a church bell across the water, and there was no doubt in Katherine's mind that, if the sleeping pirates were not already aroused by the noise, they soon would be. The boat could not be moved unless the weight was off-loaded. But before they had time to empty enough barrels to make a difference the pirates would be upon them.

Without hesitation, Katherine drew her knife from her apron and started out of the water. Oliver called, "Miss Katherine!" but she did not look back. She had no specific plan, but she had no intention of dying either. If she provided enough of a distraction, if she could buy a little time, they might yet have a chance to escape.

She was on shore when she heard sounds from the camp—first grumbling, then a sharp, alarmed shout, "The boat! The goddamn boat!"

Katherine did not know what made her do it—the memory of a long ago night and a roar in the woods, a sudden awareness of her own vulnerability with nothing but a knife for defense—but as she passed the small campfire she swept down and grasped the uncharred end of a heavy, coal-red log, and then she ran ... toward the pirate camp.

She heard Zeke Calhoun's voice shout "Abe!" before she saw him. He burst through the pine boughs that separated the campsite from the boat and stood directly in front of her.

Recognition registered in his eyes, replaced in an instant with a greedy hatred so intense that the look alone was enough to paralyze Katherine.

He saw the knife in her right hand, and the glowing log in the other, and with a low growl he sprang toward her. Katherine lifted her arm and threw the log.

Zeke gave a roar of pain as the burning wood slammed against his chest, sending showers of sparks upward into his face and hair. He stumbled backwards, lost his footing, and tumbled down the embankment toward the water while the flaming log rolled into a pile of dried leaves and began to smolder.

Katherine could hear shouts and see movement all around her. More men burst through the woods and she turned to run, but was blocked by a wall of steel and a heavy arm that clamped around her ribs and shot bolts of fire through her breasts. She twisted and struggled wildly; she struck backwards with her knife and felt the blade graze hard muscle and skitter out of her hand.

Snake McQuaid felt Katherine's knife slice his thigh, but it seemed barely more than a pinprick when he considered the victory that would soon be his. He shouted, "That's him! That's the son of a bitch I want! Kill him, goddamn it, stop that boat!"

He turned his attention back to the woman who was struggling and kicking in his arms, and the rage of triumph in his face became a leer of anticipation. He liked them better when they fought. "Cut me, will you, bitch?" he growled. "Well, by God, we'll just see about that. This is turning out to be my lucky day." He wound one thick hand into Katherine's hair, jerking her neck back almost to the breaking point, and dragged her backwards into the woods.

Byrd was halfway up the bank, his pistol drawn, when the two pirates rushed him. They were half dressed, poorly armed, and crazed with the excitement of the morning's unexpected battle. Byrd fired the weapon's single shot, and one of the men tumbled to the ground; the other came at him with knife drawn. Byrd swung at him with the pistol, knocking him into the water. He could not linger to see how well he had disabled the man, however; Katherine was screaming, and the woods were beginning to crackle and smoke from fire. His shoulder throbbed, and he was light-headed from exertion, but he pushed onward through the woods after Katherine.

On the deck of the boat Caroline frantically pried open the lids of the barrels the children had rolled to the rail while Esther and Priscilla tossed the empties overboard. Oil spilled onto the water and picked up the colors of the sunrise, glistening and winking. Maude cried from below, "It's not working! We still can't move it!"

Oliver applied his weight to the hull and shouted, "Keep emptying! It feels lighter!" Out of the corner of his eyes he saw movement in the water as the man Byrd had knocked down began to stagger to his feet.

Oliver left the boat and stumbled toward the rising man, intending to use his fists to knock him back into the water. But the pirate was not as weak as Oliver had imagined. With a roar he stood up and fastened his hands around Oliver's throat. Oliver went to his knees, clawing and trying to twist away, but the next gasp he took was filled with water, and then he couldn't breathe at all.

Snake McQuaid threw Katherine to the ground and pinned her with his weight. Her nails drew blood on his face, but his fist smashed into her jaw and the inside of her head seemed to explode in shafts of black and red. Distantly she felt or heard a violent ripping sound and realized her gown was gaping open from neck to waist.

With a surge of strength born of sheer terror, she began to fight again, each breath a ragged scream, using her fists, her teeth, her feet. But he was as strong as an ox. He batted her fists away as if they were annoying insects, his grin revealing black stubs of teeth, his breath foul in her face as he pushed her back on the ground. His hands probed and tore at her clothes, bruised and pinched her flesh until she thought she would go mad.

With a grunt of triumph he ripped the cord from around her waist and held up the bag of coins she had tied there. His eyes glinted with satisfaction. "Well, girlie, what have we here? Could it be the treasure I was promised?"

Snake gave a great roaring laugh and lunged

at her. Suddenly his eyes widened with surprise and a choking gasp sputtered from his throat. He jerked around and touched the back of his neck, which was streaked with blood. With a sob of primal joy Katherine saw Byrd's face, grim with his own pain and taut with killing rage. He held her knife in his good hand, raised for another blow.

Taking advantage of Snake's surprise, Katherine scrambled away from him, clawing at the ground with her hands and feet. But she hadn't even stood up when there was a roar of fury behind her as Snake broke away from Byrd and threw himself at her. She saw Byrd; she saw the evil, twisted face of the pirate. She turned to fight because she couldn't run and then his weight flung her backwards. There was a thunderclap of pain in her head and everything went sun-bright, then faded in waves of agony to gray. The last thing she saw before she sank beneath those waves was Byrd, lunging toward Snake with her knife in his hand.

Maude floundered toward her son as if in slow motion. She saw Oliver's head come up, his eyes bulging as his hands tore at the fingers clutching his throat. She saw the pirate pushing him under the water again. There was screaming in her ears and it might have been her own. That was her son. It was Oliver, her own, and every primitive instinct in her rose to the fore.

She hurled herself on the pirate with a thundering cry; she grabbed lengths of his greasy long hair and yanked back viciously. The pirate jerked backwards and released Oliver long enough to slam his arm back into Maude's ribs. Maude fell hard into the water as Oliver seized the chance to break free. He was stumbling to his knees, gasping and choking, when the pirate came down on them again. "No!" Maude screamed. "Stop it ... you're killing him ... Oliver, God, *no!*"

On her hands and knees she pushed toward them, and then she heard another voice screaming at her. Caroline was leaning over the side of the boat, the hatchet in her hand. Maude flung herself toward the boat, snatching the hatchet and stumbling back toward the pirate who was murdering her son.

They were locked in mortal combat, Oliver's hands braced against the pirate's shoulders, the pirate forcing Oliver under the water. Oliver was submerged, then he rolled to the surface and the pirate went under, but in only a moment the pirate slipped free and had his hands around Oliver's throat, pushing him under yet again. Oliver's face was blue, and terrible choking sounds came from his throat. Maude sprang forward with a scream of rage, swinging the hatchet.

The blade sliced into the pirate's neck; blood spurted and tendons crunched. She saw a pair of red-rimmed startled eyes. Blood bubbled from the mouth as she swung again. The pirate was on his knees, hands half lifted as though in supplication, face frozen in a bloody death mask. Maude brought the blade down again and again; blood spattered on her face, her mouth, her hair, and still she lifted the hatchet, though her arms were on fire and her hands were slippery with blood. Then someone was grabbing her, stopping her. It was Oliver. He was safe! He was alive!

Her voice emerged as grunts and sobs as the hatchet slipped from her hands into the water. Her arms went around her son, but she was too weak to hold him and he was too weak to stand. He slid to his knees, his arms still around her, his face buried in her skirts, making hoarse, gasping sounds of relief and horror.

Caroline dropped to her knees in the water, getting her arms under Oliver and helping him to his feet. "Hurry!" She was sobbing too. "The boat is drifting! The woods ... we've got to get on board ... Maude, hurry!"

For the first time Maude noticed the smell of smoke in the air, and the snapping and crackling sound from far away that had nothing to do with the movement of the river. The shore was dotted with flames and swathed in a blanket of smoke which drifted out over the water like fog.

Oliver held onto her arm. "Ma!" His voice was barely a croak; his throat was covered with redblue bruises and his eyes were enormous. "Hurry!"

Maude looked at her hands. They were slimy with blood, and the water at her feet was pink. The still-bleeding corpse of an unknown man floated face down in the shallow water. There was blood on her apron, on her bodice; she could feel it on her face. She said slowly, "Katherine."

"Ma ... come on! The boat ..."

But Maude was looking toward the smokey shore, plodding through the water, away from Oliver and Caroline.

"Maude, come back ..."

When she reached the shore, she lifted her sodden skirts and ran toward the flames.

Katherine heard the voice calling her and felt the pain that stabbed through her every muscle and sinew long before she opened her eyes. Someone was shaking her and the hands must have been made of flames because each time they gripped her, new agony jolted through her limbs.

Finally she forced her eyes open, but even then she couldn't see. Her vision was obscured by a dense fog that wavered and blurred, and when she tried to take a breath her lungs collapsed in a spasm of searing coughing.

Maude got her arms around Katherine's shoulders and pulled her to her feet. Katherine staggered and almost fell, but Maude pulled her upright again. "Hurry! No time!"

Her voice was muffled and hoarse, and Katherine saw that she had drawn up her skirt to cover her face. There were streaks of blood on Maude's face and hands, but that hardly registered on Katherine because then she knew it was smoke that surrounded them, that flames were spitting and crackling all around them. Panic obscured her own pain and confusion as she looked frantically around for Byrd.

Maude pulled on her arm. "This way! Hurry . . . the fire!"

"Byrd!" It was barely more than a whisper, torn from her throat and leaving her sobbing with the effort. She searched the area but saw nothing through her streaming eyes except the snapping flames and choking smoke. Byrd was here, he had

pulled the pirate off of her, he was here somewhere.

"He's not here!" Maude shouted. "I didn't
see ..."

"He was! I have to ..." Katherine turned and
started to run, but the underbrush was on fire
and red-orange flames were licking at the bark of
the trees, and she couldn't see.

Maude cried, "Honey, you can't get through
there! Nobody could! There's only one way out
and that's the way I came! Hurry!"

"No!"

"He might be at the boat by now! We have to
hurry!"

Maude had her arm about Katherine's waist
and was dragging her through the burning woods,
and as much as Katherine wanted to fight, she
knew Maude was right. There was no place to go
except toward the river. Byrd might be ahead of
them, going for the safety of the boat or already
there, and they had to hurry. Katherine pressed
her apron over her mouth and nose and crouched
low, half-running, half–stumbling, as Maude
pulled her along.

They broke out of the woods and onto the narrow shore, coughing and gasping, their lungs on
fire and their eyes burning to the point of blind-
ness. Katherine drew a sooty hand over her face
to clear the tears and saw the boat bobbing in the
water, heard the shouts from its deck.

Maude lifted her arm. "The boat! It's moving!"

They stumbled toward the water. Maude
splashed into the shallows and started treading
toward the others, but Katherine stopped and
looked frantically back toward the burning woods.

"Byrd!" She tried to shout, but the sound was

only an incoherent croak. Soon the boat would pick up the current and float away. She had to hurry or she would never reach it. Maude had risked her life to come back for her, Byrd was safe, he must be, and she had to go. Now!

She lifted her torn skirts and took a running step into the water, but suddenly a hand grabbed her ankle and she pitched face down into the shallows. She rolled over, sputtering. All of a sudden, Zeke Calhoun's face loomed above hers, his hands winding into her hair.

The side of his face was raw with bleeding burns; his hair was singed off above a knotted black bruise on his forehead. His lips were drawn back in a feral grimace and he growled, "It ain't over between us yet, bitch! Abe is dead! You kilt my brothers and you're gonna pay! By God, you're gonna pay!"

It was like seeing a ghost, like hearing a curse from Hell. All of Katherine's past, present, and future seemed to congeal into one terrified moment as she looked into Zeke Calhoun's bleeding, blistered face. There was no escape. The evil lived forever and no matter how far she ran it would always catch up with her.

Distantly she heard voices calling her name. Zeke's twisted face was very close; a knife blade gleamed as it descended toward her throat. And then there was another sound—a high creaking, groaning screech that caused Katherine to twist her head and scream at what she saw. A sapling birch not ten feet away was swaying toward them, its flaming trunk giving way to the force of the bellows of wind behind it.

Katherine tore herself violently away from Zeke and out of the path of the flaming tree. She didn't even feel the pain as clumps of her hair came away in Zeke's hand, for just then the tree fell between them with a mighty crash and the oil-doused water burst into flame.

Katherine staggered to her feet as the flames surrounded her in a whoosh. She could feel the heat on her face; her clothes were catching. Behind her was fire; like a spark on a fuse the flames traveled across the shallows between herself and the boat; fire was everywhere, there was nowhere to run. Frantically she slapped at the sparks on her bodice and the singed ends of her hair. She turned toward the shore where the blazing tree blocked her path, and realized she was going to die here, in a hell of her own making.

You will pass through blood, fire, and water . . .

She could feel the flames crawling up her dress as fast as she slapped at them and there was no place to turn; it was her destiny . . .

Fire and water . . .

She heard desperate, sobbing voices calling her name, women's screeches and children crying. Terror paralyzed her; she couldn't scream, she couldn't think, she couldn't move. And then it came to her again, a voice bursting inside her head, *You will pass through fire and water . . .*

No. Her life wasn't over.

She began to run, not away from the blazing water but into it. When fire scorched her face and bobbed around her on every side, and she could see neither backward nor forward, she took a deep breath and dove beneath the flames.

Zeke Calhoun staggered onto the shore. The last thing he saw was Katherine Carlyle going up in flames. He roared with triumph and lifted his fists to the sky, and then he turned and began to run, away from the fire, toward home.

Chapter Seventeen

T he settlement of Cairo was not much bigger than Mud Flats, younger but hardly more prosperous. Less than two dozen cabins were strewn along the riverbank and some further inland; they belonged to farmers, mostly, who fought the yearly floodwaters and tried to eke out a living on the thin, flat soil.

A farmer, plowing his bottomland along the bank upriver, first spotted the boat filled with women and children. Rumor had trickled into the small settlement over the past couple of days of just such a group of travelers, but no one had believed it. The farmer stared, even now hardly accepting the evidence of his own eyes. He dropped his mule's reins to the ground and ran to the bank, waving and calling as the keelboat drew within shouting distance. He sent his small son scurrying into town to spread the news, and he stopped by the cabin to collect his wife before running after the keelboat toward Cairo, anxious to get an up-close look of the strange group.

When Katherine had emerged from beneath the flaming waters and clambered on board the keelboat, she had begun a journey which should

have taken no more than two days. It had, in fact,
taken more than a week. None of them had the
strength or the navigational skills to maneuver
the sweep oars which sould have kept the boat on
course, and they had spent a great deal of time
stranded on sandbars. Once, they had drifted out
of the channel completely and would have ended
up hopelessly grounded if not for the assistance
of a family on a raft who, by shouting instructions
over the current, managed to get them on course
again. That family had brought to Cairo the
strange tale of a boat filled with women and children. Over the last few days, the rumor had been
substantiated by others who had drifted into the
settlement or tied up on the banks, lingering
where they might not otherwise have stayed
merely to wait for news of what had become of
the hapless travelers.

Every afternoon the women brought the keelboat to the riverbank to hunt for game and
prepare a meal. What once had seemed a monu-
mental task was now a routine. The earth was
good and provided for her own. Each dawn they
set out again to face whatever hazards the river
had in store, and each day traveled put miles behind them that could not have been traversed on
foot.

It was a weary, much-used group who stood on
the deck that late summer afternoon and watched
the first few cabins straggle into view. Their faces
were drawn and smudged, their hair tangled, their
clothes tattered and loose on frames which once
had been much fuller. In the distance they could
see, as clearly as if on a map, the muddy waters
of the Mississippi pooling against the cool green
of the Ohio. They saw chimney smoke and peo-

ple running to gather on the banks, shouting and waving. They were home.

Atop the roof, Caroline and Katherine worked one oar, Oliver and Maude the other. Priscilla and Esther struggled with the lines as the oars slowly turned the cumbersome boat toward shore. Tears of silent joy were streaming down Caroline's cheeks; Maude's hand covered her son's and squeezed it hard.

Katherine stood tall, filling her eyes with the flat, sweeping land, the ugly little mud-locked village that seemed to cling to the shore. Cairo. It wasn't much of a town, no more than Mud Flats. Just a stopping off place where passengers changed boats or cargo was transferred onto boats plying the Mississippi. But just as Mud Flats represented in some ways the end of an era, Cairo represented the beginning.

There was a tavern on the docks surrounded by ramshackle warehouses. Along the bank under the shade of some willow trees a dozen or so men were camped, hoping for work on passing riverboats. Only half a dozen cabins made up the town, the rest of the settlers having staked out farmland back from the river and its annual floodings.

But to Katherine, the village could not have been more beautiful or more welcome had it been the ancient Egyptian city it was named after, rising up from the plains and shimmering in the sun. They had made it. They had survived.

Several of the dockworkers rushed forward to catch the lines Priscilla and Esther tossed and dragging the boat the last several feet to safe shore. Oliver helped Katherine down to the deck and she found herself handed forward, from one to the other, for no one would alight before she did.

The banks were crowded with people with curious, gaping faces and excited voices. Women left their cookfires and men left their axes and their plows and their smithing, and they ran down the narrow, muddy trail which was the town's only street to see what all the clamor was about. A boy rushed into the crowd shouting in a high, clear voice, "Come see! Come see! It's the woman-boat!"

Katherine could hardly take it all in. A pair of strong hands grabbed her waist and swung her onto shore. Her feet sank ankle-deep in mud. She suddenly wanted to laugh out loud at the familiarity of the sensation.

"Who are you?" someone demanded.

"How'd you get here?"

"Where's your menfolk?"

"What happened to your pilot?"

Katherine looked around and said simply, "I'm Katherine Carlyle, and we are the remainder of the Dewhurst party."

An instant of silence greeted her announcement, followed by a rush of murmuring and awed speculation that rose in pitch to outright incredulity.

"Can't be!"

"But that boat was lost upriver over a month ago!"

"You mean to tell me . . ."

"By God, it's true then! All them stories . . ."

"Never seen the like! Nothing but womenfolk and youngsters . . ."

"Couldn't believe it. Heard the tales but never reckoned on . . ."

The other women and children were handed

on shore, and the voices became more excited, the press of bodies more insistent. Katherine found herself being passed forward from one pair of strange hands to another, everyone wanting to touch, to question, to stare, and to wonder. The faces and the voices blended together, and only snatches of each caught in her consciousness as she tried to smile and return greetings and answer questions. Finally she gave up and simply let the sensations wash over her.

"I heard there were Indians."

"Somebody said something about pirates."

"Look at those poor children! We'll get them fed right this minute."

". . . a tale for the two-cent papers, if ever there was one! Nobody'd believe . . ."

"Must come home with us, dear."

"They say it was that one, the red-headed one."

"Ronny, you come back here!"

"I just want to touch her, Ma!"

Katherine was pushed and jostled and touched and petted, and the movement she made through the crowd was eerily reminiscent of another walk through mud streets, other faces staring, other voices murmuring, yet with a difference that dazed her. For as intense as the wonder of triumph was, ghosts walked close beside Katherine. Hilda, baby Kitty, Matthew, Byrd. . . . There was no victory for those they had lost.

People were still rushing to the banks, filtering in from outlying farms, joining the crowd, doubling the noise. Through the blur of faces and voices that surrounded her, Katherine saw a single figure detach itself from those who pressed toward the shore and stop in the center of the road.

Katherine pushed away from the crowd as though the bodies were nothing more substantial than a handful of fog. She stood alone, staring. He opened his arms to her, and she walked into them.

Byrd Kincaid wrapped his arms around her and Katherine pressed her face against his chest. She thought then not of loss, but of miracles. Fire and water. An ancient symbol etched into the ground before a Shawnee chief. Byrd, here and alive. *We will be with you always, your family, looking out for you.*

Joy was an ache in her throat; it burned her eyes; she held him tightly, so very tightly.

"Looks like you turned out to be a hero after all," Byrd said huskily.

Katherine looked up at him and saw everything clearly for the first time. She answered unsteadily, "I just did what I had to do."

He moved against her, drawing her close. But anxiety mitigated her relief and she stammered, "I thought . . . the fire . . . how . . ."

He smiled at her. "It'll take more than a fire and a dirty pirate to get rid of me, darlin'." He moved away from her and reached inside his shirt. He brought out a leather pouch and placed it in her hand. Gran's gold coins.

We will be with you always.

"I been here a day or two," Byrd went on. "Was about ready to set out looking for you. Should've knowed there was no need."

His tone changed slightly as he added, "I staked out a little place for us, back from the river. Good land, plenty of timber for building. This little town might not look like much right now, but I got a feeling that with folks moving west the way they are, it might amount to something one of these days. We could do worse."

Katherine lifted her eyes to him, hardly daring to believe what he was saying. But Byrd was gazing over her head. "Miss Caroline, you and your brood best move in with us." Katherine realized then that the rest of her party had joined them, their faces brilliant with wonder and relief, but reluctant to intrude on the reunion between Katherine and Byrd. "Oliver, I marked off a piece for you right near our place. It ought to do to feed the family 'til something better comes along."

He looked back at Katherine. "After we get the cabins raised and shored in for the winter, I'll be going out to bring back the baby."

Katherine searched his face, hesitant, uncertain. The words she wanted to say were written in her eyes, and he answered them, soberly.

"I told you once you was a smart woman, Miss Kate. And I'm not saying there won't be times when I won't miss the high plains or the sound of the wind moving over a mountain pass, but the trouble with this land is it takes a man off by hisself too much, makes him forget what he ever went traveling for."

His gaze moved toward the opposite shore, where the Mississippi wound its sluggish course south. "It's God's country across that river, Katie-girl," he said, "and that's a fact. But God didn't make it for men to walk through. He made it for women to settle in, to build homes in, and raise up families in. And that's what we forget, sometimes, when we go a'wandering."

His face was shining with sincerity. "A woman to take care of, young'uns to raise up right and teach what he knows, a family sittin' around him

... that's what a man needs, and that's why he does all he does. That's all I want, Katie."

Katherine smiled at him. "That's all I want too," she said.

He took her hand, and they turned away from the river. Together, Katherine and her new family began the last steps of their journey, toward home.

Epilogue

The last log was set around noon, and the atmosphere was busy and jubilant. Neighboring families wandered in and out of the newly finished cabin, examining the joist work, commenting on the draft of the chimney, putting a final touch or two on the porch steps, and congratulating themselves on a job well done.

The wives had set up planks across sawhorses and stumps for tables and were spreading out the noonday feast, while laughing children engaged in a noisy game of tag. The area around the cabin had been cleared long before the first log was set; generous settlers had donated the labor of their mules and the sweat of their brows to plow the fields and plant the first crop. Now, as before, they gave of their bounty in celebration of the new settlers. Welcoming strangers was good cause for a celebration, as every newcomer to the community strengthened its chances for survival.

The guests shared what they could, and each offering was received gladly. At one end of the table were trenchers filled with fried catfish, contributed by the men who worked the docks, who knew where the biggest and best could be found.

The tavern owner and his wife supplied a keg of malt and a dozen blackberry pies, which were famous downriver as far as Memphis. There were venison and rabbit, roasted sweet potatoes, maize and blueberry bread, corn pone and johnny cake. And there were tarts of crab apple, wild cherries, and strawberry.

Maude oversaw the mealtime efforts, making sure that the children each had a glass of buttermilk and the men each had no more than two tumblers of malt. Already she was asserting her leadership in the community, just as she always had done. Construction on her own cabin would begin tomorrow, but the fields had already been plowed and planted and she was busy negotiating with a keelboat captain for goods on consignment that would enable her to open her own trading post.

Priscilla and Esther had left the day before for regions east, and it had been a tearful parting. For Oliver the goodbyes had been particularly painful. He had held Priscilla's hand for a long time, wanting to say something but not knowing how to say it. He could see the same yearning and unhappiness in her eyes, and the weight of the secret that would lie between them forever. In the end, he kissed her hand, a small salute for all he felt for her, and Priscilla moved onto the boat and out of his life without a word having been spoken between them.

The cabin was double wide, with a loft to accommodate Caroline and her children, as well as the children that would one day swell the Kincaid family. "No point in doing it piecemeal," Byrd had said, pausing to wipe his brow after the first wall went up. "Make it big enough now and you don't have to go back and add on later. It'll be stronger this way, too. Last a hundred years or more."

Katherine stood in the yard now, admiring Byrd's handiwork and that of the other steadfast volunteers who had lent their backs to erecting the cabin. It was snug and solid, with a big fireplace, a strong door, and windows to let in the river breeze. It was a good thing, home. But even as she smiled, her pleasure was tinged with sadness, for she was remembering Hilda and the aroma of pies and cakes and the flowers outside the windows.

She would plant flowers, Katherine decided. And when Kitty came back, she would be welcomed by a living memorial to her mother.

Byrd slipped his arm around Katherine's waist. He smelled of sun and sweat and the strength of a man, all welcome scents to Katherine, and familiar ones. "Well, Katie-girl," he said, "tonight you sleep under a roof."

She snuggled against his shoulder. "And not a moment too soon!"

"If I recollect," he said thoughtfully, "there was something else you said you wanted . . ."

He nodded toward the side of the cabin, where Oliver, beaming proudly, was just coming around the corner, bearing a cumbersome split-oak rocker in his arms.

Katherine laughed out loud and clapped her hands in delight as Oliver set the rocker on the ground. She ran toward it, caressing the smooth wood and exclaiming over the fine workmanship. The children lost no time in discovering the rocking chair and began to compete with her for the right of first use. Katherine cast a daring, dancing glance at Byrd. "And where's my feather mattress?" she demanded.

He grinned. "By the time you get ready to bring forth my first born, wife, you'll have your feather mattress if I have to carry it on my back from Pittsburgh every step of the way."

Katherine blushed and laughed again, and scooping up Benjamin Adamson, took her place in the rocker with Benjamin on one knee and Rebecca on the other. She leaned her head back, an arm around each child, and the years promised to unfold contentedly before her with the rhythmic creak of new wood.

Somebody said, "Well, look at that. We've had more strangers come down that road the past month than all year put together."

Katherine, lost in her own happiness, did not immediately look up. Byrd drawled, "Miz Sherrod, you'd best set another place at that table." And then Katherine turned, shading her eyes against the sun, to see what everybody was looking at.

A man was walking down the path that had been cut to the new cabin, tall and roughly dressed in a fringed buckskin hunting shirt, leggings and moccasins, and a coonskin cap. A Kentucky rifle was slung over his shoulder, and suspended from his leather belt was a small axe and a hunting knife. Under his right arm was a powder horn, and a bullet pouch hung around his neck. He was leading a spindly legged horse ridden by an Indian woman with a loosely wrapped bundle in her arms.

Just another trapper heading home, Katherine decided. Her curiosity satisfied, she started to turn back to the children in her lap. Then she stopped

and stared more closely. She got to her feet slowly,
setting Benjamin and Rebecca on the ground almost absently. She didn't even notice the cries of
protest or their querulous scrambling to reclaim
the chair. As the man walked closer her eyes di-
lated, her color drained, and her hand flew to her
mouth to muffle a cry. Then she was running, her
skirts flying above her knees, her arms outstretched.

The man let the reins drop from his hand. He
took off his hat and shook his shining red hair to
the sun and, with a whoop, he ran the last few
steps, catching Katherine up and swinging her
around until they were both dizzy.

"Boothe!" She was gasping, half–sobbing and
half–laughing, alternately clinging to him and
pushing him away to see him better, running her
hands through his hair and around his shoulders
and over his face. "Oh, Boothe!"

She pressed her face to his chest again and felt
his deep, rumbling laugh of pleasure as she
hugged him harder. Then she looked up at him,
breathless, still hardly believing it. "But where . . .
how did you find me? How did you . . ."

"Little girl," he told her, grinning broadly, "I've
been hearing tales about you up and down the
Mississippi, and it didn't take much of a tracker
to follow the kind of trail you left! Even before I
heard your name I knew there wasn't but one
woman who could've made that kind of stir, and
that was Kate Carlyle."

She smiled up at him. "It's Kate Kincaid now."

"So I hear." Boothe looked over her shoulder,
to where a group of curious onlookers were waiting. Byrd stepped forward from the group and
held his hand out to Boothe.

"Byrd Kincaid," he said, and the two men shook hands solemnly, liking what they saw in each other.

The words rushed up inside Katherine, all at once. Urgent things, sorrowful things, mundane things, and not one of them could wait another minute. Her face reflected the distress of choosing how to begin. "Oh, Boothe, I have so much to tell you!"

"I can guess you do." He ruffled her hair affectionately, but his kind, patient smile assured her that there was plenty of time. "I've heard some of them—about how you trekked through the wilderness and birthed a baby and fought the pirates and the Indians—and won. There's tales enough about your adventurin' to last three generations of campfires."

Just then there was the small mewling sound of an infant, and Katherine turned toward the woman on the horse. She had almost forgotten Boothe's companion.

She looked back at Boothe curiously, and he grinned. "I figured you might want this young'un back since you fought so hard to save her."

Boothe turned and spoke in quick Shawnee to the woman. She slid off the horse and walked over to Katherine, holding out the child to her.

Katherine's heart was beating erratically and her muscles were trembling so badly she was afraid she would drop the small, warm bundle the Indian woman placed in her arms. With a shaking hand, she lifted the blanket from the infant's face. "Kitty," she whispered.

"Honey," Boothe said gently. "I've been camped with the Shawnee since winter, laid up with a bad leg. All that time I wasn't no more than a stone's throw away."

Katherine's face was still, her eyes wide. "They knew you . . . they were bringing the baby to you."

"With her ma dead and all, they did the best they could for you. This woman here is Mirawah. She lost her own baby and has took right good care of this little 'un. I came as soon as I could travel, Katie."

The baby began to stir in her arms and Katherine looked back at her, thinking about miracles, and promises, and all the wonders of God's earth that had come home to her today.

She tightened her arms around the baby and looked up at Byrd, then turned to Boothe, her face shining, her eyes bright with questions and unbounded happiness. "There's so much I want to know, to tell you, so much I don't understand."

Boothe smiled and looped his arm around Katherine's waist. "And there'll be plenty of time for talking, little girl. I'm home to stay."

He was home, and Kitty was home. That was all that mattered. The worst was behind them, and a new life stretched before them all, wide with possibilities and rich with promise. All they had to do was claim it.

Katherine leaned her head against her brother's shoulder in a silent gesture of gratitude and love, and they started back toward the cabin. Byrd slipped his arm around her shoulders and she turned her face up to him, her eyes warm. Then she stopped and turned back.

She smiled and hesitantly extended her hand to the Shawnee woman. "Welcome," she said, "to my home."

The woman inclined her head, understanding

the gesture but not the words. She came over to Katherine and took the infant from her when Katherine offered.

Together, they all walked back to the cabin as the westward sun, glinting off the tops of the trees in the distance, etched their shadows on the land.

**If You Enjoyed Book One in
THE KINCAIDS Story,
Sample Book Two, PRAIRIE THUNDER,
Coming Soon from Avon Books**

1837

Blue skies in April were a rarity in Cairo, Illinois. In the flat, fertile peninsula at the junction of the Mississippi and Ohio rivers, rain was the norm both spring and fall; farmers plowed and planted between showers, and, like the ancient inhabitants of the Egyptian city which was its namesake, the people of Cairo had learned to plan their lives around the flooding of the river.

But on the day Benjamin Adamson came to take Rose Shipton as his wife, the day was cloudless and warm, the breeze off the river was sweet-smelling, and the profusion of wildflowers and willows that grew along the banks were at the height of their springtime glory. Later, looking back on the day, many would believe that the biggest obscenity of all was how blue the skies were, how beautifully the day began.

The wedding was to be held after services on Sunday in the church that, having been destroyed by fire and recently rebuilt, still smelled of fresh-cut pine. Reverend Morrison, whose four other churches along the river circuit allowed him to devote only every third Sunday to Cairo, preached a two-hour sermon extolling the virtues of the two young people who had vowed to devote their lives to the service of God.

After the sermon and before the wedding, grateful parishioners were given a much-needed opportunity to stretch their legs and partake of a midday meal. Baskets were unpacked and tablecloths unfurled on the banks of the river.

Children, ever mindful of their Sunday clothes, played roll-the-hoop and blind man's bluff, and tried to stay out of sight of their mothers; the women set out the food and gossiped about Benjamin Adamson and the shy young bride he had brought back from the East; men gathered in separate knots to talk about matters of more consequence. Not surprisingly, it was not the wedding that dominated their conversation but what was to come afterward; more specifically, the journey west on which Ben and Rose, along with the other missionaries, were trusting Boothe Carlyle to guide them.

There were some who said Carlyle was doing it only for the money. The more astute among them guffawed at that, for it was common knowledge that Carlyle had been approached in the first place only because nobody else would take the job for the pay they were offering. It had to be because of Ben Adamson, for everybody knew that there wasn't much in this world Boothe Carlyle wouldn't do for Ben's mother, Caroline Adamson, or any of her brood. But it remained an unspoken consensus among them that this time Boothe Carlyle wasn't doing Ben or his mother any favor.

Caroline Adamson, the local schoolteacher, was liked and respected by every member of the community. Her girls had made good matches with local boys and were raising respectable families of their own. Now Ben was back from the seminary in Tennessee with a calling to bring salvation to the savages in the West. Nobody could fault the widow Adamson or the way she had raised her family, and in fact the only taint on her name over all these years had been her continued close association with Boothe Carlyle. For one thing, it had kept her a widow longer than was decent, when there were plenty of men who needed a good wife. For another . . . it was Boothe Carlyle.

It was not that they could ever—until recently, that was— pin a specific complaint against Carlyle. In the first place, he was Katherine Carlyle Kincaid's brother and Byrd Kincaid's brother-in-law, and no one in his right mind wanted to get on the Kincaids' bad side. Secondly, over the past fifteen years or so, Boothe Carlyle had been their own private link to the rest of the world, their source of news and their liaison in trade. He traveled west along the trail to Santa Fe and south to Texas and New Orleans, north to the Erie Canal and across to Oregon. He brought back exotic delicacies and even more exotic tales. Each time he returned, his arrival was greeted with a mixture of eagerness and well-concealed resentment. Each time he departed, he was watched with envy and carefully qualified resignation by those who did not have the freedom, or the courage, to go themselves. Boothe Carlyle was by way of being a local legend, and legends by their very nature were not permitted foibles or mistakes.

In 1835, Boothe Carlyle had made a mistake, and it had affected them all. He had led a caravan west, but it had never reached the Promised Land. Carlyle had brought a dozen people into untold suffering and death, and though there were many versions of the story, only one thing counted: Boothe Carlyle had failed. For that and other sins, he had been tried and found guilty in the minds of every man in the community. For they and only they, claiming him as they did, had a right to do so.

Some folks said he'd been paid off to see that the expedition failed; others that he'd simply been drunk and careless. Whatever the reason, folks they knew had died on the trail because of Boothe's failure. Women and men, who'd trusted him with their lives.

Only the staunch support of Katherine and Byrd Kincaid and their respect for Caroline Adamson had kept the condemnation a silent one for this long. Now history was starting to repeat itself, with Benjamin Adamson and his missionaries the innocent victims, and there had been talk over the past few weeks, plenty of it. In honor of the Lord's day, however, and with no desire to account to their wives should the upcoming wedding be spoiled or in any way shadowed, today the men of Cairo kept their well-formed opinions to themselves. But they took their own satisfaction in watching Boothe Carlyle and remembering; in sharing grave, private glances; in sadly and silently predicting doom for poor Ben Adamson and all who followed him westward toward Kansas.

This was not, however, the time for bringing up past grievances, and today the most scandalous thing Boothe Carlyle did was to sit down to eat with Caroline Adamson and her family when, it was commonly held by some of the more vocal women, he should have sat with his sister and left Caroline to enjoy the last few hours with her only son before he went off into the wilderness.

It was not only the eagle eyes of the matrons and the stern, speculative gazes of the men which were focused on Boothe Carlyle. Kitty Werner Kincaid, Katherine and Byrd's seventeen-year-old adopted daughter, was filled with impatience as she sat on a blanket by the river between her younger sister Margaret, called Meg, and her brother James. She watched Boothe with an ache in her chest and frustration in her stomach.

Meg, who was fifteen years old and already putting on airs, followed Kitty's gaze and commented with a toss of her head, "Well, I don't care if Rose Shipton *did* go to school back east, I still say she's got about as much gumption as a field mouse and she's not all that much prettier, either. Ben could've found a much better wife."

Kitty ignored her. It was typical of Meg's fifteen-year-old self-centeredness to think the only important thing going on today was the introduction of a new bride into the Adamson household. Didn't she realize that at this very moment Kitty's entire world was being pulled up by the roots? Who cared whom Ben married or whether he married at all, when tomorrow her entire life would be broken apart?

Her Uncle Boothe was going away, just as he always did. And he was going with her . . . just as he always did.

Things were different now. She was no longer a little girl, a child; she was a young woman, and she knew what she wanted. What she wanted was her chance—her only chance—to be with Boothe. All her life he'd whetted her dreams with stories of his adventures, and now it was time for her to claim those dreams for her own. It wasn't as if she couldn't take care of herself. She could ride and shoot as well as any man in town. A lot better than Ben Adamson, she thought, with a touch of resentment as she looked at him. And certainly a lot better than Rose Shipton.

There were eight sharing a picnic dinner on the Kincaid blanket, with children ranging from Kitty's seventeen to Luke's age three, and almost as many voices were talking at once. It was difficult to single out a voice, much less levy a reprimand, but Katherine Kincaid's sharp ears missed nothing. She directed a stern scowl at her daughter Meg.

"You watch your tongue, miss. It won't be so long till some fine young man takes you to the altar, and how would you like it if folks were talking behind your back on your wedding day? I'll not have loose gossip at my dinner table."

"Blanket," pointed out eight-year old Sarah sagely. "It's a blanket."

James thought that was the funniest thing he'd ever heard and burst into squeals of laughter, tossing a bread crust across the blanket at his sister. Kitty could have screamed. She was straining to make out what was being said at the Adamson blanket across the way, but so far hadn't been able to hear a word. They were finishing early, probably so the bride could change into her fancy dress, and pretty soon they would leave. She had to talk to Boothe now. She just *had* to.

The food fight was cut off before it had a chance to begin, and Meg gave an impertinent toss of her head. "I don't care," she declared. "I'm never going to marry any-body anyway. Besides, she *is* a mouse. I heard Pa saying just the other day what does she think she's going to do out there with those Indians . . .".

Katherine gave her husband a sharp look, and Byrd shrugged his shoulders. "A man's got a right to his opin-ion," he said with a hint of a twinkle in his eyes.

"A man," Katherine pointed out coolly, "also has a right to remember little pitchers have big ears."

Kitty could see across the churchyard to where Ben and Rose got up and were holding hands as they walked toward the river, their heads close together. Boothe was helping Car-oline fold up the blanket. Surely, Kitty thought, he would come over now. How much longer could Miss Caroline keep him dawdling there? Kitty had counted on Boothe's eating with them today; without his support, she didn't stand a chance of convincing her parents to let her go with him. What was he doing, wasting time with Ben and Caroline Adamson when he knew her whole future was at stake?

James, who had gotten rowdy again, jostled Kitty's arm and spilled her untouched plate of food all over her clean apron. She pinched him hard and he squealed, and Katherine gave her one of those looks that each of the Kincaid children had spent a lifetime learning to avoid. Without being told, Kitty got James to stop squealing and cleaned up the mess, and by the time she looked around again, Boothe and Caroline were gone.

Meg, who did not like to have attention diverted from her for any reason, declared, "Well, I mean it! What is she going to do out there with those Indians and snakes and deserts and things? Uncle Boothe says—"

Kitty took a deep breath and knew she was on her own. She looked her mother in the eye and said clearly, "*I'd* know what to do."

It was as though everyone had suddenly been stricken dumb. Even Luke stopped squirming in his mother's lap for the cup of milk she held just out of reach and sucked contentedly on a chicken bone. Meg edged a little bit away from her sister, as though to be safely out of range of her mother's wrath, and every eye was trained on Kitty.

The only sign of emotion on Katherine's face was a slight tightening of her jaw. "We've had this conversation before, Kitty."

"No, we haven't!" Kitty cried. "*You've* had it! You haven't ever listened to me. All you did was say no—"

"That will do, Kitty." Katherine's voice remained quiet and firm, but her eyes met those of the willful younger woman with chilling force. "You're far too young to be going halfway across the country by yourself, and that's all there is to it. The whole notion is ridiculous."

"I wouldn't be alone," Kitty insisted. "I'd be with Boothe, and . . . and Ben. Besides, Rose Shipton is younger than I am and she's going!"

Young Luke squirmed in his mother's lap, waving the chicken bone, and Katherine shifted her head to avoid a greasy fist. "Rose Shipton will be a married woman," Katherine replied. "And besides, she has the call of the church."

"Lots of unmarried women go west," Kitty insisted. "I was reading in the St. Louis newspaper only the other day—"

"Is that what you *want?*" Katherine's carefully maintained control snapped, and two spots of color appeared in her cheeks. "To marry some filthy trapper and live like a squaw for the rest of your life? To be raped by some

Indian or mauled to death by a wild animal or go mad from loneliness? To die in a place so barren they have to cover your body with rocks because there isn't even enough earth to dig a grave?"

Her voice was rising, and her arms had tightened around Luke until he began to whimper. She moved him off her lap and faced Kitty with a set jaw and a voice low enough to send chills down the spine of every listener. "I'm telling you right now, Kitty Werner Kincaid, no daughter of mine will ever waste her life that way, not as long as I have a breath in my body. Do you understand that? No daughter of mine!"

Kitty stood up, her stained apron clutched in her fists, her eyes blazing. "But I'm not your daughter, am I!" she cried, and tossed the apron on the ground. "I—"

Hot tears flashed in her eyes, and she couldn't finish. She whirled and stalked away.

Stunned silence echoed in her wake for perhaps thirty seconds. Then Katherine swallowed hard and lowered her eyes. She started to stand up.

Byrd laid a hand lightly on her arm. "Stay," he said quietly. He rose and followed Kitty.

Ben lifted a low willow branch and held it as Rose ducked beneath it. He smiled at the picture she made in her delicate cotton dress, with her smooth brown hair brushed back from her face and her wide gray eyes alight with soft pleasure, the whole framed by a cascade of willow branches and bright sky overhead. She was even more beautiful than she had been the day he first set eyes on her. For Ben, it had been love at first sight.

In the year of their courtship, Ben had learned that Rose was as good as she was beautiful. Her father, the Reverend Shipton, was head of the Presbyterian teachers' college where Ben had gone to obtain his training two years ago. Rose was studying to be a teacher just as he was, but whereas Ben had planned only to return to Cairo and help his mother, Rose had higher ambitions. She was determined to minister to the Indians across the Mississippi, and when she and Ben had read the inspirational writings in the *Christian Gazette* citing the desperate need for a ministry among the savages, Ben, too, had discovered his calling. It had been like a miracle.

Through Rose's father, Ben had met the Reverend Syms and Martin and Effie Creller, who were planning an expedition to Kansas Territory, where they would join the beleaguered missionaries at the Pawnee mission. Ben couldn't ignore their enthusiasm and the nobility of their purpose. He knew at once that this was his destiny; with Rose at his side and the hand of God guiding his steps, he too would go west.

It had all happened so fast that Ben sometimes thought it had been a dream. Yet it was real, and he was glad. Had it been only three days ago that Rose had arrived on the steamboat from Louisville? And now the day after their wedding they'd be leaving with Boothe Carlyle to head west and meet the rest of their wagon train. It was only fitting that Boothe would be their guide, yet another sign of the divine hand of destiny at work. For two years, ever since the tragedy in the mountains, Boothe had refused to undertake another plains crossing. But now, when Ben needed him most, Boothe would be at his side. It was right; it was perfect.

Rose, stepping from beneath the willow, turned her face toward the sky. "Look," she said softly, "how beautiful everything is. What a perfect day for a wedding!"

"I wonder what it will be like," Ben mused, conscious of a rising excitement as he imagined the future. "Kansas and the mission."

The mission was something shadowy and mysterious to Ben. His only contact with the Indians had been as a child with the Shawnee, and he recalled the experience with the dim terror of a long-ago nightmare.

Rose, who knew even less of Indians, was full of confidence. "Just before I left home we received a long letter from one of the teachers at the mission. Of course, it was written almost a year ago," she confessed. "He didn't say much about Kansas—except that he misses the trees back east. The work with the Indians is still slow, but sometimes God puts obstacles in our way to make our success sweeter."

Ben looked at Rose in amazement. How differently she saw things. Would he ever understand her?

"Boothe says—," Ben stopped as he saw the faintest of frowns mar Rose's smooth forehead.

"I've heard stories, Ben," she began hesitantly. "Since I got here. I wonder if we did the proper thing telling Reverend Syms that Boothe was the right man to lead us through Kansas."

Ben tensed defensively. "What happened on that other expedition wasn't Boothe's fault; in fact, without him the consequences might have been even more tragic. He's a hero, not a villain, despite what certain low-minded people say. All my life, ever since we came to Cairo with Miss Katherine, Boothe and Byrd have been the two most important men in my life."

"It must be hard to grow up without a father."

"But I had Boothe; that's what I'm trying to explain," Ben said. "Would I trust the life of the one I hold most dear in the world to anyone in whom I did not have perfect confidence?"

Rose touched his arm, her expression sweet and soothing. "Oh, Ben, you know I trust your judgment. And I know Boothe Carlyle must be a good man, if you're so devoted to him."

Ben covered her hand with his. "He is, Rose," Ben assured her. "And if you love me, you'll trust Boothe."

"I do love you, Ben," she replied, her eyes glowing. "And I will never question you. Nothing will spoil this, the happiest day of my life."

Kitty did not go far; there wasn't far to go in a town like Cairo. There was a spreading oak set back from the riverbank; for most of her childhood she'd climbed over its exposed roots or hung from its lower branches. She stood there now and leaned her head against the cool, rough bark, absently rubbing the scar on her shoulder and trying not to cry.

She had been raised on the story of how she had gotten that scar from an Indian arrow before she even left her mother's womb. Katherine said it was a mark of greatness, a reminder that God, having spared her, would expect big things from her. But how was she supposed to do big things, or even find out what greatness meant, if she was never allowed to leave this riverbank?

She did not hear Byrd come up behind her, but knew when he sat down on one of the big roots a few feet away from her. He sat there silently, as was his way, waiting until she was ready to speak. Her father was the most patient man Kitty had ever known.

"It's not fair, Pa," she said at last, without turning around. Her voice sounded choked, and her fist tightened on her shoulder. "She won't even listen to me. She won't even *try*. It's just not fair."

"No," Byrd agreed slowly. "I reckon it's not. And I guess it don't help much that she's got her reasons."

"What reasons?" Kitty demanded bitterly to the tree trunk. "I'm seventeen years old. I'm not a little girl anymore. She treats me like a baby!"

There was a thoughtful silence. "I reckon to her, you always will be."

Kitty whirled on him. "But it's not fair!"

Byrd took up a twig and spun it absently between his fingers. His expression was calm and his tone mild, as they always were. "When your ma weren't much older than you, she lit out on her own for the trail west. Before she'd been gone a week, she saw half a dozen men die in a bad way. She was left to do a man's job in the wilderness, and I reckon she saw the devil's red eyes looking over her shoulder more than once ... and it wasn't just herself she had to be afraid for, but the folks she had to take care of. She lost some of them."

He fixed his quiet blue gaze on her. "She lost your ma, Miss Hilda. She lost you, and I ain't never seen a woman so tore up as she was when them Indians took you away. It took near about all the strength I had to hold her back, and I'm here to tell you it ripped a piece out of me big enough to choke on, to stand back and watch it happen. You don't get over a thing like that. I reckon sometimes when your ma looks at you, she still sees a babe in arms and that big Shawnee carrying you into the woods. She promised Miss Hilda on her deathbed, you see, that she'd take care of you. And she's still keeping that promise, the best way she knows how."

Kitty turned back to the tree, her throat thick. "Stop it, Pa. You're making me cry. I hate to cry."

Byrd smiled a little. "I know you do, little girl. You're that much like my Katie."

Kitty squeezed her eyes tightly shut, and the tears hurt. Her voice was barely audible, no matter how she struggled to make it strong. "I didn't mean what I said."

"I reckon she knows that. But I want you to understand something. In a lot of ways, you're always going to be more of a daughter to your ma than the ones she gave birth to. She chose you, and she made promises to you even before you were born. You've been through life and death together, and that's a special thing. There ain't nothing you can ever do to change that."

Kitty took a cautious, somewhat stifled breath and lifted her head, staring up into the lacy network of leaves. She said steadily, "I know that, Pa. But . . . all my life I've known what it means to be a Kincaid. And I'm not one. I'm different, Pa, and nothing can ever change *that*. I need different things. I need . . . to find my own place."

Byrd was silent for a moment. Then he said, "Turn around, little girl, and look at me."

Reluctantly, she complied.

"Now I want you to look me in the eye," he said quietly, "and tell me that your place is out on the Solomon River, preaching the gospel to the Pawnee."

Kitty tried, but she couldn't hold his gaze. He knew she wouldn't be able to, and that shamed her. She turned away from him with a quick, frustrated gesture toward the riverbank. "Oh, Pa, don't you know how much of the world there is out there? Don't you ever look at the river and wonder where it's going or what's on the other side?"

Byrd smiled. "Yeah, girlie, I do. And every time your Uncle Boothe starts down that trail, it's near 'bout all I can do to keep from slinging on my pack and walking beside him."

She looked at him in surprise. "But—you never said . . ."

He tossed the twig aside. "There's a time for wandering and a time for staying. I got all my wandering done when I was a younger man. But your Uncle Boothe now, he's a different breed."

Kitty said swiftly, lowly, "He's not my uncle."

A new alertness came into Byrd's eyes, and Kitty felt her cheeks grow warm. She had to look quickly away.

"No, I reckon he's not," Byrd said slowly. "Not by blood." He stood up. "But I wouldn't be surprised if you didn't have more of the Carlyles and Kincaids in you than you think, little girl. It's not always something that's passed down through blood. Now, come on. We're gonna miss the wedding, and your ma won't take kindly to that."

Kitty hesitated. "In a minute, Pa. There's something I have to do first."

He looked at her for another minute, then nodded and walked away.

Zeke Calhoun had ridden hard, stopping only to water and rest his exhausted horse before pushing on. He was a whipcord-tough, trail-dirty man with a seventeen-year-old thirst for vengeance in his heart. At last satisfaction was within sight. He had finally found the bitch who'd killed his brothers. The time of judgment was at hand.

For years he had thought she was dead. She *should* have been dead. But all this time she'd been hiding out on some farm outside Cairo, married and with a new name. And now she was his.

He'd been drinking with a keelboater in a saloon in Mud Flats, Kentucky, who'd told him about a red-haired trapper he'd had a run-in with. A man by the name of Boothe Carlyle. *Carlyle.* He had to be related to the lying, cheating bitch who'd killed Abel and Early. The Calhouns had had more than one run-in with that witch-woman, tracking her all the way from Mud Flats down the Ohio where, in the end, she and her band of ragged refugees had just about done them all in. Only Zeke had escaped, and it was up to him to take revenge in his brothers' names.

Well, he'd finish it now. He touched the Patterson Colt in his belt; the newest model and worth a dozen of any rifle. He could get off five shots without reloading, but one was all he needed.

A cold, thin smile tightened his lips when he remembered the face of that red-haired witch-woman. It wouldn't be long now.

Boothe helped Caroline pack away the remnants of dinner in the wagon. It had been a good, easy meal together, not unlike others he had shared at her table over the years. A lot of the talk had centered around the bridal couple, and Caroline didn't flinch anymore when Ben talked about the journey west. She had never once looked at Boothe with accusation in her eyes. All in all, the day was turning out better than he had a right to expect, but still there was an uneasiness in him, like the shadow of a thundercloud gathering in the back of his mind.

It could be because of Caroline, and what he was leaving behind. It could be because of young Ben, and what lay ahead. It could be because he knew how folks were thinking and talking, and none of it was good. Or it could be something else.

His grandmother had been what some folks called a seer, and she wasn't the first in her family. The gift was passed down through the generations, and though most times it landed with the women, occasionally it was picked up by a man. Sometimes Boothe knew things, in dreams or waking visions, or by just knowing. Not all the time, just sometimes. More than once his grandmother's gift had saved his life, and more than once it had failed him when he needed it most. But he couldn't argue with it or ignore it any more than he could stop the heat of the sun by closing his eyes to the brightness. He didn't understand it and didn't particularly want to; it just was.

Sometimes it felt like something he should know but didn't, something he should see but couldn't. Sometimes it meant nothing at all.

He stood by the side of the wagon while Caroline fussed with the blankets and the leftovers, looking across the way at the church. He had helped build that church, and the one before it. A lot of his life had been put into this town, and now, getting ready to leave it once again, he couldn't quite remember why he had never been able to stay.

He looked back at Caroline. Her face was shaded by a sprigged sunbonnet with a circle cut out of the back to show off her hair. There wasn't a streak of gray in that hair, and though he knew she had changed over the years, just as he had, when he looked at her now she was just as young and pretty and gentle-faced as the day he had first laid eyes on her.

He had a lot to say to her, so much he didn't know where to begin. The trouble was, he should have started saying it ten years ago.

"I don't know if I ever told you," he said, "but you raised a fine boy. You don't have to worry about Ben."

Caroline glanced at him. "You did a lot of that raising, Boothe. Whatever man there is in him is due to you and Byrd Kincaid."

"A lot of folks're saying you've got no cause to be grateful to me now. That I put notions in the boy's head, when he would've been better off at home."

"They're a bunch of fools." Caroline's voice was stern, but he saw the hurt come into her eyes before she could hide it, the look a mother gets when she knows she's losing her son. She softened the look with a smile. "It was never my wish for Ben to go west, but a mother doesn't have much of a say in what a man does. Ben has to listen to a higher calling. I guess all men do," she added softly.

She looked Boothe straight in the eye. "If he has to go, you know there's not a man on earth I'd rather trust him with than you."

Boothe shifted his gaze away. "Maybe you're wrong in that," he said quietly.

"Boothe Carlyle, you hush that kind of talk! It's bad enough that you sit back and let everybody else go on with their wrongheaded notions without your starting to believe it yourself. Well, I don't have to listen to it, I'll tell you that much!"

Caroline Adamson was slow to anger, but she could be as fierce as a lioness in defense of her own. Boothe saw that anger blaze in her eyes for his sake, and he loved her. He wanted to tell her that. He wanted to tell her that hers was the face that stayed with him when he was cold and wet and aching from sleeping outdoors. Hers was the laughter he heard in the high mountain passes. Hers was the shadow that walked beside him on the trails. When he thought of home, he thought of her. When he measured goodness, he thought of her. He supposed she might have known all those things, in the way women have of knowing, but still he wanted to say them. He had just never felt he had the right to, not in all this time. And he certainly had no right now.

"A lot of years between us, Miss Caroline," he said quietly. "And I wasted most of them."

She held her head high and met his eyes without condemnation. "Yes," she said. "You have."

"And now I reckon it's too late."

"Is it?"

She had a way of looking at him that was half joy, half sorrow. It reminded him, all too poignantly, of all those lost years.

"I've waited for you before," she said. "I waited while you went down the river to sell a load of furs. I waited while you went over the mountains just to see what was on the other side. I waited while you wintered with the Kansa and summered with the elk, and I waited while you ran off with Sam Houston to fight his stupid war. I've spent half my life waiting for you, Boothe Carlyle," she said softly, and into her eyes came a smile that was so sad and so beautiful and so full of things Boothe did not deserve that it hurt him, deep in his chest. "You'll be coming back, and I reckon I can wait a little while longer."

The thundercloud in the back of Boothe's mind grew darker.

"I wish I was a different kind of man," he said gruffly.

She laid her hand, very lightly, very briefly, on his arm. "If you were, I wouldn't wait."

For a moment they stood there, just looking at each other, and then Caroline stepped away. People were starting to drift toward the church. "I'd better go see what I can do to help Rose," she said.

Boothe watched her go with the darkness nagging at him in the bright sunshine, and then he felt a touch on his sleeve.

"Boothe?" Kitty was flushed, and seemed a little breathless. "Can I talk to you?"

Boothe turned around, and Kitty saw the troubled, unhappy look on his face vanish into a smile. He always smiled when he saw her, and not the distant, patronizing smile most people gave their youngers when they were too tired or too busy to be bothered. Boothe was always glad to see her. Boothe had always, even when she was a child, made her feel important. He talked to her as if she was an adult, and as smart as he was. Even before she knew that she loved him, and that her destiny was to be always at his side, he had been her hero.

When people said awful things about him, she got mad enough to fight, and she had fought, too, sometimes with boys twice her size. Over the past year she had grown too big to fight with her fists; Caroline Adamson said it wasn't ladylike and, next to her mother, Miss Caroline was the finest lady Kitty had ever known. So these days her fights were on the inside. Now she was in the middle of the biggest battle of her life, a battle for her future, and for Boothe's. Boothe would not fail her now. They would win together.

"Well now, Miss Kitten," he said. "What can I do for you this fine spring day?"

He was the only person in the world who called her Kitten, and for that reason she loved the name. He extended his arm to her, just like a gentleman would to a lady, and she slipped her hand around it. She tried to calm the excited pace of her breathing as they walked toward the church. She tried to find just the right words, just the right tone of voice. She wasn't worried about Boothe not taking her seriously; he always took her seriously. But this was so important . . .

It was so important that she couldn't wait for the right words and she blurted out, "Let me go with you. Talk to my mother."

Boothe slowed his pace a little, and though he didn't answer right away, he was already shaking his head. He was a tall man, with thick red hair now slightly dulled by gray, and a ginger-colored beard. When the sun struck his hair, as it did now, flames seemed to dance around his head. The Shawnee used to call him the Firebird.

"Now, Kitten," he said. "You know I can't do that. I'm not about to get between you and your ma."

She stepped in front of him. Her heart was beating so hard it hurt, and the words she spoke had an airy, breathless quality. "But you want me to, don't you? You want me to go with you."

Boothe regarded her gravely, for a long time. Kitty saw

the answer in his eyes, and it made her so happy she thought her chest would explode.

He cupped her cheek in a gentle, stroking gesture he was fond of using. "Sweet girl, it don't matter much what I want. What's meant to be, is. That's all."

"But I'm meant to go with you." She could barely whisper it. "Isn't that right?"

He didn't shift his eyes away, but it was as though he were looking at something else. It seemed it took an effort to bring his attention back to her, and he smiled. "Can I tell you a secret?"

She nodded, desperately holding back her impatience.

"Some time ago—I reckon it must be nigh on three, four years now—I had this dream. Had it a couple of times since. You were in it, looking just as fine and strong as you are today, racing bareback on a white pony down a buffalo trail on the plains, your hair flying out behind you and your body bent low against the wind, that pony kicking up dust . . . I can see it as clear as yesterday. I couldn't make much sense of it. You'd never been in plains country, and I didn't have any reason to think you ever would. Not then."

The pace of Kitty's pulse was so quick, so hard, that she could barely breathe. "Your dreams always come true, don't they?"

"Not always, but most times."

"Then I *am* meant to go with you! But how can I, if you won't talk to Mama?"

"It's not what your ma wants," he said. "Maybe not what I want for you, either. But if there's one thing I've learned in this life, it's not to fight what is." Then he tweaked one of her curls in a playful way. "Don't you fight it either, Kitten. You'll wear yourself out."

That was not the answer she wanted, not the answer she knew he wanted to give. But the church bells started ringing, and there was Katherine, waving to them from the steps. Boothe started to hurry Kitty along, but she caught his arm again. "We'll talk more about this?"

"Sure we will," he said, and that had to be good enough.

Nobody wanted to a miss a wedding, and each one of the hard-slatted pews was filled to capacity. Some of the men lined up along the side to allow the elderly and gravid women to sit. The young children, even those who considered themselves far too old to be held, resigned themselves to finding places on their mothers' laps. Within moments the scent of fresh pine mingled with the odors of perspiration and wilting broadcloth, and the sunlight, slanting through motes of dust from the high windows, heated up the little building like an oven.

The bride wore a long lace veil, yellowed with age, over her Sunday dress and carried a bouquet of pink peonies picked from Katherine Kincaid's flower garden. Ben Adamson, blond and handsome and bursting with pride, couldn't stop smiling at her. Caroline Adamson sat in the front pew with her two daughters and their husbands, her eyes bright with tears and her face glowing. The Reverend Morrison, his collar starched and his shiny face cherubic, opened his prayer book and smiled benignly.

"Friends and neighbors, we are gathered here on this most happy of the Lord's days to unite these two fine young people in the holy bonds of matrimony . . ."

Kitty had arrived too late to sit up front with her family, but that was all right, because Boothe had, too. She squeezed into the back pew, and Boothe stood against the wall beside her, and it was almost as though the two of them were together, a couple. Just having him near her made her ache with despair and strain with hope. She listened to the words of the ceremony and watched the bride turn shyly toward her groom, and she tried very hard not to hate Rose Shipton for what she had and Kitty did not.

But it wasn't going to happen. Boothe was not going to leave her behind. Somehow, some way, something she could do would change her mother's mind. If only Boothe would speak for her. Katherine had never refused to listen to her brother. If only he would go to her, and . . .

If only he knew how I felt. Kitty's eyes widened in surprise and a flush warmed her skin. That was it. Boothe didn't know that she loved him, not as a child but as a woman. He didn't know that her destiny lay with him. She had to tell him, and then he would understand, then her *mother* would understand. Then Boothe could not refuse to take her with him. Katherine could not refuse to let her go.

I have to tell him, Kitty thought, and her heart was beating so crazily with excitement she could hardly swallow. *As soon as the ceremony is over, I—*

There was a commotion behind her as the door opened and a bright square of sunlight was cast across her face. Several people stirred to look around. Then someone shouted, "Hey, what—"

Thunder exploded.

It was fast, as fast as it takes a man to fire three shots from a Patterson Colt revolver, but each action stood out in such separate, brightly colored detail that it seemed to take forever. A blossom of bright red burst upon the bride's white dress as she pitched forward into Ben's arms. The roar of horror from the congregation was like a single, distant scream, and they lunged to their feet, not all at once but in spurts and starts, like a wave trying to gather force. Children scattered. Mothers clutched their babies. Men lurched forward to push their womenfolk down. Not one of them had a gun. No one carried a gun to church anymore.

Kitty watched as Caroline rushed toward Ben and was thrown forward beneath the impact of another ear-splitting thunderbolt. There was a roaring in her ears, like the scream of a mad animal, and Boothe was turning, moving, pushing past her toward the door.

It took seconds. Only seconds.

Katherine Kincaid struggled to break the grip of her husband's arms, screaming Caroline's name. Byrd pushed in front of her, trying to force her to the floor, and the bullet that was meant for Katherine struck him in the throat. Kitty was screaming; she was on her feet and she did not know how long she had been there, her hands pressed against her ears, screaming.

She felt Boothe's hand against her shoulder, shoving her down hard, and instinctively, hysterically, she fought back, spinning around, tripping . . .

And he was there, the mad man with the lean stubbled face and the dirty hair and the flaming eyes, inches before her, his gun raised and his lips parted in a wild, triumphant grin. She couldn't stop her forward momentum and she didn't want to; she lunged toward him, fists upraised, clawing at him, and he never once looked at her.

Boothe slammed against him and the gun discharged once more into the air as the three of them crashed on the floor. Kitty smelled the smoke and felt the heat; the odor of him, madness and filth, seemed to penetrate her very pores. There was iron between her fingers and Boothe's hands were grappling with hers, then thunder and fury and blood splashing in her face, and the man beneath them jerked and lay still.

She never knew who pulled the trigger.

She never knew.

The silence was unnatural. Broken only by the occasional hiccoughing sob of a child, the stillness pressed down as thick and as acrid as the gun smoke that still tainted the air. No one moved; no one spoke.

Somehow Kitty was on her knees beside the body of the gunman. There was blood all over her hands and on her best Sunday dress. She could feel the wetness on her face and in her hair. But she couldn't feel anything else.

Boothe grasped the dead man by the hair and turned his face upward. The eyes were still open, the lips still split in that ghoulish grin.

"Zeke Calhoun." The soft voice belonged to Katherine Kincaid. Her skirts brushed against Kitty's face as she slowly dropped to her knees beside her. Her voice held no remorse, no anger; her eyes seemed to see far away. "It's only fitting," she said. "The past comes full circle."

And that was all.

Boothe got up and walked to the front of the church. His face was hard and his mouth tight. He knelt beside Caroline's body and lifted her into his arms. The congregation parted to let him pass, and he looked neither right nor left as he carried her from the church and into the sunshine.

Katherine's arms came around Kitty. Kitty turned her face to her mother's bloodstained bosom and wept.